House of Apache Fires

Morgan Jameson

This book is dedicated to the 'greatest generation' and in particular to my Grandparents, Bob and Marian, my Uncle Vern and Aunt Vi, as well as Uncle Ralph and Aunt Alma who all did their part during a dark time in history.

Acknowledgments

No book like this is written alone. These people helped make it possible:

First of all, I never would have tackled a second or third novel without the support and encouragement of my wonderful agent, Kimberley Cameron. She believed in me when no one else did. Thank you, Kimberley.

I could not have done it without Harry Weisberger's knowledge of aerobatics, and of course his editorial skill. If there is an error, it's likely something Harry told me about which I chose to ignore for the sake of telling the story. Thanks Harry. Likewise, having Jeremiah Horstman as my "go to guy" when referencing WWII Germany was a true blessing. He helped me see the German soldier as a soldier, and not just as 'Nazis'.

Alexandra Caldwell dragged her butt out of bed even when sick and miserable to hike to the top of a nearby butte just to take my author's pics. Thank you Alexandra – I will never forget your kindness.

James Wallis offered to tackle the graphic design of the cover, and I can't imagine what it would have looked like without his help. A.L. Bentley, an incredibly talented engineer, did the drawings of the Horten and was generous enough to allow me to use one for the cover. I encourage you to buy some of his aviation prints at: www.albentley-drawings.com No one does it better.

I'd also like to thank the Sedona Historical Society, the Flagstaff Historical Society, and the great folks at the Lowell Observatory, especially my long-time friend Emily Clough for giving me a behind the scenes, personal guided tour. Tim Sinson lent me a book: *Arizona's War Town – Flagstaff, Navajo Ordnance Depot and WWII* by John S. Westerlund which was invaluable to me. Thanks Tim.

It's also important to mention Randall D. Reynold's wonderful tribute site to the Frye's : www.sedonalegendhelenfrye.com - it was on this site that I first heard of the House of Apache Fires. This site gave me the seminal idea that a book might be built around. I highly recommend it if you are interested in Sedona history. Thanks Randall.

I'd also like to thank Jason Anderson of Polygarus Studios for the fantastic job he did formatting the book. I highly recommend them. Thank you Jason.

Several people beta - read the book and the input I received from each of them was invaluable. Their input made the final manuscript much better. My father — Deac Jones, Robert Allison, Harry Weisberger, Mike Callahan, and Jeremiah Horstman all suggested important changes and provided encouragement. I cannot thank you guys enough. Your comments meant a lot to me.

Ed and Estella Santana have not read the entire thing, but helped me get the Spanish right. Muchas gracias. I also want to thank Ramiro Muñoz and Jose Guevara for "loaning" me their names for a couple characters. I did it as a tribute to our friendship. I hope you like the book guys.

Lastly I'd like to thank my oldest friend Robert Allison for not only helping with suggestions, reading multiple drafts and helping me with the naval scene from hell, but for helping me in a million other small ways, even though he is busy raising a family and running an IT department. If any one person helped make this happen, it was him. Everyone should have such a pal. I can't thank you enough, old friend.

– Part One –

Sedona, Arizona, November, 1944

THE KILLER had pulled tumbleweeds over the body in a sorry attempt to hide it. It was almost as if he didn't care, or wanted the body found, the sheriff said. Jake stood for a minute after closing the car door, the heat of the metal against his palm a reminder that he was still breathing and she was not, amazing to him considering the circumstances.

There were times during the war when he was sure he would never make it home, yet here he was, alive, while Lily lay mere yards from him, never to laugh or cry again; a sweet young girl with a shy smile who'd once brought him lemonade on the porch where her sister Laurel and he had sat holding hands on the swing in the summer darkness, listening to the hum of cicadas and the song of crickets, long before he could imagine the horrors human beings were capable of visiting upon each other.

He forced himself away from the car, away from the past, towards the uncertain, scary future. Towards the lovely young girl he'd once considered his sister. Who indeed would have been his sister, once he and Laurel were wed.

Ben looked at him sadly as Jake limped slowly toward the murder site, then he bent down, pulled the blanket, away and stepped aside.

It was the mundane things that struck Jake - the way the body lay on its side as if she were asleep, the beer cans on the ground, the remains of a small fire nearby...and oddly, an eagle feather in front of the body. He pointed this out to Ben, who nodded, a tired look on his face. Then he noticed the dried blood on the pale skin, the blood which had seeped from wounds too numerous to count. Stab wounds, slash wounds...awful testament to the killer's twisted psyche. He had seen things like this during the war and worse; bodies that had ripened in the sun like grapes, the foul smell of decomposition everywhere, polluting the clean Mediterranean air.

He leaned heavily on his crutches as he slowly walked around to the front of the body. The sheriff had already taken pictures with his Brownie,

3

and so Jake knelt in front of her, and with a trembling hand, lifted aside the hair veiling her face. Animals had been at work, but the killer had started the process with a series of brutal slashes that were awful to contemplate experiencing.

What was left of Lily's face was drawn in a contortion of horror he knew he would never forget. Her mouth was open as if screaming, her open eye sockets staring at some distant point he couldn't fathom, as if she'd seen death coming for her in that final moment, the eyeballs long gone to scavengers, likely vultures, who always went for the soft parts first. The ground was dark beneath her torso, where blood had soaked into the hard ground like it had with so many other westerners. Jake waved off one of the many flies, felt his gorge rise and fought it back down, trying not to look at the rest of her body, but the gaping wound above her heart drew his eyes lower. He closed them against the pain she must have felt.

He could already smell the decay; the putrescence of rotting flesh that he remembered all too well from the war, but what shook him was the earring she was wearing. It was one of the earrings he and Laurel had bought her for her sixteenth birthday. They were Navajo, silver and turquoise, but small and pretty, like tiny unreal feathers. One was missing.

Jake thought about the hug she'd given both him and Laurel when she'd opened her present that day. Until that moment when he'd seen the earring, he couldn't believe that it was actually her; that this pile of rotting meat was actually someone he'd cared about. He stood up, shaking with anger, and looked at Ben, fury beginning to burn inside him.

"What do you think? Is it her?"

Jake nodded. "It's her. It's Lily. That earring is one Laurel and I gave her for her sixteenth birthday several years ago. Dammit, who could do such a thing?"

Ben pushed his hat back and scratched his head as he did when something puzzled him, then settled it back, lower in front this time, to keep the morning sun out of his eyes.

"Jake, I've seen a lot as an officer of the law...things I'd rather not discuss, but I've never seen anything quite this brutal. No one who's right in the head could do such a thing." The sheriff shook his head, looking down at the body as the coroner's station wagon pulled into the draw behind their car.

"Here comes Doc now. I was pretty sure it was Lily, but I needed a witness. Sorry you had to see this, Jake. Soon as I get Doc going and we load up Lily I'll drive you home."

Doc Edwards wiped his brow as he came up to them. Like most everyone else in the area, Jake had literally known Doc his entire life. Doc had delivered him, nursed him through whooping cough, chickenpox and measles, but he also doubled as the local coroner.

"Sorry boys. I need a new battery. Had to get the neighbor to give me a jump- start. That old Packard wagon of mine needs some attention." He looked past the sheriff's shoulder at the body beyond.

"Who is it, do we know?"

Ben Goodwin looked at Jake sadly, then back at Doc. "We're both pretty sure it's young Lily Hausen. I'll warn you Doc, it ain't pretty. Not telling you your job, but it's clearly murder."

"My God… and she was such a sweet girl. Let's take a look," Doc Edwards said, moving to the body. Jake turned away, making his way slowly with his crutches over the rough ground back to the car. He got the door open, and slumped into the seat, his feet still outside. He sat there sweating from the effort as Doc and the sheriff knelt over the body. Suddenly he felt sick, and he wanted to fall out of the car to his knees, and puke on the hard ground at the thought that it was Lily's body they were looking at, but he just leaned his head back against the seat and closed his eyes, the agony in his heart overwhelming the ache in his legs.

Hungary – Eastern Front, 1944

KESSLER WAS cold. Not just a little cold, but the kind of cold that made you think you'd never be warm again. He knew better than to strike an officer, so he really couldn't blame anyone but himself for banishment to this SS punishment battalion. He knew he'd been sent here, to Hungary, the new eastern front, to die. He didn't care anymore. He huddled in the drafty shell of a destroyed tank, clutching his rifle to keep it warm so it wouldn't freeze up, his zeltbahn wrapped around him, waiting for the bastards to attack. He had very little ammo left, and hadn't had any food in three days.

Kessler was a survivor, but he knew death when he saw it, and he hoped the Russians would attack soon so he could die a soldier's death instead of being found here in the snow. Goddamn snowstorm and it wasn't even December yet. He wondered what it would be like in January.

He couldn't feel his toes anymore, and wondered if when the time came, whether he'd even be able to stand up. His toenails had been slowly turning blue with frostbite. He hunched down a little more, dozing even as the bitter wind threw spindrift in his face and down his neck. He was too tired to even curse. Like the rest of Hitler's vaunted Wehrmacht, these days Kessler just endured.

The crunch and squeak of feet on frozen snow woke him. He didn't move, but peered out from beneath his helmet at the men in front of him. It looked like Schiller, hunched inside his greatcoat, stamping his feet and rubbing his hands, with an officer behind him. The officer did not hunch, rub his hands or stamp his feet. His boots were polished, and his clothing was new and untorn. His demeanor was as if the snow were not there at all. Great, Kessler thought, another hard-on. He wondered how long this one would last before his troops dropped a grenade into his bunker.

Schiller was yelling something, and with the wind and the frozen state of his brain, it was a minute before Kessler understood that they were yelling his name. Mein Gott, he thought, probably reconnaissance again. He cursed softly as he struggled out of his snow bank, realizing just how warm he'd actually been as soon as the wind hit him. Still, it was good to be moving. He slung his rifle but carried his submachine gun, as always, tucked under one arm.

Schiller and the officer had moved on, up the trench line, and it took him several minutes to catch up with them, his muscles numb from the cold and immobility. When the officer turned, he looked familiar, but they all did these days. He didn't look happy.

"Unteroffizier Heinrich Kessler?" he shouted above the wind. Kessler nodded.

"You are wanted elsewhere. Come with me."

"My gear," Kessler said, aiming a thumb back over his shoulder at his position. He had nothing but his tornister and zeltbahn on him. All his spare drum magazines for the Russian submachine gun he'd liberated and his cooking gear were still back at the tank.

"Leave it. You won't be needing it. In fact give that to him," the officer said coldly, pointing at the Ppsh-41 submachine gun Kessler had taken off a Russian. "You may keep the rifle." Then the officer turned and strode up the trench. Kessler gave the submachine gun to Schiller. He was going to miss the mean little thing. It'd saved him several times when his Kar98 was useless, and had never jammed, despite the cold.

He nodded to Schiller who gave him a little good luck wave, then followed the officer. He wasn't sure what this was about, but it didn't bode well. He tucked a thumb under the sling of his rifle and leaned into the wind, wondering what he had done wrong.

The command post was warm and dry. He'd thought at first that they'd pulled him out of the field to shoot him, but instead he was shipped to the rear on one of the few transport planes he'd seen make it in recently, then given a clean uniform and a hot bath. He guessed he was somewhere in Austria.

When he finally got out of the bath he'd been surprised to find that his rifle had been cleaned and oiled and the scope polished, the rags he'd tied around it for camouflage torn off. He'd also been supplied with a new pair of boots, and the dress uniform of an unteroffizier with copies of his medals and ribbons was waiting for him. He had no sooner finished dressing than an orderly had appeared with an officer's fur-lined greatcoat, denuded of rank but new, slung over one arm, and a ham sandwich in the other.

Kessler nearly inhaled the sandwich, then promptly thrown up in the washbowl. Too much, too soon, he thought. He wiped his face and cleaned up, the face in the mirror so thin and gaunt he barely recognized himself, then he shrugged on the coat and grabbed the rifle, his sidearm - a little Walther HSc, and the small tornister pony pack that had followed him across Europe, then reported back to the verwaltung for his orders.

When he saw the name on the orders he couldn't help but grin. He fell asleep on the plane to Berlin after eating again, this time with more success. He was met by two SS troopers at the airfield, relieved of his rifle and pack, and driven to the SS Hauptamt on Prinz-Albrechtstrasse, where he was shown to a waiting room with several others, mostly officers. Finally his name was called and he was told to report to an office on the third floor, that Colonel Skorzeny required his presence immediately.

3

L T. COLONEL Otto Skorzeny was a legend in the German military. Even as a student he was a fighter, receiving the famous scar on his face in the tenth of thirteen sword duels he fought while attending university in Vienna. Joining the Austrian Nazi Party in 1931, he soon joined the SA, yet successfully survived the SS takeover.

In 1940, as a young second lieutenant, he came to the notice of German High Command after coming up with a design for special ramps to facilitate the loading of tanks onto ships. He fought in Holland, France and then the Balkans, where he earned a promotion by forcing a large Yugoslav force to surrender.

In 1942 he was hit in the back of the head by shrapnel from Soviet Katyusha rockets, but refused all aid except for a bandage, a few aspirin, and a glass of schnapps. Despite his protestations he was evacuated to Berlin and hospitalized.

He received the Iron Cross for bravery, and while recuperating outlined a blueprint for the training of an unconventional guerrilla commando force which eventually crossed the desk of SS Brigadeführer Walter Schellenberg, head of the SS Foreign Service department of the Reichssicherheitshauptamt; the Reich Main Security Office, and a star was born.

Once put in command of the so - called"Werewolf" schools he designed, Skorzeny trained operatives in espionage, sabotage, assassination and other dark arts, building a trained cadre of special forces operatives, or sonderkommandos, whom he deployed in a number of successful operations in Iran, the Balkans, and other countries in the Mediterranean theater.

Although Operation Long Jump, a bold plan to assassinate Stalin, FDR and Churchill during the Yalta conference was foiled before it began, he did succeed in leading a daring mountain - top rescue of Mussolini in 1943, freeing Il Duce from Italian partisan forces holding him at the Campo Imperatore Hotel, atop the Gran Sasso massif.

Skorzeny and his commandos, Kessler among them, crash-landed nine gliders near the hotel, which was accessible only by cable car, and freed Mussolini without a shot fired. Il Duce was then flown from the mountain in a STOL aircraft - a Fiesler Storch, cementing Skorzeny's reputation as Germany's greatest commando. He received another promotion and a gold and ivory cigarette case from Hitler himself as a thank you.

Kessler found Skorzeny pacing like a lion, hands clasped behind his back; staring at something in the floor only he could see. A feeble glow came from the coal heater in the corner, which was fighting a losing battle against the cold which had seeped into the room overnight. He looked up as Kessler entered, shut the door and saluted.

"Good to see you again, Kessler," Skorzeny said with a grin, ignoring the salute and extending his hand to Kessler, who shook it, returning the smile.

"Good to see you as well, Herr Standartenführer. I apologize for taking so long to get here. The bombing last night brought additional rubble into the streets. We had to find an alternate route."

Skorzeny waved the explanation away. "Sit. I have some information for you, and time is short," he said. Kessler did as he was told, taking a small notebook and a stubby excuse for a pencil from the breast pocket of his uniform.

"Now listen to me carefully. I leave this afternoon for the Ardennes. This may be the most crucial battle of the war, and the Führer himself has given me a critical task. I will be taking charge of the 150th Panzer Brigade. Unfortunately, this causes some problems for our little operation. There are things which must be done while I am gone, or the timetable will be thrown off, and that is *not* an option."

"What is the mission Herr Standartenführer?"

Skorzeny smiled. "We are going to attack where the Allies would never think we would go – the very heart of the United States. It is a three-pronged attack, in conjunction with experimental fighter bombers. The fighters will be armed with American bombs, and we will use their own bunker-busters to destroy the Hoover Dam in Nevada. Their war production in Los Angeles is dependent upon the electricity from the dam. It will be a catastrophe for the Americans. Production of heavy weapons built on the west coast will come grinding to a halt.

"The second part of the attack in western America will be centered around Navajo Depot, the largest arms depot in the U.S. *Your* commandos, acting in a werewolf role, will use the extra ordnance we recover from the depot itself and blow the tracks. They have trains full of ordnance backed up nearly 40 miles – all the way to Flagstaff. A chain reaction explosion there will cut a major rail supply line straight through the heart of America. There will be two zugs involved in the operation – the second zug will handle this task."

"And the first zug sir?"

"The first zug will attack the spa compound at Warm Springs, Georgia, and assassinate the president of the United States. We have reliable information that he will be there in early April. We have until then to get our forces into position."

"Mein Gott. No offense, but it sounds like a suicide mission, Sir," Kessler said.

Skorzeny raised an eyebrow. "Now Kessler, are you refusing to take the mission?"

"Nein! I am yours to command Herr Standartenführer!" Kessler said, coming to attention.

"Gut, because although I do have other people I can use for this mission, you were my first choice…do you understand, Herr Obersturmführer?"

Kessler thought he had heard wrong. "I'm sorry Sir, but I thought you said…"

Skorzeny gave him a thin smile. "Yes, Kessler. You are now an Obersturmführer, a lieutenant. My tailor is waiting to adjust your uniform."

"But Sir…"

Skorzeny waved the objection away. "Listen to me," he said, presenting a folded piece of paper which he held up like a warning.

"This piece of paper is your *Führer Befehl*. Signed by both the Führer and myself, it gives you carte blanche. Whatever you need for this assignment you will get. Simply show this document and it will be done. It will be *your* job to find it. You will have an assistant, a corporal by the name of Danzig. He knows the distribution system better than anyone I know. If he can't find it for you, no one can."

Kessler took the folded letter and inspected it briefly.

"Now, even though I have no doubt that you will wield that letter like a sword, as a sergeant you will have less success than as an officer. No one would dare cross an officer with such a letter, even a lowly Obersturmführer. I am making use of my power and giving you the advantages of rank. As an officer you will have to work harder to find someone of superior rank to assault. This should keep you off the Eastern Front, I hope," Skorzeny said wryly, referring to the reason Kessler had been sent to a punishment battalion in Hungary. Kessler knew enough to keep his mouth shut. The officer's poor judgment had been getting his men killed, and in Kessler's opinion was lucky he was still alive.

"This mission is of the utmost importance to the Reich. It comes from the highest authority. *Führer befehl ist führer befehl.* You cannot fail. If you do, the Reich will be destroyed. If, on the other hand you succeed, we may have a chance for an armistice with the Amis, or at least a delay, allowing us time to rebuild our forces. It has come to this."

"But Sir, I don't know how to act like an officer."

"You know how officers act though, correct?"

"Yes Sir. Usually they're assholes."

Skorzeny laughed. "Thank you, Kessler, I needed that. Now, you will put on your new uniform and be an asshole. Verstehen?"

"Jawohl, Herr Standartenführer."

"Now pay attention. I am tasked with creating a unit for the Ardennes offensive that will be a faux American unit. We will wear American uniforms, drive American jeeps, and paint our tanks to look like Shermans.

Dressed as Americans, and speaking only English, we will play merry hell with them. We'll turn road signs around, even remove them. We'll set up fake roadblocks, even walk into American positions and set charges. I based the idea on the mission I'm giving *you*…it should be interesting."

"Also dangerous."

Skorzeny nodded grimly. "Yes, which is why I'm giving you this command. If I fall, there will be no one but you to carry on. I cannot reveal everything to you just yet, but there are papers in my safe outlining the operation in whole. You will receive them, as well as use of this office. You will use my notes to duplicate my efforts in creating an English-speaking, faux American commando force for part of this mission. I've already collected a number of men for this. Unfortunately, I now need them for Operation Grief in the Ardennes.

"It's not the best use of them in my opinion, but I have my orders as well. I will have no time for what I consider the most important mission of the war, the mission I'm handing over to you. Many of these men I've recruited will not return…for one reason or another. We need more men for this mission anyway. I have a list of people you can start with. You are to handpick them, teach them English if necessary, and get them ready to move.

"I have left detailed instructions as to their dispersal, the type of training I want them to have, as well as more details as to required equipment, including American. Pay close attention to that list. The rest is up to you. You will have great latitude past my initial orders to carry this out as you see fit. I trust your judgment, which is why you are here. It is *critical* we get these men and have them ready to go in six weeks, no more."

"Six weeks?" Kessler asked incredulously.

"Ja. We are on a timetable. If anyone can do it, you can Kessler. You cannot fail. Klar?"

"Jawohl," Kessler replied, wondering what he'd gotten himself into…and how the hell he was going to get the men he needed.

"You will be able to pick anyone you want. Anyone. Remember, you are an officer of the SS now. You will *not* be denied. Not with such a letter as you have in your possession. You will have to twist, maybe break a few arms. Do what ever is necessary, verstehen?"

"Jawohl."

"Now, there is another thing I need you to do. I will have a letter for you to deliver to Adolf Galland, General of Fighters. You know who he is, ja?"

"Of course. He is a legend, Sir."

"Yes, and for a reason. He is a superior officer in every respect. I require that you coordinate the next step of the operation with him. This will give you a better view of the operation as far as what I can tell you to date." Skorzeny handed a thick briefcase to Kessler.

"Guard this with your very life. It contains most of the operation. A temporary safe will be installed in your office this afternoon for you to use until I leave for the Ardennes and you take over this office. It may be a few days, perhaps a week. Change the combination immediately, or we will be sharing everything with the damn Gestapo.

"The second part concerns experimental aircraft. Galland is not even aware of the role these planes will play, but he is training pilots to fly them as we speak. You will brief him on the second part of the plan once you have read the briefing. I know Galland and he can be trusted. You will need his help sooner or later because Göring is involved, and he has spies everywhere."

Kessler raised his eyebrows as he took the briefcase. "Yes, Sir. Ist klar."

"Gut. When I return we will finalize the final plan together. I will answer any questions you have then."

"Jawohl, Herr Standartenführer."

"Your commando gruppe has been given the designation S33, for 'Sonderverband 33'. I want these men equipped and ready when I return. If I do not return…well, the mission will be in your capable hands."

Skorzeny rose from his chair. He looked very tired. Kessler stood with him and Skorzeny reached across the desk to shake his hand.

"Welcome to the officer corps, Heinrich. I know you will make a good one. After you get refitted in a proper uniform I recommend you use some of the money in the briefcase and visit the Konditerei on the Bilderstrasse. Tell them I said to give you my table, that I wanted you to try the potato blintzes, and that you have access to my wine stock.

"It is a private booth, and you will be able to review the documents there. Trust me, it's more secure than this office, which I have swept daily for bugs. If I do not return for some reason, remember to do the same. There are ears everywhere, Kessler. I don't like sharing with those animals in the Gestapo."

"Jawohl, Herr Standartenführer."

"Now get out of here, get yourself a good meal and get some work done." Kessler saluted and let himself out. His last glimpse of Skorzeny was the lieutenant colonel's tired figure slumping into his chair as Kessler closed the door.

4

THE FOLLOWING morning, Jake was up early as usual but, because of his injuries, instead of going out to the barn to saddle up and help with the cattle he was watching the sun come up over Sedona, the yellow light slanting in over the Mogollon Rim, gradually giving shape to the giant spires of red rock, first turning them pink then purple, then gradually to their true colors.

Jake never got tired of watching the light play on the mountains and, if anything, he loved the twilight more than mornings like this, for that was the time the light and shadows played across the rocks in ever changing focus, illuminating one giant formation as if with a spotlight, while another in front of it was bathed in blue shadow. Though he'd grown up in the area, it had always held great mystery for him, and he could understand why it was considered sacred by the local Indian tribes. Sedona was a place of magic.

His legs ached terribly, just from walking a little, but he was determined to get back in the cockpit of a plane again, and walking was the best way he knew of to start rehabilitating his legs, shredded as they had been by antiaircraft fire. He still had shrapnel working its way out in several places - the doctors said there had been a great deal of muscle damage, and that he would likely never fly again. Jake was out to prove them wrong.

Jake Ellison was not raised to spend time feeling sorry for himself, but lately he just couldn't seem to help it. He sat on the wood-chopping stump holding his crutches, watching Jose and Ramiro work their horses around the strays, waiting for one to make a break for it, then chasing it until it ambled back to the herd as if it'd just needed reminding. They were getting together a small shipment of beef for the army - their main customer these days. He was glad the two vaqueros were around, because the sheer effort of merely walking pained him severely, let alone having to gallop a horse after some fool heifer. Still, part of him ached to be beside them, spinning the horse as he shook out a loop to snare an unruly calf.

Cates was out by the barn getting the mule ready to go on one of his prospecting trips into the mountains, and Jake found himself looking at the early morning sun illuminating the peaks, wishing he could go out there with him. There was no help for it though, his legs weren't ready, as he'd found to his dismay the day he'd returned to Sedona and tried to get on a horse for the first time since he'd left for the war. Horses and planes were all he knew and loved, and he couldn't have either one of them. It just ate at him to have to sit and watch the world go by.

He watched the sky turn robin's egg blue, then struggled to his feet, tucked the crutches under his arms and turned back towards the house. Jake Ellison was being forced to admit that he now had physical limitations, and while the idea didn't sit very well with him he found the reality to be far worse. If it hadn't been for the sheer joy of being home he would have been in a foul mood indeed. He had barely managed to get off the stump when he heard Rosa's cry from behind him, as he had heard it so many times growing up:

"Jake, mi Tomatillo…" she said as she threw her arms around him. He could rest his head atop her graying head now, but he remembered a time when she towered above him. Her word in the house was still law, and no one, not even Cates, dared defy her on matters of household. When she went on a tear she'd grow quiet, but slam things down on the counters and look at you with such an evil eye you would swear she could turn a body to stone if she really set her mind to it. On the other hand, when you were in her good graces, as Jake was now, there was no better place in the world to be.

"It's so good to be home Rosa. I missed you…and your jalapeño cornbread, too."

Rosa swatted him with one hand, but did so with a smile, holding him around the waist as he turned to limp to the house. It was slow, painful going, and the look of concern in Rosa's eyes grew until finally she yelled for Jose in Spanish to come help Jake or she would fry his gizzard for breakfast…at least that's what Jake got from it.

Cates, Jose, Rosa and Ramiro all helped him, of course, but every time they did Jake couldn't help but feel a twinge of resentment. He knew he was lucky to be alive, but he hated the crutches with a passion. He couldn't wait to burn the damn things. His teeth were clenched in pain as they reached the welcome shade of the huge cottonwoods which shaded the front training arena, but he managed a smile.

Jose took his arm and walked next to him in case he tripped and fell, something which Jake seemed to do on a fairly regular basis these days, his legs on fire as Rosa went into the kitchen. Before he knew it he was sitting in a rocking chair on the porch and a cold glass of lemonade was sweating in front of him. He drank most of it down, and looked up to see Rosa watching him.

"What?" he asked.

"Toma. Todo," she said, bringing her palm up as if to tilt the glass for him, just as she had when he was little and wouldn't finish his milk. He emptied the glass, and she smiled with satisfaction, taking the glass from him and handing him another with the other hand.

"Bueno. No so fast theese time eh? I am making breakfast, but is not done. I will get jou something to hold jou, yes?"

"It's okay Rosa. I can wait."

"I will get jou something," she said, walking away, and Jake knew from the finality in her voice that there was going to be no arguing with her. Not if he knew what was good for him.

Cates slapped the dust from his jeans with his hat as he came up the wide, ancient juniper steps and hung it on the pronghorn antler hat rack screwed to the outside wall near the door. He saw the big glass of lemonade in Jake's hand and grinned.

"Bet she's back out here in ten seconds with something for you to eat."

No sooner had he voiced this prediction but the screen door swung open and Rosa came through with a steaming plate of verde corn tamales and a bowl of fresh guacamole.

Cates looked at Jake and winked. "Say, Honey, think I could ge of that lemonade?" he said.

"Chure. It's in the icebox where it always is," she said, placing the food on the table in front of Jake.

Cates looked at Jake soberly, then looked back at her. "Are you tellin' me I can't even get served in my own house?"

"Si, this is what I'm telling jou." With that, she kissed Jake on the top of the head and shook his skull gently with both hands just as she'd done when he was a boy.

"I have to finish breakfast," she said, and was gone.

Cates chuckled. "See what I put up with? I'll be right back. Gonna go get some lemonade. You want more?"

"No, this is my second glass."

"Bet you forgot what a tyrant she was eh?"

"It's good to be home."

"I'll bet," Cates said with a smile.

"Hey Cates, looks like a car's coming."

The sheriff's black '39 Plymouth came up the road slowly, kicking up a small cloud of dust then coming to a shuddering halt, dieseling a couple times before finally dying, clearly in need of a tune-up. Ben Goodwin climbed out and slammed the door. Ben clearly wasn't suffering from lack of food, despite his wife passing some years earlier from consumption.

He wasn't a fat man, but he was carrying around a few extra pounds. By the looks of it, the sheriff was spending quite a bit of time at the café. Still, Ben Goodwin was one of those people who are hard to dislike. His disarming smile was his most effective weapon. Cates had once told Jake a story about Ben walking right up to the Dominguez boy while he was holding a shotgun, and talking him out of it. Most cops just would have shot him. Ben wasn't that way. His usual pleasant smile was missing this morning however.

"Hello Cates, Jake. How are the legs?"

"Fine, Ben. Better every day," Jake lied.

"Ben, why don't you set awhile? Rosa just made some fresh lemonade this morning, and we finally got the freezer unit fixed on that damn gas fridge, so we've got ice," Cates said. Ben said Rosa made the best lemonade around, which could have been due to the fact that she usually splashed a little tequila in it for him.

"I can't, Cates, but thanks. I actually came to ask Jake if he'd do me another favor."

"Not another body, I hope."

"No, one's enough. Actually I was hoping Jake would go with me up to Hausen's and break the news to Laurel. I thought it might be better coming from you, Jake, since you were so close. I'm sorry, but I don't know who else to ask."

Jake looked out at the mountains again, the sun crowning them with golden light. He'd dated Laurel, Lily's older sister, for nearly four years during and after high school, starting in the summer before their junior year. They'd run into each other at Slide Rock one day and talked, really talked, for the first time. He would never forget how Laurel looked that day, her hair golden in the sunlight, her smooth legs beaded with water…her smile warm and coy at the same time. It had been a less than idyllic love affair, but one both of them had been sure at the time would end with marriage and children - all the things one normally expected from life.

Pearl Harbor had changed that dream. He'd been in Alaska working on a fishing boat at the time, and had signed up like every other red-blooded American boy. Laurel had yelled at him, then cried, and they'd sworn to each other that love would find a way, that neither would give up the other, that she would wait, that he would return to her, and they would pick up where they'd left off. Neither of them had counted on the war changing everything. Things had always been up and down between them, but the war seemed to have been the final straw.

She'd written for a while, but then the letters seemed to come further and further apart. By the time his squadron had left North Africa to support the new offensive in Italy the letters had nearly ceased altogether.

Jake was up to his ears in German and Italian fighters for several days, and his best friend at the time, Tops Miller, had been killed in his P-38 while covering Jake's back over the ruins of Monte Cassino.

Retribution was the word for the day, and Jake had doubled the kills stenciled below his cockpit, but he didn't care. He'd lost a friend. Afterwards, he was sitting on a sandbag with Italian writing on it, smoking a cigarette and someone handed him his mail. "Dear Jake," her letter began...

"Sure, Ben. I need to sit for a few minutes first. Sure you don't want some coffee, or maybe some of that lemonade while you wait?"

A poor cousin of Ben's usual infectious grin crept onto one corner of his face. "I guess one glass wouldn't hurt," he said as he hung his hat on the antler rack and knocked on the screen door politely.

"Go on in. You'll have to get it yourself. Rosa's on a tear this morning. Jake made her mad," Cates said.

Jake looked at Cates, who ignored him as Ben pulled open the heavy wooden screen door.

"Oh, and Ben, the tequila's in the corner cabinet."

5

THE DRIVE north to the Hausen place had been all too quick. Jake could see the familiar mailbox at the end of the long driveway, the driveway he'd driven up so many times filled with a sense of anticipation, of excitement even, but never, until this moment, of dread. This time the long driveway was the road to hell, the corridor down a cellblock to the electric chair, the path to perdition. Laurel was the last person he wanted to see, especially under these conditions.

He was painfully aware of everything around him; the crunch of gravel beneath the car tires, the soft squeak of the shock absorbers as they wound their way up Route 89A, the pale sun beating on the dusty dashboard...some kind of news about GIs in Paris on the radio. Ben kept the police radio turned down most of the time, only turning it up if a call came through. There wasn't a lot of crime in this part of the world, and he spent much of his day holding down a stool at Purdymun's café. He pulled into the drive, shut off the car and looked at Jake.

"Want me to come in?"

Jake shook his head no in response, opened the door, swung his crutches out of the car and pushed himself up and out, bracing himself on the car door. There was no breeze, although it was cooler and shadier here in the canyon than at the ranch. Most of the leaves had fallen - winter was around the corner; a few yellow leaves left shadowing trees a harbinger of things to come.

The house looked pretty much the same as he remembered it, except that the red begonias that Lily's mother had been so proud of seemed to have died with her. It made him sad when he looked at the dry, brown plants spaced ever so carefully on the short, red rock stem wall which ran between the big piñon pine posts holding up the front edge of the veranda.

The mesquite floorboards of the porch, always carefully swept in his experience, were now adrift in sand and dried leaves. No rug lay in front of the door to wipe your feet on, no one holding a pewter pitcher of ice water to greet you at the door. The door was closed in fact, something he remembered as a rarity at this house.

He had loved Laurel and Lily's mother almost as much as his own, and she'd shown him the love due an adopted son in return. It had pissed Laurel off at times - that her own mother seemed to side with him, love him even more than her. Of course that wasn't true, but it spoke of her mother's true heart - the one that gave solace to strangers, that fed you without question and welcomed you with open arms.

When she had died, the place had changed. It had lost its polish, its gleam, its ready, loving openness. Laurel had written him in North Africa about her mother's death and it had hit him hard. He'd gone for a walk on the dunes, feeling as if he'd lost his own mother. He missed it, and he missed her. She'd been one of a kind. Now he brought pain to her house.

He stood in front of the door he'd stood before so many times, raised his hand to knock, paused, then let it go. The sounds felt ominous and lonely in the stillness. He knocked again, waited a bit, then turned to go.

He was halfway off the porch when he heard the door open. He turned stiffly, and there she was, as lovely as he remembered.

"Hello? Oh God. Jake? JAKE. It *is* you. Jesus!"

He felt something go out of him, and for a moment he forgot why he had come.

"You changed your hair," he said inanely.

She touched it self-consciously, a small smile lighting her face. "Years ago. You were still overseas…" she began, but the light left her. She gave him another smile, this one forced. "Whatever are you doing here?" She looked over his shoulder at the sheriff sitting in his car. "What's Ben doing here?"

"Please, Laurel. Can we go inside?"

The look of quiet amusement on her face turned to a look of fear, as if she already knew what was coming. She nodded, and gestured for him to come in. Jake looked back at Ben, who had decided to stay in the car for now. He found himself wishing he'd never told Ben he'd help him.

23

Stepping into the house was like stepping back in time. He took a deep breath. The smell of the lemon water Laurel's mother had used with the ammonia for cleaning had faded, but was still faintly present…or perhaps he was imagining it. It was cool inside, but stuffy. Rebecca Hausen would have had the French doors to the garden in back open even this time of year, but they were closed now and no longer sparkling clean. The rug was the same deep red and black Navajo as he remembered, the drop-leaf mesquite table her son Harold had built stood against one wall; the one she'd been so proud of despite having to shim one leg so it stood level. Harold had died in '38 in an auto accident.

He ran a finger over it and was rewarded with a fine coating of dust. He wondered where Abby Begay was. Their maid was Navajo, and he tried to remember if she'd ever spoken to him. He remembered her letting him in the door, and leading him into the living room, or just nodding with her head to indicate direction. Not much for talking, that Abby.

Laurel came from the kitchen with two glasses and thrust one at him.

"Tom Collins, our favorite."

"Thanks…but no," he told her, neglecting to tell her that he didn't drink them anymore, because every time he did he thought of her. Besides, it was barely 10:30 in the morning. He wondered if she began drinking so early every day.

She shrugged. "More for me, I guess. Want me to make you some coffee?"

"No thank you. Let's sit down."

Jake followed her into the living room, where he collapsed with difficulty into one of the low Mission-style chairs that flanked the fireplace. A new Zenith bakelite radio played Benny Goodman softly and she rose again to turn it off. As she sat back down Jake noticed she'd finished her drink already and was starting on his.

"All right Jake, what's this all about?"

Jake looked at the woman he'd once loved…still loved a little, if you wanted the absolute truth. He hadn't been sure of it until this moment, but now an ache in his heart amplified the terrible thing he had brought with him.

"It's Lily isn't it? Is she all right? In jail? You wouldn't believe what a little wildcat she's turned into…out until all hours, coming home reeking of booze. She's only nineteen for God's sakes. I've done my best, but ever since Mom died she's just gone crazy. It's really not her you know, it's those friends of hers…"

"Laurel."

"I've tried everything Jake, but I'm just not up to it. She wants to dig her own grave, fine. I'm washing my hands of her if she's…"

"LAUREL."

She looked at him, mouth slightly open.

"Lily's dead."

It came out just like that. He'd wanted to break it to her gently, but that's how it came out. He supposed there was no good way, but it still felt brutal.

"What? DEAD? How can she be dead? I just saw her!"

Jake could hear her panic rising, the shrill note in her voice finding a scale that wasn't in her range…eyes wide, uncomprehending the madness her ears had borne witness to.

"I'm sorry, Laurel."

"No. She can't be… She's just a kid. If this is a joke…"

"It's no joke, Laurel. I'm sorry, but Lily is gone from our lives."

"But…but how? I mean, when she didn't come home, I just thought it was another fling. We'd had an argument…Oh God," she said, this last in an almost wheezing tone as the wind left her. She reached for a pack of Lucky Strikes on the table next to her and took one shakily from the pack, tried to light it.

Jake reached over gently and took the matches, lighting it for her. She drew the smoke into her lungs and closed her eyes, one hand supporting the arm of the hand with the cigarette, with which she held her head. Blue smoke roiled towards the ceiling. Her mother never would have allowed smoking in the house, but Jake supposed it didn't matter much anymore.

She raised her head to look at him, tears starting now, running down her cheeks.

"How? A car accident? What?"

Jake shook his head, hating what he had to tell her.

"Jake?"

"She was murdered, Laurel."

"*Murdered?*"

"Yes."

"You're sure of this."

"I'm afraid so."

"How?"

"I can't tell you that."

"Jake, she was my little sister, and I want to know."

"No. Dammit, Laurel I just…can't. I wish I could," he lied, knowing that he could never give her the gruesome details of her younger sister's death, also knowing that soon the rumor mill in town would be working overtime, and it was just a matter of time before she heard something horrible. It was his job *not* to tell her, to keep the details confidential, but he knew that even if it weren't, that he still wouldn't be able to tell her. It was just too horrible for words. "I saw her body," was all he could get out.

He looked at her. The tears had stopped for now, and she stared out the window vacantly. Jake wondered what was going through her mind. He forced himself up and off the chair, his legs protesting the movement. She stood and embraced him, and he held her awkwardly, wishing he didn't have to, wishing that it wouldn't end, and wishing he had never joined the goddamn Army Air Corps - maybe he could have prevented this.

She held his shoulders at arms length and looked at him. His hand dropped from the smooth, remembered curve of her shoulder blade to the inanimate curve of his crutch as he looked back into her eyes, the eyes he remembered so well.

"Thank you, Jake. Thank you for coming to tell me. I wouldn't want to have heard it from anyone else…" the tears took over then, and she fell back against him, nearly dropping them both, but he managed to hold on somehow.

"Ben wants to ask you some questions as soon as you're ready. Said he can come back in a few days, but the sooner the better."

"I'm the last one, Jake. The last one," she sobbed softly in his ear, the hot wetness from her eyes on his neck and cheek. Her family was gone: Her brother Harold before the war, her father years before that, her mother in '43 of some mysterious flu…now this. She had no one left.

"Don't leave me alone, Jake. *Please.*"

Jake closed his eyes against her, the smell of her, the feel of her, just the way he remembered her, just the way he'd imagined it sitting in a filthy, rumpled uniform, waiting for orders on a captured landing strip in Italy, not knowing at the time just how much he had lost in the war already, nor how much he was about to lose.

"I'm here, Laurel. I'm here," was all he could say.

6

KESSLER'S RETURN to Berlin came as a shock. The city he loved had been under nearly constant bombardment since he'd been sent to the eastern front, with the Americans bombing during the day and the Brits taking the night shift.

Everything was in short supply; food, fuel, even clean water. The beauty of the Lindenstrasse, the famous, broad boulevard named for the linden trees which lined both sides, which despite having been covered with camouflage tarps to present less of a landmark, had been ravaged as whatever trees that hadn't been shredded by Allied bombing raids had been cut down for firewood by desperate Berliners. There was simply nothing left. Coal and kaffee were as good as gold. Everywhere he looked was devastation and horror.

People were hanged from lamp posts just for being in the wrong place at the wrong time. Ostensibly, the death squads were looking for deserters, but when they didn't find real ones, anyone who crossed their path would do, and there was no one to stop their predations. A woman cutting rancid meat from a dead horse would be shot as a thief, an old man too crippled to serve hanged as a traitor, boys far too young for war were rounded up and forced into badly fitted uniforms, then sent to face tanks with nothing but a panzerfaust, or *"armor fist"* which was only effective within 60 meters. The Wehrmacht got the 80-meter panzerfausts of course, and the Hitler Youth and the Volksturm "volunteers" got what was left.

When they got to the warehouse on Heerstrasse it was total chaos. Trucks and forklifts fought for room to maneuver, their drivers blaring their horns and shouting epithets at each other and waving their arms in frustration. With the war on the eastern front expanding and the Americans getting closer and closer to Berlin, the warehouse was being emptied at an alarming rate.

Danzig corralled an irritated looking NCO with a clipboard who was directing the loading of containers full of rockets onto the back of a flatbed Mercedes truck. Kessler watched impatiently as Danzig argued with him fruitlessly, then returned to where Kessler stood, hands clasped behind his back, only the white knuckles of the hands clutching his gloves an indicator of his displeasure.

"I am sorry, Lieutenant. He says they are far too busy to be troubled with a few measly uniforms and field gear. He said to come back later in the week."

"You showed him the letter?"

"I tried to...he turned his back on me."

"Give it to me. Raus."

Danzig handed him the letter and Kessler drew himself up to his full height as he strode forward, his new boots clicking on the damp concrete, his sniper's eyes on his target's back.

"SERGEANT."

The NCO looked over one shoulder, then seeing an officer approaching him turned quickly and snapped to attention.

"Yes, Herr Obersturmführer. What can I do for you?"

"My adjutant came to you with a request for some tropical uniforms and load bearing gear. I require your help. Immediately."

"I am extremely sorry, Sir, but I have been given the responsibility for loading these trucks supplying troops on the Russian front."

"Do you see this letter?" Kessler said, waving the letter in his face, "It is from Standartenführer Otto Skorzeny and has the Führer's signed endorsement. I am to be assisted in any way that I require."

"I'm sorry Obersturmführer Kessler, there's Major Schnelling. Perhaps he can help you. He is in charge here."

Kessler gave the NCO a look that would curdle milk just as the major to whom he had been referring stomped over to them.

Kessler clicked his heels, bowing his head briefly in deference to the major's rank.

"Herr Major, I apologize for the interruption, but I require you to read this," he said, extending the letter stiffly.

The Major snatched it from his grasp, snapped it open and ran his eyes over it briefly, then looked at Kessler with the beginning of a sneer.

"Your bonafides are impeccable, Herr Obersturmführer, but I'm afraid we're too busy at the moment to search for a small lot of dusty tropical gear that at this time of year is undoubtedly buried at the rear of the warehouse. In case you haven't heard, the Russians are coming, and so are the Americans. I need every man I have to load ammunition for the front. The SS came by yesterday and took a third of my men. Come back tomorrow. Better yet, don't come back at all."

With that the major crumpled the letter and threw it to the ground, turned his back and began walking away. Kessler drew his Walther, pointed it at the back of the Major's head and pulled the trigger. The Major crumpled to the ground like a sack of flour as the enlisted men looked on in horror.

Kessler calmly walked over, picked up the crumpled letter and smoothed it out carefully, then raised it above his head so everyone could see, the smoking pistol still in his hand at his side.

"This officer treated a letter of authorization from the Führer himself with contempt. This letter says I am to be given *complete and total cooperation*. Nothing else will do, *verstehen*? Now I need three men to help my adjutant find what we require and load it into my staff car. Who would like to help me?"

The loading dock had gone quiet. Forklifts had stopped, men whispered to each other while others stood by silently. Finally an NCO snapped an order at three men who sprinted forward to salute Kessler, the fear in their eyes plain to see. Kessler smiled at them.

"Danzig. Have these men drag this body out of the way, then help the sergeant with the list. I want to be out of here as soon as possible."

Danzig looked pale. "Jawohl, Herr Obersturmführer."

Kessler looked at his watch as Danzig and the other men ran into the warehouse. He figured they had half an hour.

7

LAUREL HAD finally cried herself to sleep, and Jake had removed her shoes, covered her with a blanket, and closed the door to her room softly. As he crept out of the house however, something pulled him down the hall to Lily's room. It was in the east wing of the house, far away from Laurel's room, the separation of the two girls in order to give them each their privacy, their parents' gift to them both.

He paused with his hand on the doorknob, not sure why he was doing this, but he knew he had to.

The room was neat as a pin, in stark contrast to the whirlwind he'd always encountered in Laurel's habitat. Lily had been the deliberate, careful one, although she'd had the biggest heart in Arizona.

Jake eased off the crutches and sat down on the bed, still covered with the turquoise chenille bedspread she'd had since she was a young girl. It was a velveteen rabbit of a bedspread, growing thin in spots, soft as only love can make things, and when he lowered his nose to it he found a vague remnant of her favorite lilac scent. Lily had been like a little sister to him, more sweet and lovely than the harder edged Laurel.

He had thought it rather sweet, the young girl bringing him lemonade or something else to eat or drink every time he came to pick up her sister. They'd become pals of a sort, and he had learned more about the family from Lily, the little chatterbox, than he ever did from Laurel, who'd always been somewhat reserved.

He wiped the blur of tears from his eyes and wiped his nose on his sleeve. Big strong war veteran, he thought. He'd seen death up close, had smelled the charred corpses of fellow pilots, had seen first hand what men do to each other in the heat of battle, but for some reason the death of this sweet innocent girl had hit him hard.

Everywhere he looked in the room he saw her, saw her memories hanging from every corner. A picture of her goofing at the Grand Canyon, one that Jake had taken himself years before when the three of them had gone up there for an overnight, was stuck in the corner of the mirror, next to a picture of Dick Lawson. Were they dating? Could he be her killer?

Somehow he couldn't imagine that – he had gone to school with Dick, who was just one grade behind him, and they had been friends, although not close ones, and had played baseball together. He hadn't seen Dick since before the War began, heard he'd joined the Marines and was in the Pacific somewhere.

A white, milk-glass vase whose knobby surface matched the texture of the chenille bedspread stood on one corner of her dresser, next to the jewelry box her brother had made her for her twelfth birthday. Lily had always loved fresh flowers, had gotten it from her mother, he guessed, although Laurel had always seemed fairly immune to their charm.

It was Lily who had often picked and changed the flowers in the house, like the ones that always stood in the cut glass vase in the entrance, and they were always beautiful bouquets; tulips, lilies and Black-eyed Susans vying for attention with a sprig of baby's breath or a bit of Queen Anne's lace. Daffodils were her favorite as he remembered, along with lilies of course; her namesake.

The roses in the vase were brown and dead, and suddenly he couldn't stand them anymore. He picked up the vase and one crutch and limped outside where he threw the dead flowers away. He looked towards the car, but Ben had his head back on the seat, and it looked like he was asleep. Jake canvassed the yard without seeing anything, but in the garden behind the house he found a few stray poppies going to seed and some ragged white chrysanthemums still oddly blooming.

Kneeling awkwardly with one crutch, he picked some and took them back to the house, cut them off and refilled the vase, carefully wiping the bottom with a dishtowel just as Lily always had, before setting it on the lace doily that covered the dresser. He paused at Laurel's door but heard nothing but the sound of her breathing, which was soft and slow. After three Tom Collins by his count, he wasn't surprised.

He limped back down the hall on one crutch and put the flowers on the dresser in Lily's room then stood looking at them a moment. The flowers stuck out awkwardly, at all angles, not bunched gracefully together as they always were when Lily cut them. He tried half-assed to make them look better, but it was no use. He leaned heavily against the dresser, his eyes closed, legs aching, the tears trying to come back as he thought of her. He looked up at the ceiling, in search of the God he wasn't sure existed anymore, not after all he had seen, and asked "Why? Why her? Of all the rotten bastards you could have taken, why *her?*"

Furious, he turned and kicked the wall, kicked it hard, with his 'good' leg, then slumped back down on the bed in pain. As he was looking down at the floor, out of the corner of his eye he noticed he'd dislodged the baseboard a bit with the kick, which puzzled him, since the house was so well built. He immediately felt terrible – he was tearing their house apart. He knelt awkwardly between the bed and dresser and saw that a short piece of baseboard had been cut out then refit, an obvious repair, but he could see a gap behind it. He wiggled it a bit and it came right out. Inside was a small treasure trove.

There was a silver locket of whose provenance he had no clue, a small bottle of Kentucky bourbon - three-quarters full, a monogrammed handkerchief, and wrapped in it, a small, worn copy of Jane Eyre. As he pulled it out he saw that it inside was a letter, in an envelope with foreign stamps on it. Curious, he pulled it from the envelope, but it was unreadable since it was in German. It was simply addressed to a Post Office box in Sedona.

German? Why would Lily have a letter written in German? It didn't seem as though it were addressed to her, it just opened with "Liebchen," which from his very limited German he knew meant sweetheart. Other than that, he literally couldn't make heads or tails of it. There were two pages, and a signature he couldn't make sense of either. Why would she keep such an odd thing, and where did she get it?

He ran his hand inside the cavity to double check, but all he found was a few dusty marbles and some stale chewing gum; a child's treasure. He put everything back except the letter, the handkerchief and the book, which he pocketed out of curiosity, and slipped the baseboard back into place. He would not reveal her secret.

Jake groaned as he got up off the floor, his legs shaking. He was through grieving now and felt a coldness inside him that he had only felt before in a dogfight. He was going to get to the bottom of this and kill the son of a bitch who had hurt her if it was the last thing he did. He gritted his teeth as he crept from the bedroom, leaning heavily on his crutches now, the pain from kneeling in that cramped space pure agony. It mixed with his anger to become a red blur. He found his way to the car and fought with the door, startling Ben, who awoke with a snort.

"Sorry…couldn't help it. Been up since 3:00 a.m."

"No worries. Laurel's sleeping too. Hell, even I feel like a nap."

"You all right?" Ben asked as he started the car.

"Define 'all right'," Jake said, but Ben didn't reply, just backed the car out of the drive and headed back down the canyon towards Sedona. Neither of them noticed the beige Ford sedan parked down the road pull out behind them and follow at a distance.

8

3,000 MILES away in Berlin, Kessler was making the tour of warehouses, collecting material for the mission. He had a shopping list, and this late in the war things were getting harder and harder to find. The German Army had always been efficient, but the lack of materiel was endemic, and to get what you needed you had to show up with a letter such as he had in his pocket and threaten someone. Kessler's descriptions and threats of the eastern front had so far netted him a number of badly needed items, but he was still shy the weapons he needed. Today he would fix that.

They had given him a small staff car, a well-used Mercedes Geländewagen with four-wheel drive and four wheel steering, missing its doors but with a decent canvas roof and fortunately, a good heater. Instead of the ever-present Danzig, Schmidt, his best NCO had come with him as Kessler wanted his opinion.

Their driver, Rudi, was a sullen Hitler Youth who yearned for battle in the way only those who have not yet been in battle do, and he repeatedly begged Kessler for stories until Kessler had yelled at him for leaving the car running while they were inside the last warehouse on yesterday's list. He knew it was cold outside, and that he'd been given all the gasoline he needed, but Kessler couldn't help but think of the Panzers in France enduring the same cold, and needing the very fuel he was using so much of. The boy had been quiet and sullen ever since. Kessler didn't know which was worse, the voluble boy or the quiet one.

The building they had come to was smaller than the distribution centers they had so far visited. It was stone, not brick, except where the high arches of the windows had been bricked over. It reminded him a bit of a church without a steeple. A high razor-wire topped fence surrounded it, and regular SS guarded the gates, a far cry from the Volksturm and Wehrmacht guards he'd seen everywhere else. Their papers were examined, then they were waved through into a courtyard.

They left Rudi to sulk in the car, and showed their papers yet again to two guards wearing Waffen SS oak camouflage standing guard outside the door. They seemed bored, and Kessler recognized tired veterans when he saw them. The place was well guarded for as small as it was. As he stepped into the building he began to understand why. With the exception of a couple small offices, most of the building was one huge workroom, and it was filled to overflowing with weapons of every type and description strewn everywhere – on top of benches and leaning against them, on the floor, even hanging on the walls and from the beams and rafters.

Despite being officially banned, the soft strains of Mendelssohn wafted through the room and a small group of men were working at benches on various items. The only one Kessler recognized as being anything was a mortar, but it looked smaller and lighter than any he had ever used. It looked like it had Japanese writing on it. He reminded himself to take a look at it before he left.

A thin, sallow-faced man with a permanently sad demeanor rose from his bench to come greet them.

"Herr Seiler. Thank you for seeing us," Kessler said. The older man shook their hands solemnly.

"Colonel Skorzeny called me himself and asked me to help you. How could I refuse? I know his family. Now what is it you require, Lieutenant?" Seiler asked, looking at Kessler.

"MP40s, panzerfaust…and a rifle," Kessler said. Seiler was already shaking his head.

"No, I have no MP40s. Well, I actually have one, but it's being gold-plated for Himmler, and you can't have it."

"I have a letter from Standartenführer Skorzeny. For whatever I deem necessary."

"I don't care if it's from the Führer himself - Himmler would have my head. Come in, tell me your requirements. Perhaps we can do something for you."

They followed Seiler into the crowded workroom, and he quickly cleared off a couple of chairs piled high with papers and machine parts.

"Kaffee? Seiler asked them.

"Danke," Kessler said, and Seiler yelled at an underling to bring two mugs.

Kessler could smell that it was real, a pleasant surprise. He sipped with pleasure from the chipped mug given to him.

"Danke, Herr Seiler. This is very good."

Franz Seiler nodded and waved them into chairs. His desk was strewn with more papers and machine parts. Kessler recognized a receiver from a ZB26 and a trigger group from an MG42 peeking out from the drift of loose papers. He looked at Schmidt, who just smiled over his coffee mug at him.

"Now. Your requirements?"

Kessler took his list from the breast pocket of his uniform along with the letter of authorization from Skorzeny and handed it to Seiler. The old man glanced at the letter as if he had seen it before and turned his attention to the list.

"Hmmm. The weight is the problem eh? You want all this gear but you have not weighed it. You simply cannot take all this. Perhaps you should get a bigger plane?"

"The plane is already quite large. We have definite limitations on the weight, as you can see."

"Then you have a problem."

"Which is why we came to you, Herr Seiler," Schmidt interjected, trying to be diplomatic. Franz Seiler sighed and put on his reading glasses.

"You are outfitting 24 men."

"Yes."

"They will be jumping."

"Half may. The weight requirements are the same either way, however."

Seiler looked up at this. "You are sure?"

"Positive...the issue is fuel consumption," Kessler said, wondering how much he should tell him.

"Ahhh. I see," Seiler said, nodding his head as if he really did. Kessler wondered how many times he'd been through this kind of thing. "I do have something that may work, although finding you 24 of them might be problematic… KARL, *kommen zie heir,*" he barked, causing a younger man to drop something on his bench and walk over.

"Yes, Herr Seiler?"

"Do you remember those Beretta 38/44s we modified for the Italians?" Karl nodded. "Whatever became of them? We shipped six of them for them to evaluate, but they couldn't make up their minds on the changes, remember? Are they still here?"

"I think so mein Herr…in fact, I think I know where they are."

"Get me one will you?"

Karl nodded and disappeared through a door.

"Let's move on to something else. The ammunition is no problem. The Panzerfausts…I have a couple I can let you have, but the weight issue again…you must look at this list carefully and decide what you can live without. Pare it down to the minimum. We will do our best with the rest, but…" he shrugged, "I do not know enough to know what you really need for this mission.

"The American weapons are not a problem, but they are fairly heavy. The Thompson weighs 12 pounds, the Garand nine and a half, over ten fully loaded. 4.63 kilograms to be precise. The .45 pistols are not a problem. I have the 8 you require, although there is a colonel in the SS who is going to be very disappointed."

"Let him be. The future of the Reich hangs on this mission," Kessler said.

Seiler smiled for the first time. "Do you know, Herr Kessler, just how many times I have heard that? Now, what about the rifle?"

"8mm, four-power scope. I need a hardcase, and it would be preferable if it broke down into two sections. Good trigger."

"How far will you be shooting with it?"

"I don't know yet."

Seiler frowned at this. "Guess."

"Probably no more than 300, perhaps 400 meters at the most."

"HESS," Seiler barked again. Another man, one older than he this time, looked up from his bench where he was working on the tiny mortar Kessler had seen earlier. Seiler waved to him and the man walked over, wiping his hands on a towel.

"What's the overall length on that G43 you built?"

"110 centimeters."

"Get it for me will you? He turned back to Kessler and Schmidt. "You have fired the G43 eh?"

"Yes. A good weapon, but not as accurate as a bolt action," Kessler said.

"I carried one during Stalingrad. It is a good weapon but the scope is fragile," Schmidt opined.

"Ahh. Here's the boy with the Beretta," Seiler said.

His helper had appeared magically with a greasy burlap sack. He handed it to Seiler, who reached in and pulled out a submachine gun. Kessler recognized it as a Beretta 38/44, but it had a folding stock. He couldn't hide his excitement. He liked the Beretta, had used it in Italy. He actually preferred it over the MP40. It was lighter, more accurate, simple and very well made.

Seiler wiped the grease from the weapon carefully with a towel, checked the chamber and inserted an empty magazine. He unfolded the stock, which Kessler recognized as an MP40 underfolding type, and handed it to Kessler. Kessler brought it to his shoulder, and was surprised at how light it was.

"Nearly a full kilogram lighter than an MP40. We tried bakelite for the stock, but it cracked for some reason we could never determine, so we kiln-dried some wood and laminated it. The pistol grip panels are bakelite however. We used alloy parts where we could, such as for the grip frame. The barrel is not much shorter than the MP40 however, so it shouldn't bother you.

"The barrel was originally fluted to save weight while maintaining accuracy. The flutes also help dissipate heat under high volume of fire conditions, but it was decided to simplify the manufacturing process, especially at this point in the war. Unfortunately, I only have ten of them.

Tell me, you do have some weapons already, don't you? Some MP40s perhaps?"

"Yes, but they are very worn."

"Hmm. The best I can do is to service your current weapons. I have run out of the solution I need to re-blue them, but I can replace the barrels and any other worn parts. Give me what you have and I will have Karl rebuild them. A good job for an apprentice. Perhaps he can even paint them for you."

"I will have them delivered to you immediately," Kessler said. "Schmidt?"

"I will take care of it right away. Herr Seiler, do you have a telephone I may use?"

"Over there…beside the American Browning," Seiler said.

"Do you have a range here? I would like to shoot the Beretta," Kessler said.

Seiler smiled yet again. "Of course. Karl, take Herr Kessler out to the range."

Kessler was taken outside to a well-equipped 50-meter range surrounded by a high stone wall banked with sandbags. There were a number of targets already set up at 10, 25 and 50 meters, as Karl set a box of loaded magazines at his feet.

"Do you require anything else?" Karl asked. His lack of obsequiousness made Kessler intensely aware that his rank didn't matter here. He doubted it would even if he had been wearing the shoulder boards of a field marshal, so he thanked the young man, whom he noticed walked with the limp of a club foot, and turned to the range.

The Beretta had two triggers, the front for single shots, the rear for automatic fire. Kessler had found this difference from the MP40 disconcerting until he had actually used it in battle, then he had decided he liked it since it saved on ammunition…an important consideration in the mission to come, since resupply would be impossible.

He adjusted the sling to support the weapon and fired several bursts, then ran through the targets firing single shots. He inspected the targets with satisfaction. He fired several more shots aimed as carefully as he could, and was once more impressed with the little weapon's trigger pull and its accuracy. He was remembering why he liked the Beretta submachineguns. Satisfied with the weapon's performance, he handed the gun to Schmidt, who seemed eager to try it. Schmidt ran through a couple magazines, which put a big smile on his face.

"Good, eh?" he asked Schmidt.

"Yes, Sir, but truthfully I prefer my MP40...although it would be nice to get a new barrel for it."

"I'm sure Herr Seiler will make them as new,"

They went back inside, where Seiler was talking to the other, older man he had sent for the G43. As they turned to greet Kessler and Schmidt, Kessler's attention was taken by the semiautomatic G43 the technician held in his hands. It was familiar, but there was something about it that was different.

"Well?" Seiler asked in a slightly bored tone.

"The Beretta will be perfect. Even Schmidt liked it."

Seiler smiled slightly. "I'm glad it meets with your approval, Herr Kessler."

Kessler could tell that the old man had had no doubts about the Beretta. Seiler took it by the sling so he wouldn't burn his hands and handed it to Karl, who took the weapon to clean it. Seiler nodded at the other man, who held out the G43 for Kessler to inspect.

As Kessler took the weapon, he realized what was different about it. First of all, the barrel was shorter, along with the handguard, which made the rifle lighter, as well as more compact overall. The second was the scope, which was not the ZF-4 common to these weapons, but a slightly longer, six - power scope similar to the one on his K98 but shorter, mounted on the same quick-release mount as the regular G43.

The receiver itself seemed slightly shorter, and had what looked like a short STG44 magazine. The gun also had two large, very strange oval cutouts in the butt o the stock running at a forty-five degree angle to the longitudinal axis. He brought the rifle to his shoulder and swung it. It was very fast point-to-point, and he imagined engaging multiple targets with it. He inspected the chamber to make sure it was empty, then let the bolt slam home and dry fired it. The trigger was every bit as good as his K98, maybe better. Kessler smiled.

"I not only shortened the rifle, but I accurized it as well. G43s are good rifles, but I didn't want the shorter barrel or the new chambering to be a liability. The receiver is actually shorter, and it is chambered for the same 7.92x33 round as the STG44. I never liked the original strap-style scope mounts either. You will see that this uses the top of a short side mount for a Mauser. As usual, the entire scope assembly is quickly removable but still retains zero.

"You lose a bit of velocity from the 8mm Kurz round but at the ranges you gave me, you should not even notice." The man looked at the rifle as if he hated to see it go. "The stock is laminated wood. Not pretty, but stable in extreme temperatures, and the sling is one used by the Afrika Korps. We can, of course, supply you with a different sling, perhaps leather…"

"No, iss perfekt," Kessler said, admiring the rifle in his hands. "I don't suppose you have more of these?"

Seiler laughed. "No, just the one. The cut-outs in the stock look strange, I know, but they reduce the weight a bit, and make it easier to lash the weapon to a pack. It was designed as a replacement for the G33/40, to give the mountain troops a higher rate of fire while keeping the package compact and light. As a former gebirgstruppen I'm sure you can appreciate that."

Kessler was a bit surprised that the old man recognized the edelweiss pin on his hat, identifying him as a member, or former member, of Germany's elite mountain troops.

"Now that we have the STG44, everyone wants them instead of G43s, even though the G43 chambers the more powerful 8x57 round, better for long distance, so we built this as a test. The Gebirgsjäger would be better served by this rifle, but they've decided they like the STG44 better. Personally I think this is a superior weapon. What it gives up in added weight, it gains in accuracy. I do not think it matters at this point in the war."

"I would like to test it."

"Of course.

Kessler looked at the older man and the tiredness in his eyes made him wonder what the old man had done before the war. Hunting rifles? Clockmaker perhaps? He would never know.

"When I told you this mission was essential to the survival of the Reich, Herr Seiler, I meant it. I understand that you may not believe that we can win this war at this point, but you and I will do our parts to save the Reich. These weapons you have given me will make a difference. I promise you that. Now, I want to shoot my new rifle."

Seiler looked at Kessler with a look of amused patience. Perhaps he believed him, perhaps not. Kessler didn't care. He just knew they could not afford to fail.

"Of course, Herr Obersturmführer. Karl will take you out and set up new targets."

"Danke schoen, Herr Seiler," Kessler said, thinking things were definitely looking up.

9

THE SOUND of raccoons muttering outside his window woke Jake. He pulled the alarm off the bedside table and peered at it in the dark. It was only 3:00 am. He tried to get back to sleep but it was a no - go. He got up without turning on his light and found jeans and a sweater, struggling into them, ignoring the ache in his legs; the pain that had become a constant companion. He wondered if once the pain had gone he'd miss it. He guessed not. Jake decided he could live with it as long as his damn legs began working better. Not being able to ride, or fly, or even walk had turned him a little surly, and other people in the house had began giving him a wide berth.

Lately Jake had been rising early, about the same time, driven out of his bed by the pain in his legs, sometimes even beating Cates to the kitchen. They would sit there quietly in the predawn darkness with the lights off, watching the glow in the east slowly spreading across red rock country, the shapes of the mountains quiet sentinels in the dark, slowly becoming real in the spreading light as if coming out of a mist, often not speaking at all, simply sharing the miracle of another morning on earth.

He flipped a light on in the kitchen and made himself some coffee. He poured himself some of it, and it was good, but strong, and he could taste the chickory that Cates had thinned it with. It tasted like home. He poured the rest into a thermos with a string Cates had tied to the handle so they could ride with it and decided to leave one crutch in the mudroom so he had a hand free for his coffee.

He stumped to the kitchen door as quietly as he could, juggled the coffee to open the door and slid out into the darkness. There was no moon, but the stars took his breath away. It was cold, but he was warm enough in the sweater, and part of him felt as if the chill were the price he paid for the beauty of the night sky. He had flown many missions at night, and he could almost hear the drone of *Arizona Annie's* engines, remembering the moonlight on the Mediterranean and the cold, high altitude air biting at his sheepskin flight jacket.

He decided to go see the Jenny, in the barn, which became his destination. It seemed to take him as long to limp the 90 paces to the barn as it had taken to fly from Sicily to Italy, all the time the yellow circle of light outside the door taunting him.

By the time he made it to the man door cut into the slider his coffee was gone, much of it onto the ground, and he was sweating despite the cold. He pulled the door open and stepped through. He flipped on an inside light, found a wooden nail keg and slumped onto it like an old man, setting his crutch on the ground beside him.

Jake sat on his barrel looking at the plane that had made him a pilot, remembering once more the first time he'd flown through a cloud. He could almost feel the mist on his face. His parents had been flyers too, and when they had died in the crash outside Yellowstone, his godparents, Cates and Rosa, had raised Jake as their own.

The Curtiss Jenny was a sad sight with its wings removed, covered with two years of dust and hay that had filtered down on her. No airplane looks right with the wings missing…it was like a man who'd lost his legs…something Jake had a pretty good reference for.

He'd learned to fly in this plane, and as he ran his hand over the taut linen memories of soaring above Sedona, free as the proverbial bird, filled his head. He could hear the engine even though it wasn't running, feel the control stick in his hand despite standing on the ground. The old plane was as familiar to him as his own body.

He found a crate and used it to climb up so he could see into the cockpit, brushing a mouse nest from the seat, grimacing as he strained to see. He frowned at a hole in the fabric he hadn't seen, where packrats had chewed through the side of the plane to get into the cockpit, where they'd built a nest. Little bastards. Then he found that they'd chewed on some of the bakelite control knobs, and that really made him angry.

Before he knew it however, the calming influence of the plane had taken over, and he found himself grinning, remembering sitting in the plane as a boy with Cates' flying cap on, making plane sounds, yelling *"Contact!"* to an imaginary ground crew. He had fought the Red Baron many times in this plane, long before he had ever flown it.

Cates had taken him up for the first time on his sixth birthday, and Jake had loved flying ever since. He learned to roll the plane at 12, and by 15 was known as a local terror, swooping down on cattle so low his wheels were touching the treetops. Cates had a talk with him about that, and told him if he didn't shape up he wouldn't teach him anymore of what he knew about aerobatics, which was to say, a lot.

Cates had been a volunteer with the Lafayette Escadrille in the First World War, and had flown Spads. He said the Jenny wouldn't turn like that Spad, but he'd put her through her paces anyway. An Immelman turn in that Jenny was pretty thrilling to a boy in his teens, and Jake remembered the first time he'd done it in a P-38. At the time it was like dating the prom queen, the older woman left to molder in the barn with his memories.

Now he had come home to her. He decided right then and there that whatever it took, he was going to fly the Jenny again. Right now though, all he could think about was Lily. Who had killed her, and why for God's sake? Jake knew the world could be an evil place, but he just couldn't imagine a world where a young woman with the wit and grace of Lily could be so much of a threat to anyone that they'd do such a thing to her.

He heard a scuff on the floor behind him, and thinking it was Cates, began to turn, but strong hands grabbed him from behind and clamped an evil-smelling cloth over his face. He tried to fight, but in his weakened condition Jake didn't have a chance. Everything went blurry, then the lights went out.

The heat brought him to, and he heard a crash. Still dizzy, he looked up and saw the hayloft was on fire. Pieces of burning wood and straw were swirling through the barn, dropping from the ceiling to start new conflagrations. Jake rolled over with a groan, trying to clear his vision, then began crawling toward the door. He heard another crash behind him, and a whoosh of heat as the loft collapsed on top of the Jenny. The fire was about to get hotter – the highly flammable nitrocellulose dope which the fabric - covered fuselage and wings were treated with in order to stiffen and strengthen them would act as an accelerant. Jake fought to get to his feet, coughing and gasping for breath, but the room swirled around him and he hit the ground again, then passed out.

10

THE ANTIAIRCRAFT rounds were shaking the P-61 Black Widow as they hit it, jerking him from side to side, then his copilot was yelling something at him, and he realized the plane was on fire and someone had their arm around his neck and was trying to pull him out of the cockpit. Every night the same dream…had they landed? But he thought they were still in the air…

The world spun crazily, then the heat from the fire was gone and he was lying on the cold ground, looking up at the stars. There was a face above him, but it was blurred. He tried to sit up.

"Just stay down, you're okay. I used the phone in the house and called the fire department. They'll be here soon."

"Harry? What the hell?"

"What happened Jake? How'd the fire start?"

Harry Weaver's face finally came into focus. Jake still wasn't getting it – he hadn't flown with Harry since they were kids. What was he doing…then he realized where he was. He was at home. He turned his head to find the barn in flames, instead of his plane in Italy. His head was pounding as if someone had cold-cocked him and he could still smell chemicals.

"Harry - where's Cates and Rosa?"

"They're okay. Your foreman Jose and his son…what's his name again?"

"Ramiro."

"That's right…they're trying to wake them up. They're groggy like you. Looks like someone tore your house apart looking for something. They tried to set fire to the ranch house too, but we got that out. Good thing I stayed out late tonight, old pal. I was on my way home when I saw the fire."

The Weaver ranch was a few miles up the road, and Harry and Jake had grown up together, had been close as kids, but Jake hadn't seen Harry since he'd left for Alaska, before the war. Cates had taught Harry to fly in the

Jenny as well, and the two had taken turns scaring the bejeezus out of each other.

"You're in uniform," Jake said inanely.

Harry grinned at him, a streak of soot on his face. "You know the ladies can't resist a man in uniform. C'mon, let's get you further away from here."

He helped Jake to his feet and they moved further away from the fire. Jake turned back to look, and saw the barn was fully engulfed. There was no saving it. Then a huge fireball exploded out the front, blowing the sliding door 50 feet and knocking them both to the ground.

"The Jenny…" Jake began.

Harry looked at him sadly. "I'm sorry, Jake. The fire was too far along to put out. It was all I could do just to get you out of there."

"Thanks, Harry. I owe you one."

"Forget it. Now let's get you inside and see how Cates and Rosa are doing. I hear sirens, so the fire truck should be here soon. Why would someone do this, Jake? What were they looking for in the house?"

For some reason Jake had the strange idea they had been looking for the letter and the book he'd taken from Lily's room, but he didn't tell Harry that. Best to keep him out of it. He wondered if they'd found his hiding spot, but Cates and Rosa never had when he was a kid, so he doubted it. Could a letter in German, a copy of Jane Eyre and a handkerchief be so important that someone would kill over it? Jake didn't know, but he was sure as hell going to find out.

11

L IKE MOST people, Kessler had known love once. He had found it in a
villa in Belgium, at the home of a retired German general with a wife
two-thirds his age. Katya was a child refugee from Russia during those
terrible days in 1917 when the corn stubble of the steppes was fertilized
with the blood of aristocrats and poets. Her husband was recently back
from the front of that first terrible war, and Germany - even in those late
days - had no inkling quite how badly things would go for them.

The general had been a major then, in his late forties, she but a girl,
barely seventeen, but he was smitten by her doe eyes; the same eyes which
had so ruthlessly captured Kessler twenty-five years later. The general had
taken her into his house, and later married her. She told Kessler there had
never been love in it for her, but just safety and the sureness of her next
meal. No small thing for one who had lived through the Bolshevik
revolution.

They had to be careful - the general remanded to his wheelchair now,
the squeak of his wheels loud in the quiet rooms of the country house,
breaking them from their embraces. The general was doing his duty for the
fatherland he said, but you could see it ate at him to have soldiers in his
house. Kessler wondered if he would have minded having officers being
billeted there as much.

Finally they had orders to leave, and he had given Katya his spare pistol,
just in case. It was a dangerous time in a dangerous world, and they'd been
playing a particularly dangerous game, for the one thing the old bastard
they'd been cuckolding had left was his pride, and despite his apparent
frailty he was no one to be trifled with.

Kessler never figured out how the general found out, but when he had
returned to take Katya away with him, she was already gone, taken by the
SD. Suspicion of working with the underground, they said. Of course they

had found the pistol he had given her and some black-market goods in her possession, which damned her.

Kessler knew the old fool had something to do with it...he had seen him peering out of the upstairs window the day he had left, trying to figure out whom it was Katya was waving to. Kessler let himself into the house one dark night and strangled the Prussian with a lamp cord, then volunteered for duty on the eastern front...he wasn't sure why.

Now he had a woman in Berlin, nothing special for either of them, but comfortable. She would pretend to be glad to see him when he showed up at the scabby blue door to her stale little apartment, and he would pretend he didn't see that what she was most glad for was the potatoes, turnips and cabbage he brought with him. As an officer he was now able to source chocolate, coffee and barely stale bread as well, and she tried a little harder. Kessler didn't know what would happen to them, but sometimes at night with her arms around him, he could almost believe he was holding his Katya again. He didn't know he called out her name in his sleep at times, and of course she didn't tell him, despite her curiosity.

Every night after meeting with the men, Kessler would arrive and she would take his coat, the apartment somehow prettier now that they had a little coal for heat, and tea, and ersatz coffee. He would sit at the table and drink schnapps and read the paper, which was mostly dreck and propaganda, but it filled the silence between them along with the radio or the phonograph, and the busy sounds of a woman preparing the best meal she could from next to nothing.

Oh, they ate better now; sardines, turnip and onion soup, sometimes a sausage, even a pumpkin from which she made a pie with real sugar, sometimes tripe, and once, just once, some real beefsteaks he commandeered from the officer's mess which they ate cold, cut thin with horseradish, like beef tongue, wrapped in heavy black bread with some sharp cheese she'd found.

He knew the time was coming when he would have to go, and knew also that he might not return...in fact probably would not. He saved every ration he could for her, as well as money he made on the black market by selling things that were not actually his, but the government's. Everyone did it. It was the only way you could survive. Berlin was slowly turning to rubble day by day.

If the night bombing raids earlier in the war hadn't been bad enough, now the American Eighth Air Force was bombing them during the daytime as well, with the British RAF still taking their turn at night. You could almost smell the fear in the streets, with air raid sirens going off all times of the day and night, firemen running like rats, nothing but shock and exhaustion on people's faces.

Rumors that Patton was nearing Berlin ran rampant. Better him than the Russians, people said. The Russians were animals. Stories of what they were doing to civilians outside the city were on everyone's lips. Everyone prayed for the Americans - that is, except for the SS, the Gestapo and some Hitler Youth. There weren't many of the true believers left, the ones who hadn't been killed by the war and who could afford it having taken their valuables and left for warmer climates, but the ones who were left were out of their minds with fear and hatred, and as dangerous as the Russians. The Gestapo had become particularly enthusiastic in these final days, as if their brutality could stop the American bombs. If it had been madness before, Kessler had no idea what to call it now.

Finally his orders came. He was to take S33 to Jagdverband 44, General Galland's new fighter gruppe in Brandenburg-Briest, and coordinate training with the planes, then later a train to Pillau, near Bremerhaven on the Baltic Sea, where they would meet the planes and the pilots. When he told her he was leaving and not to wait for him, she pretended to be upset but her lack of tears betrayed her.

He gave her some money and his extra gas and food chits, along with some perfume and a scarf. She gave him a cigar she had been hoarding and the only other thing of value she had to give him: herself. In the morning Kessler bathed, dressed, kissed her goodbye and walked down the decrepit stairs for the last time. When he looked up at the window from the street she was looking down at him. He began to raise a hand, but she turned away and disappeared from his sight. It was just how it was between them.

Kessler didn't think about love anymore. In fact, he wasn't at all sure there was any left in the world to have.

12

ILY WAS buried at the Pioneer cemetery near the turn for Soldier's Pass Road. The Cook family was building rental cabins and a small grocery in front of it, near the side of Route 89A, and there were plenty that thought it was a poor place to put it, but with all the Hollywood folks coming to town to make films in the last few years no one could say it was a bad idea. Plus having another grocery in town would be a godsend.

It seemed like everyone in town had turned out for the funeral. The strangest part was that there would be no wake, no food afterwards at the house. There was plenty of talk about it, tongues were wagging on the sidelines for sure, but Laurel just said she couldn't take another funeral. Some of the women apparently volunteered to help her set things up at the house, but she was adamant. She wanted a simple ceremony at the grave and that was all. That's what Lily would have wanted, she said.

The problem with that was that it left plenty of people unsatisfied. Lily had touched a surprising number of people in her short time on this mortal coil, and her friends needed to console each other, to share memories of her, to review all the good things she had done for people, but they couldn't. The ceremony was indeed brief, and Laurel seemed withdrawn and strangely angry. Jake heard a number of people mention it, but in the diminished tones one reserves for the newly bereaved. Different people take things in different ways, they said.

Laurel had always been a little different. Jake well knew she had a temper, and at times she was like this: withdrawing inside herself to some place she didn't let anyone into, even Jake. It was one of the problems they'd always had. Jake had been brought up differently, to talk through everything. He pretty much wore his heart on his sleeve. No problem was so big it couldn't be talked out, Cates had always said. Laurel just wasn't like that. She'd never been the social butterfly Lily had been, and had in fact made some enemies. Jake heard *"not like her mother at all"* several times, and knew they weren't talking about Lily.

Finally Laurel broke down at the grave and ran through the crowd, jumped into her car and tore out of there, headed home presumably. Suddenly it seemed like everyone was looking at Jake.

"What do you think we should do, Jake…should we go after her?" Alice Purdyman said.

He shook his head. "No, better to leave her alone. She's made it clear she doesn't want to be around a lot of people right now. We should finish the service, then if people want to meet somewhere, maybe have a cup of coffee together, I think Lily would like that."

That seemed to be the answer people were looking for, because when they all met back up at Purdymun's Café everyone had a story about Lily, something sweet she had done for them, or for someone they knew. There was plenty of laughter, and tears, as they remembered her antics, her bubbly enthusiasm, and her genuine empathy for others. "So much like her mother, a gem of a woman. It's a real shame, cut down in her youth like this," Jake heard several times.

The only time Jake got angry was when someone mentioned that they heard an Indian did it, that they'd found eagle feathers at the scene. He told that particular person in no uncertain terms that Indians had nothing to do with her murder, and he was, by God, going to find the killer. Suddenly he realized people were looking at him. Jake grabbed his crutches and excused himself.

"You all right?" Cates asked, catching him at the door.

"Fine."

"Don't know about you, but I'm about ready to go. Let me say goodbye and I'll come get you."

"I'm ready any time," Jake said, pushing out the door. He fought with his crutches and slid out through the door with difficulty. He needed some fresh air. He sat down on an old cottonwood stump and lit a smoke. That was just like Cates, he thought. He'd go in and make peace, collect Rosa, and everyone would understand. Jake wondered where he'd gotten his to get along with people from. Everyone liked Cates. Well, almost one. Cates had a tendency not to suffer fools lightly.

The remark about Indians cut deep. Jake's adoptive "uncle" was Yavapai Apache. Jake had first met Tom Crow Flies in the eighth grade, after he'd gotten his clock cleaned in a few fights at school - his nose broken in one of them. Cates had taken him to see Tom, who had taught him how to fight the Apache way, which was to say, not exactly by Marquis of Queensbury rules. Tom had not only taught Jake how to fight, but how to track deer across dry rock, how to sit still for hours without moving, and how to stay warm in a blizzard, making a fire with flint and steel in the rain.

The training had been rough, hard work, but Jake had loved it, and had grown close to the old man. Then puberty had hit, and Jake had given up catching lizards and crawling up on deer for chasing girls and the new thrills they promised. Tom had even showed him how to make his own moccasins, and he still had a knee high snake-proof pair the old Yavapai Apache had made for him before Jake left for Alaska. Tom had gone back to his people, down by Camp Verde. Jake wanted to go see him as soon as his legs were good enough to drive that far.

"Jake?"

He looked up in surprise. It was Dick Lawson.

"Dick. My God, how are you?" Jake struggled to his feet and Dick extended his hand…his left hand, which is when Jake realized he was missing his right arm almost to the shoulder. Jake took it, and Dick pulled him to him, giving him a one-armed bear hug, surprising him. He let him go and raised his stump.

"Left it on Tarawa a year ago. Takes some getting used to. I heard you got shot up a little as well."

Jake nodded. "Messerschmitt over Italy. It's good to see you."

"Good to be home. Sorry I missed the service. Damn car's broken down again," Dick said.

"I'm sure Lily would understand," Jake said.

"I was just up there. The guys filling the grave said everyone came down here."

They both fidgeted in awkward silence for a moment. The ghost of Lily stood between them, a subject too large to ignore.

"Look, Jake, I've never been a beat around the bush kind of guy. My little brother said you called to tell them about Lily when it happened."

Jake nodded. "I can believe such things happen in war, but here?"

Dick nodded in agreement. "I got a letter from my brother a few weeks ago. The Marine Corps still hadn't released me. I was wondering why she hadn't written…" his voice broke and he stopped. When he looked up at Jake his eyes were shiny.

"I was going to ask her to marry me, Jake."

"I know, Dick. I'm sorry. More sorry than you can imagine."

"She was waiting for me to come home…" he said, looking off at the mountains.

"I'm truly sorry, Dick. I miss her too." There was an awkward silence.

"I understand you've been looking into how she died."

"She was murdered, Dick, by a sick, twisted, sadistic bastard."

Dick nodded. "I know, but something's not right about it. You see, she was investigating something herself."

Jake stiffened. "What do you mean?"

"She wrote me a couple times, telling me there was something strange going on here. It had something to do with some people in Flagstaff she said, and she was trying to get more evidence so she could turn them into the FBI. A spy ring she said."

"*A spy ring?*"

"I told her not to get involved, to just give what she had to the authorities. I didn't want her getting hurt. She wrote back and said she thought she had what she needed…that was her last letter. She never did listen well."

He looked at Jake intently. "Jake, I want to find the bastards who did this to her and hurt them. I want to hurt them bad." The former linebacker's eyes were still glistening, but this time it was rage Jake saw in them, not sorrow.

"I want to help you, Jake. Two heads are better than one. Show me what you have. I can be your leg man." They both smiled at this.

Jake told him about finding the letter in Lily's room, what Doc had said about the state of her body and his conviction that Indians had nothing to do with it, that he was convinced that it had something to do with the letter, and the book, but he couldn't imagine what. He'd been reading up on book codes, but hadn't figured anything out so far. The idea that Lily had somehow stumbled onto a German spy ring was hard to believe.

"So, tell you what. You work on this code thing, and while you're doing that I'll go do the 'old buddy back from the war' thing and see if I can find out anything about what she got herself into. She pictured herself a real Mata Hari. Did I ever tell you she wanted to go to Africa on safari?"

"Lily?" Jake was trying to assimilate this new picture of Lily with the shy, quiet young girl he had known. She must have really blossomed, he thought, then had a pang of regret that he had never gotten to see it.

"Yup. Not the wallflower type, our girl. So, you rest those legs, figure out that damn code without giving yourself a cerebral hemorrhage while I poke around and find out who we should talk to."

"Sounds good, Dick. I agree. Two of us can cover more ground and brainstorm through this better than one."

"Partners?" Dick said, extending his huge paw of a hand.

"Partners," Jake said, shaking it.

"Just one thing, Jake. If you find out something that you think might hurt my feelings, I want you to tell me anyway. I'm a big boy now and I can handle it…no matter what it might be. Agreed?"

"Agreed. Same goes for you."

Dick grinned. "All for one and all that."

Jake grinned back. "And all that."

"I'll catch you later."

"Take care Dick."

"We're gonna catch this bastard, Jake," Dick said, giving him a piercing look before turning and walking away.

13

A S SOON as they got back to the ranch they all went and changed out of their good clothes. Jake had an appointment with Doc Edwards in Cottonwood, so they decided to make a day of it, pick up groceries and feed for the ranch, and maybe even get some lunch. Rosa was trying to turn it into a party, but Jake just couldn't shake the feeling of gloom that had followed him the last several days after Lily's murder.

Jake climbed into the old pickup along with Rosa and Cates, and with Jose and his youngest son Antonio in the back, they headed for town to buy supplies. Ramiro stayed at the ranch to watch things and finish chores.

The ride out to Route 89A was bumpy, and hurt his legs quite a bit, despite Cates' careful steering, but once they got out on the main road it was better. 89A was the main road from Prescott to Flagstaff and they took pretty good care of it, even though most road maintenance had suffered during the war. It was a nice temperature, about 65 degrees, heading for 70, and the sun promised to raise it a bit more by the end of the day.

They were coming down the hill to the Cornville Road cut off when they saw a plane glint in the sun as it flew over, turning into a long, low approach just over the hill from them.

"That's Jack Frye's Lockheed Lodestar. He had an Electra but this one's even bigger. Can you imagine owning your own airline? Flying your own personal plane like that around? Look, he's coming in - let's go take a look," Cates said, flooring the gas.

The Lockheed Lodestar was a beautiful plane. It looked as though it were going three hundred miles an hour even with its props not moving, sitting on the ground. It reminded Jake of a P-38 Lightning that way. You just never got tired of looking at it. The gleaming aluminum body with red lettering was mirror-bright in the morning sun, and as Cates and Jake leaned against the truck waiting for the occupants to emerge, they looked at each other and smiled. Rosa just gave them a dirty look from the truck, not happy that they'd stopped.

"Give my left nut to fly her just once," Cates said.

"You can say that again," Jake responded.

Finally the door opened and a man in an Army uniform leaned out and set the steps on the ground.

"Huh. Is that Jack Frye? Didn't think he was young enough for the service…" Cates began, but Jake wasn't paying attention. There was something familiar about the man as he stepped out and turned to take the hand of a woman Jake assumed was Helen Frye, and as she stepped from the plane he turned and Jake realized with shock who the man was.

"My God, that's Elliot Roosevelt."

"*The* Elliot Roosevelt? The president's son?" Cates said, but Jake was already hobbling towards the plane, a huge grin plastered on his face. As he drew nearer, another, serious-looking man came out the door behind him took one look at Jake suspiciously and reached into his coat pocket, but Elliot Roosevelt put a hand on his arm.

"Jake! how are you?"

"COLONEL," Jake said, coming to an abrupt halt, nearly falling in the process, then drew himself up to his full height and saluted rigidly. He felt silly doing it in jeans, a sweat-stained straw hat and moccasins, holding crutches, and he wondered for a moment whether he was out of uniform, then realized Elliot wouldn't care. Colonel Elliot Roosevelt, son of Franklin Delano Roosevelt saluted back, then launched himself at Jake, grabbing his hand and pumping it with both of his like a campaigning politician, although far less ingenuously.

"What the hell are you doing here? I heard you were sent back to the States, but I wondered what had happened. Last I heard you were, well…"

"It's okay, Sir. I was shot up pretty bad."

"That's a bit of an understatement isn't it? I don't know how you managed to land that P-61, Jake. Took a bit of flying. Hell, we had to scrap the damn airplane; too many holes. The plane had more air than aluminum."

A pretty, blonde woman had come up behind Elliot as they talked, and Jake wasn't sure, but he thought she looked familiar.

"Elliot?"

Elliot turned and slung his arm around her, then turned back to Jake.

"Jake, I'd like you to meet Faye Emerson."

Oh right, Jake thought, the movie star. How could he forget? Elliot had kept a picture of her on his desk. She extended her hand to shake with a wide smile. Her hand was cool and soft, just a like a movie star's hand should be, Jake thought.

"Jake was in my squadron. If I'd had a few more like him the war would already be over."

"Pleasure to meet you Jake."

"Same here…but don't let Elliot fool you. He likes to stretch the truth a little."

"Don't I know it," she said.

They all laughed at that. Jake looked around for Cates, who was hanging back. He waved him up.

"Elliot, Faye, This is my godfather, Roman Cates."

"Pleasure to meet you, Roman," Elliot said, pumping his hand.

"Call me Cates. Everyone does."

"I'm Faye."

"Of course you are," Cates said with a wide smile. "Recognized you right off Miss. I just saw *Crime by Night*. You were great in it."

"Why thank you, Mr. Cates. I'm no longer a Miss however. Elliot here finally decided to make an honest woman of me."

"Why congratulations! When did this happen?"

"Oh, about three days ago."

"You're kidding - I had no idea. You should have told me, Elliot," Jake said, wondering what he could get them as a gift.

"Sorry, kiddo, I had no idea where to get a hold of you. I meant to, really, but well, I had other things on my mind," he said, looking down at his pretty bride.

"All right, Elliot. Who are these folks taking up space on my landing strip?"

They turned to find Jack Frye, president of Trans-World Airlines, hands on hips, trying to repress a grin and failing. His wife, Helen, a woman beautiful enough to be another actress, wasn't suppressing her smile at all. She looked at Jack and rolled her eyes as if she had been through this before.

"C'mere Jack. Want you to meet somebody," Elliot said, waving him over.

Another round of introductions were made, and soon Cates was involved in an animated conversation with Jack Frye, obviously having to do with the plane. Jack was waving him inside to show him the cockpit as Helen came over.

"You know, I love flying, but right now all I want is a hot bath and a martini, and Jack is bragging about his baby again. You men and your planes."

"She is a beaut, you gotta admit," Jake said.

"We'll have to take you up some time," she replied, surprising Jake.

"So you obviously live around here, right Jake? Why don't you come for supper tomorrow? We're throwing a little shindig," Elliot said.

"Oh yes. Do come Jake. Bring a friend…and your godfather…or parents. Hell, bring anyone you like," Helen agreed.

"That's very kind, but…"

"That's an order, Captain," Roosevelt said with a look that tried to be stern but didn't quite succeed, probably because of the smile that framed it.

"Okay. I will. We should let you go though. I'm sure you're tired. HEY CATES."

Cates stuck his head out the door of the plane and Jake waved to him, pointing at his watch. Cates stuck up a finger meaning one minute, and disappeared back inside.

Helen Frye shook her head.

"Sorry Mrs. Frye. I'll go get him."

"Oh it's fine. Let them be. Jack doesn't get a new audience every day. There is one thing though."

"Yes?"

"If you don't stop calling me Mrs. Frye and start calling me Helen, I'm going to put rat poison in your food tomorrow night."

14

RUNNING DOWN the list of names Skorzeny had given him had taken Kessler more time than he had liked. He had drawn lines with a red pencil through the names of the men who were reported as deceased. The number of red lines depressed him. He had recognized several of the names, and a deep sense of loss for his fallen comrades filled him whenever he looked at the list for too long.

He'd had some luck however, and had collected a total of 27 men, all veterans, all SS or fallschirmjäger, most of them skilled commando operatives. A few had been with Kessler and Skorzeny in Italy, participating in the daring mountain top rescue of Mussolini from Gran Sasso in 1943. They all had another thing in common however...they were all exhausted. Kessler recognized the tired, haunted look in their eyes, and knew that inspiring them would be his greatest challenge. He decided the first thing they needed was some R&R.

Rest and recreation were not easy to find in Germany in 1944, but Kessler did his best. He found new uniforms and razors for the men, commandeering an entire hotel for a week while the unit was assembled. He put Danzig in charge of finding decent food for the men, but he had to do some real arm twisting to get what he needed. He was required to be in Brandenburg-Briest in three days to meet with Galland and he was taking the men with him to begin their training on the planes. They would have to function as a ground crew during the mission, so Galland's men were going to drill them on refueling the planes and loading armament.

He stocked the hotel bar with champagne and various liquors...and of course, bier. He also found enough women who were willing to spend a few days with his soldiers in return for food. It was one of the easier tasks. He told them to wear their best clothes, and even supplied them with new dresses and makeup when that was not possible. He felt a bit like a pimp, but he knew this would be the only party his men had seen, or would see, for years, and would possibly ever see again. He knew that without such a blowout, they would be worthless to him.

But even Kessler did not expect the raw exuberance which filled the hotel during the next three days. It was as if he had managed to turn back the clock to 1940, everything and everyone clean and bright, wearing new uniforms, cries of *"Prosit!"* echoing through the rooms…it was eerie, but he realized what was happening. It was as if everyone had chosen to forget the present and live in the past for a few days.

No one spoke of the war, the music played endlessly, the bright lights nearly driving the darkness out of Kessler's heart. Nearly, because he knew what was coming. He only hoped it would be enough. He couldn't help but feel, however, like they were fiddling while Rome burned.

On the third day the party ended. The men were to board a train for Brandenburg, and Kessler was touched by the scenes of goodbye between the men and their chosen lovers, of the teary kisses and whispered goodbyes. It reminded him again of the early days, when the German Army still ruled Europe. The short train ride to Brandenburg was uneventful, and Kessler and Schmidt went ahead in a staff car, after being assured that a couple trucks were on their way to pick up the men.

They were strafed by two Mustangs on the way to the airfield, and had to take cover in a ditch. The car was destroyed, and the lack of German planes in the air was notable. They walked the rest of the way, and Kessler was glad when the mist came in, the fog drifting through the tops of the trees, giving them cover from Allied air marauders. Kessler was in a foul mood when they were challenged at the gate, and demanded to see Galland, doing his best to live up to his idea of what a German officer should be. The sentries got the message, and a car was sent from the HQ building to pick them up.

Galland met him on the porch with a polite smile, but it was not long before they realized that they had much in common as professional soldiers. Over schnapps in Galland's office, Kessler gave him as many details as he could…and perhaps a few he shouldn't have. He could not give Galland the specifics of the target, but Galland wasn't stupid, and he could see that the mere requirements for the aircraft and their estimated fuel usage had already given Galland most of the answers.

He also asked for Galland's help with the Kriegsmarine. Galland pledged that he would do everything in his power, but protested that being a flyer he lacked much influence with the Navy. When Kessler reminded him that a general would certainly have better luck than a mere lieutenant, Galland responded with a hearty, friendly laugh and said he had been a mere lieutenant not long ago. Perhaps Kessler wanted to be a general?

Kessler protested heartily and honestly, which amused the General of Fighters no end, so he addressed Kessler as 'Herr General' for the remainder of his visit...at least when they were speaking privately. It embarrassed the hell out of Kessler and amused the hell out of Galland.

They discussed the realities of the war frankly, and Kessler found this at once refreshing and disturbing...refreshing because he was used to dealing with SS types who refused to see the writing on the wall, and disturbing because it was clear that Galland, General of Fighters of the Luftwaffe, saw that same writing clearly. He was equally glad that Galland realized that inherent in this operation was a real possibility to literally pull the rabbit from the hat and get the Americans to see reason, and to force an armistice. Fortified with schnapps and with the dried mud from the ditch brushed from his uniform, Kessler gladly accepted Galland's invitation to see the new planes before the men arrived, the planes they would be taking on the mission with them. After seeing them, and talking with Galland, for the first time in a long time Kessler felt as though there might be a chance for Germany after all.

15

AFTER LEAVING the Fryes and Roosevelts at the plane, Jake and company crossed the Verde, passing through the deep shade of the big cottonwoods that lined the banks of the wide, muddy river, and headed for town. Trees were just beginning to shed their leaves in earnest this deep into November, the cottonwood and aspen leaves bright yellow in the sun.

Jose and Antonio jumped out with the list at the feed store, then Cates dropped Rosa at the Mercantile, telling her he'd be back as soon as he took Jake to the doctor's. She told him with a smile not to worry, that they could meet at the new soda fountain for some ice cream later, and Cates told her that he'd park the truck there so she could put stuff in it. He knew she looked forward to this occasional trip into town, something they did less now with gas rationing, and Cates knew they'd be getting back late since Rosa usually stopped to visit with friends on these outings. She was more of a social person than he, and he understood she needed these trips just as he needed the silence of the woods at times.

Doc lived near the Verde River, in a small white clapboard house shaded in part by an orchard next door and by the languid efforts of an ancient cottonwood in the yard, which was tidy and well-kept, with tiger lilies fighting tulips for room in the flowerbeds. It would be months before they bloomed, but when they did a riot of color surrounded the house. A large lilac stood at the corner of the house nearest the steps.

Doc Edwards and Cates went back to the Great War, Cates having flown in the Lafayette Escadrille and Doc having served, prior to his medical career, as an artillery officer. They'd met on the troopship coming home, among a boatload of soldiers sick with the Spanish flu. They'd both become impromptu nursemaids to the sick and dying, had gotten to know each other, and had been close friends ever since.

Cates parked right in front of Doc's so Jake wouldn't have far to walk, but he struggled to get out of the truck anyway, and had broken a sweat by the time they reached the door. The ride in the truck had jarred his legs more than he'd expected, and he thought he felt a trickle of blood down one leg from a wound that was still seeping.

He fought with the screen door and made it inside just as Cates came up behind him and caught the door. He heard him mutter something about not being able to train a mule, but ignored it.

It was cool and dark in the waiting room, just as he remembered it. Jake had been there dozens of times as a kid, and the dark shellac of the beaded groove paneling was as familiar as an old friend. A faint smell of antiseptic hung in the air, and he eased himself into one of the wide, heavy, wooden chairs next to a side table full of National Geographic and Life magazines.

No sooner had Cates slumped into the chair next to him and picked up a Farmer's Almanac than the door to the examination room opened and Doc stood there, looking at him with the stern look he saved for recalcitrant patients.

"Might as well come in. Let's have a look," he said, reaching forward to take Jake's arm as he stumbled towards the door. "Cates, you wait out here for now, eh?"

Cates shrugged and went back to his reading as Doc closed the door behind him. "Sit," he said, helping Jake up onto the table.

They went through the normal procedures, with Doc listening to his heart, thumping on his chest gently, and taking his blood pressure with one thorny hand clasped on his wrist while he watched his pocket watch. When he was satisfied he helped Jake get his pants off so he could look at his legs. He found that he had been right, the wound was seeping, and he'd torn some stitches, which seemed to make the doctor inordinately angry.

"Breaking horses?"

"No," Jake laughed. "Rode one a little…"

"Just as I thought. Let me ask you a question," the Doc said as he cleaned the suppurating wound, "How'd you like to lose your leg?"

"Huh?"

"I'm serious about this, son. You have a lot of vascular damage - that's damage to major blood vessels. Now, we stitched you up once, and by the look of it whoever did the job knew what they were doing. I'm sure they would not appreciate your attempts to undo their work, I know I wouldn't. Now, I'm going to re-stitch them, and I want to see you next week and every week after that until such a time as I deem necessary, understand me?"

Jake shook his head meekly.

"Next time you come in here with more stitches pulled out, I'm going to get out the saw and just get it over with. Am I making myself clear, Captain? You are *not* doing yourself any favors by pushing your recovery."

"Yes sir. I understand," Jake said meekly, as Edwards looked over his glasses at him. He was preparing a shot, which he stuck directly in the wound, making Jake swear.

"Son of a..."

"See now, if you'd taken better care of these stitches, you wouldn't be going through this. That should numb it. Can you hold the leg like this? Here, put this cushion under it. Better? Good. Now look. I know you want to get back in the cockpit as soon as possible. Pilots are impossible that way. If my son ever said he wanted to be a pilot I think I'd just drown him. Save us both a lot of trouble."

"I just want to do my part, Doc. They need pilots," Jake said.

"Not dead pilots or ones with no legs. I'm serious, Jake. You keep this up you're going to lose at least one leg. You want that?"

Jake nodded no.

"Then you do as I say, or I promise I will just cut the damn thing off and be done with it. Know who will be giving you clearance to get back in a plane?"

"You?"

"Yes, me. Remember that."

Doc Edwards finished sewing, swabbed the stitches again with betadine, sprinkled sulfa over it, and stripped off his gloves. "Okay, that's it. Let me just dress this, then we'll check the other wounds."

"Doc? Can I ask you something?"

"As long as it's not about flying."

"Who would do such a thing?"

Doc sighed. "You mean Lily."

"Yeah."

"Someone who isn't right in the head, Jake. Someone sick."

"The Indian signs around her, the feather... Jake said. "I just can't see any of the Indians I know doing it."

"I'm sorry you had to see that, Jake. No one should have to identify the body of a loved one...unfortunately it's necessary."

"I've seen worse."

Doc put his hand on Jake's shoulder. "I guess you have. Still isn't right. Tell you one thing, I don't think an Indian had anything to do with it."

"I don't either, but why do you say that?"

"You know eagle feathers are sacred. They wouldn't leave them lying on the ground like that. No beadwork or rawhide attached either, just a feather. She was butchered, not killed in some ceremony. Another thing, she didn't die there."

"How do you know?"

"Lividity. That's the blood pooling in the body after death. Most of the lividity was in her back. She was stabbed from the front, and laid on her back for a time. Most of the blood settled in her back. When they moved her, they arranged her on her side. There was a little lividity on the side of the torso, but not much. Besides which, the human body holds approximately six quarts of blood. If she had been killed there, the blood would have soaked the sand in a much wider pattern."

"Jesus."

"Jesus doesn't have anything to do with this, son. Now listen to me. Finding her killer or killers is a job for the police, not a shot up pilot who should still be in a hospital, got me? They'll figure out soon enough that Tom didn't do it. You stay out of it."

"Yeah, Cates says the same thing."

"Yeah, but what do a couple old coots like us know, right? If you're smart you'll learn to listen when Cates tells you something. It's for your own good."

He wrapped Jake's leg, then carefully cut off the other bandages one by one, poking and probing with his fingers, asking Jake if it hurt, which by God it did. Finally he treated all the open wounds and re-covered them. Jake noticed there were less bandages though, and in their place he could see the tiny white worms of scars where there had recently been scabs. He was healing, just not fast enough. The muscles still hadn't recovered, and that was the worst part. It hurt worse than it looked, and it looked like hell.

The Me110 had taken his plane down, but it was the shrapnel from antiaircraft fire that had done the number on his legs. He guessed he was lucky – if he'd been hit directly by one of the Messerschmitt's 30mm cannons he'd be lying in a pine box draped with a flag.

"All right, next week, same time. One more thing. I want you on those crutches for a while yet. You aren't ready for a cane, and I would bet the Army doctor who stitched you up would agree. Now take care of yourself, and that's an order."

"Uh…Doc?"

"Yes?"

"I hate to add to your low opinion of pilots, but when do you think I'll be able to fly again?"

Doc Edwards sighed, removed his glasses and rubbed his nose, the other hand at his hip, holding his white coat open. He looked tired.

"Son, you have to understand that those anti-aircraft guns did a hell of a job on you. Frankly, I don't know how you managed to land the plane at all. You're lucky to be alive. You're going to have pain in your legs for a long time - probably the rest of your life. How much you can endure it depends on you, but until the torn muscles and blood vessels heal, I'd personally prefer you in a wheelchair.

"Now, I know you don't want that, and it's good for you to exercise a little, but no more than 50 yards a day for now, understand? 50 yards, *that's all*. You're already over your quota for the day. Now, take it easy, and I'll see you next week. And remember what I said about those stitches," he said as he helped Jake to the door and out to the waiting room. Cates stood up as they came out.

"Hey Cates, I told this young man if he didn't stay off those legs we'll just chop them off."

"You hold him, I'll handle the ax, Doc," Cates said. "I'll make sure he does what you say."

Cates helped Jake out to the truck, where he collapsed, in obvious pain. Cates slammed the door as he got in.

"Why don't you lemme take you home. I'll come back to get Rosa and the boys and get our groceries. You don't rest those legs, you're gonna be in Dutch with Doc."

"No sense wasting gas. Just drop me off downtown and I'll wait while you and Rosa do your shopping." Cates gave him one of his looks.

"Hey, I'd just be sitting around at home anyway. Besides, I could use a break before we hit that damn road to the ranch."

"Well...okay, but no walking around. I want you to sit down and relax for awhile."

"Cates, I'm not totally helpless."

"You don't take that tone out of your voice you're gonna be."

16

JAKE'S OLD friend from school, Harry Weaver, had come by the ranch to get Jake and take him to lunch. On the way he filled Jake in on his new job teaching dive-bombing at the Navy school in Kingman. One of his duties was to pick out dummy ordnance for the students to train with and to arrange its shipping, so he made the trip to Navajo Depot quite often. Despite regulations against it, Harry being Harry, he usually drove down to Sedona on the Navy's dime. He told Jake he could probably do it on the phone now, but technically it was classified information and besides, what fun would that be?

They ended up at "The Corral", a tiny watering hole in Cornville that was popular for its cold beer and evaporative coolers in the summer. Being winter, the swamp coolers weren't running but the beer certainly was. They usually had a decent bar lunch, which today was venison stew with biscuits and a side of home fries. As usual, Harry had cheese melted over his, which Jake couldn't understand. He'd been telling Harry what Doc had told him about the state of Lily's body.

"Jeez, Jake, I'm trying to eat here for cryin' out loud," Harry said out of the side of his mouth. Despite his complaint, it didn't seem to be affecting his appetite in any real way.

"There's something else. I found a letter in her room…in German," Jake said in a low voice.

Harry looked at him between bites. "Personal letter from Hitler?"

"No dummy, from her grandmother."

"Oh. Yeah…clearly it's a coded message from the Nazi spy ring she was working with. Did you decode it? I still have my Captain Midnight decoder ring if you want to borrow it."

"Okay smart-ass, I know her and Laurel's family came from Germany and her grandmother still lives there, but she hid the letter in a secret spot, and it's only one page…why not the whole thing?"

"First of all, maybe that particular page meant something to her personally, so she kept it…or maybe she lost the rest of the letter. Secondly, where and how'd you find it?"

"In her room. I was putting flowers in a vase and happened across it."

"Uh-huh. Flowers in a dead girl's vase, snooping around in her room…you aren't going funny on me are you good buddy?"

"No, it's just…shit; I just want to catch the bastard who hurt her."

"We all do Jake, we all do, but it's the sheriff's job, not yours. They catch you snooping around the edges of this, interfering with their investigation, Ben will nail your hide to a tree and you know it."

Jake nodded, staring at his plate, his food growing cold.

"Listen, come up to Flagstaff with me tonight. We'll roll some craps, chase some women…"

"You know I don't like gambling."

"On dice or women? Look, you can watch. Have a few drinks…then a few more drinks. Get your mind off this murder business."

"All right, but there's someone I'd like to see."

"Who's that my friend?" Harry asked, pushing his plate aside and lighting a cigarette.

"The family of my copilot."

"Sure. I think we should ask Laurel to go with us, maybe she can drive so we can tip a flask of giggle water in the car on the way up."

"You're incorrigible Harry, anyone ever tell you that?"

"Nope, never. You gonna eat that?"

17

THE TWENTY four men Kessler had chosen were lined up at attention outside the hangar when he stepped back outside. When they saw Kessler and Galland, they immediately saluted as one, and Kessler felt a slight thrill - that sense of pride that every commander has in a group of good men - realizing at that moment that he had truly become an officer. It was a heady feeling, one he would never forget.

Galland and he returned the salute, and when Galland even made an open comment about what a fine looking group of soldiers Kessler had brought with him, Kessler saw why he was a general. He had a way with men, and inspired them as easily as he breathed. Kessler was learning there was much more to being a good officer than just a uniform, and he was learning from the best. He could almost see the men swell with pride, and suppressed a smile. Galland then opened the door and stepped back inside. Kessler tilted his head at Schmidt, his best NCO, and stepped in behind Galland. The men followed. Galland flipped on the lights in the hangar and Kessler heard the men gasp.

The plane was like nothing any of them had ever seen, including the Me262s they'd seen taking off from the airfield. It was one gigantic wing, sweeping back into gracefully curved wingtips, which then curved back to a flattened, pointed trailing edge, above which the huge exhaust pipes of two jet engines could be seen, buried in nacelles in the wing itself. It looked like a huge, virile, man-made bat.

A graceful bubble canopy held two seats, one behind the other, but there was no real nose, unless you could call the point of a triangle a nose. That area was rounded, almost like that of an Me410, but the canopy was flanked on both sides by the gaping maw of the jet intakes. So dramatic was the departure from a regular plane that the sleek Me262s it shared the hangar with drew barely a glance.

"The engines are at present the same Jumo A4s that the 262 uses...but there is a new engine in the works, a BMW, which should be more reliable. I shouldn't tell you this, but they are working on an auxiliary rocket such as used in the Me163s, but smaller, to get the plane off the ground more quickly...one of the 262s few faults. As it is, this aircraft is much easier to get into the air due to its large wing area. It can also easily take off from grassy fields, something the 262 has difficulty with."

Galland continued the briefing as he walked slowly around the craft, and not one of them, not even the General of Fighters himself, could resist running a hand over it.

"The framework of the wings is laminated wood. The British Mosquito bombers use this material to great advantage...it tends not to show up on radar. The radar signature is diminished even further by the use of a special paint...they won't even tell me what's in it. Of course, the very shape of the plane helps as well."

The open-mouthed response from Kessler's men when they saw the Hortens was gratifying, and mirrored his of a few hours earlier. As they left the hangar Kessler could hear the murmuring about the new plane behind him. He whirled on the men, who had forgotten that he was an officer now and not an NCO anymore.

"QUIET. You will not speak of this in ordinary conversation ever again. If you do, I will shoot you myself, *verstehen?*"

"JAWOHL, HERR OBERSTURMFÜHRER," the men responded in unison, snapping a salute again, as one.

Kessler repressed a smile and turned to his non-commissioned officers. "Schmidt, Giesler. Find the barracks and get the men settled. We will begin training with the ground crews in the morning. Give each of the men a small ration of Bier and one schnapps, no more, with their meal. When I see you later I will brief you all on our part in the operation."

"Jawohl Herr Obersturmführer!" Schmidt and Giesler barked.

"Heil Hitler."

"HEIL HITLER," the men shouted as one, raising their arms. Kessler dismissed them with a simple salute, then spun on one heel and strode off.

Behind him he could hear his NCO's yelling for the men to double-time back to the barracks. Then he heard one of the men start singing the Horst Wessel song: the song of the Hermann Göring division, and as the others joined in another chill went down his spine.

He resisted the urge to turn and watch them jogging across the airfield. He knew at that moment, when they had broken into song, that all was not lost. Not yet. If they did not succeed it would not be for lack of commitment. Kessler allowed himself a small smile as he strode up the steps to Galland's office, on his way to battle once more.

18

HARRY WAS one of those guys who just won't take no for an answer, and over lunch had suggested that a trip to Flagstaff might cheer up Laurel. He told Jake he'd already talked to her about it and said she was game. Jake said he'd go on one condition, and that was if Laurel drove instead of Harry. Harry had suggested in return that they stay in Flag for the night, considering the weather, and that way they could hang out downtown and not worry about driving. Jake was sick and tired of the ranch, so he agreed to go, although he was a little surprised that Laurel had wanted to go after the way she'd been at the funeral. Maybe a little fun was what they all needed, Harry said.

The streets in Flagstaff still had snow on them but it was melting rapidly. Laurel stopped at the outskirts of town so they could take the chains off the rear wheels, and for once Jake was glad for his infirmity as Harry got back in, cursing the snow.

"I'm soaking wet!"

"Gee, I didn't get wet at all."

"Me neither," Laurel said.

"Screw you both. Let's go find that drink."

The slush splashed against the bottom of the car as they drove into the center of town, the late afternoon sunlight hard against the windows. The smell and sounds of the town were just as Jake remembered. The only difference was there seemed to be more trains than usual, which was really saying something. They waited 35 minutes on San Francisco Street for two trains to pass, with Harry grumbling about dying of thirst. Finally they were waved across, and found a parking spot directly in front of the Monte Vista Hotel.

"How about that? They saved my parking spot," Harry said. They all laughed at that. It was beginning to feel like a party.

"Listen. I have to find Red's folks first. I don't want to show up there filled to the gills, if you know what I mean. Let me find a phonebook and I'll take a cab over there, that way you don't have to move the car. We'll never find another parking spot this close"

"You always were a spoilsport, Jake," Laurel said.

"Now look, I promised Red I'd look them up. Besides, I'm wondering how he's doing. Maybe they've heard from him."

"We'll be right here, Jake. You take as long as you want," Harry said.

Jake got a phone book from the Monte's front desk, found the Thompsons' address and called a cab. Raucous laughter and loud swing music drifted up from the Monte's bar, but he wasn't tempted - this was something he really needed to do. The last time he had seen Red was when he'd come to see Jake in the military hospital, just before he was moved to the hospital ship which would take him back to the States.

Red had been given his own P-61 and copilot, and Jake had said he was glad for him, but lying there with his legs shot up, he was a little jealous. Now, with time, he was really glad Red had gotten his chance at his own plane. It just made him wonder if he would ever fly again himself.

The cab driver hit every pothole on Route 66, and by the time they reached their destination, just off Steve's Blvd, Jake was feeling sore. He climbed out with difficulty, the cabdriver not even getting out to open the door for him. Jake didn't leave him much of a tip, telling him he'd call a cab when he was ready. The cabbie shrugged and roared off without a word, leaving him standing at the base of a set of flagstone steps leading up to a dark brown, well-kept bungalow. It was a job getting up those steps, which still had ice on them in places where the sun hadn't hit the flagstone yet, but he made it, and stood perspiring at the top.

Jake composed himself and forced a smile to his face. He reached for the doorbell, but to his surprise, the door opened before he could ring it. A pretty, red-haired young woman stood there holding her sweater shut, glaring at him.

"It's Tiny...isn't it?" she said. Jake blinked, trying to figure out what she was talking about. An older man appeared behind her.

"Let him in, Morrie. He's just here to do his job," then he turned and walked slowly into the depth of the room. The screen door swung open and Jake looked at the young woman. She was lovely, but pale, her auburn hair the same shade as Red's, and he surmised that this must be his sister. He forced a smile to his face again, stuck out his hand.

"Hi. I'm Jake Ellison. Red was my wingman in North Africa. I promised him I'd come by and say hello."

Red's sister didn't take his hand as expected, instead her eyes filled with tears and she ran off, and Jake could hear her feet pounding on the stairs as she flew up them. What the hell is with this crazy family? he wondered.

"I'm sorry, son. Please, come in," said the older man, whom Jake assumed was Red's father, as he took his hand in a strong grip. Red's mother was nowhere in sight. Jake hobbled into the room on his crutches, gritting his teeth from the pain as Red's father closed the door.

"Please, take a seat. We thought you were here about Tiny."

"Tiny?"

"Red's brother. He's with the Marine Raiders in the Pacific."

"You thought I was here…"

"Yes. Then I saw that you were wearing an Army Air Corps uniform, not a Marine uniform. All those damn uniforms look the same to us."

"I'm terribly sorry. I didn't even think. I should have called you first," said Jake, thinking about the scare he must have given them. They had thought he was an officer come to give them the bad news about their younger son. He remembered the nickname now. They called him Tiny because he was the biggest of them, over 6' 5", and looking at his old man Jake could see where he'd gotten his size. He sank heavily into the chair he was shown to.

"I feel awful. I promised Red that I would come see you when I got home. This is my first trip to Flagstaff since I've been back. He told me so much about you all…I feel like I know you."

An older woman who looked tired, as if she'd been crying, came out of the doorway which must have led to a back bedroom somewhere. Red's father got up and went to her with concern. "Patty, you shouldn't have gotten up," he said, taking her hands and leading her to the couch.

"Stuff and nonsense. I heard you talking about Red."

Jake tried to get up, but his legs just wouldn't cooperate.

"No, please, sit. Would you like some coffee? Something else?" she said.

"Coffee would be fine ma'am, thank you."

She turned and went through another door that apparently led to the kitchen. The old man watched her go with clear concern. He sat down on the couch heavily and looked at Jake.

"She's had a rough time of it."

"We all have. I hope this war will be over soon. Now that we have the Germans on the run..." Jake replied, trying to fill the silence with conversation. Red's mother quickly returned with a tea tray with steaming coffee mugs, sugar, a milk pitcher and some shortbread cookies.

"How do you take your coffee, Captain?"

"Call me Jake, ma'am. Just black please."

"The smarter way...the milk is powdered I'm afraid, and the coffee is just coffee substitute of course."

"That's fine. Thank you," he said as she brought him a mug. As she handed it to him, she did an odd thing; she made sure he had it by wrapping both hands around his. Her hands were soft and cool, and there was some sort of message in her eyes that Jake couldn't decipher. She returned to the couch as her husband was taking a mug for himself from the tray on the coffee table.

"I'm sorry for the lack of hospitality when you first knocked. Ever since we lost Red we haven't much wanted to see another uniform on the porch," she said as she sat.

Jake stopped with his mug halfway to his lips. They looked at him and saw the shock in his face, and looked at each other, then back at him again. She covered her mouth with one hand.

"Oh Lord. You didn't know, did you?"

Jake looked at the coffee without tasting it and held it with both hands. The black liquid was the color of the Mediterranean at midnight.

"We just assumed you must have heard. Oh Jake, we're so sorry."

"When? What happened?"

"Just before Thanksgiving. He was shot down over Germany."

Jake closed his eyes. Red had become his best friend in the short time they flew together. When he opened them they were blurry.

"He was a fine pilot. He talked about you all the time," he said inanely.

"He said in his letters that he was flying with the best pilot he'd ever seen. He said it was strange that you two grew up just 30 miles from each other but had never met..."

Jake nodded, afraid to talk. He willed the tears back into his eyes. He couldn't look up at them for some reason, so he didn't see the looks they exchanged.

"Son, we feel awful having sprung this on you. We just didn't know. We just want you to know, whenever you come up to Flag, you have a place to stay. As far as we're concerned, you're one of the family now," Red's father said.

Jake took a deep breath and looked up. "I told him we'd come back here and paint the town red," he said. "He said he'd already done that before he left, but that it would probably need a new coat by the time we got back."

They both laughed in relief. "That sounds like Red. He said you had an old plane? He was looking forward to flying it," Mr. Thompson said.

"The Jenny? Yeah. I was going to take him up over Sedona....aww hell. I'm sorry. I guess I need to go. This is just too hard right now," he said, pushing himself from his chair and pulling himself up onto his crutches.

"We understand, Jake. Listen, I'll have Morrison take you back into town, it's no trouble. MORRIE."

Apparently Morrie had been on the stairs listening, because she appeared immediately as her parents stood and came over to help Jake.

"I'll get the keys," she said, disappearing into the kitchen, the look on her face telling Jake she'd heard every word.

Red's mother took his hands, then gave him an awkward hug. "Thank you for coming by, Jake. It means a lot to us. I'm sorry you had to hear it this way."

"We mean what we say, Jake. You always have a home away from home here," added Mr. Thompson, putting a fatherly hand on one shoulder, shaking Jake's hand. Jake just nodded; numb with the idea that Red wasn't around anymore. He just had to get out of here.

"Thank you. And thanks for the coffee."

"You're very welcome, Jake. Stop by anytime. We mean it."

Morrie had come back with the keys by then, and without saying anything she took Jake's arm and helped him down the flagstone steps to the curb, where an old Chevy sat waiting. The sun had melted most of the snow, but Jake didn't notice. She helped him in and went around to the driver's side to start the car. The house disappeared as she took the first left, and he found himself staring numbly at the scenery without seeing it at all.

19

KESSLER HAD been awakened by a polite but insistent knock at his door. It was the orderly, who saluted and handed him a telegram. Kessler closed the door in his face and tore it open, only to find that it was from Skorzeny. He was to round up his men and materiel and make his way to Berchtesgaden as soon as possible where S33 would receive gebirgsjäger training.

Kessler shook hands with Galland, both of them knowing they would likely never meet again, then wearing his field gear and carrying his dress uniform in a bag, along with a small tornister pack which he had managed to hold onto throughout the war, he slung his new rifle and made his way through the mud to the car they'd provided him. The new G43 felt good in his hands; solid and dependable. He handed the bags to the driver and climbed into the back.

Kessler had called ahead to the barracks, so the men were ready, chomping at the bit, all of them in the SS snow camo anoraks Kessler had told them to wear. Except for their Afrika Korp issue load-bearing gear, which they were wearing, the rest of their desert gear was stowed in their packs. Kessler could see they were excited to finally be getting underway. None of them were men who took naturally to a sedentary existence.

They were soon on their way to the Alpenfestung in Berchtesgaden, the alpine fortress they had heard so much about in the propaganda films and radio broadcasts. Field Marshal Kesselring was in charge of southern forces, and Kessler wondered if he'd get a chance to see him. He had pushed Kesselring into a trench during a mortar attack on his command post in Italy and the general had given him his first sergeant's pips. He wondered what he would think of him as a lieutenant.

The car they were assigned to was strangely silent as the train made its way across the countryside. There was none of the boisterous camaraderie of previous campaigns, no jokes, no gambling, no one singing the Horst

Wessel song. The men read the Völkischer Beobachter, slept, or stared out the window at the ruined countryside.

Kessler smoked quietly and watched the dirty white fields roll past, muddy bomb craters and skeletons of farmhouses dotting the landscape. Occasionally they'd see a woman or a child standing near the tracks, watching the train go by. Kessler could sometimes see the anger in their eyes from where he sat, and he wondered what they blamed him for.

The train was strafed twice and bombed once but they were lucky, only a couple of guards who were on top of the flatcars got hit. The second time had been a close thing however, with bullets whizzing through the car, seeking flesh. One of his men was hit, but it was just a scratch, and the medic took care of it. They stuffed crumpled newspaper in the bullet holes in the sides of the coach to keep the cold December wind out, and once more they were on their way.

They got off the train in Nuremburg, and commandeered two trucks, which did not endear Kessler to the local garrison, but he couldn't care less. The mountains were beautiful, and as the trucks wound slowly up the long, winding, narrow roads Kessler could not help but wish the war was over, and he could once again climb the high peaks to hunt or just climb, with nothing but a backpack full of food, water, and maybe a little schnapps.

He'd started out in a Gerbirgsjäger mountain regiment, then transferred to the fallschirmjäger, then was finally commandeered into the SS. Salzburg, where he had grown up, was just a few miles away, Now here he was, back in the mountains again. He felt the pull of his hometown, but doubted he'd have time to return there. It made him sad for some reason he couldn't quite fathom, and he found himself wondering for the first time if Germany might really lose the war.

Checkpoints seemed more common here, and there were a number of ENTRITT FUR ZIVIL VERBOTEN signs along the roads splitting off from the one they were on. Kessler couldn't help but wonder what was down those roads. Finally they made it to Berchtesgaden and reported.

It was late, after 11 p.m., and the officer in charge told them they would most likely not hear anything until morning, but after calling up the hill to the verwaltungsbau - the admin building, he found Kessler a temporary billet in Villa Bechstein, a house formerly owned by the famous piano makers, and made room in the SS barracks for the rest of the men. When he heard Kessler was reporting to Skorzeny, he said he was not aware that the Colonel was on Obersalzburg, but he would see what he could do to find him.

When Kessler heard this, he began to have a bad feeling about his orders. They had come as a telegram, not in Skorzeny's own hand, and he cursed his own stupidity. Some general may have decided to hijack his men and send them to the Obersalzburg to help defend what was left of the Reich…If so, he had little chance in getting to the Baltic Sea, where they were supposed to rendezvous with the pilots and their planes.

He and his men had to be there in just a few weeks or the mission would be scrapped, and he had no doubts as to which newly minted lieutenant would swing for the error…even if it were someone else's. He was exhausted however, and decided a good night's sleep wouldn't hurt matters any. He had just seated himself on the bed in his room and was pulling off his boots when the knock came on his door. It was the same officer, a Major Goetz, who had met him when he reported.

"Yes, Herr Major. Is there a problem?"

"No problem, Herr Obersturmführer. You are required at the Haus Göring immediately."

"Yes, Herr Major. Where would I find that?"

"I have a driver waiting outside. He will take you."

"And my men?"

"They are fine where they are for now. The request was for you only."

"Danke, mein Herr."

"Hurry now, we wouldn't want to keep Herr Reichsführer Göring waiting."

Göring, Kessler thought. So *that* was it. An SS sergeant with a back like a steel rod met Kessler at the car and saluted, opening the door. Kessler saluted him back and got in the back, wondering what it was all about. Just in case, he had brought all his paperwork, but he knew the plan by heart. He wondered what the head of the Luftwaffe wanted

20

"I'M SORRY about the scene at the door," Morrie said.

"Don't worry about it. I understand."

"I don't think you do. See, Red and I were twins...fraternal, but we still have...had the same birthday. I feel like I'm missing something in my life now."

Jake took a deep breath. "We both are. Red was the best friend a guy..." was all he could get out without being choked up. Her hand snuck over and took hold of his on the seat, squeezed. He couldn't look at her, he just squeezed back. The scenery was getting blurry.

"Where can I take you, Jake?"

"I...um...we're at the Monte for the night. If you can drop me there..."

"Sure, no problem. Listen Jake, I understand. Really, I do," she said, putting a gentle hand on his forearm, then removed it so she could shift.

"When we lost Red I couldn't do anything for ages. I just didn't care about anything, but then I thought about how he was...I don't have to tell you how much he loved life. I decided that I had to keep on going, that he would be disappointed in me if I didn't. Sounds stupid, I know."

"No...no, it doesn't sound stupid. It's exactly how he was. He would just look at me when I was moping around the tent feeling sorry for myself, and toss some water on me or throw a football or baseball glove at me and make me go outside. Before I knew it, I had forgotten all my problems and was enjoying myself."

Morrie chuckled. "That's Red all over. Do you know the night of my prom he painted the bottom of my shoes bright red just before I left the house? I was *furious*. I had red paint on my hands, there were red shoeprints all down the stairs...OH! I could have wrung his damn neck. I asked him why, he just stood there and grinned and said something about painting the town red. Now strangely, it's one of my favorite memories of him."

Jake could hear it coming in her voice as she finished, and saw her sniffling. He cleared his throat.

"You know, it gets cold in the desert at night, right? Well, when we were in North Africa I had this favorite sweater my godmother Rosa sent me. It was just a simple sweater, but really warm, handmade...well, I wore it all the time, whenever we had a night mission. Days were warm enough I was fine with just the coat, but at night, well, that sweater made things a lot better.

So one day I go to put it on and it seems just a little tight. Not bad, mind you, just a little smaller. Well, I figured I was just gaining weight, and I started exercising a little more. I didn't wear the sweater for two or three weeks, but I got back from ferrying a transport plane to Tunis and went to put it on, and it was smaller yet! I just couldn't figure it. It was like someone had washed it or something. I got it on, but I really figured that I had gained a bunch of weight since my pants hardly fit either.

Finally next time I went to put it on I couldn't even get into it. I mean, I couldn't get my arms into either of the sleeves, and my pants wouldn't button, came halfway up my leg. I saw Red eyeing me and went after him. Boy, was I sore. I wanted to tar and feather him. Seems he found a woman in the local town and had her take just a little more off the sweater each time he took it to her. It only happened when we weren't flying, which wasn't often, so it took a while. Then the rotten so – and – so swapped my pants out with his, then with a guy half my size. Man, I really wanted to kill him!"

Morrie was laughing hysterically by this time, tears running down her face. It made Jake feel better somehow. She grabbed his arm again.

"When we were kids, Red decided he didn't want oatmeal for breakfast. Of course, that's what we ate almost every day...Well, one day he swiped two bottles of milk from the milk bin. Mother complained to the milkman of course, who said these things happen, and got her two more, but that day we had pancakes. Next day, same thing - no milk. Well, my mother was just beside herself. Then it was a week before anything happened. We went back to cereal everyday.

Finally one morning she went to get the milk and it was bad...I mean Phew, really awful. Both bottles. Well, she poured it down the drain and called the milk company. They gave her a discount, but said they couldn't be responsible for the deposit on the bottles. Oh, she was raging. Someone was swapping out their bad milk with our good milk. She was determined to catch the thief of course, and two days later she did. Red was taking the fresh milk out of the box and replacing it with the milk he'd stashed in the garage, figuring if it was sour he wouldn't have to drink it or eat oatmeal. Boy oh boy, did he get a hiding for that one!"

Now it was Jake's turn. Tears fell freely, but he was laughing so hard he didn't care. It got suddenly quiet in the car.

"I miss that sonofagun," he said softly, looking at Red's sister.

"Oh Jake, I miss him too," she said, turning the corner off Cherry. They drove in silence for a few minutes.

"Listen. I've got an idea. Why don't you come out with us tonight? Tommy Dorsey is playing at the Orpheum and it should be a hoot. We'll get an extra ticket for you. Ever hear Frank Sinatra sing? We can talk more about Red...you can tell me more stories about him."

"I wish I could, Jake, but I have an early class in the morning that I can't miss. I'm sorry."

"That's okay. I can't dance yet anyway," he said with a smile.

"Well, when you can dance you come see me again, okay sailor?"

"Hey, watch what you call me now," he said.

She laughed as she pulled over to the curb. "Wait a minute, I should have gone the other way, Jake. Let me turn around."

"No, just let me out here. I don't want to go in just yet."

"You'll catch your death."

"I'm fine."

"Are you sure?"

"Positive."

"Well, okay. But you take care of yourself okay? And next time you come up to Flagstaff you'd better come by and say hello. I know my folks feel awful. You simply *must* come for dinner."

"I promise, cross my heart. You take it easy on the way home, okay? The roads are slick. No accidents now."

"I will. Goodbye, Jake." He looked at her like he was seeing her for the first time, her smile bright in the darkness.

"Goodbye, Morrie."

Jake slammed the door and watched her drive away, already wishing she'd stayed. It was snowing to beat the band now, so that even the sound of the trains was muffled. The band in the Monte was hitting their stride from the sound of it. He heard the sound of a car sloshing its way down the street just before he heard the music. He looked up as the car passed, just in time to see a young woman in a blue dress leaning out the window to the waist, nearly sitting on the window, her head thrown back, eyes ecstatically closed, her bare arms raised to the sky.

He could see the happiness on her face as she passed, the slush splashing against his boot. He could hear the saxophone's lament of friends lost, of love found, and it suddenly seemed like it held all the heartaches in the world and all the joys of living at once. Then she opened her eyes, looked straight at him and smiled, clearly happy to be alive.

She waved, a carefree summer festival queen from her float, and he waved back. Then she did something odd. She raised her face to the sky and stuck out her tongue to catch a snowflake, found something there that amused her, then she was gone, dropping back through the window to whatever had so pleased her.

Jake looked up into the sky and closed his eyes, feeling the cold flutter of the snow on his face. Goodbye Red, he thought. I'm gonna miss you, you son of a bitch. Then he wiped his eyes, took a deep breath, crossed the slippery, snow-covered street and pushed his way into more havoc than he'd seen in ages.

21

THE RIDE up the mountain was almost like traveling through any small town in Germany or Switzerland, except for the guards. They were checked carefully at the guard shack which hung off one side of the road, and Kessler had to show his travel documents, which were examined carefully. The gate was raised, and they drove past the guards with their dogs, their panting breath hanging small clouds in the night air.

As they came past one of the first driveways, Kessler recognized the Führer's house - the Berghof, and just up the hill from there, the famous Hotel Zum Turken. They went straight on up, past the SS barracks on the right, then turned left at what looked like a small café, closed for the night from the looks of it, and continued on up. The wheels of the car crunched on the hard snow then spun a little as they hit an icy patch, but the sergeant was an experienced driver and made it to the top without any more difficulty. They stopped before a chalet that looked for all the world like a hunting lodge.

When Kessler got out of the car he could not help but look around and gasp. It seemed that they were on top of the world, and the Hoher Göll loomed high above them. The famous Kehlstein Haus, or Eagle's Nest, as it had come to be known, sat on a high promontory atop Kehlstein Mountain overlooking the valley below, the entire scene covered in white. The moon was out, and with the faint strains of music coming from somewhere down slope it would be easy to believe that the world was at peace.

Kessler breathed in deeply, and though the cold air stung his lungs, he felt alive for the first time in months. After the hell of Berlin, after being bombed nearly every day, every night, the silence was bliss. Artillery lightning flickered off to the northeast, but there was no sound.

"Please, Herr Obersturmführer," the sergeant beckoned him, not wanting to get in trouble, or perhaps he just wanted to get a midnight snack from the kitchen. Kessler looked around one more time and steeled himself for Göring.

He was shown into a long room with a fireplace at the far end. A polished Mp-38 submachine gun hung beside the fireplace as if it were a hunting arm. The room was clean and plush...not as luxurious as the pictures he had seen of Göring's castle, but nice nonetheless. A long table split the center of the room. A lone figure in a powder blue uniform standing near the fire holding a drink turned when Kessler came in - Reichsführer Hermann Göring.

Kessler wiped his feet politely and took three great strides into the room, coming to rigid attention as the sergeant let himself out. The click of his boot heels reverberated in the still room.

"HERR REICHSFÜHRER, HEIL HITLER."

"Heil Hitler, Herr Lieutenant. You have come a long way."

Kessler was unable to discern whether Göring's comment referred to distance or his career, and he correctly assumed it was both.

"Yes, Herr General."

"Would you like a drink?"

"Yes, Herr General, thank you." The last thing Kessler wanted was a drink, but he knew better than to refuse Göring's hospitality.

"Over there. On the table. The American whiskey is very good."

Kessler placed his briefcase on the least expensive looking table he could find, and pulled off his gloves. The bar was well-stocked, and he decided to go with Göring's recommendation. He was right. It was excellent. He joined the head of the Luftwaffe near the fire, attempting to maintain an air of discipline and attention, but in a relaxed way. It didn't work. He felt uncomfortable without Skorzeny to guide him. He knew very well that one false move or wrong word and he'd be in front of a firing squad within minutes.

"Relax, Kessler. You have done well with what little Skorzeny gave you. I'm impressed. Tell me, how is the training going?"

"Very well, sir. The men are motivated, experienced, and I have no doubt of their success. They are looking forward to the gebirgsjäger training"

Göring chuckled, then fixed one beady, dangerous eye on Kessler. "You realize of course that this is a fool's errand?"

Kessler blanched. Was this some sort of test? "I'm sorry Herr General, I don't know what you mean."

"I mean that Germany's losing the war Kessler. I mean that the only thing that matters now is getting as many SS as possible back here to the Obersalzburg to help in finishing construction of the Alpenfestung. If we can consolidate our power here, before next fall, the Allies don't stand a chance."

"But...I understood the Alpenfestung was already a reality...isn't this part of it?"

Göring chuckled. "Ahh, my newly minted Lieutenant, our propaganda minister has a talent for, let us say, *creative exaggeration*. The stories you've heard are true enough...to a point. It is true that there is a defensive line built on the old WWI defensive line from Bregenz on Lake Constance, up through Klagenfurt, along the Yugoslavian border, all the way to Hungary. It is true that underground bunkers exist, full of foodstuffs, weapons, even factories where we are building new jets and manufacturing munitions....but there are not enough of them. Most of them exist only here. Even now we are blasting out underground runways for aircraft and making room for as many supplies as we can. With 20 divisions, we can hold out here until we rebuild our forces, then take back Europe."

"But the mission..."

"The mission is over. I need you here," Göring said, draining his glass.

"But Reichsführer, I thought the Führer..."

Göring spun to look at him, and a chill went through Kessler. He had seen much evil in this war, and he recognized its face.

"You forget yourself, *Herr Obersturmführer*. You are here at *my* pleasure. You DO NOT want to incur my wrath. Verstehen?"

"Yes, mein general," Kessler replied, bowing his head in deference, knowing he had come close…too close. Göring refilled his drink and returned to the fire, holding out the empty hand to warm it. He turned to Kessler and smiled. Something about that smile of his chilled Kessler more than Göring angry.

"You should be grateful, Kessler, *especially* with your record. You began your career as a gebirgstrüppen. Now you are back in your beloved mountains. I understand you are a fine skier. You will find that being stationed on the Obersalzburg has its benefits."

"Yes, mein General."

"Good then. You are dismissed."

"Herr Reichsführer, one thing."

Goring gave him a look that was a clear warning. "Yes?"

"The planes, sir. They are being loaded as we speak."

"Yes…of course. That is being taken care of. You needn't worry yourself about it. Report with your men to the verwaltungsbau in the morning for your new duty post."

"Yes, Herr Reichsführer, and danke schoen. The whiskey was very good," Kessler said, suppressing his anger.

Goring waved him away with a hand which clearly meant he was to get out. Kessler set the nearly untouched drink down, grabbed his gloves and briefcase, clicked his heels and saluted his general one last time, and in the way of all smart young officers before him, made himself scarce.

The beauty of the night sky and the mountains draped in snow had somehow lost its appeal, and Kessler's mind raced as he wondered what he would do now. The mission was over…yet it hadn't even begun. He sighed and wondered again if Germany would really lose the war. He had no illusions about the war – he knew that things had gotten very bad, but he still felt there was hope…this mission might be Germany's only hope. He truly felt that way.

He knew better than to argue with Göring, for fear of his neck, but it seemed to him that this mission had merit. If it were a success it might just bring the Allies to the table. Surely an armistice was better than total defeat?

It was an unhappy Kessler who got back in the car to be driven down the mountain.

He looked around as they drove. So this would be his new home. It was better than some things he could imagine…but what about the mission? What would Skorzeny say? What lie would Göring tell the Führer? Had he already changed his mind?

Kessler was trying to think of some way to get a message to Skorzeny when they stopped at the checkpoint. A guard wearing the ribbon of the Leibstandarten division knocked on his window. Kessler rolled it down impatiently. It was after midnight and he was exhausted.

"Yes? *Vas ist?*"

"You are required at the Berghof, Herr Obersturmführer."

Kessler's blood ran cold.

"In the morning you mean?"

"Nein, Herr Obersturmführer. Immediately. Der Führer wishes to speak with you."

22

O F ALL the battles Kessler had been in, of all the tight spots he'd never expected to come out of alive, he had never been as fearful as he was at this moment. He had never met the Führer, although he had seen him at a rally once. Still dressed in his battle fatigues and winter camouflage, Kessler was intensely aware that he was anything but a spit and polished officer. Why hadn't he taken the time to shower and change?

His car was met in front by one of Hitler's aides, who looked none too happy to be standing in the cold in the middle of the night, waiting for some SS lieutenant who had undoubtedly raised the Führer's ire. Light came from a large window on the front of the house overlooking the drive, and Kessler followed the aide, a lieutenant colonel, up the wide steps he had seen so many times in newsreels, thinking *Mussolini stood on these steps.*

They went in through a large, heavy, arched side door, which was swung shut by a guard with some effort. Kessler could smell bread baking somewhere to the left. The adjutant turned to the right and Kessler followed him down a hallway to a door flanked by two guards. As the aide placed his hand on the knob, he turned to Kessler with warning in his eyes.

"Do not upset the Führer. He has a great many things on his mind right now. This is a great honor. He has asked to see you alone. This is almost *never* done. Give me your sidearm."

Kessler undid the flap of his holster and handed his pistol to the colonel.

"Good luck." He opened the door and Kessler stepped through it, surprised that there were steps. He went down them into a long room with high ceilings.

The famous huge window that could be lowered into the basement was at one end, but was of course closed against the cold. To the left of the window was a piano, above which was one of the most beautiful tapestries he had ever seen. The room was full of comfortable, expensive furniture.

He was alone. Kessler decided to stand. He was drawn to the window for some reason, and closed or not the view was magnificent.

The valley which lay before him, nearly at his feet, was one of the most beautiful and dramatic he had ever seen, the Alps rising majestically to the stars, illuminated in the moonlight, visible even with the lights on in the room. It was breathtaking.

Kessler stood for a moment with his hands behind his back, just looking at the view that Hitler enjoyed every day, when he heard a door open behind him. He spun, clicked his heels, and saluted, trying not to tremble as the Führer came down the steps towards him and crossed the room. He was shorter than Kessler thought he would be, and strangely, he had a wide smile on his face.

"Obersturmführer Kessler. I am very pleased to meet you. I understand you have been accomplishing great things in my behalf at this difficult juncture in the war." Hitler held out his hand to shake his, and Kessler took it automatically, hardly believing this was happening. Hitler's grip was cool and firm, surprisingly so, although he held his other hand behind him.

"I am doing my very best, mein Führer," he responded, lowering his head in a bow as Hitler let go of his hand.

"Please, relax. This is my home and you are my guest. Would you like some tea? Kaffee perhaps?"

"Nein, mein Führer. Danke."

"Oh come now. You have been traveling all day, and have just come from meeting with Reichsführer Göring, now you are here. It is past midnight…well into the new day actually, and you are telling me you could not use a cup of kaffee?"

Kessler knew better than to decline. Actually, kaffee was a welcome thought. "Danke, mein Führer. It would be an honor."

Hitler pressed a button beneath the edge of a nearby table and a servant appeared.

"Yes, mein Führer?"

"Ilsa, I would like some tea, and some kaffee for Kessler here. Also some of those cookies Bernard made this morning… if there are any left?"

"I'm sure there are, mein Führer."

"Gut. Danke. Oh, and send Traudl in when she's finished."

"Yes, mein Führer."

Hitler turned to Kessler and looked him over. "You look tired, Kessler. Please, take a seat."

"Thank you, Führer," Kessler replied, sliding nervously into a soft chair. He felt a grittiness in his eyes that was not there an hour ago. It must be past one by now, he thought, but he must remain alert. Hitler sat across from him and crossed his legs, resting his arms across the back of the wide sofa.

"It is always good to meet a real soldier who has come so recently from the field. I understand you have come recently from Berlin."

"Yes, mein Führer."

"How is Berlin?"

"Holding up well, mein Führer. The German people are strong. Their resolve is unshakable."

Hitler looked at Kessler shrewdly as if deciding something.

"You need not give me the party line, Herr Obersturmführer. I understand better than most the tribulations that are being visited on the people of Berlin. I also know that the German people are strong...but when I ask you something, I expect the truth from you. I can get any number of people to tell me what they think I want to hear. I have decided to give you a measure of latitude in speaking with me, because I have to make a decision. So please, the truth."

Kessler looked at the floor wondering how to tell the Führer just how awful it was in Berlin right now. The same door Kessler had come through opened and Ilsa came in with a tray holding a silver kaffee carafe, a small but lovely porcelain tea pot, two cups and a selection of cookies. She placed it on the table between them.

"Would you like me to pour, mein Führer?" she asked with a smile.

"Nein, Ilsa. I have kept you up far too late. Please, go to bed. It is late and you need your rest," Hitler replied with a smile, his manner that of a kind old uncle speaking to a favorite niece. Ilsa smiled back at him.

"Danke, Führer. I will see you in the morning."

"Yes. Guten nacht."

"Guten nacht, mein Führer."

As the leader of Germany leaned forward to pour his 'guest' a cup of coffee, Kessler shook himself. He must be dreaming. Hitler was actually pouring him a cup as if he were an honored guest. He knew it was meant to disarm him, but ever since he'd been a boy he'd followed this figure across the table from him, and now here he was, treating him like family. It was disorienting.

"So. Berlin. Tell me about Berlin," Hitler said as he handed him the cup of coffee. Kessler knew an order when he heard one. He took the cup carefully and sipped it. He hadn't had real coffee in weeks. It was better in its way than the American whiskey Göring had offered him. He looked up and Hitler was looking at him over his cup of tea, not taking his eyes from Kessler as he sipped.

"Berlin is in trouble, mein Führer. The Americans bomb us during the day, then the British take their turn at night. Coal, fuel and food are in short supply. The black market flourishes, mainly because people cannot find enough to eat any other way. Everyday we dig ourselves out of the rubble and begin again. It is very…trying."

Hitler shook his head as if this were exactly what he expected to hear.

"So, morale is suffering?"

"Yes, mein Führer. You must understand. The people still love you, still believe in the cause…but they are tired. Simply tired of being bombed and not having enough to eat, or hot water, or…"

"Danke, Herr Kessler, I get the picture."

Kessler sipped the wonderful kaffee, wondering if he'd stepped over the line. Hitler had a grim look on his face. He had placed his tea back on the tray and was tapping his fingers on the arm of the sofa as he stared at Kessler, who quickly finished his coffee and went to put the cup back on the tray.

"Please, help yourself to more. Iss gut, no?" Hitler said with a small smile.

"Ja, mein Führer. Danke," Kessler replied as he refilled his cup from the silver samovar, more from a need to do something with his hands than a desire for more.

Hitler poured himself more tea and sipped. "When you leave I will send a few pounds of my private stock of beans with you. I don't drink it myself, I prefer tea, but it is a pleasure to see someone really enjoying it. Kaffee should not be so hard for our people to obtain, don't you agree?"

"Yes, mein Führer, danke schoen." Kessler didn't know what else to say.

"Now, on to the reason you are here."

A chill went through Kessler. He could see that Hitler understood the carrot and stick theory very well. He steeled himself for what was coming next.

"You have a letter, I believe? Given to you by my dear friend Otto?"

"Yes, mein Führer."

"May I have it?"

"Of course, mein Führer." Kessler reached into his inner jacket pocket where he always kept the letter, handed it over to Hitler and sat back in the chair, wondering whether they would hang him or shoot him. He found, to his surprise, that he was so tired he no longer cared. Hitler unfolded the letter and looked at it briefly.

"It is crumpled. You should take better care of such things."

"I am sorry, mein Führer, I shot the man who crumpled it."

Hitler raised an eyebrow at this. He smiled at Kessler. "Then I hope you do not shoot me when I tear it up Herr Obersturmführer," he said, refolding the letter, then tearing it in four pieces and throwing it on the tray.

23

KESSLER SAT stock still, wondering what was happening, when Hitler suddenly laughed at his own joke, slapped Kessler on the knee and stood, walking slow circles around the room, hands clasped behind his back.

"I understand your meeting with Reichsführer Göring did not go well?"

"I am here to serve you, mein Führer. You know best how I can help."

Hitler smiled at this, his hands clasped behind his back. "Yes. Yes I do. That is why you will disregard what Herr Reichsführer Göring told you tonight. The mission will continue."

Kessler tried not to show his shock.

"Yes, mein Führer."

"You will remain here for as long as it takes to finish training your men. You will have the run of the facilities, absolute priority at the underground firing range, and access to whatever you require. This mission is of the utmost priority...verstehen?"

"Yes, mein Führer," Kessler said, standing. Another door opened and a pretty, blonde secretary came in with a piece of paper. She stifled a yawn as she crossed the room, covering it with her hand. She seemed comfortable in the room with the Führer. Kessler wondered what it must be like to work with him every day.

She smiled at Hitler. "I am sorry, Führer. It is late. Here is the letter I redrafted. Is it acceptable?"

Hitler took the letter from her and looked it over. "Yes. Perfekt. Thank you, Traudl," he said with a smile. "Please, get some rest. Thank you for staying up so late."

Traudl Junge curtseyed. "Anytime mein Führer."

Hitler reread the letter as she let herself out. He reached into his lapel pocket and removed a fountain pen, shook it once, and signed the letter with a flourish, then blew on it to dry it. He handed it to Kessler, who took it gently, trying not to let his hand shake.

"There. That should be clear enough to anyone who reads it."

Kessler looked at the letter.

By direct order of the Führer, Sturbannführer Heinrich Kessler is to be given any and all assistance he requires, whether material, manpower, or transportation, without regard to rank or prior orders. His orders are to be treated as if they were an order directly from myself. His mission is of the utmost importance to Germany. Anyone not complying with Herr Sturbannführer Kessler's direct orders will be summarily executed.

Hitlers' signature was a large black scrawl in the middle of the bottom of the page. Kessler could hardly believe it. The mission was on.

"Mein Führer? May I ask a question?"

"Of course, Heinrich."

"Have I been promoted?"

Hitler laughed heartily at this as if it were a rich joke. "Yes, *Sturbannführer* Kessler, you have. It is of necessity. You see, it turns out I am a bit short of majors right now, and no one will believe that a mere lieutenant would be carrying such responsibility, or have a letter like that. May I have it for a moment?"

Kessler handed him the letter and Hitler examined it in the light to make sure his signature had dried, then folded it carefully in thirds and placed it within the envelope Heidi had brought with it. He handed it back to Kessler.

"You see, Kessler, Otto was needed for other duties. He was the only one I felt I could trust with this. You apparently have the same relationship with him. He trusts you implicitly, which means I can as well. He tells me you were on the mission with him in '43 to rescue Mussolini."

"Yes, mein Führer."

"That mission was important, and dangerous, but nowhere as complicated as this one. There are some aspects to it that you need to be made aware of if you are to lead it." Hitler looked at a clock on the table. "It is, however, very late. Please get some rest. I will send a tailor to see you in the morning…not too early eh?" he said with a smile.

"You will return here for lunch. I will send a car. We can discuss the mission at length then. You must consider any questions you have for me because soon I will return to Berlin to lead the defense of the city. Klar?"

"Yes, Führer. One question?"

"Yes?"

"What about Herr Reichsführer Göring?"

Hitler smiled. "You leave the reichsführer to me Herr Major."

"Yes, mein Führer."

Hitler held out his hand and Kessler shook it.

"Until tomorrow then. Thank you for coming, Kessler."

"Thank you for your faith in me, mein Führer. I will not let you down."

"I am counting on that Kessler. I am counting on *you*."

Kessler left the room, then the Berghof, in a dream. The combination of whiskey, caffeine and his meeting with Hitler was a heady mix. He felt drunk, and although he knew he was exhausted, he also knew he would not sleep well…yet when he was returned to his quarters he had barely enough energy to removed his boots and the letter from his pocket before he fell into a deep, untroubled sleep for the first time in months, his last thought being "Sturbannführer Kessler. Mein Gott."

24

THE GHOST in Room 305 hadn't bothered Jake that night…perhaps because he had been too drunk to notice, he wasn't sure. When he awoke with a splitting headache he found that he couldn't remember much at all of the night before, except proposing multiple toasts to his lost friend, Red. They had lucked out and found two rooms; Laurel got one and he and Harry shared the other.

He looked over at the other bed to see if Harry was up yet, but the bed was empty. He rolled to look at his watch on the nightstand. Nine-thirty. My God, he thought, I haven't slept this late in years. He didn't feel like getting up, but the pressure in his bladder forced him out of his warm cocoon, and the ache in his legs reminded him that he had spent way too much time on his feet the night before.

When he had performed his morning ablutions, showered and shaved, he limped to the window with the help of his cane and looked out. The sun had come out and had melted a great deal of the snow, which was quickly turning to slush, water rushing down to the gutters in miniature, street-bound rivers. Jake finished dressing just as a knock came and the door opened. It was Harry, looking none the worse for wear, dressed smartly in a fresh set of Class As. He grinned when he saw Jake struggling with his tie.

"How you feeling, partner, rough night?"

"The night was fine. Rough morning."

"You ever get that thing tied and we'll go get breakfast. Laurel's gone to do a little shopping. Said she'll meet us over at the diner."

"I'm not feeling too hungry right now."

"Best thing for you, though. Pickle your liver otherwise. C'mon, let's go. I already checked us out."

This surprised Jake. "Paid up?"

"Yep. All set. Don't worry, you can owe me."

Due to his extravagant lifestyle Harry was usually broke, so the idea of him actually having money to pay for the room, and doing it, came as a shock to Jake. Maybe the boy has turned over a new leaf, he thought.

They crossed Aspen, then San Francisco, and made their way up the other side of the street to the Downtown Diner. The minute they walked in the smell of home fries, sausage and bacon frying assailed them and Jake found to his surprise that he was actually hungry. He slumped into a booth opposite Harry and took the menu out of the holder at the head of the table.

"With the weather the way it is I thought we might stay an extra day before we go back. Laurel has to go back to work later today, so you and I can cat around a little, stay one more night, then we'll drive back down in the morning."

"Fine. I just wish I could help drive. The right leg's a lot better, but it's still hard to work the clutch."

"S'matter? You don't like my driving?" Harry asked, a mischievous grin on his face.

"Not much, no. I hope you don't fly like you drive."

"Of course I do."

"Like a bat out of hell?"

"Like a bat out of hell," Harry replied with a grin.

Laurel came through the door nearly running, tossed her packages on the seat next to Harry and slumped down next to Jake, looking like a million bucks.

"How you feeling, Jake?" she asked impishly, winking at Harry.

"Anyone get the number of that truck?" he replied.

Harry laughed. "I told you to watch out for those Gin Sours, ol' buddy. They'll spank you if you're not careful."

The waitress's return saved Jake from a response. She took their order efficiently and spun behind the counter to get their coffee.

"So, Laurel, you're working today right?"

"Yeah. Wish I didn't have to, but you know how short handed we are."

"I can imagine."

"No, you can't. We've got trains backed up all the way to Flagstaff, full of munitions needing repair. Can you imagine what would happen if the Germans bombed those trains? It'd take out the tracks for *months*."

"The Germans are getting their asses handed to them. The war will be over soon."

"A girl can dream though, right Jake?" Laurel said, winking at him with a smile.

"I'm shocked. What a thing to say," Harry said.

"Oh hell, Harry. You can't imagine what it's like to work your fingers to the bone every damn day, then walk outside for a cigarette and see trainloads and trainloads of more munitions stacked up on the sidings. I'm beginning to feel like Sisyphus, constantly rolling the boulder uphill. Can't a girl wish for one little, itty bitty German or Japanese raid just to shake things up?

"Besides, I doubt that could ever happen," she went on. "We're pretty safe here. Too many air miles between here and the coast. That's why they put Navajo Depot here, I guess."

"I guess," Harry said, pulling out a money clip swollen with cash.

"Geez, Harry, where'd you get all the cabbage?" Jake said.

"Got lucky at cards."

"*You?* Lucky at cards?"

"Aw shaddup. I bought breakfast and you're complaining?"

"Hey, it's just such a new experience for me."

With breakfast finished, Jake looked up at the sky as he pushed out the door of the diner onto the sidewalk while Harry settled the check. The sun was hard and bright, making the windows on the upper stories of the surrounding buildings glow as if lit from within.

Jake loved Flagstaff although he hated larger cities. It was still small enough to feel friendly, although these days it was bustling with life, being centered as it was on the railroad, which ran directly through the center of town, east to west. As Laurel had mentioned, the sidings were currently full of railcars filled with ordnance waiting to go on to Williams, to be repaired or decommissioned at Navajo Depot, where Laurel worked.

The buildings were brick and slump block, and just high enough to give the downtown area an established, yet cozy feel. It was so different from the red rock formations and wide open terrain of Sedona that it could be in a different state. It reminded Jake of a town in Colorado, or maybe Oregon, instead of Arizona. He looked up at the sky and sighed. He wasn't looking forward to the ride home. Despite an attempt by all three of them to keep things light, the entire time they'd spent together seemed a bit forced and unreal, Jake wasn't sure why. Maybe you couldn't go home again.

"Jake?"

Jake turned to find Morrie facing him with a wide smile.

"Morrie! You missed a good show last night…" he began.

"I bet. I just couldn't Jake, I had a 7 a.m. class. I went by the Monte, but they said you weren't in."

The diner's glass door swung open again as Harry and Laurel came out of the café, talking sub-rosa, looking serious. It made Jake wonder what the problem was, then he wondered if they were talking about him. Just as quickly he dismissed it. Who cared? The past was past.

"My parents feel awful about what happened, Jake. You shouldn't have learned about Red that way. I was sent to find you and tell you we want you to come to dinner so we can make it up to you."

"Don't worry about it, Morrison. It wasn't anybody's fault, it just happened. Red wasn't the only friend I lost in this damn war, and I learned to put it behind me. If I had thought too much about them I wouldn't have been able to do my job. As bad as that sounds, in the war I learned to put it behind me and get on with life. Red and I were like brothers though, and I just wished that I had stayed and talked with you all longer. See, I was the rude one. You all have nothing to apologize for."

"Then you'll come to dinner?" Morrie said, her smile as radiant as the sun reflecting off the windows. It warmed Jake in a way the sun never could. He realized he was falling for her already…though they'd just met.

"I'd love to. Tell your folks…" he began.

"Hello, who's this? Laurel said, inserting herself into the conversation. Jake didn't like the smile on her face.

"Oh, Laurel, this is Morrison Thompson. She's the sister of my ex-wingman Red Thompson. Morrison, this is Laurel Hausen."

"Pleased to meet you," Laurel said a little too pleasantly. She didn't extend her hand though, nor did Morrie.

Uh-oh, Jake thought.

"Pleased to meet *you*, Miss Hausen. I was just inviting Jake to dinner. You're certainly welcome to come as well." Morrie was smiling as she said this, but Jake couldn't shake the feeling that the two women immediately disliked each other.

"Morrison, this is one of my oldest friends, Harry Weaver," Jake said, holding out his arm to sweep Harry into the conversation.

"Hello, Morrison. Very nice to meet you," Harry said with his most vivacious smile, extending his hand to her.

Morrison shook his hand and gave him a flirtatious smile.

"Nice to meet *you*, Harry, but if people don't stop calling me Morrison and start calling me Morrie there's going to be trouble," she said, winking at Jake.

"Sorry," he said with a grin.

"Well, *Morrie*," Laurel said, "I'm going to be late for work if we don't get going. These gentlemen are going to drop me off. Come on, Jake. You wouldn't want me to get in trouble with the boss would you?" Laurel said, sliding her arm through Jake's and turning him away.

"Wait a sec," he said, turning back to Morrie. "Can I call you?"

"Sure. I'll give you my number," Morrie said, reaching into her purse for a pen.

"Jake, we need to *go*," Laurel said, tugging gently at his sleeve.

"Wait a minute," he said, pulling his arm away. "She and her folks invited me to dinner. Besides, the way Harry drives, we'll be early."

"Fine. I'll be in the car, Nice meeting you," Laurel said over her shoulder as she pulled her arm out of his and walked away.

"I'll go with her," Harry said, waving goodbye.

"Hope I didn't make your girlfriend mad, Jake," Morrie said, tearing a piece of paper from a notebook under her arm.

"She's not my girlfriend," Jake said, trying to put a lid on his anger.

"She sure acted like she was."

"Yeah, well, we have some history, but it's been over for years."

"I like Harry, though."

"Yeah, he's a good egg. We've known each other since third grade," he said as she scribbled down her number and thrust it at him.

"I'm sorry, but my ride is with them. I should go. Can we do this another time?"

"Sure. Is the weekend best for you?"

"Doesn't really matter – the main problem is getting up here. I'm still getting used to the cane, but it's just too hard to drive yet. I'll have to get a ride."

"Why, I'd be happy to come get you. I haven't been to Sedona in ages."

"Well, you're always welcome at the Diamond - S. The way Rosa is though, you might be too full for supper later. It's just a long haul to come get a cripple."

"It's no trouble, really. It'd give me an excuse to get out of the house and waste some gas. Just one thing Jake…"

"Yeah?"

"I don't want to hear you calling yourself a cripple anymore, okay?"

She had such a serious look on her face when she said it that Jake couldn't help but break out laughing, which brought her smile back.

"I promise. Do you like to ride? I've been trying to ride a couple times a week to strengthen the legs, but I still can't go very far. If Doc knew I was doing it at all he'd skin me. We could pack a picnic lunch and ride over to Oak Creek – I know a couple nice spots."

"That sounds wonderful, Jake. Just one thing though."

"What's that?"

"Do me a favor. Don't invite Laurel." Just like that she had him laughing again.

– Part Two –
Christmas, December 1944

25

THE WEIGHT of the heavily laden mountain pack was a familiar friend to Kessler. Something within him reveled in it, even in the sweat pooling in the small of his back and the heat in his boots. The familiar feel of ski poles in his hands was like an old friend as they traversed the steep slope, listening carefully for the rumble of avalanche. It was still early though, the snow frozen and stable, and Kessler planned on being well off the mountain before the sun hit the slope, softening the snow and increasing the danger.

The shortened G43 strapped to his pack shot well, and he was glad he'd been able to acquire it. Snow sifted down through the snow-laden trees, a small creek burbled along the rocks, and Kessler realized that he was happy. He hadn't realized how much he missed the mountains, missed being on skis.

He led his men across the rocky, tree-covered slope in the dim pre-dawn light, training for the mission to come. To tell the truth, everyone was looking forward to the holiday, to toasts around cheery fires, to the excellent Black Forest hams they had been promised for dinner, and most of all, a brief respite from the war.

After Russia, Kessler swore he'd never be happy to see snow again, but his heart sang a different tune now. These were not the windswept, frozen steppes he had fought his way across in the darkness of the arctic winter, these were the mountains of his home, breathtaking in their raw beauty, their ragged steep faces and hourglass moraines bordered by hardy pines and firs clinging tenaciously to the steep slopes, with the highest of the mountains, the Hoher Göll, rising above them.

They had been in the mountains now for four days, and Kessler was proud of how the men had adapted to living on snow and rock, working together to not only survive, but to obtain their objective – in this case a mountain. The peak they had climbed was not nearly the toughest Kessler had ever done, but it had enough technical problems to test what little training he and the gebirgsjäger training cadre had been able to put together on such short notice. The men were getting an abbreviated version of the course Kessler had suffered through when he'd first joined the army in '39. He only hoped it would be enough. They no longer struggled with the ropes and karabiners, and were setting pins and handling the ropes like they'd been doing it for years. Not everyone could handle the rigors of mountain training, and he was glad to see he'd selected the right men.

Incongruously, since they would be operating in mountainous desert or swamps, the men were also getting desert and jungle training, shivering in a cold classroom warmed only by a small coal brazier while snow flurried on the other side of the windows while learning about warfare in temperate climates. It felt strange, and brought out the class wit in several of the soldiers, especially Hans Meier, the class clown.

Kessler struggled to maintain decorum, without stifling the exuberance of his young soldiers, knowing that if they were to succeed in their mission they would need to work as a team, and their morale must be high.

Morale in Germany, in these dark days of the war, was a rare commodity and the toughest part for Kessler. Although they were clean, surprisingly well fed and had new uniforms, even here in Berchtesgaden news and rumors of the war intruded. The allies had crossed the Siegfried Line and were approaching the Rhine; the Russians were threatening the Elbe on the eastern front, and though several divisions had been sent to reinforce the lines, a sense of despair flitted about the edges of the collective unconsciousness, whispering that the war was already lost. Everyone felt it, even Kessler.

The Führer wasn't helping. He would suddenly break into maniacal tirades during staff meetings or dinner, in the middle of a speech meant to inspire, and while everyone cheered desperately when he was finished, it was out of fear and for the lack of anything else to cheer about.

Kessler knew they would be leaving their idyllic mountain community soon, possibly before Christmas, although he privately hoped the men would be able to spend the holiday here in the mountains as a last reprieve before battle. Frankly, as his skis sliced through the fresh powder, the wooden tips submarining then poking briefly from the snow ahead of him, he wished they could all just stay here forever.

He stopped the zug with a motion of his arm, side-slipping to a gentle stop, his troops sliding in below him, lining up facing out at a virtual sea of mountains, the snow on them turning from grey to blue in the early morning light, the glow to the east growing stronger every minute.

Kessler was sure the men were wondering what they were doing, just standing there, looking across the German alps, shivering in the pre-dawn chill, but suddenly the sun began peeking up over the horizon behind them, and a thin line of light began creeping slowly across the sea of blue black massifs until they were glowing yellow and orange, the snow suddenly changed into a mirror, intensely colored by the suns rays.

Someone let out a breath, then there was a whoop of *"BERG HEIL"* from somewhere downhill, and Kessler would have bet money it was Hans Meier. Then they all started clapping and yelling, and Kessler let them. He wanted them to remember this moment during the rest of their very likely short lives, because in this moment, with the sun shining gloriously off the jagged peaks, the war didn't exist at all…they were just a group of friends greeting the dawn, about to ski down through silky, morning fresh powder to a hot cup of kaffee, a fire in the hearth, a good meal, and the warmth of shared experience.

Kessler actually smiled at the thought of them as a ski-mountaineering club. Some of the men had never been on skis, and their attempts to become proficient were quite comical. As an officer it had been difficult at times for Kessler to keep from breaking out laughing, but he doubted they would need skis where they were going, the rope and navigation skills being the main reason for the gebirgsjäger training. It had the added effect of getting these men from different units used to working together as a team. He had mainly insisted on the skiijäger training as a break for the men, who had been working incredibly hard.

The intensity of the early light was beginning to fade from the mountains, turning them light yellow, then white as Prussian china once more, the sky delft blue. Kessler turned his thoughts downhill, stepping into a turn he scribed into a series of sweeping, beautifully perfect turns, dancing down over the wide crest of the hill above Berchtesgaden, savoring each one, selfish for the moment, leaving his men struggling down the hill as best they could.

These few minutes were his - a last reprieve before the killing began again, and he wished again that the war was over, and he could just come back here and ski. As it was, Kessler knew it was likely these were the last ski turns he would ever make.

26

THE HOUSE was lit up like a beacon, making it easy to find. Jake was glad he hadn't had to walk up the hill though...his legs ached at the very idea of it. Cates had dropped him off, saying he wasn't much for parties even though he'd been invited. Jake had the idea from the volume of laughter coming from the house that this one was going to be a doozy.

Helen Frye opened the door, giving him a radiant smile when she saw who it was.

"Why Jake! I'm so glad you could come. Please, let me take your coat...my Lord, What *is* that huge thing?"

"Present for Jack," he said as he shifted the cane clumsily back to his right hand as he stepped inside. "Here, this is for you. It's some of Rosa's Prickly Pear jelly."

"How wonderful! But I told you not to bring presents, Jake...here, let me take it. Now give me that coat as well."

Jake let her take the package from under his arm with no small relief. He shrugged out of the greatcoat with some difficulty, even with Helen helping him.

She aimed him at the living area while she hung up his coat, but he could have found his way just by the noise. He had thought about asking Laurel, but had decided against it. It just didn't feel right. He wasn't in the room ten seconds when Elliot Roosevelt spotted him and came over with a drink in his hand.

"Glad you could make it, Jake. I was getting worried. Thought we might have to send the posse out after you."

"Aww, you know how it is."

"No, I don't. Now, there are some very pretty and available women here so don't you be going after my girl hear?"

"Yes Sir."

"None of that 'Sir' stuff tonight, Jake. The war's nearly over. Hell, Patton is almost to the Rhine. Another month and all we'll have to worry about is the Pacific campaign, and that's going pretty well right now. You're retired, so I don't want to hear any 'Sir' nonsense from you tonight."

"With all due respect, I'm not retired *yet*," Jake answered seriously. Elliot just laughed.

"Spoken like a true pilot."

"Now Elliot," Helen Frye interjected, "You aren't giving him orders are you? Look what he brought for Jack. I'm just dying to find out what it is. Now Jake, what would you like to drink?"

"Just some bourbon would be fine, Ma'am."

"Now, what did I tell you about that? Let's get you a drink then we'll give this to Jack," Helen said, taking Jake's free arm in hers and steering him to a table loaded with bottles, two ice wells, and a stack of cut crystal tumblers. Next to it was a long buffet full of hors d'oeuvres, with martini glasses and champagne flutes littering the nearby table. So this is how the other half lives, he thought.

He was glad he wore his class A uniform now; he didn't have a decent suit. Jake decided then and there that he would fix that first chance he got.

She poured him a tumbler of 12 year-old whiskey big enough to drown in and steered him towards Jack, who was deep in conversation with an intense-looking financial type wearing a grey pinstripe that Jake was sure cost more than he made in a year, while nearby several people stood around a piano player jangling out a passable version of "Take the A train".

Helen barged right into the middle of Jack's conversation, saying "Jack! Look who's here and just *look* at what he brought you."

Jack turned at her voice and saw Jake, giving him a wide smile and sticking out his hand. "JAKE. Glad you could make it," he said as they shook. "Now what in blue blazes is this? I thought we agreed, no presents..."

"Hell, it's not much anyway, Jack. Merry Christmas."

"May I unwrap it?"

"Don't see why not."

Jack set his drink on the table and looked at the long, narrow package with a puzzled look, running his hands over it for a minute before giving up and tearing the paper off it.

"Why I'll be damned! It's a propeller."

"It came off the Jenny. It's not serviceable, but when we replaced it a few years ago we hung it in the barn. For some reason it survived the fire. Cates had the idea of giving it to you, so you should really thank him. All I did was polish the brass and re-varnish it."

"It's beautiful, Jack, really," Helen said, and it *was* beautiful, the rich wood of the laminated curves fighting the polished brass center for attention. It gleamed in the lamplight, and quickly became the center of attention, which Jake found a bit embarrassing. Everyone wanted to touch it. Even the piano player stopped playing to come over and take a look. They all seemed to think it was wonderful. Hell, it's just an old, worn-out prop, Jake thought. Cates had been right though – it was the perfect gift.

"Cates and I thought it might look good on the wall of your office or study," he said.

"Hell yes it will. That's *exactly* what I'm going to do with it," Jack Frye said. "Wait till they see this at TWA. Every damn body'll want one!"

"Where's the rest of the plane' Jack? Buying them a piece at a time now?" Elliot said, provoking laughter.

Everyone laughed as if it were the funniest thing they'd ever heard, and pretty soon everyone in the room was getting introduced to him before he knew it Elliot had refilled his glass twice, and a brunette by the name of Nancy Clark was hanging on his every word, even though he was saying nothing of importance. Suddenly he heard a spoon on a glass, getting everyone's attention. It was Helen Frye, still looking radiant, but more than a little drunk.

"Gentlemen, Ladies, Please find yourself a seat at the table. Dinner is served."

As Nancy steered him to a seat next to her, he found that he was suddenly ravenous. He slumped heavily into the chair, wondering what was for dinner.

The trout almondine and the spinach salad settled his stomach and his head, and he decided to lay off the booze for a while. Since he'd been back Harry had been taking him out every chance he got, and Jake was just tired of it. He couldn't blame Harry, since it been years since they'd seen each other, but his old boyhood chum had more of a penchant for bars and fast women than Jake did.

Overall, Jake preferred the quiet peace of the backcountry, the smell of a wood fire, the taste of coffee boiled over that same fire, and fresh juniper honey on biscuits made to rise with hardwood ashes. Harry had always been the cosmopolitan one, chasing women, wearing fancy suits, gambling whenever he had the chance. Jake, on the other hand, had never understood gambling. It was like throwing money out the window of the car to him, only less productive. An occasional poker game was okay, but it was the camaraderie Jake enjoyed the most.

And so he found himself out on the porch, leaning heavily on the railing, looking out over the valley which stretched out below him. Oak Creek burbled its way south and west to join the Verde River, the red rocks rising on each side. Just two miles away Cathedral Rock rose majestically above the entire scene like a coliseum built for giants, the moonlight casting it in spooky shadow, the red rock pink in the light of the half moon.

"Beautiful isn't it?"

Jake turned to find Helen Frye standing behind him. She came to the railing smoking a cigarette, and set her drink on the rail.

"I fell in love with this place from the air…made Jack buy it for me. We built this house in '42, which is why it's still not done, and the rock was all quarried from right up there," she said, pointing at the top of a small knoll.

"It's an incredible spot."

Helen laughed. "It is, isn't it? Of course, there's no running water, being up here on the butte like this; we have to haul it in and fill a cistern. We live in the other house for the most part. Jack has his office up here though, and I have my studio…and it's a great place for parties."

"I understand it has a name."

She nodded, sipping her drink. "A friend of mine came to visit while it was being built, and we were standing out here one night. Of course the railing wasn't here yet, but the workers and their families were staying down there, on the creek. They had cookfires going, and of course many of them were Yavapai Apache…so she said we should call it 'The House of Apache Fires.' It just seemed to fit. It's so evocative don't you think?"

Jake nodded.

"We were a little surprised you didn't bring someone with you, Jake."

"No one special right now," he said, but of course that was a lie. He felt a bit guilty because he realized he wished he had asked Morrie to come to the party with him. Laurel was the past…but was Morrie his future? He hadn't been able to stop thinking about her since they had met.

"No one?"

"Well, there was one girl, but…well, the war changed that," he said, not wanting to jinx himself by saying Morrie's name out loud.

"I'm sorry to hear that, Jake," she said, placing her warm hand on his arm for a moment. "There's lots of fish in the sea, as my father use to say. Tell you what, I'll make sure there's more single women at the next party."

Jake laughed. "Sure, it's a deal."

"You should wear your medals though, Jake. I understand you're an honest to god hero. You know us women, we love heroes."

Jake laughed. "I'm no hero. I was just doing my job."

"That's what all heroes say, right Jack?"

"Right."

Jake hadn't heard Jack Frye come up behind them, but now he felt a good-natured slap on the back.

"Trying to make time with my wife, Jake? Doesn't look good, you two out here on the veranda in the moonlight." Jake didn't know what to say, but he felt the embarrassment climb his neck like the bloom on a rose.

"Oh stop, Jack, you're embarrassing him. Jake's too much of a gentleman to make a pass at me. We were just discussing his lack of a date. I told him at the next party I'd make sure there were lots of single women for him."

"Just kidding, Jake," Frye said, his wide, salesman's smile illuminated in the dim flicker of the Tiki lights. "Come on back inside for a few minutes, we're talking planes."

"Sure." He wasn't sure what to think of all this cosmopolitan joshing. Where Jake came from, a man accuses you of hitting on his wife, you'd better be ready to fight.

Jack Frye guided him slowly back inside, helping him navigate the other guests, tables and the wayward chair with a firm arm. Jake was sweating from the pain in his legs by the time he got to the study, where Jack steered him towards a high-backed leather chair that was about the most comfortable chair Jake had ever sat in, or at least that's what he thought as he sank into it gratefully. He barely noticed the other men in the room until Jack closed the door, muting the noise from the party outside. He looked up to find Elliot Roosevelt pressing another glass of whiskey into his hand.

"Looks like you're ready for another painkiller, champ. The doctor give you any pills?"

"He wanted to, but I don't like taking stuff like that. I've heard of too many guys ending up with a monkey on their back."

Roosevelt laughed. "That's good thinking, Jake, but I don't like seeing you in pain. I know a good doctor…"

"Thanks, Colonel, but I have two dictatorial old bastards on my case already. I don't think I could take another doctor."

The whole room laughed at this, and Jake realized there were five or six others scattered around the sumptuous study, hanging on the arms of chairs, drinking or smoking, almost as if they were waiting for something.

"Now Jake, I'm Elliot to you in this room. You'll be a colonel yourself soon enough if I have my way," Roosevelt said. Jake didn't know what to think of that, but he wasn't getting his hopes up. What could a gimpy ex-flier like him have to offer his country? he mused bitterly.

"All right, everyone. I'd like you to meet a new friend of mine," Jack Frye began. Oh shit, Jake thought. It's a damn hero worship meeting.

"This is Jake Ellison, and he's a local boy back from the war. Flew P-38's and P-61 Black Widows in North Africa and Italy with Elliot here. He was shot up by an…"

"Me110," Roosevelt interjected.

"Thanks, Elliot. Me110 nightfighter, over Italy. What's amazing about it is that he managed to get the plane home at all with something like seventy percent of his control surfaces shot up."

There was a low murmur from the room, appreciative smiles as the others looked at each other.

"That's some damn fahn flyin' if you ask me, gentlemen," commented a tall, dapper man with slicked back hair and a thin mustache that Jake had barely noticed, ensconced as he was in a corner chair. There was general agreement at this statement, and one of the other men bent to whisper to this man, who nodded, and raised his glass full of what looked suspiciously like milk to Jake. He looked familiar, but Jake couldn't quite place him. He hadn't noticed him at the party earlier.

"He landed the plane successfully after manually deploying the landing gear…which he had to do himself as his copilot had been shot up and was unconscious. Elliot here says Jake is the best natural pilot he's ever seen, and I thought we ought to include him in our little club."

"HERE, HERE," they all shouted. Jake looked up at Elliot Roosevelt curiously.

"Everyone here has either been shot down or has crashed a plane and walked away Jake. Welcome to the Crash Club."

Now Jake felt better. These men understood him. They were fliers themselves. They understood. He relaxed into the warmth of his chair.

"Now you tell Cates that we're all a little bit put out that he didn't show up for this little shindig, and he'd better come to the next one. I don't think anyone here except Howard has crashed a WWI plane. I understand Cates flew with the Lafayette Escadrille in the Great War?"

Jake nodded. "He flew Spads. Crashed one behind enemy lines. He's a tough old coot. We had an old Jenny in the barn with her wings off that I wanted to get back in the air." The words came unbidden, and he knew he was talking too much, but no one seemed to care. "We lost her in a fire recently."

"Would've lahked to see that plane, Jake. I have a special place in this black heart of mahn for old bahplanes," the man in the corner said.

"I learned to fly in her," Jake said sadly.

"Ah understand, Jake. Fella's first plane is lahk his first girl…"

"How many biplanes did you buy for Hell's Angels again Howard?" someone asked.

"Flying or for parts? At one time I owned the fifth largest air force in the world."

Suddenly Jake knew who this man in the corner was. It was Howard Hughes! He swallowed hard. My God, who are these people? Then Elliot was trying to introduce him to someone.

"Jake, this is Jack Northrop. He was an engineer over at Lockheed, but he's got his own company now. Likes it better that way he says. He designed and built the P-61 Black Widow you flew in Italy, Jake."

"Shhh," Jack said, holding a finger to his lips. "I've got Howard convinced he's going to buy me out for a fortune," he said with a smile.

"Listen, Jake," Elliot said, "I know you want to get back into the war, but that part of it is over for you. Hell, the war in Europe will be over by Christmas at this rate anyway. We're working on a few things that we'd like to talk to you about. You'd be compensated of course, but it might require some travel…if you're feeling up to it. We need the input of experienced pilots like yourself in this final design phase…just to make sure we haven't missed anything. You know, two heads being better than one and all that."

"Well, sure. I mean, I still technically work for the Army…"

"We'll get you a temporary duty assignment to Lockheed as an Army consultant, Jake. Don't you worry about that. In the meantime, I want you to get those legs in tip-top condition. You take care of yourself and listen to your doctors, and that's an order," Roosevelt said seriously.

"Yes Sir."

"Jake, I want you back in a cockpit just as bad as you do. Patton is the only man dumb enough to say what we've all been thinking, but when we defeat the Germans, we're going to be in a technology race with the Russians. The next war we fight will be with them, and we need to be ready. How'd you like to be a test pilot?"

"Damn, Sir, I'd give my eyeteeth for a chance like that."

"Well you've got the chance. It's up to you now. You get those legs in shape and we'll find a way to keep you busy in the meantime. Deal?"

"Deal, Sir."

"Now, I thought I told you to quit with all that 'Sir' business tonight?"

"Okay, Elliot."

"That's better. Now tell us, what was your most memorable flight in the war?"

"Hmm. Well, I can't talk about the specifics, but one time I was tasked with picking a guy up in the Greek Islands. I got to fly a captured German Arado seaplane. Other than Germans everywhere, it was a pretty nice flight…until the shooting started."

The other pilots all laughed, and began talking about their own experiences. As he took a long swallow from his drink, Jake looked across the room at Howard Hughes, who was looking at him with a sly smile on his face. He raised his glass of milk again, and Jake toasted him back, wondering what other surprises lay in store for him.

27

THE BAD weather hadn't lent itself to training outdoors, so Kessler got permission to set up interior walls in the underground firing range beneath the SS barracks and lay out a course like a house, which they ran backward and forwards, first with empty weapons, and in various teams so he and his NCOs could see which men worked best together.

They were then reorganized into different twelve-man zugs, and teams of three and four were run through the "house" clearing targets. The underground range was heated by steam pipes running through it to other parts of the building, and they sweated through the training as Kessler had Schmidt start a timed competition between the men to keep their minds off the mission, and off of Christmas.

Weihnachten was coming, and the kitchens were bursting at the seams with food. Kessler had never seen so much, and after the deprivations of Berlin it seemed almost pornographic, but even he was looking forward to a traditional Weihnachten dinner of goose stuffed with apples and prunes, washed down with glüwein, or "glow wine", a hot, mulled wine which never failed to live up to its name.

Ornate, hand-painted signs proclaiming *"Christusmansionem Benedicat"* were beginning to appear over doors in the village, along with banners stating *"Ein Volk, Ein Reich, Ein Führer."* As far as the Führer went, Kessler wasn't sure if he was trying to play Sankt Nikolaus or Krampusse - the ill-tempered imp who accompanied him to punish bad girls and boys with his switch.

Kessler rarely saw him, but at the few staff meetings he attended, the Führer's mood had been increasingly mercurial, smiling and benevolent one minute, angry and raving the next. He'd sat through a forty minute rampage just that morning with several other officers, all of them higher ranking, that made him wonder briefly if Hitler wasn't losing his mind.

Just as with Göring - a known drug addict since injuring his back in the 1923 bier hall putsch - there were dark rumors of the Führer receiving regular injections of pure methamphetamine from Dr. Morell, who had replaced Brandt as his physician. Some claimed it was just B12 and other vitamins, but Kessler had his doubts.

He stayed busy hunting down and requisitioning the final supplies for the mission, overseeing the training of his men and coordinating the transport of the Hortens with Galland's help. Through it all, his new Luftwaffe "aide" Herr Gothe, stuck to him like glue, and he was sure the little weasel was reporting his every move to Göring, who for the most part stayed in his house on the hill.

"I have to change and see to my men," Kessler told Gothe as they left the shooting range, dropping the hint that he never seemed to take.

"Of course," the Luftwaffe officer responded politely.

Gothe had come into his life in a most unwelcome way. Kessler had returned to his quarters one day and was wading through the last of his requisitions wishing he was an NCO once more when a knock came on his door. Answering it, he found to his surprise a young Luftwaffe officer standing outside. The officer cracked his heels together smartly and saluted, which Kessler returned half-heartedly.

"Herr Sturbannführer Kessler?"

"Yes? What is it?" Kessler growled, wanting nothing more than to finish his duties and put some time in at the range with his new weapon.

"I am Major Friedrich Gothe. I have been assigned to your command by order of Herr Reichsführer Göring.. I am your new Luftwaffe liason. I have brought you my orders." He handed Kessler a sheaf of papers held together with a clip and a sealed envelope, obviously his orders. More paperwork, Kessler thought. Mein Gott.

"Bitte, Kommen innen zie, Herr Major," Kessler replied, inviting him in at the same time wondering how he was going to get rid of him. Göring undoubtedly had assigned the young officer to keep an eye on Kessler and his men.

"Why have you been assigned to me? I have been coordinating all Luftwaffe business through General Galland quite nicely," Kessler said, already impatient with his new "liason" as Gothe closed the door behind him.

The major had looked at him impassively, but Kessler could sense his arrogance beneath the polite surface.

"Obviously Herr General Göring disagrees Herr Sturbannführer," he said, a note of disdain in his voice as he looked around Kessler's simple, but relatively, at least in Kessler's experience, luxurious accommodations.

Kessler had come to understand that there was a hierarchy here among the officers, and it had little to do with actual rank or command, and everything to do with whose son you were, where you were from and who you knew, or who your parents knew. Nepotism was alive and well in the Nazi party, and Kessler had no illusions about where he fitted in.

This young Luftwaffe officer, on the other hand, was clearly one of them, the kind who moved pins around on maps for generals, who had never seen battle except from afar, had never worn a filthy, lice-ridden uniform, had never watched a friend choking on his own blood while lying in a muddy ditch as artillery screamed overhead.

When he'd first come here, Kessler had been happy. Happy to be in the mountains he'd grown up in, happy with the training, happy to be out of the war for now. He'd even taken a day for himself and gone to Salzburg to see his family. Despite the holiday exuberance, however, Kessler found he was antsy, ready to begin the mission and more than ready to get out of Obersalzburg and away from the back-stabbing politics that infected the entire command structure.

"I have good news, Herr Sturbannführer Kessler," Gothe said, as they exited the Kaserne and the range and headed for the Platterhof, where Kessler had been quartered more permanently. They could have gone through the tunnels, but Kessler needed fresh air. It was a beautiful, sunny day, and the only thing that ruined it was Gothe's presence.

"Ja? And what would that be, Herr Major Gothe?"

"Reichsführer Göring has kindly granted my request to accompany you on your mission. I am coming with you, Herr Sturbannführer."

Kessler gritted his teeth and forced a small smile. "Wonderful news indeed, Herr Major. Wonderful news," he said, as he wondered if Gothe might have to have a terrible accident soon.

28

IT WAS two weeks before Jake saw Dick again. He'd been busy with Christmas shopping, just like everyone else. He'd gotten Cates an ancient book about the Lost Dutchman mine he was pretty sure he didn't have, plus a new magneto and plugs for the Jenny that were now useless. It made him sad just to look at them.

He'd found a bolt of material he was sure Rosa would like, and got Jose and Ramiro each a new pair of gloves and a lariat, while Antonio got a new cap pistol and belt, as well as a real pair of chaps. Harry would get a new deck of naked lady cards and a bottle of Johnny Walker Red, but he still hadn't gotten Laurel anything…to tell the truth, he'd been thinking about Morrie more and more and Laurel less and less. He hadn't spoken to Laurel since their trip to Flagstaff, and Jake found to his surprise that this didn't bother him one bit. When he looked in store windows during his forays to Flagstaff and Cottonwood, it was Morrie he found himself thinking about, not Laurel.

As a result of Christmas, he'd had less time to spend on deciphering the letter, and he felt more than a little guilty about it. He'd tried every book code he'd read of, and a few some mathematicians at the college had helped him with, but he wasn't having much luck. Dick, as it turned out, had done much better with his task. He came bouncing into the kitchen with his news.

"Let's go for a ride."

"Where?"

"I'll tell you when we get there," Dick replied, being deliberately mysterious.

Jake clumped his way awkwardly into the mudroom off the kitchen and struggled into his coat. He was glad Dick didn't try to help him as some people did. He hated feeling like a cripple, hated the damn crutches, and couldn't wait to throw them away.

"Ready?" Dick asked, coming into the mudroom.

"Yup. I'm taking my coffee with me though. Want some?"

"Sure, I could stand some."

They poured their coffee into a couple of old, chipped mugs so Rosa wouldn't bitch, and went out to the car. The mud was still frozen, and a cold wind had swept the yard clean. There were gray clouds hanging low over Sedona, obscuring the rocks. Jake hoped it would snow; he loved the way the red rock formations looked frosted with fresh snow. It was one of the things he had missed most during his time in North Africa.

Dick took it easy through the potholes after seeing Jake flinch, or maybe it was just so they wouldn't spill their coffee, but either way, after riding to Cottonwood a couple times with Harry, Jake appreciated it. Instead of going right to 89A though, Dick turned left on Sterling Pass road, and headed towards the mountains.

Having grown up here, Jake knew the area every bit as well as Dick, so when they turned into the drive going to the old Indian ruins at Palatki, he looked over at him.

"I've seen the ruins before, if that's what we're doing."

"Just hold your horses," Dick replied, clamming up. He followed some older tracks for a while, then pulled up into the shade of an ancient juniper near an empty corral and shut off the motor. There were no sounds but the wind and the ticking of the engine as it cooled.

"Okay, I'll bite. What's this about?"

"My brother David told me it's a popular place to bring a girl to neck. No one bothers you here."

"You put your arm around me and I'll punch you right in the snotbox, you weirdo."

Dick grinned at him. "Naw, you ain't my type. Reason I brought you here is, there's another reason people come out here."

"Which is?"

"To make deals. Illegal deals, if you catch my drift."

"So?"

"So you remember Ed Shelton?"

"How could I forget? He broke my nose in eighth grade."

"You got a few licks in yourself if I remember correctly."

"You telling me he's involved in something illegal? Who cares? He always was a little scumbag."

"He was seen hanging around Lily…and not just once, but several times."

"I don't believe it. He was definitely not Lily's type."

"Don't I know it. The question is, *why* was she interested in this guy?"

"He's meaner than a Mojave rattler nailed to a tree. What are we gonna do…ask him?"

"Exactly."

Jake looked at his friend as if he'd lost his mind. "You want to corner the meanest guy ever came out of this part of the country and just ask him politely if he knows anything about Lily's death?"

"Something like that."

"He was a Marine too, I understand."

Dick shook his head. "Yeah. He was a Raider like me. See, us Marines stick together. I'm just going to ask him real polite, brother to brother."

"First of all, I'm pretty sure that the war just made him meaner and more dangerous than he was before. Second of all, that piece of shit will never be your brother. He's swimming in a completely different pond, bud."

"So we appeal to his business sense."

"Like how?"

"Like if he doesn't tell us what we want to know, we'll beat the snot out of him. He won't be able to do business with broken arms."

"Have you lost your mind? Neither one of us is in condition to mess with a guy like that, a guy I might add who probably comes to do 'business' packing heat, if not with backup."

"I think we can handle him."

"Oh, well that makes me feel so much better."

"You turn into a chickenshit all of a sudden?"

"No, but I didn't leave my brains in Italy, just a few pieces out of my legs."

"Trust me will you? I told you, I set it up."

"What'd you tell him?"

"That we were interested in some extra-special Christmas presents."

"You have lost your ever lovin' mind."

"Listen, I have a plan."

"Enlighten me."

"He works out of his trunk, see? When he opens it up to show us the merchandise, we push him inside and lock it on him. We refuse to let him out until he tells us what we want to know."

"*That's* your plan?"

"Pretty much."

"Gee, too bad Eisenhower doesn't have you on his staff, the war'd be over by now."

"Oh come on. It's not going to be that bad."

"He's a dangerous criminal, probably armed. His whole family are criminals. They love hurting people. It's what he *likes* to do. He had the same training as you and saw combat...by the way, why's he out of the service?"

"Dishonorable discharge. He raped a girl overseas. Beat her up too, from what I understand."

"That's our boy. His father must be so proud."

"Probably, knowing *his* old man."

"You really think he'll tell us anything?"

"He's the best lead we've got."

Jake took a deep breath and looked at Dick. "Then let's lock the sonuvabitch in the trunk and weld the lock shut."

Dick grinned. "I knew you'd see things my way."

"I get shot again I'm going to be pissed."

"I'll get you another Purple Heart."

29

THE MOOD on the Obersalzburg was exuberant. German forces had smashed through the Allied lines at a thin point between American and British forces, capturing hundreds of soldiers, and had surrounded the small town of Bastogne, which sat at the crossroads to Paris, the coast and, more importantly, Antwerp. Once they took the town, the road to Belgium would be clear, and the Allied forces would be cut off from their beachhead. Without fuel and ammunition, it was just a matter of time before the German army swept the Allies back into the ocean. They were on the offensive again.

Model's forces had taken the Americans by surprise, and Hitler was calling the winter storm that had blanketed the area, grounding American fighter bombers *"A storm straight from the heart of Germany."* Everyone said they would be in Belgium by the end of the month. Even the SS, an organization not known for good cheer, had caught the holiday spirit.

Kessler had even seen an off-duty group of Schutzstaffel singing carols in the small café at the top of the hill near the barracks. Of course, the large quantity of bier they had consumed surely had contributed to their enthusiasm, but after being bombed day and night not just by Allied bombers but by constantly bad news from the front of the enemy's march across France, the news that the German Wehrmacht was again taking it to them was welcome indeed.

News from the eastern front was not nearly as rosy. The Russians were steadily driving into Germany. Kessler had spent enough time on the eastern front in winter to know what his compatriots were going through. As they crossed Hungary and Czechoslovakia the Russians were burning and looting everything in their path, raping and killing, much of it in direct revenge for the depredations visited upon their country previously by German forces, but Kessler didn't care. He felt hurting civilians was just a line you didn't cross. Combatants however, were another matter.

Kessler had just returned from a day of close quarters combat practice. He had the carpenters build a representation of the Warm Springs compound, and he and Schmidt had spent the last week working with the men, storming through it until it was second nature. He now knew which men were fastest loading the planes with ordnance and which were fastest through the houses, and he and Schmidt had spent the last two hours separating the men into their final two teams. He was exhausted.

As he was removing his tunic, a knock came on his door. When he answered it, a messenger handed him a wax-sealed envelope. Kessler signed for it, thanked the aide and closed the door. The wax seal had been impressed with the Führer's personal stamp, and he felt a chill as he tore the end of the envelope open and pulled out his orders.

By order of the Führer, you are to report with your men and all necessary material to Munich to receive transport to Königsberg then to Bremerhaven where you will rendezvous with the rest of your gruppe and proceed on your mission. This will be done immediately, within the hour.

Hitler's now unsteady scrawl accompanied it. They would miss their holiday dinner, but that couldn't be helped. It was time to go. Just how they would get all the way north across Germany to the Baltic, with the Americans on the west and the Russians on the East, he had no idea. He had no doubt that it would require a fight...or several. It didn't matter. They were ready.

30

E D SHELTON showed up fifteen minutes late, driving a beat-up '35 Ford that had seen better days. It had no hubcaps, but the tires were good ones, and Jake could hear the tight burble of a well-tuned engine, just the thing for outrunning the cops on a dark night. Jake would have bet that there was a cut-off switch for the brake lights under the dash as well.

The Ford pulled up to their car head to head, but Ed waited for them to get out before he shut off his engine. Cautious, Jake thought, like a coyote. Jake fought with the door and his crutches and followed Dick over to the Ford. Ed had finally shut off the car and climbed out, and now gave Jake an evil smirk as he took in the crutches. Jake could feel his blood boiling in his ears already. He never had liked this guy, and he was wondering if they were doing the right thing.

"Well, well. Look who we have here. How's the nose, Jake?" Ed asked, even though the broken nose episode had been eons ago.

"Just fine, Ed. Want another chance at it?"

Dick put his good hand up in the air between them. "Now c'mon guys, we're here to do business. Let's not get into it."

"Naw, you didn't tell me you'd be bringing *him* with you. Deal's off," Ed said, moving to get back in his car.

Jake didn't know what he was going to do before he did it, it just happened. He dropped one crutch to the ground as he picked up the other one and swung it at Ed's head like he was hoping for a home run, which in fact he was. Ed took the blow square in the temple, and his eyes rolled up as he fell to the ground, unconscious. At least Jake hoped he was unconscious.

Dick looked at him and shook his head. "What happened to 'let's push him into the trunk?'" he asked as he knelt to check Ed's pulse.

"Sorry, just seemed like the thing to do."

"Well, we're in luck, I don't think you killed him."

"Broke my damn crutch though," Jake said sadly, looking at the splintered wood.

"Shit, he's carrying a piece. Let's get him over in the shade and wait for him to wake up. Check the trunk and see if there's anything to tie him up with."

Jake went around to the back as Dick dragged the unconscious smuggler by the shirt over to the shade of a large alligator juniper. He popped the trunk, and sure enough, it was full of booze, several guns, paper sacks filled with the most obscene magazines he'd ever seen, and some smaller tins and bound packages which he was pretty sure were illegal drugs.

He found some old clothesline in the wheel well behind the spare, and yanked it out. He closed the trunk and limped over to the juniper using the one crutch, already regretting breaking the other one.

Dick had relieved Shelton of a snub-nosed .38 and was playing with it. Jake threw him the rope.

"Quit messing with that thing, it might go off."

Dick just grinned at him. "I'm a trained killer remember? Don't worry about this little peashooter. We had *real* guns in the Marines. I carried a BAR."

"Yeah, well help me tie him up," Jake said, slumping to the ground.

"How?" Dick asked, raising what was left of his right arm.

"You can hold your damn finger on the bow, now help me roll him over."

They rolled Shelton over with some difficulty, eliciting a low moan from their victim.

"Hurry, he's waking up."

"*You* want to do this?" Jake asked, as he hog-tied Shelton like a heifer they were getting ready to brand. Actually, not a bad idea, Jake thought as he finished the last knot, but he didn't have a branding iron.

"So now what?" Jake asked.

"So we ask him a few polite questions."

"And if he doesn't answer?"

"Use the other crutch on him."

"I only have one left. Besides, eventually we have to let him go, and he's gonna be pissed."

"*Now* you're getting cold feet? Should've thought about that before you cold-cocked him."

"Oh, and locking him in his own trunk wouldn't piss him off?"

"Hey, he's coming around."

"Ohhh. Shit." Ed's eyes slowly opened then grew confused. He tried to move his hands and legs, then realized he was tied. He lost it, struggling and straining against his bonds like a wild animal.

"I GET FREE I'M GONNA KILL BOTH OF YOU," he hollered, followed by a few choice expletives, the general gist being the legitimacy of their parentage.

"Ed, calm down or you're just going to make things worse," Dick said.

"Screw you. You let me loose right now or so help me…"

Dick calmly smacked him on top of the head with the barrel of the .38, eliciting a howl of pain from his victim.

"OWWW. You son of a …"

"Now, I warned you once Ed, don't make me hit you again. That's gonna be a lump tomorrow."

"You're gonna be a corpse tomorrow," Ed growled. Dick tapped him again, and Ed yelled again.

"SHIT. CUT THAT OUT. What the hell do you guys want? What'd I ever do to you?"

"You broke my nose you so and so," Jake said.

"That was in eighth grade for chrissakes. What do you want?"

"We want to know who killed Lily Hausen, asshole," Dick said, his face clenching up in rage. Strangely Ed went quiet for a few seconds.

"Don' know nuthin' bout that."

"Oh, you don't? You know she was my girl though, right Ed? We was gonna get married when I came home. Some low-life offed her though."

"I swear, I don't know nuthin'."

Dick took a deep breath. "I was afraid you were gonna say that, Ed." He pushed himself to his feet and aimed the .38 at Ed's head.

"Jesus, Dick, don't do it," Jake said as Dick thumbed the hammer back.

"I swear to Christ risen that I don't know nuthin'," Ed yelled, seeing the huge bulk of the ex-linebacker standing above him. Dick pulled the trigger, and the sound was deafening in the still air. When the dust cleared, Jake expected Ed's head to be gone, but then he saw him rise up. His face was covered in sand from where the slug had hit next to his skull, spraying him with sand. Ed was really swearing now.

"One more time, Ed. I've got five more shots here. How'd you like one in the kneecap?"

"Dick…"

"Shut up, Jake. Now tell me something Ed."

"I swear, I don't…"

BAM. This time Dick had missed his head on the other side, by mere hairbreadths again, splashing sand into Ed's eyes and mouth. Ed screamed and struggled, scared and furious at once.

"Last chance, Ed. Next one is in the leg."

Ed spit sand from his mouth. "All right, so I saw her a couple times. She came to me, not the other way around."

"Tell me," Dick said, his eyes dark and terrible, the smoking revolver held unwavering by his left hand.

"She wanted me to get her something."

"What?"

"Drugs."

"Drugs? Lily?" Dick asked incredulously. "I don't believe it. Try again."

"No really. She wanted some morphine…but it was weird you know, like she wanted to know how to use it, like if you didn't want anyone to know you were using. I told her some girls injected it between their toes…that way there's no tracks. Nobody looks between the toes."

Jake felt sick. Lily a hophead? It didn't make sense.

"I don't believe you," Dick said, cocking the hammer again.

"I swear. Then she wanted to know if I could get a letter to her grandmother in Germany. I told her it'd be tough, but I had some people I could ask."

"Why does that not surprise me?"

"Hey man, you asked."

"So you sold Lily dope?" Jake said, looking at Shelton with disgust.

Ed blew the sand off his lips again. "Don't blame me – she asked for it specifically. I told her she should start off with a little something else first, you know? She was a babe in the woods, man, trying to act all grown up and tough, but you could see she wasn't. Trying to be all worldly and grown-up. Truthfully I think it may have been for someone else. You guys may not like what I do, but I just provide a service…to people who already got the need. I'm not looking for new customers, I got plenty."

"Bullshit."

"I swear, man. I wouldn't do that to a sweet young thing like that."

Dick drew back his leg and kicked him in the gut. All the air went out of him, and Ed lay gasping on the sand like a fish yanked ashore on a line. Finally he got his breath back.

"You'd better kill me now because when I get loose…"

"Shut up, Ed or I'll take you up on it," Dick growled, his finger tightening on the trigger. Jake had never seen him so pissed. "What do you think, Jake?"

"I hate to say it, but I think he's telling the truth…mostly."

"Yeah, it's the mostly part I wonder about."

"Look, I heard she was spending time with some guy in Flagstaff. That's all I know," Ed said, looking up at them with red, sand-filled eyes. When he saw the look on Dick's face, he laughed. "You didn't know, did you? Hey Dick, maybe she just wanted a guy with both his arms…"

Dick started kicking Ed as if he were trying to punt him downfield. Jake staggered to his feet and threw himself at Dick, knocking him off balance, and catching one of his kicks in the stomach as a result. They both fell to the ground, Jake wheezing atop his friend until he pushed him off.

"Dick, STOP," Jake managed to get out as Dick got back up to stand over Ed, his eyes black with murder.

"You'd better not be lying, you piece of shit, or I'll find you and finish the job."

"Yeah? Well you'd better leave the county, my friend, because next time I see you and your buddy I'll have friends with me."

"Sure. What are you gonna tell them? That you got beat up by a couple of cripples?" Dick tucked the gun under his bad arm, reached into his pocket and flicked out a folding knife, quickly slicing through Ed's restraints. Ed rolled over rubbing his wrists where he was bound, looking up at Dick, who now held the gun on him again.

"I get my gun back?"

"I don't think that's a good idea right now," Dick said, as Jake found his crutch and struggled to his feet.

"That's theft."

"You oughta know."

Ed got slowly to his feet, a look of pure hatred on his face. He spat at Dick's feet, then staggered off to his Ford. Just before he got in he looked back at them and spat again. "Like I said, better be watching over your shoulder asshole. You messed with the wrong guy this time."

"I'm shaking in my boots," Dick answered, the gun still pointed at the smuggler. Ed got in and the car started with a roar, then he put it in gear and dumped the clutch, spraying a huge rooster tail of dust in their direction as he tore out of there, giving them a one-finger salute as he went.

"I think you made a new friend," Jake said.

Dick looked down at the gun in his hand and stuck it in his belt, then looked at his remaining hand. He made a fist, then opened his fingers again. This time when he looked at Jake the rage had turned to sadness.

"I hate to say it, but I believe that asshole."

"It could be something entirely innocent," Jake said.

"He told us the truth, Jake. He knew it would hurt me, so he told us the truth."

"Maybe," Jake said, but they had both seen it in Ed's eyes, and heard it in his voice.

"Let's get out of here and go have a drink. I don't want to think about this shit anymore today."

Jake nodded in agreement as they headed for the car, wondering if they'd ever know the truth about Lily. A turkey vulture circled high above them in the hot, blue sky, signaling death for something or someone as they followed the road back out to civilization.

31

THE ROADS north of Munich were madness itself. They were blocked everywhere by civilian handcarts, bicycles, small automobiles pulled by horses or mules, the occasional large flatbed truck full of people and their possessions which had either run out of fuel or had gotten stuck in the deepening snow on the road, and of course soldiers, many of them bandaged and hollow-eyed; entire units fleeing south to the Alpenfestung: the alpine fortress Goebbels had praised so lavishly on the radio, which Schmidt now knew to be a mere fraction of the size reported.

Kessler had sent Schmidt ahead with a small contingent of men to clear the road, which they did in the usual efficient SS fashion: move out of the way or you will be shot. It reminded him of hand – to – hand combat; the pressing mass of people was cloying, the stench of dead animals and improvised latrines beside the road mixing with spilled petrol and worse, the smell of hundreds of unwashed Germans, without running water for months; like one giant, fetid hand pressing against your face.

At one point a madwoman, eyes wide with worry or sheer lunacy, had grabbed Schmidt by the lapels and began screaming at him about the Russians. He could smell the fear on her. There was nothing to do but harden your heart and push through. After five years of war, Schmidt's didn't need much hardening.

At Würzburg they checked with the stationmaster and found, unbelievably, that the tracks were undamaged nearly all the way to Berlin. No one was interested in going north however, thank you. The trains were piling up on the sidings, unable to continue south.

Schmidt talked to Kessler and they decided to risk it, since they were getting nowhere on the roads. A few imprecations and a pistol pointed at the head of an engineer's son however soon got them their ride north. They quickly transferred their packs, jump containers and other gear to the waiting train, while Pieter, who had worked for the railroad before the war, held his submachine gun on the engineer to provide encouragement. Ten minutes later they were on their way.

The engineer was clearly worried; the main reason the trains weren't running back and forth was that communication lines were down, and there was about an even chance that they might meet another train on the same track, coming the other way. Despite the worsening weather, Schmidt posted Meier on the small front platform to warn of broken track, large drifts or oncoming trains. Kessler ordered all the men to keep their weapons and packs with them at all times and to be prepared to jump if it looked as though a crash were imminent.

Twice they had to stop the train and dig through snow drifts too large even for the engine to bull through, and ten long hours later they were approaching Luckenwalde, just south of Berlin when a warning shout came from the front, and the engineer reduced throttle, then reversed it, and brought the train to a halt. Pieter climbed up into the cab, covered with snow and shaking from the cold, to tell them the tracks were gone ahead, likely from bombs. They could go no further.

Schmidt ordered him to report the blockage to Kessler in the main car and warm himself by the small coal burner while the rest of them unloaded the gear. As Schmidt began climbing down from the cab behind him, the engineer grabbed him by the shoulder, saying, "You can't leave me here like this. How will I get home?"

Schmidt tore himself free and gave the trainman a hard look.

"Would you prefer I just shoot you, mein Herr?" The railroad man shook his head and Schmidt climbed down and waded back through the shin-deep snow to the main car where Kessler was waiting.

After forming the men back into two zugs, they split the gear between them, each soldaten carrying not only his own load - bearing gear, weapon and pack but also one end of the jump containers filled with MG-42s, Panzerfausts and the like. Other men shared the burden of the spare ammo boxes. No one complained. They were not Hitler Youth, they had all been here before. They worked their way through the fields, towards Berlin, and other than being fired upon once by a defensive position, reached the city without further incident.

If the road had been madness, Berlin was an asylum. Other than an increased sense of panic, it was likely no worse than it had been before they left for Obersalzburg, but a few weeks in the quiet of the mountains put it in a new light. Kessler and Schmidt shared a look as an old man was executed in the street by soldiers for cutting meat from a bloated horse carcass.

Snow had converted much of the rubble into ersatz hills within the city. Hungry children watched with black eyes as they passed, a four – year – old child clutching a doll in one hand, her older brother's hand in the other, stared at them shamelessly. His men tried not to let him see as they slipped the children some of their precious rations, and to Kessler's credit he pretended not to see them doing it. They bent their heads against the wind and marched on.

With so much of the city gone they had trouble finding their way, then once they had, would find the street blocked with rubble and have to backtrack. The men were exhausted from carrying so much weight, and it had begun snowing again when Kessler called a halt.

"It's getting dark. We'll stay in that building there for the night if it looks safe. Set up a machine gun each side of the street and rotate the watch every half hour. Have the men check their feet for frostbite. We won't get much further without a truck or two. In the morning I'll take a couple men and see what I can find. I doubt there's anything to burn, but if you can find something, start a fire for heat. No cooking besides tea. The smell of food cooking here could cause a riot. Cold rations only."

"Jawohl, Herr Sturbannführer. Immediately." Schmidt turned to find his sergeants.

"Oh, and Schmidt?"

"Ja?"

"The mission comes first. When I'm gone tomorrow, do not let some hard-on try and appropriate the gear just because he outranks you. Do whatever you have to. Verstehen?"

"Jawohl," Schmidt said grimly.

32

ROSA LOVED Christmas and the house showed it. Every shelf, ledge, nook and cranny was strung with tinsel, ornaments, and long white and red strings of popcorn and cranberries. Jake had always hated making the strings as a kid, because half the time he'd stab himself in the thumb trying to get the needle through the hard, red berries. He vowed when he left home that he'd never make another damn cranberry – popcorn string as long as he lived, but here he was, stabbing a needle through the damn things, his fingers already sore and red, the mixing bowls full of supplies in front of him barely half empty, a long string laid out carefully across the floor.

Cates was asleep in his chair in front of the fire, a book lying across his stomach, his reading glasses rising and falling gently as he snored. He'd conveniently fallen asleep just as Rosa had come into the room with the two mixing bowls of agony, a spool of thread and a pack of needles. Jake strongly suspected him of faking it to get out of making decorations…not that he could blame him, he just wished he'd thought of it first.

The Christmas tree they'd cut themselves up on the rim stood green and lush in one corner, still devoid of ornaments. Trimming the tree was a job they normally left for Christmas Eve. The tree would stand only until the New Year, by Cate's decree of course. If it were left up to Rosa, she'd leave the damn thing up until June.

Rosa came into the room with a paper sack and before Jake could object, poured yet more popcorn into the half-empty bowl, making Jake groan.

"Rosa, come on. How many damn strings of these do I have to make?"

Rosa shook her finger at him. "Jou watch jour language en mi casa. We are done when we are done," she said sternly, then her face changed into a vision of sweetness as she smiled, her hand going to his shoulder, the proprietary touch of a mother with her son.

"Jou wan' some cookies, maybe?"

Jake grinned back at her. "Maybe? Cookies and eggnog are all that's keeping me going, Rosa."

"Bueno. I make jour favorite," she said, heading to the kitchen.

"Hey, bring me a couple," Cates said, conveniently rousing from his slumber.

"Left me to make all these stupid things myself, you can get your own damn cookies," Jake grumbled.

"Don't know what you're bellyachin' about. You're warm, dry, plenty to eat...imagine those poor bastards pinned down in Bastogne, surrounded by Germans, no warm clothes, nothing to eat for days, running out of ammo...why, it reminds me of a time during the Great War..."

"Cates, please. I've heard the story about you crashing your plane in the mud and spending Christmas in the trenches a hundred times. Soon as the weather clears, the Air Corps will drop supplies and bomb the snot out of the Germans."

"Hasn't cleared yet from what the radio said. Could stay like this through Christmas," Cates said.

"Poor bastards," Jake said.

"At least they got gumption. That General McAuliffe telling the krauts to shove it? That took balls."

"I think he said 'Nuts', Cates," Jake said. He heard the phone ringing in the kitchen and wondered if it were Morrie.

"Whatever. It still took brass ones."

"Tomatillo, telephone...Jake? Jou hear me?" Rosa yelled from the kitchen.

"Si, Mama. Un momento," Jake yelled back.

Jake's legs were gradually healing, and he was using a cane instead of crutches now, but he was still sweating by the time he got to the kitchen, the phone handset laying on its side waiting for him.

"Hello?"

"Jake? Ed Shelton here."

Jake recoiled in surprise. "The hell you want?"

"That's not a very nice way to answer the phone, especially at Christmas."

"What do you want, Ed?"

"I want my damn gun back. I had it engraved and nickel-plated, and I want the damn thing back. Also, I heard something about Lily you'll want to hear."

"I'll have Dick send it to you."

"Uh-uh. I want my piece back, then I tell you. I didn't know your asshole buddy's phone number or I'd a called him."

"Why would you want to help us?" Jake asked.

"I told you. I want my pistol back. Besides, Lily was a sweet kid. She didn't deserve what she got."

"For the first time in our lives, Ed, I think I actually agree with you."

"Same place as last time, 5:00 p.m."

"I'll talk to Dick about it."

"This is a one time offer, asshole. I figure we're even otherwise. I sucker punched you when we were kids and broke your nose; you nailed me but good with that crutch, but I want that damn gun back."

"If we're there, we're there."

"Don't be late. I'll wait fifteen minutes, then we have an issue."

Jake opened his mouth to respond, but a click on the other end of the line told him the conversation was over. He hung up the phone just as Rosa came back into the kitchen.

"Rosa, Mamacita, I have to go see Dick. I'm going to take the Model A. It has more gas."

"When jou be back?"

"Probably seven or so. It depends."

She shook her head angrily. "I have a good supper planned, now jou tell me jou no be here? AIY," she said, throwing up her hands in disgust.

"Rosa, I'm sorry, but I have to go," he said firmly.

She looked at him, and shook her finger at him the same way she had when he was a kid. "Jou be careful, jou hear me? Theese business with theese dead girl is no good. Muy malo. Don' go, Tomatillo, es no bueno."

"Rosa, I'll be back later," he said as he headed for the living room and the gun cabinet. If they were meeting with Ed Shelton again, this time he'd by God have a pistol with him.

"FINE. Jes don' expect la comida you get back. I GIVE JOUR SUPPER TO THE DOGS," she yelled from the kitchen.

33

T HIS TIME they weren't the first to arrive. Ed's mean-looking black
Ford coupe sat facing towards them. The sun was fading, getting ready
to sink behind the mountains, but Jake could still see two people in the car.

"Shit. I guess I can't back you up from the side, they got here first.
Should've let me out up the road, I coulda' hiked in and flanked them,"
Dick said.

"Yeah, well, nothing for it. We'll just have to go straight in."

"They might have a guy in the trees…or in the backseat with a
shotgun."

"Well, we won't know until we get out, I guess," Jake said. Racking the
1911's slide to chamber a round, he put it on safe and tucked it into the
back of his pants, in the small of his back, cocked and locked. He saw Dick
struggling with his .45, trying to do the same thing, but having trouble
one-handed.

"Need a loop welded on the slide so's I can grab it with this hook," he
muttered.

"Here, let me get it for you," Jake said, taking the weapon and
chambering a round. He put the safety on and handed it back, and Dick
stuck it in his waistband just as Jake had, but left-handed.

"Ready?"

Dick nodded and they got out of the car, leaving the doors open. Jake
pulled his new cane from behind the seat and struggled out of the car. He
limped slowly to a point halfway between the cars, Dick next to him on his
right, his ears straining for any sound from the sides, in case there really was
someone in the weeds with a gun.

Ed didn't get out until they'd stopped, then he and the man beside him
in the front seat, a tall, skinny, angry-looking hillbilly type, got out slowly
and began walking towards them. Jake stood next to Dick and waited, his

right leg aching from the effort of trying to support himself on the sandy ground. They stopped about ten yards away.

"You bring my piece?" Ed said.

Dick pulled up his shirt and pulled the nickel-plated .38 from his waistband, holding it up so Ed could see it.

"Let's have it," Ed said, extending his hand.

Jake could see the outline of a gun under Ed's shirt, and he figured the thin man was packing as well. He figured Ed knew they'd be armed as well – they'd be stupid not to be. He nodded to Dick. "Give it to him."

Dick tossed the gun to Ed, who caught it deftly, looking it over carefully, a small smile creeping over his face. He stuck the .38 in his pants pocket and reached around behind him. Both Jake and Dick had their .45 autos out in a blur and pointed at them, Ed's friend returning the favor by whipping out his own pistol, another nickel-plated monster, a Smith and Wesson by the look of it.

"HOLD ON. Just settle down boys," Ed said, but the three men stayed as they were, safeties off, guns pointed at each other. At this range, somebody's gonna die, Jake thought as Ed slowly brought his hand out from behind him. In it was a plain white envelope. He'd had it tucked in his rear pocket and had been reaching for it, not a gun.

"Lester. Put that goddamn cannon away."

"Not until they lower their guns."

"Two guns to one, asshole," Dick said.

"I'm better. You two are dead men," Lester said.

"I SAID TO PUT THE DAMN GUN AWAY, LESTER." There wasn't much question who was in charge on that side of the fence.

Lester looked at him, then looked at Dick again and lowered his weapon. Jake breathed a sigh of relief as he and Dick safed their guns and returned them to their waistbands.

"What's in the envelope?" Jake asked.

"A name and address for a guy who was dating the girl you asked about. He's a German...and a junkie. I understand he was in the Bund in Chicago."

"That's a damn lie," Dick said hotly, clenching his remaining fist.

Ed smiled evilly. "Hey, maybe she got lonely and needed some comforting. Maybe she decided she wanted a little weiner-schnitzel while you were off killing Japs…all I know is, they spent a lot of time together."

"Where'd you get the name, Ed?" Jake asked, giving Dick a warning glance.

"Not part of the deal," Ed said, tossing the envelope at him. It fluttered to the ground. "We're done here. Far as I'm concerned, we're even. You ever see me again, you'd better head in the other direction."

"We're just ready to start cryin' over here, Ed," Dick said flatly.

"Try me and find out," Ed said. "Let's go Lester." The two of them headed back to their car, Lester backing away while keeping one eye on Dick as Jake limped forward to pick up the envelope.

He heard the Ford start up and back up in a three-point turn, then head out a back way he hadn't realized was there. The full-sized envelope was slightly wrinkled from being in Ed's back pocket. He tore the end open. There was a single, folded sheet of paper inside and he pulled it out, squinting to read it in the rapidly failing light.

"Hans Gruber, 412 West Cherry Ave, Flagstaff. No phone number."

"It's bullshit, Jake. She wouldn't cheat on me."

"So you don't think we should check it out, Dick? This is the only lead we've got right now. I say tomorrow we go find this guy and talk with him."

"You really believe that asshole?"

"I don't know *what* I believe anymore, Dick, but Lily was caught up in something. I don't know what, but whatever it was it got her killed, and dammit, I want to know why, don't you?" Dick just shook his head angrily as they walked back to the car, a bird trilling in the twilight as the light faded into darkness.

34

BY MORNING the snow had stopped, but they were all stiff and cold. All of them had fought in the winter before though, so it was just another inconvenience. When it was full light Kessler left Schmidt in charge and took five men with him in search of transportation. A couple of half-tracks would be perfect, he thought, but he doubted he'd find one in Berlin.

Although Kessler had lived in Berlin for a time, he wasn't that familiar with the city, which after two years of nearly constant bombardment was now nearly unrecognizable anyway. Miraculously Schenk, who had grown up in Berlin, said he knew where they were, and led them through the huge maze of rubble and half-destroyed buildings with the contents of their rooms displayed openly to the world like a giant shadow box.

It was strange to see the intimacies of the former tenants' lives – family portraits and paintings still hanging on the walls, green flowered wallpaper, a metal pitcher on a table with two chairs as if the owners had just gone into the next room; open doors leading who knew where, a piano with the music still pinned to the stand and the keyboard cover up - these were the images that fought for Kessler's attention until he stumbled over something in the snow. Looking back he saw the bare, frozen arm of a young woman sticking up from beneath the rubble, wrist bent almost demurely. After that he kept his eyes on the street.

It was slow going, but they made better time without their packs and the heavy drop containers. They turned onto a wide avenue which Kessler recognized with shock as the Lindenstrasse; the heart of Berlin. As bad as he remembered it, with camouflage netting covering the trees and street itself, it was far worse now. The netting and most of the trees were gone, nothing left but shreds of cloth and the shattered remnants of the trunks, the magnificent boulevard itself torn and holed by bombs.

Schenk called a halt and waved to Kessler, who ran forward. "Look," he said, pointing just off the street, at a wide park edging a frozen pond where a group of civilians were being herded off a truck and handed shovels by a small number of soldiers.

"Safeties on," Kessler said. "Follow me."

When they were 25 meters away, the officer, a young lieutenant in a filthy feldgrau longcoat holding a pistol at his side turned and saw them. He pointed the gun at Kessler, shouting "HALTEN ZIE" in a high voice.

Kessler's anger came boiling to the surface, but he did not stop. "Do you normally point a weapon at a superior officer, Herr Leutnant? Lower that pistol. NOW."

"Jawhol, Herr Sturbannführer," the young officer replied, chastened, but Kessler could still hear anger in his voice. By now the civilians were scraping futilely at the hard, frozen ground with picks and shovels, or in the case of one man who was getting some special attention from one of his guards, with his bare hands.

"Denn hier los?"

"These men are criminals. They are digging graves, Sir."

Kessler glanced in the back of the truck, but saw no bodies. It wasn't a grave detail, it was an execution squad. The men would dig until the animals guarding them tired of the game, then they would be shot.

"What did they do?"

"Illegal appropriation of Reich resources. They are thieves."

"What did they steal?"

"Does it matter, Herr Sturbannführer?"

The officer was young, with a sallow, cruel face, and one drooping eye. Kessler recognized the type; persecuted and bullied his entire life, he was now paying the world back for the pain inflicted upon him by others. Despite Kessler's rank, his manner was surly, his eyes bright, and Kessler recognized madness there.

He looked at the guards the young lieutenant commanded and saw they were just boys in ill-fitted uniforms, but angry, cruel boys, who with the exception of one who looked to be about eleven and who was having trouble just holding up his Mauser, seemed to be enjoying this. Kessler had little doubt this was their first such execution.

"This is your truck?" Kessler asked.

"Yes, Herr Sturbannführer."

"We will require it. Let these men go and return to your CP for new orders."

"You are not my commanding officer, Herr Sturbannführer. I cannot give you that truck. You and your men look like criminals to me. Put your weapons down and your hands on your head," the young idiot commanded, raising his pistol once more.

Kessler looked at him in amazement. "Perhaps you did not hear a superior officer give you an order, Herr Leutnant. Tell your men to put their weapons down. NOW," he commanded. Beside him he heard Schmidt click off his safety.

"I just hung a colonel yesterday, Herr Sturbannführer. There are many criminals in the streets. NOW TELL YOUR MEN TO LOWER THEIR…"

Kessler pulled his pistol and shot the young fool in the forehead as Schmidt and some of the other men opened up on the others, who were still fumbling with their weapons. The execution squad went down in a hail of bullets, while their victims cowered in the graves they were digging.

When the smoke cleared, Kessler said to Schmidt, "Tell these men to throw the bodies in the graves they were digging, then get lost. Get the men on that truck – it'll be tight, so when we get the rest of the men they'll have to stand. Let's get out of here before some other maniac comes around. We still need a second vehicle. Check this one for fuel."

"Jawhol," Schmidt said, turning to give the orders. They had three weeks to get to Königsberg, then the port at Pillau to meet the ship. According to reports, the Russians were attacking all along the Eastern front so they had no time to waste. If they got cut off, the mission was over. It would be a fight getting there, and they had no options but to go by road. Kessler had a feeling it might take every bit of that to get through what were now front lines.

Kessler looked down at the young idiot he'd just shot, staring at the sky in amazement, mouth open, with a small, neat red hole in his forehead.

"I'm afraid the war is over for you, Herr Leutnant," Kessler said before turning towards the truck.

35

B Y THE time Jake and Dick got to Flagstaff the rain had stopped, but
the sky was still dark, ominous - looking clouds blocking their view of
the San Francisco Peaks, making it look as if they almost didn't exist. It was
snowing on the mountains, and looked as if it would start snowing where
they were at any minute. The weather matched their mood. Jake parked,
legs aching, wondering why he'd insisted on driving, and checked the
address again.

The building was a run-down tenement built of yellow slump block that
looked as if it might have been a motel in a previous life, but had been
converted into apartments at some point. The trim was dark brown, the
paint peeling and scabrous. The bushes surrounding the place were
untrimmed, the crabgrass and dandelions having long since choked out any
vestiges of flowers in the narrow beds flanking the walkway. Water from the
storm pooled in potholes in the parking lot.

"Nice place. What's the number?"

"2C," Jake said.

"So it's probably on the second floor. Let me go check it out first. No
sense in you climbing those stairs with those legs of yours if he's not even
home."

Jake nodded gratefully. Dick chambered a round in the .45 one-handed
by pushing the slide against the dashboard and gave Jake a wink as he
tucked the weapon into his waistband again. "Be right back."

Dick slid silently out of the car, and clicked the door shut, the patter of
the rain on the roof covering his movements. The air that came into the car
as he did so was freezing, and Jake watched as he ran up the walk, then
disappeared into the shadows. He asked himself for the hundredth time
what Lily could possibly have in common with German spies - if that's
what was really going on. After all, there was probably a perfectly
reasonable explanation for why she had that letter, but why would someone

want to kill her, particularly in such a terrible way? Nothing made sense, and the deeper they delved into it the less sense things seemed to make.

Rain falling on the windshield blurred the street, each droplet refracting the light from the streetlamp like a tiny prism. For some reason it made him think of Morrie and the first day they met. He was tempted to call her, since he was in Flagstaff, but it seemed a little selfish with Dick having just lost Lily so recently. He could see them as a couple now in his mind's eye, imagining for a moment a better world where Lily still lived and the four of them could go on a double date together, then he thought of Laurel and wondered how Lily would feel about him dating someone besides her sister.

The car door opened and Jake gripped the steering wheel involuntarily. Dick slid back into the car and shut the door, his wet hair glistening in the dim light seeping through the car windows.

"I was right. It's on the second floor. Window's dark, so unless he's sleeping this early he's not home. I say we stay here for a while and see if he shows. I'd hate to have driven all the way up here for nothing."

Jake nodded in agreement.

"You're awful quiet."

Jake shrugged. "Just been thinking about this girl I met here in Flag. She's the kid sister of my former wingman. Her name's Morrison, but everyone calls her Morrie. A real sweet kid. I was just wondering how Lily would feel about her if she were still alive."

"You mean, because of your history with Laurel?"

"Yeah, well that and she was the little sister I never had. Hell, you can't imagine how many dates we went on with Lily riding along. Don't get me wrong, she wasn't a third wheel or anything, although there were a few times when we wanted to be alone when she didn't make it too easy, know what I mean?"

Dick nodded. "Lil felt a little bad about that I think. She really enjoyed hanging out with the two of you though."

"She shouldn't have felt bad; it was fun having her along. She was always an instigator. She'd come up with some crazy idea and we'd go along with it, and usually have a blast. Laurel was always more serious, kind of a stick in the mud to tell you the truth. Hell, if it hadn't been for Lily it might not have lasted as long as it did."

Dick looked out the window and Jake glanced at him, unable to tell if it was rain making his face wet or something else. Suddenly Dick sat up straight. "Someone's coming up the sidewalk."

They peered out the windshield, although it was a bit like looking at yourself in one of those wavy, funhouse mirrors, the rivulets of water distorting everything. A short, ascetic man wearing a thin jacket was coming quickly up the sidewalk, his hands jammed into the jacket pockets, his shoulders hunched against the rain. He wasn't wearing a hat, and Jake got the feeling he probably couldn't afford one.

He turned sharply at the walkway to the apartments and picked up his pace, clearly wanting to be out of the weather, finally disappearing into the shadow of the walkway. Whoever the landlord was, he didn't believe in unnecessary use of exterior lighting. A minute later a light came on upstairs, illuminating a small window.

"That's him," Dick said. He looked at Jake. "You ready?"

"Maybe I should go talk to him alone."

"Why you say that?"

"Dick, you may not like some of the things he has to say about Lily."

The expression on Dick's face darkened. "Screw that. I'm here for the truth. I told you, I just want to find the son of a bitch who did that to her. Nothing she could have done would make me love her less. She didn't deserve what she got, even if she *was* a goddamn German spy. No way *in hell* am I staying here."

Jake nodded. "Okay then, let's go."

"There're two staircases. Maybe I'll walk around back and check for a fire escape. I'll meet you upstairs," Dick said, climbing out of the car.

Jake nodded and struggled out of the car with his cane, his legs already aching from the drive, facing the long fight up the stairs. His legs were getting stronger every day, but he'd truly come to hate staircases.

By the time he made it to the top he needed to sit down. Not just wanted to, but really had to. He slid down the wall and sat with his legs straight out, his back against the cold slump block, waiting for Dick. One of the "prescriptions" the doctors had given him to rehabilitate his legs was stair climbing, but there just weren't many stairs in Sedona, and they had warned him about overdoing it. He had a feeling the 30 or 40 steps he'd just come up was exactly what they had meant by that.

He closed his eyes against the burning ache in his legs, leaning his head back against the freezing block. It helped, but he only had a brief reprieve before Dick was standing in front of him.

"Hey," Dick said softly.

"Jeez, you startled me. I can't believe I didn't hear you come up."

Dick grinned at him. "Gotta be quiet in the jungle fighting Japs. You aren't the only guy who's spent time in the woods you know." He squatted down in front of Jake.

"No fire escape that I see. 2C is two apartments down, near the middle...you okay?"

"Yeah fine. Gimme a hand up willya?"

Dick reached down and Jake took his hand, letting him pull him up off the floor and despite wanting to sit right back down Jake said "Let's go."

It was colder now, the rain finally beginning to change to snow, and Jake realized he really didn't want to be here, didn't want to hear what this guy Gruber had to say, didn't want to hear that Lily had been working with the Germans - that's what they were both thinking after all, the unspoken thought he and Dick had both shared coming up the canyon. By the look on Dick's face, he was feeling the same way.

"Well, let's get this over with," he said.

Dick nodded grimly as they turned towards apartment 2C.

36

KESSLER LOOKED at the ship with a dubious eye. It had been mothballed for years, and didn't look like it had ever been much of a ship to begin with. *This* was one of the famous Q-ship raiders he had heard so much about? The trawler in front of him looked as though it had an equal amount of black paint and rust, its lines were slack, and although men swarmed over it welding, carrying supplies and making repairs, Kessler was beginning to have second thoughts. It was nothing like the sleek U-boat he had envisioned. This ship was big, slow and ugly. The name Orion stood out in rust-streaked white paint on the stern.

"Doesn't look like much does she, Herr Sturbannführer?"

Kessler turned to find a tall man wearing the long gray leather coat and epaulets of a Kriegsmarine captain.

Kessler clicked his heels and nodded. "Herr Kapitan. Mein namen iss Kessler."

"Kapitan zur See Kurt Weyher, mein Herr, at your service."

"A pleasure, Captain."

"So, you do not like my ship Herr Sturbannführer?"

"This is not meant as an insult Kapitan, but I am having second thoughts as to her suitability for this task."

"Then let me show you her hidden charms, Herr Kessler. Perhaps you will change your mind."

Intrigued, Kessler followed the captain aboard where they were met with salutes and a piped warning to all hands that the Captain had arrived. Schmidt and the other men had stayed to unload the supplies from the train they had taken to Bremerhaven from Königsberg, but Kessler wanted to see just what made this old hulk suitable in the eyes of Donitz for such an important mission.

"Her name is the Hilfskruezer Orion. She was recommissioned briefly as a gunnery training ship and renamed the Hektor. She is a good ship, but her engines were always her weak point. She was the third ship to receive them, and they were literally antiques, totally unsuitable for a long-range raider. Despite that, we were able to keep her at sea for 511 days, sinking over 73,000 tons in the process. Her original armament was one 75mm gun, one 37mm gun, four 20mm guns, and six torpedo tubes."

Kessler raised his eyebrows at this. "Torpedo tubes? On a trawler?"

Kapitan Weyher smiled in response. "Of course she was stripped of armaments, so we are rearming her. She received two 88mm guns while she was briefly used as a training ship which we have rearsenalled and reinstalled, along with her original 20mm guns.

"This time, however, she has also received three 37mm guns, and instead of the two Arado float planes she was originally designed to carry, she now carries just one. We are however carrying more torpedoes for her, of the new acoustic homing type, which have proven quite effective in the U-boats. Her new engines were 'borrowed' from the aircraft carrier Graf Zeppelin, which is no concern as they were too small for that particular ship anyway.

"She is 148 meters bow to stern, with a beam of 18.6 meters, and an original draft of 8.2 meters, although we will be sitting a bit lower in the water with our additional cargo and armaments. We are also adding additional armor and cosmetics such as false scuppers to make her look more like an Allied liberty ship. We will be flying a Norwegian flag on this trip, mein Herr, since our best weapon is camouflage."

Despite the beat-up exterior, Kessler could see as he toured the ship that everything was in its place, that the sailors were well-trained and met their captain with clear respect, almost awe. It was clear that Weyher ran a tight ship, which Kessler was glad to see. The tour took a solid hour, from the engine room where the final connections were being made to the new steam turbines, to the bridge where they watched as a new 88mm howitzer was placed forward on a mount built on an elevator, then lowered beneath the deck silently, completely concealing it. Kessler was impressed and said so.

"I assume you are going back ashore to get your men and supplies?"

Kessler nodded in the affirmative, eyeing the other armaments being loaded.

"Ober-maat Schenck here will accompany you to coordinate the loading of your materials onboard. The other supplies have already been loaded, as has the main cargo."

By this, Weyher meant the planes, which Kessler knew had been disassembled for the voyage and crated, the contents marked as pianos.

"I had no idea the SS were such music lovers, Herr Sturbannführer," Weyher said with a wry smile. "Of course, I have never seen a piano that required 37mm cannon rounds to operate," Weyher finished, winking at Kessler, who failed to repress a smile.

"The 1812 Overture will never be the same, Herr Kapitan," Kessler replied with a smirk. Weyher snorted and shook Kessler's hand.

"Let me know if there is anything you require. Once we are underway perhaps we can share a cigar and a small cognac?"

"It would be my pleasure Herr, Kapitan."

"Gut. Then I will leave you to your labors. Schenck will take you to the railhead and make sure you find your way back to the ship. Now I must return to my duties," he said, saluting Kessler who technically outranked him, even though as captain he was in command of the ship.

Kessler saluted back. "Danke for your graciousness, Herr Kapitan. I must see to my men."

"Don't forget, a drink later in my cabin. Come find me when you get back aboard," Wehyer said.

Lieutenant Schenk met Kessler at the gangplank with a crisp salute, which Kessler waved off. He gave Schenk a smile. "Your captain runs a tight ship," he commented.

"Jawohl, Herr Sturbannführer. I would follow him into the gates of hell."

"Let's hope it doesn't come to that, ja?"

A kubelwagen with Kriegsmarine markings was waiting at the end of the dock with a driver who saluted them both. The train station was two kilometers away, and Schenk suggested that after securing their cargo perhaps he could treat the Sturbannführer to a quick schnapps in town? Kessler didn't really want any schnapps, but he agreed, thinking perhaps a kaffee or hot chocolate would be a nice diversion. When they got to the train however, he could see two lines of men, one of them his, facing each other with weapons drawn.

"SCHNELL," he yelled to Schenk, who put his foot in it.

Kessler could see his men had their submachine guns out and were spread out in a half circle around a loading ramp. Facing them were at least 40 armed panzertruppen, all of whom looked serious. One of the boxcars that held their gear and munitions was apparently in the process of being unloaded when something had gone wrong. Kessler leapt from the staff car before it even stopped moving, striding forward like a Panzer running down a country road.

"What's going on here?" he demanded.

Schmidt didn't even look at him, but kept his gaze on the men he was covering with his MP40. "Herr Sturbannführer, these men say they have orders to confiscate our weapons, munitions and supplies."

"Schiess. Who is the idiot who gave that order?"

"That would be me, Herr Sturbannführer."

Kessler turned to find General Otto Lasch himself standing to the side, holding his gloves in front of him. Kessler walked quickly over to him and came to attention.

"Herr General. There must be some mistake…" he began.

"There is no mistake, Kessler. These weapons and materials are required for the defense of the Reich."

"But Herr General, I have a letter from the Führer himself," Kessler said, pulling his trump card from the outer pocket in his coat sleeve. He handed it to Lasch, who looked at it briefly and gave it back.

"I, too, have a letter signed by der Führer, Herr Sturbannführer," he said.

"No offense, Herr General, but this mission is of the utmost importance to the Reich."

"Ja, ja. *Everything* is important to the Reich these days, no? You will order your men to stand down. You may remove your personal gear, nothing else. Then you will report, with your men, to my headquarters for new orders. Your mission has been rescinded."

"But Herr General…"

"That's an *order*, Kessler."

"With all due respect, Herr General, may I see your paperwork regarding this matter?"

The general looked at Kessler as if he were a bug he was about to step on. "Are you calling me a liar, Herr Sturbannführer? Because if you are you will find yourself and your men out on the eastern front so fast it'll make your ears bleed. The fighting is not far from here you know. There are plenty of Russians to go around."

"Nein, Herr General. I simply have to know how to report this. I am going to be brought on the carpet for losing this material. I must simply see the paperwork."

This the general could understand, and he pulled his papers from an inner breast pocket and handed them to Kessler. The first was a letter from the Führer as he had said, very similar to Kessler's own, permitting the general to requisition any and all supplies he required. It said nothing about the general taking control of his men, and was dated earlier than Kessler's letter. Kessler suddenly understood the real problem was politics.

The second was a letter from Göring detailing what was on this particular supply train, suggesting that it might be of some use to the general in his defense of the Reich, and that the unit's orders had changed, perhaps the general had use for them? The letter was dated just two days previously.

Kessler could feel the blood pounding in his ears. He was ready to kill someone, preferably Reichsführer Göring, but what could he do? He folded the papers neatly and handed them back to the general, who took them with a bored look that Kessler wanted to smash from his face. Göring, you fat bastard, he thought.

He saluted the General. "We will comply immediately, Herr General," he said.

At this Lasch became more jovial. He didn't want a shoot-out with SS paratroopers anymore than Kessler did.

"I apologize for any inconvenience, Herr Sturbannführer, but as ranking officer I must do what is best for the Reich. We have important use for you and your men here in the defense of Festung Königsberg. I think you will find that a posting here will not be totally without benefit."

"I understand, Herr General," Kessler replied, thinking *I understand all right.* "My men will remove their gear immediately, Herr General. The rest is yours. May I ask one favor?"

"Vas ist?"

"We would like to keep the drop containers themselves. Your men will not require the containers, just what's inside."

"Nein. You will not need the containers without the materials inside. You will be detailed to ground defense. You will not be jumping."

With this the general gave him a quick salute, which Kessler returned, then Lasch turned his back and walked away. For a brief moment Kessler considered drawing his sidearm and shooting him in the back.

Kessler dropped his salute, turned crisply and strode back to Schmidt who gave him a quick look out of the corner of his eye.

"Sergeant Schmidt."

"Jawohl, Herr Sturbannführer," Schmidt replied, coming to immediate attention this time.

"Herr General Lasch and his men require our supplies. Have the men remove only their personal gear and chutes from the train. Nothing else. Verstehen?"

"Klar, Herr Sturbannführer. Does that include our jump containers?"

Kessler understood his NCO's dismay. In the jump containers was the panzerfaust, extra ammunition and medium and light machine guns, including the MG-42s.

"Nein, Sergeant. Packs, personal weapons, ammo and chutes only." He gestured him closer so the general wouldn't hear.

"Now listen to me. Herr General is trying to hijack us. When you are done, get the men on the ship as quickly as possible. I don't care what you have to do. Get them on that ship and hide them. Salvage whatever you can. *Whatever you do, get the American gear.*"

"Jawohl, Herr Sturbannführer."

As the men lowered their weapons Kessler could see a visible relief in the faces of the panzertruppen. They didn't want to get in a close-quarters battle with the SS. He knew his 24 men were easily better than 40 panzer troops, and would immediately respond, but he didn't want them hurt. Besides, what was the world coming to when German troops began fighting *each other*? He sighed and put his hands behind his back, watching his men begin unloading all the gear he had so painfully acquired.

37

2C'S DOOR matched the rest of the wood trim on the building; dark brown and scabrous, indicating a lackadaisical attitude regarding building maintenance by the management. Snow was beginning to drift down intermittently, a flake here and there, and Jake was wondering what the drive back down the canyon would be like. He wasn't looking forward to it.

"You knock and I'll cover you," Dick whispered outside the door.

"He didn't look particularly dangerous to me, Dick."

"Just being careful."

"Fine. You ready?"

Dick nodded and Jake took a breath, switched his cane to the other hand and knocked on the door, then knocked again. They waited, but nothing.

"Knock again."

Jake gave him a look, then knocked again. Finally they heard movement inside through the thin plywood door.

"Who is it?" a querulous voice asked.

"Mr. Gruber? Mr. Hans Gruber? I'm a friend of Lily Hausen's."

There was silence on the other side for a moment.

"Vaht do you vant?"

"I have some information."

"Go vay."

Jake took another breath. "Lily's dead, Mr. Gruber. Can you open the door please?"

There was another moment of silence, then the sound of a chain being drawn back came to them through the door, which looked so cheap Jake figured Dick could probably kick his foot right through it. There was another click of a lock as the deadbolt was thrown, then the door opened a few inches and Hans Gruber peered out at them.

He wasn't as young as Jake had thought in the car, in his late thirties perhaps, with the thin, drawn face of a man who had seen much pain in his life. He looked at them suspiciously.

"Iss true? Lily is kaput?"

"Yeah, Lily is kaput, now let us in," Dick said. Always the diplomat, Jake thought.

"Mr. Gruber, as I said we're friends of Lily's. We're just trying to figure out why she was killed."

"Vhen dis happen?" Gruber asked. Jake could feel Dick coiling up behind him, ready to kick the door in and sent him a mental plea to calm down.

"A few weeks ago. Please, we only want a few minutes of your time."

Gruber looked at the two of them with something akin to fear, and Jake wondered if he'd ever been visited by the Gestapo in the middle of the night. He had the look of a man who had.

"Please Mr. Gruber – a few minutes."

Gruber grimaced but opened the door wider, waving them in.

The apartment was little more than an efficiency, with the tiny kitchen part of the living area. A closed door likely led to the bedroom and bath, the furniture all matching; beat-up and scarred from years of abuse, looking as if it had been rescued from the trash, which Jake felt was likely. The curtains were brown with cigarette smoke, the smell of which lingered in the air, a large glass ashtray full of butts confirming it.

The walls were a horrible burnt mustard color, and there were several brown water stains on the ceiling and upper corners, bearing witness to a leaking roof and confirming the landlord's commitment to ignoring maintenance. The place was clean, but the worn rug matched the rest of it, and Jake figured the Monte Vista had nothing to worry about.

"Sit, please," Gruber said, waving a hand at a couple rickety chairs, which surrounded a scarred table of similar vintage. Dick remained standing but Jake sat gratefully. His legs were getting better every day, but the drive up the canyon had really tested them. Holding in the clutch in traffic was the worst. He twirled his cane between his hands, unsure of where to begin. Gruber was lighting another cigarette.

"She vas such a nice girl," Gruber said, blowing smoke out his nostrils.

"How did you know her?" Dick asked. Jake looked at him, could see violence coiled within him like a diamondback readying itself to strike.

"She got my name from a man I sometimes do business with," Gruber said.

"And what exactly *is* your business Mr. Gruber?" Jake said.

Gruber gave him a shrewd look, and Jake realized they may have underestimated him. "I have a variety of interests."

Jake felt Dick edge forward. "Mr. Gruber, we have no desire to get you in trouble. We're only trying to understand why Lily came to you. Understanding what you do might help us with that."

"Ja? Vell, Let us just say I move tings around. Necessary tings. I do not ask questions. It would be…unvise."

"Unvise? I'll give you unvise…" Dick said, moving closer.

"Dick, settle down," Jake said, holding up his hand. He'd seen a flash of fear cross Gruber's face for just a moment as the big man moved closer, but now it was gone again. He smiled at Gruber, who was holding the cigarette palm-up in the European manner, sucking on it like a pacifier.

"Mr. Gruber, can you please tell us why Lily came to see you? Did she buy something?"

"She bought my services. I have little money as you can see. My memory is not so good after my injury…" Gruber gave him that shrewd look again and Jake realized what he wanted. He pulled out his wallet. He had fifteen dollars he kept for emergencies, and he pulled the notes out and laid them on the table. It wasn't a fortune, but it was a couple of weeks groceries…or drugs, he thought, remembering what Ed Shelton had said.

"This is all I have. Please, what did Lily want from you?"

Gruber's bony hand snatched the money from the table as he squinted against the cigarette smoke. He made a small disappointed expression with his mouth, then put the bills in his pocket. He lit a new cigarette from the stub of the old one and stubbed the rest out in the ashtray. Smoke once more from the nostrils.

"She wanted me to translate somezing. A letter in Cherman. It meant nudding, from her Grandmere. She was nod happy."

"That's all?"

Gruber made a face, shook his head. "She came back a week later with a note, again in Cherman. It was the name of a book, a scientific book, and an address…or a place rather. She seemed happy zis time, and left."

"What was the address?"

"I do not recall," Gruber said, giving Jake the shrewd look again, clearly indicating he wanted more money.

"Dick?" Jake said, without taking his eyes off Gruber. Dick moved in quickly, towering above Gruber, who shrunk away from him as Dick reached down and placed his hand on his shoulder. His eyes told Jake he knew what was coming next, and he was surer than ever that Gruber had been down this road before.

"ALL RIGHT. I wrote it down after she left. I kept it just in case…chew never know when these tings become useful."

"Where is it?"

"In the bedroom. I will get it…chust don't hurt me. Please."

Dick looked at Jake, who nodded. Dick took his hand off Gruber's shoulder, and Jake could see Dick was trying not to smile, but it was there in his eyes.

"Get it," Dick said.

Gruber sighed with acceptance and stood, leaving his cigarette burning in the ashtray.

"Don't try anything funny," Dick said, pulling the .45 out so Gruber could see it.

Gruber's eyes grew large and he held up his hands. "Please, no guns. I get chew zee note."

"Go," Dick said, gesturing at the closed door with the Colt. Gruber went to the door as Dick turned back towards Jake, smiling openly now. Gruber opened the door and there was a slight click, which Jake assumed was the latch, but suddenly the look on Dick's face changed to one of sheer terror and he threw himself at Jake, hitting him like a football tackling dummy, knocking him over backwards in the chair to the floor, landing on top of him as he screamed "DOWN!"

38

THE MEN had been sick for a week, including Kessler himself. They were soldiers, not sailors. He felt like he was beginning to get his sea legs a little, and hadn't thrown up in two days although he still wanted to at times. He kept his mind clear by concentrating on the mission, going over and over it to make sure he hadn't missed something.

He took the men into the hold to double check the Hortens, and check the webbing holding them to the hull, but Kapitan Weyher's men had already seen to it. Despite the seemingly casual attitude towards military discipline onboard, there was nothing slack about the Kriegsmariners. They were professionals through and through. He was amazed at how quickly they could change a flag, or how casual they could be when waving at the British or American planes which had haunted them for most of the crossing. He recognized excellence in their every action, and was beginning to think that they just might make Mexico alive at this rate.

When they were in safe waters he would sometimes have the men come up on deck to practice firing their new American weapons on targets he threw out into the water. It was surprisingly difficult, since the targets were moving in two planes and the boat another. Not surprisingly, Kessler was still the best at it. He grew fond of the G43, although he still wasn't sure he completely trusted it. Any self-loading weapon could misfeed and jam at a critical moment, a fact which Kessler knew from experience. He just hoped that when the time came everything would work properly. Schmidt liked the G43 also, which was good, because Kessler had decided to change the plan a bit.

They also practiced their deception, wearing the American MP uniforms both above and below decks to break them in and get used to them. They patrolled the deck in the uniforms, and more than once had waved off American planes successfully. Cheering the American planes had seemed strange at first, but after the first few times of pulling the wool over the

American's eyes in this fashion it had become a popular pastime, and never failed to raise both blood pressure and morale. It turned his men's fear of being at sea in an Allied - controlled ocean to confidence that they could handle whatever was thrown at them.

The Abwher had done a particularly excellent job on their documentation, and Kessler went over their individual papers every evening, searching in vain for a mistake. If there was one there, he didn't see it. He made the men speak only in English when they were together, getting them used to using their second tongue again. He was surprised to learn that a few of the Kapitan's men also spoke English fluently, and he used them to trip up his men, knowing that it would just take one slip of the tongue to give things away.

Below decks he dressed his other men in American POW uniforms, and made the "guards" work with them without using German. Mistakes were made, which he expected. He wanted all their errors to be made now, before they got to their objective. They had one chance at this. Once they were on the ground there could be no mistakes.

On the night of the 17th as they approached their rendezvous with a sub they were tasked to resupply, Kessler waited on the bridge nervously until he couldn't keep his eyes open any longer and decided to take a quick nap until the sub showed. For the first time in his long career as a soldier, Kessler had trouble getting to sleep.

A knock on his door came at 3:00 a.m., and Kessler was immediately awake.

"Come."

It was Giesler. "The submarine is approaching the ship, Major. I knew you wanted to know."

"Danke, Giesler."

"That's *Thank you Sergeant Thomas*, Sir."

Kessler had to smile. He'd been caught at his own game.

"Yes, well you got me, you bastard. What's the pot up to?"

"$200 dollars, Sir."

"That's about four hundred reichmarks isn't it Giesler?"

"Wouldn't know, Sir. I mean, hell, I look like a kraut to you?" the sergeant said with a grin.

"Very good, Sergeant Thomas. And no, you don't resemble one of those kraut bastards a bit," he responded with a small smile. Giesler and he went way back, all the way to the early days, when Field Marshall Erwin Rommel was still a young gerbirgsjäger commander.

Kessler fished a ten dollar American bill out of his wallet, wondering for the umpteenth time about the man who had owned it.

"Would you deposit this in the kitty, Sergeant? I need to get up on deck."

"Of course, Major. My pleasure, Sir."

"Sergeant Thomas" took the money and closed the door. Kessler ran his fingers through his hair, splashed some water from his new American canteen on his face, and threw his officer's cap on. He had grown somewhat partial to the leather American sheepskin-lined jacket he had been issued, but it was warm here in the Caribbean, so he didn't put it on.

When he got to the bridge he found Captain Weyher giving terse directions to the engine room to come about into the wind. When he was satisfied with the heading, he told the helmsman "Back two thirds," and the huge, lumbering ship seemed to come slowly to a halt in the water, precisely where he wanted it. It never failed to amaze Kessler. The captain fed just enough power into the engines to keep steerage. This would be their last resupply duty before reaching Mexico. Kessler had argued against using the ship to resupply U-boats at all, arguing that it put the mission at risk, but he was overruled.

The captain turned to find Kessler on deck. "Well, well. Look what we have here. Who let this American onto my bridge?" he said, drawing a hearty chuckle from the other officers.

"Everything all right?"

"So far yes. No radar contacts. The cloud cover is perfect for this, and rare this time of year in these latitudes. There's a light chop, and the radar room says we are in for a bit of weather in a few hours, but for now, we're safe."

Kessler groaned inwardly. He hated storms, as did the rest of his men. No dinner tonight, he thought grimly.

He followed the captain out to stand at the rail and watch the transfer. He could see no movement except the waves, when suddenly an antenna surfaced beside them. It stayed even with the ship, and he found it amazing that the two ships, one a submarine running blind, could run together so perfectly that neither seemed to move. All sense of forward movement stopped as he watched the superstructure break through the waves, followed by the deck of the sub.

"A type XIV. I am impressed, Herr Major. It is not everyday you see one of these. They are too vulnerable. No torpedos. Our U-boat fleet has been decimated by the Amis the last two years. This mission obviously is important…but of course, you cannot tell me anything," the Captain said, giving Kessler a sidelong look, an amused smile painting his face.

"I'm sorry, but no," Kessler replied, not wanted to tell him that this was a standard milch-cow delivery and had nothing to do with the mission.

"I am no fool, Kessler. I might be able to help you more if you trusted me."

"There is a limit to what I can tell you, Captain."

"I understand that, Kessler. I just want to help - one officer to another. Let's go out and get a closer look."

Men had come up onto the deck of the sub and were preparing for the transfer. Weyher and Kessler leaned over the rail to watch the rubber dinghy being lowered over the side. Despite the lack of radar contacts all the men wore black and had their faces painted. They looked like commandos about to make a raid.

Kessler suddenly realized that in fact that's what these men were; they were, in their world, every bit as skilled as his own men. He watched their movements and the way they handled the boat, and recognized the simple, matter-of-factness in their actions that told him they knew what they were doing and had done it many times before.

The sailors aboard the sub fired a line across, which was secured to the deck, then the boat crew clipped onto it and pulled themselves across to the sub despite the increasing waves. The wind was picking up, and the Captain looked up at the pennant snapping in the wind, a concerned look on his face. Another line shot over the rail, and a crewmember just 20 feet from them retrieved it and anchored it expertly around a cleat on the deck as a second boat crew prepared to lower their dinghy into the water.

This one was a wooden dinghy capable of carrying more weight, but with inflatable rubber bumpers tied to its gunwales to prevent it from smashing itself to bits against the submarine in the rough chop. The first boat crew was already taking on cargo from the sub; mailbags, both fresh and dried fruit, and so on. The heavier material to be transferred back to the sub, like ammunition and bulk food supplies would go into the wooden dinghy. The milch cow supplied diesel to other subs, and could take on diesel from their ship, but the u-boat had signaled that their its tanks were nearly full, so it was unnecessary.

Kessler watched, fascinated, as the first boat made its way back to the ship and supplies were loaded into a cargo net lowered by a boom crane, then raised quickly and dumped on the deck. He estimated that the whole process had taken no longer than 20 minutes, and was surprised when the captain growled at one of the officers standing next to him, "This is taking too long. Tell them to move it. Weather's coming in."

The officer moved off along the rail, yelling "Schnell" at the top of his lungs, letting them know they were slacking. They weren't slacking. Kessler could almost see the sweat on their brows from where he was. The difficulty of working with weight in a moving, rubber raft in an ever-increasing sea was clearly draining them. He shook his head in amazement as the men redoubled their efforts.

"I hope there's some fresh brandy in there," the captain said, elbowing Kessler in the side. "If there is, perhaps you'll join me for a drink later?"

"It would be a pleasure, Herr Kapitan."

The first boat crew had finished and had clipped a sling to their raft, then to the hook lowered to them from the crane. It raised the entire thing, men and all, out of the water as its occupants slumped in clear exhaustion against the sides of the raft. They were given a small cheer by the men on deck as they cleared the rail and were swung inboard; welcoming hands steadying the rubber dinghy as it was lowered gently to the deck. Kessler found to his amazement that the second dinghy was already on its way back.

"Your men are very skilled," he told the Captain.

"Danke, Herr Sturbannführer. They should be…they've done it enough times. Every man on the deck crew gets his chance in the water. It is only fair after all, and there is no training that can replace real experience."

The dinghy was approaching the ship, with about 30 feet to go, when a junior-grade officer Kessler didn't recognize stepped from the door and called to the captain.

"KAPITAN. RADAR CONTACT ZERO ONE-SEVEN DEGREES."

The captain ran to the bridge as if the deck were not pitching and yawing. Kessler had noticed the weather getting rougher and that the deep blue of the cloud formation to the south of them had gotten closer, the wind whipping the waves in the trough between the two ships into a frothy nightmare. It had come out of nowhere, and suddenly the crew of the second dinghy was having trouble catching the line. The captain stuck his head out of the bridge door and yelled to his second officer: "RIG A PULLEY AND GET THAT DINGHY BACK ABOARD - *NOW*."

Men ran every which way as Kessler hung tight to the railing, watching the drama unfold. Another rope was dropped to the dinghy, this one with a line attached to it, and the crew of the small boat snapped it into the bow and waved. A petty officer who looked as though he knew what he was about clipped the line into a pulley and handed it to a man waiting in a line with other sailors. In unison, they began pulling the rope, hauling the dinghy back to the ship.

Kessler looked at the bridge window. The lights had gone red - a bad sign. The Kapitan was yelling at another officer, who was in turn yelling at a seaman just outside the bridge door who in turn was flipping a signal lantern as quickly as he could in the direction of the submarine. Kessler looked over at the sub and saw the last of the men on its narrow deck already dropping into the hatch. He watched as it disappeared quickly below the waves, and silently wished them luck.

By the time he looked back, the dinghy was lined up next to the ship, and the crane was dropping a hook. They weren't taking the time to rig things up correctly this time, they were just trying to get it onboard. The dinghy was bouncing against the ship in slow motion in the rough sea, dropping eight feet or more in a heartbeat. His question was not when they would get the men on board, but how.

He watched, horrified, as a sailor trying to grasp the hook, stumbled and fell against the side of the small boat, his arms falling over the side to be crushed between the heavy dinghy and the ship as it rose, a steel behemoth, his screams lost in the wind.

The NCO in charge of rigging the line to the dinghy yelled at his men holding the line and one of them peeled off the end and ran for something. The crane began taking up the slack as the men in the boat tried in vain to hook the dinghy to the hook dropped to them from the crane. The sailor came running back and threw a line with another padded loop on it over the side, dropping it miraculously right into the boat.

Two men helped the injured man, whose agony Kessler could see clearly even from the railing, into the loop and cinched it down. By this time the dinghy rope had been tied off with two men left to tend it as the others ran to the railing. The injured man was hoisted unceremoniously to the deck, then gently lifted over the rail by multiple hands and carried below as the others returned to their duty, the petty officer snapping terse orders that no one seemed to need.

They finally gave up on getting a hook on the bow of the dinghy as more loops were dropped to the men in the boat. One man, clearly the petty officer in charge, helped the others into the loops as the same young officer Kessler had seen before came out of the bridge and began yelling something about fire, then Kessler felt, rather than heard, the round go overhead, and realized that they were being shelled.

The NCO in the boat had just finished with the last of the loops as his men were being pulled roughly up the side of the ship, their feet scrabbling on the rusty black surface. He was jumping for the loop left for him as the others were helped aboard, but it kept floating in the wind, just out of his grasp. Everyone on deck was busy, and Kessler realized that this man was going to die if he didn't get hold of that loop.

He lunged for the rope tied off to the rail and yanked the free end, undoing the knot. He dropped the loop to the grateful NCO just as the order was given to cut the boat loose. The towline used to pull the dinghy across was severed with a fireaxe as another round went overhead and exploded in the water just 60 meters from them.

The salt spray soaked Kessler and stung his eyes as he fought with the rope, slinging it around his shoulders to belay the man as the NCO got the loop around himself just as the dinghy washed out from beneath his feet and disappeared to the stern.

Kessler could hardly see the man in the darkness, but knew he'd had no time to secure himself in the loop, his feet dragging across the boat as it swept out from under him. He braced his feet against the scuppers and pulled, knowing that with no belay device, without the rope set properly, he was the only thing between the sailor and the sea. He took a new hold on the rope and pulled again, nearly horizontal to the rail as he pulled the man aboard, wrapping one arm in the line to secure it as he took a fresh hold with the other. Yet another round screamed overhead as he strained in the darkness, the only sign that the man was alive his weight on the line.

He set himself and pulled again, the rope cutting into his arm right through his coat. He didn't care. Pain was nothing new to Kessler, and he knew this kind of work. As a mountaineer the rope was familiar territory, and this was merely 50 feet, not 150. He pulled again and a hand grasped the rail.

Then there were helping hands all around, grasping the NCO, while others held Kessler from flipping over the rail, grasping the rope. The man he'd been helping crawled exhausted over the rail as Kessler untangled himself from the line and was helped to his feet. The NCO caught his eye as they both stood, and nodded, too tired to speak. Kessler nodded back, and smiled.

"KESSLER."

Kessler turned towards the bridge, hands still clapping him on the back. It was the captain, and he was unhappy. Kessler made his way as fast as he could as the horn for battle stations sounded again. Men were running everywhere, and the deck suddenly pitched sideways as it changed direction abruptly. Somehow Kessler made it to the doorway, where the captain grabbed him roughly and yelled in his ear so as to be heard over the general quarters alarm klaxon.

"I NEED YOUR MEN ON DECK, READY TO FIGHT IF WE GET BOARDED."

Kessler nodded his assent. He was shown to the intercom and depressed the handle. "THIS IS KESSLER. I WANT EVERYONE ON DECK IN FULL COMBAT GEAR IMMEDIATELY. SCHNELL."

He turned to face the captain. "What are we facing?"

"A destroyer, Kessler. A damn British destroyer."

39

IT WAS a small explosion by war standards, but in the enclosed space of the apartment it felt like a 1,000 pounder had gone off. Jake shook his head, coughing in the dust and smoke. He couldn't see a thing, and his ears were ringing. Last thing he remembered Dick was knocking him to the floor. Frantically he felt around the floor next to him, finally hitting a shoe, attached to a leg. He pulled on it, and realized with horror that it was no longer attached to a body. Had Dick survived the Japanese only to be killed here at home? Jake's mind recoiled at the thought.

Dropping the leg, he scrambled around on the floor until he found Dick, who had been thrown against the wall by the force of the blast. Dick looked whole, but in the dim, smoky light it was hard to tell. Jake hit something with his knee and reached down to find it, afraid it was another body part, but it was just Dick's Colt, which he tucked in his waistband.

He grabbed the ex-football player by the shoulders and shook him, which he realized might not be the best thing for the victim of an explosion, but he knew they had to get out of there. He heard the crackle of fire from behind him and pulled on Dick's shoulder, rolling him over on his back.

Dick's face was black with soot, giving Jake some idea of what he must look like himself, but he groaned and blinked, and as Jake checked him over in the dim light he looked like he was mostly there, so it must have been Gruber's leg he'd picked up.

Suppressing a shiver, Jake slapped Dick's face, making him groan again.

"COME ON DICK, TIME TO RISE AND SHINE," he yelled, his words still muffled by the dull roar in his ears. He grabbed his friend's arms and pulled him to a sitting position, then got to his knees as Dick came around, shaking his head.

"WE GOTTA GO, PAL. *RIGHT NOW*," Jake yelled at him, the words still sounding to him like they were underwater and far away. He struggled to his feet, his aching legs forgotten, and pulled on Dick's left arm, urging him off the floor. Dick made it to his feet, but staggered back against the wall, and Jake could see some blood coming from one ear – the sign of a busted eardrum. He slung Dick's arm over his shoulder, gritted his teeth, and began staggering to the door, the flames from the bedroom licking at what was left of the walls now, hungrily searching for oxygen.

The front door had been partially blown off its hinges and was leaning at a crazy angle, and Jake had trouble getting through it with Dick leaning on him, but he turned them sideways and then they were outside on the upper walkway. He turned left and headed for the stairs, his legs screaming at him, Dick shaking his head and opening his mouth like a fish, trying to equalize the pressure in his sinuses.

"We need to get you to a doctor," Jake said as they struggled down the stairs, nearly falling several times. He could hear himself talking better now, although his ears still felt like they were full of cotton.

Dick shook his head. "NOT HERE. HOME," he said loudly, and Jake realized he was right – they wouldn't be able to explain this to the police, whose sirens he could now hear in the background, his hearing slowly growing better. A man came rushing up to them, clearly a neighbor.

"You all right?" he asked. Jake kept his head down as if he were in pain, so the man wouldn't get a good look at his face, not a very difficult job considering how he felt.

"My buddy's hurt. I need to get him to a doctor," Jake said, as they got to the car. He reached for the door, but the good neighbor was there first, and held it open while he helped Dick in.

"Maybe you should wait for the ambulance…" the man said, a look of concern on his face.

"Thanks, but we'll be okay. You need to get the fire out in 2C or the whole building will go! Better make sure everyone is out safely," Jake said, as he slammed Dick's door and limped around to the driver's side.

The neighbor nodded and ran back towards the building without a second glance as Jake fumbled for the keys, got the car started and tore out of there like he was trying to set a record, hoping the guy hadn't gotten a look at the license plate. He looked at Dick, who was oddly, considering the circumstances, grinning at him.

"You okay?" he asked him.

"WHAT?"

"ARE YOU OKAY?"

"OKAY? WHY, I HAVEN'T HAD THIS MUCH FUN SINCE THE WAR."

Jake shook his head and turned back to driving, wondering what they were going to tell Doc. Neither of them saw the beige Ford sedan pull out behind them.

40

KESSLER LOOKED at Weyler, dismay obvious on his face. The mission would end here if they let the destroyer board them. It wouldn't take the British long to realize that this was no normal transport ship.

"Can we beat them?"

"I'm going to try. We don't have much choice do we?" the captain asked, looking at him. "By the way, thank you. That was a brave thing you did out there."

"Nein, herr Kapitan, your men were the brave ones. I have never seen anything like it."

Another shell screamed overhead, exploding close enough to the ship that they both staggered from the concussion.

"I'm afraid this conversation will have to wait until later, Kessler. I'm a bit busy right now. Can you stay on the bridge?"

"Of course. I am at your disposal."

"Gut. SCHENK?"

"YES KAPITAN."

"Vas iss der heading of the enemy ship?"

"RELATIVE BEARING ONE EIGHT FIVE KAPITAN."

"Come right to heading zero three zero."

"COMING RIGHT TO HEADING ZERO THREE ZERO."

As far as Kessler could tell, that would put them angling away from the destroyer at approximately 20 degrees.

"Range?"

"8,000 meters and closing sir," the navigator said as a shell screamed overhead.

The captain looked at Kessler and smiled, but the smile was grim. "Don't worry Kessler. You never feel the one that gets you," he said with a wink. "We'll have to postpone that drink until later."

"I'm looking forward to it," Kessler replied, meaning it. His mouth had gone dry, as it did whenever he was being shelled. He just never thought he'd end up being shelled at sea...

The captain stepped to the chart table and immersed himself in his work as yet another round screamed overhead, this one much closer... or maybe it just seemed closer. "Prepare forward torpedoes one and two."

"PREPARING TORPEDOES ONE AND TWO," the lieutenant sang out. Kessler could hardly believe that the old tub had torpedo tubes below the water lines, as well as the 88mm guns and other surprises hidden below decks. What a surprise the British are in for, he thought, as the 88mm and 37mm guns appeared through hatches in the decks.

They all strained their eyes looking for the destroyer in the dim light. It would be dawn soon, and they were maneuvering by radar contact only.

"Contact changing course to our relative bearing one eight zero. Directly astern at 7800 meters, Kapitan."

"Gut. Continue on this heading."

"Yes, Kapitan."

"When I give you the word, I want you to come around to two niner zero."

"Two niner zero, yes Kapitan."

Kessler watched helplessly as the Kriegsmarine did what they were best at. The captain's unflappable attitude gave him confidence, as it was meant to. Kessler knew that his life and his men's were in this man's capable hands. After what he had seen so far, he couldn't ask for more. They would all do their best.

The long moments stretched into eternity as Kessler sat watching the captain and his officers scan the horizon. One of the junior officers was using binoculars despite the darkness, but the captain just stood and faced forward, consulting his watch periodically. "Contact heading?"

"Relative bearing still one eight zero, Sir. I expect them to come around to port shortly and return to us. They are hunting the U-boat as far as I can tell."

"Range?"

"7,200 meters sir…They are definitely coming after us. Sonar reports their engine speed has increased."

"Gut. Let them come to us. Let them think we are running away, but decrease engine revolutions to one-third. Prepare to go to flank speed on my command."

The chief of the boat relayed the captain's orders to the engine room as Weyher turned back to Kessler, looking casually at his watch.

"I estimate six minutes to contact," he said.

"Seven minutes to contact," the officer of the watch said, as if to confirm the captain's prediction.

"RADAR CONTACT TWO TWO FIVE DEGREES," The watch officer announced.

"Forward torpedoes loaded and ready?"

"Loaded and ready sir."

"Range to target?"

"6000 meters sir."

"Damn these new destroyers are fast. How quickly did they cover that 1200 meters since last contact, Lieutenant?" the captain asked, already knowing the answer.

"Four minutes sir."

"Very good, Hessel. We'll make an officer out of you yet. I want to know immediately if they change course. Keep engines turning at one third but prepare for flank speed on my command. Let me know when they turn."

"They are coming right at us sir. I don't think they intend to turn."

"You think they'll collide with us? Trust me young man, they'll turn. You let me know when. Begin calling out range when they reach 800 meters."

"Yes sir."

A few tense minutes went by as they waited for the enemy. From what Kessler could tell on the radar screen, they were nearly 90 degrees, or perpendicular to the oncoming destroyer, which was moving to intercept them.

"Contact 800 meters sir," the young JG said tersely.

The captain didn't speak. He just stared out the windscreen, waiting.

"700 meters sir."

"All ahead full. Flank speed."

"ALL AHEAD FULL. FLANK SPEED," the young officer yelled into the horn. Kessler was reminded suddenly that this was no destroyer, merely a merchant vessel loaded with guns. He realized suddenly that he was sweating. A merchant ship, albeit heavily modified and heavily armed, taking on a destroyer? It was madness.

"Destroyer moving to intercept captain. They think we're running," the JG said with a small smile. Why aren't we running? Kessler wondered. Surely they can't hope to beat this thing? Of course, they'd never outrun it…

"Contact heading?"

"Their relative bearing to us is two two five…no, two five zero Sir."

"Prepare to turn into them, full port rudder on my command."

"Yes Kapitan."

The captain looked completely unperturbed, but intent. Kessler saw him glance at his watch again. Time to distance, he thought. The bastard is fighting the whole thing in his head, blind as a bat.

"Sir, they are moving to parallel us. They are changing course to come alongside," the young officer manning the radar said calmly.

"How far behind us are they?" Weyler asked, as Kessler heard a boom and heard an explosion in the water nearby.

"800 meters astern, Sir, and closing. They are moving parallel to us now captain, angling in toward us at 15 degrees on our port side."

Weyher ran to the port hatch and raising the binoculars, peered out, judging the distance. Suddenly he turned and yelled at the helmsman.

"PORT ENGINE ALL STOP. LEFT FULL RUDDER. COME TO TWO NINER ZERO. ALL BATTLE STATIONS PREPARE FOR CONTACT." Wehyer said loudly.

"COMING LEFT TO HEADING TWO NINE ZERO. ALL BATTLE STATIONS, PREPARE FOR CONTACT," the lieutenant yelled into the ship's comm The orders were followed down the pipe and the ship seemed to shudder, then stand still, then Kessler suddenly found himself being thrown forward as the ship turned and the deck tilted.

"All ahead full. Make ready forward torpedoes. Prepare for contact." The helmsman repeated the command.

"Full light in six minutes, Sir."

A hush came over the bridge.

"Sir, they're slowing, preparing to turn into us."

"Fire number one torpedo."

"FIRE NUMBER ONE TORPEDO," the command went down the pipe.

There was no sound from outside, but Kessler tried to imagine it, the frothy wake of bubbles marking the bomb's passage in the water, the panic of the men onboard the destroyer.

"Sir, they've begun turning away from us. I think they hear the fish in the water but I don't think they're going to make it."

"Time to contact?"

"Fifteen seconds Sir. Ten, nine, eight, seven, sir, they are continuing the turn, we still have their starboard flank exposed...four, three, two...."

There was silence on the bridge as the heavily armed Q-ship steamed straight for the destroyer. No one needed to be told what would happen if they missed; the destroyer would turn on them and proceed to live up to its name.

"I'm reading a name on the stern Sir. It's the H.M.S...."

BOOM. The explosion from the hit on the starboard stern corner lit up the early morning sky and was followed by several more deep thumps.

"Close quarters. Ready second torpedo."

"SECOND TORPEDO READY SIR."

"Fire number two."

"FIRING NUMBER TWO."

Kessler watched as the flames ran up the side of the now visible ship. It was nearly full light, and he could make out the list of the British destroyer as it tilted to its starboard side, clearly sinking.

"All slow."

"ALL SLOW. Ten seconds to impact. Eight, seven, six…"

"All right, Ensign, that's enough," the captain said. They watched for the last few seconds wondering if the second torpedo would miss or not. The ship had been nearly stern to bow with them at the time of launch, but was now slowly swinging about to port, away from them, following her rudder despite her disabled engine.

A huge white bloom suddenly came from the ship and Kessler raised his forearm to shield his eyes. Cheering broke out in on the bridge and other parts of the ship, but Kessler noticed that the captain did nothing but continue squinting at the glare, watching British sailors launch themselves into the sea as they tried to get away from the flames, which were spreading out on the water, following the spilled diesel even as the stern of the destroyer began settling into the water. Kessler watched as a burning man ran to the railing and threw himself overboard.

The radio crackled.

"H.M.S. Surrey to the German vessel, over."

They all looked at the radio.

"H.M.S. Surrey to the German vessel that just sank us, over."

"Don't respond captain," Kessler warned. "Remember, we are not here."

The captain turned to him with eyes ablaze. "There is a law that is older than our laws, Kessler. That is the law of the sea. We will pick up those men."

"Nein, Herr Kapitan, we will not. This is my mission. Need I remind you of the letter I hold from the Führer?"

"The Führer is not here and I am the captain of this ship. Sailors help sailors. It's the law of the sea. We are 350 miles from land. You are condemning those men to a slow death by shark and dehydration otherwise. It could just as well be us."

"But it is *not* us, Herr Kapitan. I am as sorry for the loss of those men's lives as you are, but I have a mission, and it will *not* be compromised."

"H.M.S. Surrey to the bloody Hun ship which just blew hell out of us. We require immediate medical attention and relief, over."

"Tell them we'll pick them up," Weyler said to the radioman, turning to give him the order. When he turned back, Kessler's pistol was pointing unwaveringly at his face.

"I would prefer not to kill you, Herr Kapitan. You are a brave man, and the Reich needs brave men. I am sorry, but I wish you to belay that last order."

"You *bastard*. This is *my ship*. I am in command here. There are men dying out there, and we are going to help them."

"No, Captain, we will not."

"So, you plan to machinegun them in the water? You and your SS criminals?"

The radio stuttered again, this time with a different voice. "H.M.S. Surrey to the German ship. This is the captain speaking. As you can see, our ship is about to founder. We would deeply appreciate any assistance you rotters could extend to us at this time. We'll even eat your bloody sauerkraut, just PLEASE get my men out of the water. I know that as an officer, and a sailor, you are as aware as I of the laws of the sea. You are required to tender assistance. I say again, *required* to tender assistance. My men are burning in the water. What kind of men are you?"

Kessler looked at the captain. "Order us back on course. Now."

"I always knew I was going to hell for the things I've done, Kessler, but at least I know now that there will be someone ahead of me in line. Come with me. I want you to see this," he said, as he brushed the pistol aside and stepped out the door. Kessler had no choice but to follow him.

They exited the bridge and moved to the railing. Men were thrashing in the water as the stern of the British destroyer slipped beneath the waves. Other men's screams came from far off as the flames devoured them, others huddled together in groups, raising their hands to wave at their assailants, knowing they were dead otherwise.

The storm was passing to the north and the sun was shining incongruously, as if God had aimed a spotlight through dark clouds onto the terrible carnage. As the destroyer slid beneath the waves the last men bailed off like rats...men who had waited until the last possible moment.

Some were sucked under by the vortex created by the sinking ship while others flailed about in the water aimlessly, crying for their sweethearts or mothers, as their shipmates who were first off the boat swam towards them intently, trying to help.

"This is your sin, Kessler, not mine. Yours and yours alone. I beseech you once more…let us pick them up."

Kessler saw the pain and hatred in the captain's eyes as he looked at him. Schmidt came up behind him to stand at Kessler's shoulder as the young lieutenant who had been so thrilled moments earlier came to stand behind his captain, his feelings clear in his eyes. He turned to his captain, ignoring Kessler and Schmidt.

"Your orders, Herr Kapitan?"

"I am no longer in charge here. Ask Herr Sturbannführer Kessler whom he wants us to butcher next in service to the Reich," the captain said without taking his eyes off Kessler.

"In the name of the Führer, I invoke the letter of privilege given to me by him, and command you, Herr Kapitan Weyler, to move this ship back on course immediately. We have no time to waste."

The captain took a deep breath, looking once more at the men in the water, some of whom were trying to swim to his ship. His men were leaning from the rail, urging them closer, while some others were preparing a couple lifeboats to pick up survivors. He stood there watching for a long moment, his anger and pain clear in his face.

"You heard him, Herr Leutnant. Get us underway."

"But Herr Kapitan, the men in der wasser…"

"I KNOW ALL ABOUT THE MEN IN THE WATER, LIEUTENANT. NOW I GAVE YOU AN ORDER. GET THIS SHIP UNDERWAY. SCHNELL."

All the men on deck stopped what they were doing and turned to watch him.

The lieutenant came stiffly to attention, saluted, and strode back to the bridge, giving Kessler a dirty look as he passed him. A long minute went by as the ship began moving and the German sailors starting talking amongst themselves. Kessler could clearly see they weren't happy, but he didn't care.

As the ship picked up speed, the sailors in the water stopped swimming towards the Orion and started cursing them. The German sailors just looked sadly down on them, or went back to their stations. A few threw life preservers off the aft deck covertly.

"My first officer can handle the course changes from here. If I may return to my cabin, Herr Sturbannführer?" Captain Weyler said coldly, his eyes ice.

"Of course, Herr Kapitan."

The captain brushed past Kessler as if he didn't exist, as the cries of the doomed British sailors grew fainter. Kessler looked out at the horizon, purposely avoiding looking back at the men he had abandoned to certain death beneath a tropic sun. He holstered his pistol and took a deep breath.

"Sir?"

Kessler turned to find Schmidt, who looked very serious...more serious than he had ever seen him in fact.

"Ja?"

"Your orders, Sir?"

"The men are to keep weapons on them at all times. The Kriegsmarine are no longer our friends because of what happened here today. They will do their duty, but they will not be friendly. We have two more weeks onboard this tub. Let's just get through it."

"Yes sir."

41

DOC PUT down the ear scope which he'd been checking Dick with and looked at Jake. "You really expect me to believe you two were prospecting? You must think I'm dumb as a box of rocks," he said angrily.

"Why, no sir," Jake replied defensively. He'd thought their story about using a little dynamite to blast a glory hole had been a good one. How'd the old man know?

"For one thing, I know Cates keeps his dynamite locked up tight. I also happen to know he hasn't been able to get any since the war started. So tell me, what have you juvenile delinquents been up to?"

"Hey, who you callin' juvenile?" Dick said from the examination table.

Doc gave him a look that would curdle milk, and Jake wondered what it had been like for the men who'd had him as a commanding officer in the Great War.

"Doc, we really can't talk about it," Jake said.

"Oh. Top Secret, eh? Well Dick's got a ruptured eardrum and a torn ligament in one shoulder. I haven't checked you out yet, but I can see your scalp is bleeding, and I would bet money some of the wounds on your legs that hadn't healed completely are torn back open. You're both covered with soot and plaster dust and you were limping more than normal when you came in. By the way, where's the cane I gave you?"

Jake looked at the floor.

"Now boys, I just heard on the radio about an explosion up in Flagstaff at an apartment building. Turned into a three-alarm fire. No one got killed, but several people were treated for smoke inhalation."

Dick looked at Jake.

"I'm guessing you two drove all the way down here to see me rather than going to the hospital up there...I'm right, aren't I?"

"Listen Doc, we don't want to get you involved," Dick said.

"I'm already involved. I'm treating you, and any suspicions I have about illegal behavior I am duty - bound to report. Now what the hell happened?"

Jake looked at Dick and he nodded, a grim look on his face.

"Well, first of all, someone did die. I have a feeling they know that by now," Jake said.

"And how do you know that?"

"We were in the room with him when he set the bomb off," Dick said.

Doc raised his eyebrows. "Since it's generally not standard operating procedure for bomb builders to be there at the time of ignition, I'm assuming you two are not responsible…at least not directly?"

"Doc, how could you even think that?" Jake said.

"You come here to me, covered in soot, smelling like smoke, to be treated for explosive shock and give me some cockamamie story about prospecting with dynamite? If you'd lie to *me*, how the hell do I know what you are capable of?"

"I thought it was a pretty darn good story," Dick muttered.

"If I was an idiot it would have been, but I was an artillery officer, son. You're clothes are covered with detritus from a building, not rock dust. You come here and treat me like I'm stupid, this is what you get. Now tell me what happened. *All of it.*"

Jake and Dick went through the whole thing with Doc while he cleaned their wounds, stuffing cotton in Dick's ear and putting his arm in a sling, then stitching up Jake's scalp and checking his legs. Finally they'd finished their story about Gruber, and Doc had finished his examinations. He washed his hands in the exam sink, then turned to them, rubbing his hands on a small towel, a grim look on his face.

"You two were damn lucky, you know that don't you? If Dick hadn't heard that click and reacted the way he did, you likely wouldn't be here talking to me. It sounds like they used a shaped charge hooked to the bedroom door, and by Dick knocking you to the floor he put you both under the shock wave…or most of it anyway. If you'd remained standing? Well, I'd rather not talk about it.

"Now listen to me, boys. I'm going to give you some advice. One, get cleaned up and have something to eat, then turn yourselves in to the Flagstaff police and tell them what happened. They have got to be wondering what the hell happened and your testimony may break something loose for them. The second piece of advice is, leave this damn thing with Lily alone. She was obviously mixed up in something she shouldn't have been. You both had a close call, and if you continue down this road, you might not be so lucky next time."

"Cates says the same thing," Jake said.

Doc raised one eyebrow. "But he's dumb as a stump too right? Look, I may just seem like some old coot to you young men, but Cates and I have both been through a few things ourselves. Now I know both you boys have seen the elephant, and survived, thank God, but that doesn't qualify you to conduct a murder investigation."

"Doc, with all due respect, the sheriff isn't doing much," Dick said.

Doc sighed and shook his head. "I understand how you two feel...I do, but you're on your way to becoming vigilantes and no good can come of it."

"Doc, we find the killer, we'll turn him into the police, we swear - but if we turn ourselves in now it's going to muddy the waters. What if the killer has access to police records somehow? He'll know we talked to Gruber, maybe think that Gruber told us something. Then we *will* have problems," Jake said.

Dick nodded in agreement. "We know the killer or killers know that Jake has the letter, and they know we haven't been able to decipher it. They want it back, but I'm betting unless they think we're getting too close they'll leave us alone, but if we tell the cops about this, well all bets are off."

"Listen to what you two are saying, will you? I'm not going to tell you what to do, and I won't turn you in, but you are witnesses in a murder, and you should talk to the Flagstaff police. I'm trying to do you a favor here boys – I really don't want to be called to identify your bodies. Despite the fact that you both are insufferably stupid, I brought both of you into this world, and I've grown quite fond of the two of you."

"So, you won't tell the cops about this?" Jake asked.

"No, I won't. But it's against my better judgment. Doctor – patient confidentiality aside…but I do plan on having a word with Cates about this."

"Shit. I'd kind of rather you told the cops," Jake said.

"You can't have it both ways, son. Now go get cleaned up and try not to get yourselves blown up, or shot, or stabbed or whatever. Dick, if the pain in that ear continues more than a couple weeks you come see me. Keep clean cotton in it, and water out of it. Wash gently. I want to see you again in three weeks. Your balance is going to be off for awhile, so be careful. No motorcycles or horseback riding. Now get out of here, both of you, before I put you both in straightjackets."

Dick and Jake left Doc's office and climbed wearily back into the car.

"So Dick, you want to quit?" Jake said quietly before starting the car, his hands on the wheel.

"Hell no. In fact, I'm more than a little pissed off now. Someone trying to kill *you* is one thing. Someone trying to kill Mrs. Lawson's favorite son is another. This runs deep Jake, and I'm not sure where to go with it, but I can't just let it lay. What about you?"

"I was taught to always see things through once you started something. I guess this is no different. One way or another, we're going to find out who killed Lily."

"I'm with you. Now my head's killing me and I'm starving. Let's go."

"Dick?"

"Yeah what?"

"I want to bring Morrie in on this."

"Think that's really a good idea? I mean, we just nearly got blown up ourselves."

Jake grimaced. "Yeah, I know, but we're missing something here. She's smart as a whip. Maybe she'll see something we don't."

"So whatta we waiting for, hero? Let's go find her."

42

THE REMAINDER of the crossing had been surprisingly trouble free. The *Orion* had its name changed to the *Tropic Sea*, and was flying a flag of repatriated Norwegian registry. Of course the papers were false, so if anyone checked too closely they would find discrepancies, but Kessler was counting on that not happening. He and his men always stayed in character, wearing the American uniforms and carrying the American weapons on deck, making sure to wave and smile at the PBYs and other long range sub hunting planes they saw.

His radio operator, Karl, had lived in England and had the most believable Cockney accent he'd ever heard, and handled all the radio chores. If anyone had wondered what a bunch of American soldiers and a British radioman were doing on a Norwegian registered freighter, no one had asked. All kinds of strange things were possible these days, and if the Abwher said it was believable cover, then Kessler was inclined to believe them.

They were due to rendezvous with U-1238, a type IXC, at 0100 hours, where the first zug would transfer their equipment to the submarine for the remainder of their journey to the east coast, while the ship would continue with the second zug to Mexico. Concerned about the men slipping into German at the wrong minute, Kessler had put the best English speakers in the second zug, except for Karl, who would go with the first group, as his British accent wouldn't match a cover as an American soldier very well.

Kessler wanted Schmidt with him on the primary mission, but he didn't see any way around it. Schmidt was best qualified to lead the second zug. Tenacious, smart and unyielding, Schmidt, Kessler knew, would either accomplish his mission or die trying, no matter what went wrong. The two of them had fought together on Crete, in Italy and the Balkans, and Kessler had the ultimate confidence in his abilities.

There was one problem that needed to be handled however, and that was Gothe. Kessler had tolerated him until now, but he could not have Göring's spy on either mission. Whether Gothe would stab him in the back literally or figuratively didn't matter – he couldn't be trusted. A knock came on the door of Kessler's cabin.

"Come."

The tiny metal door opened and Schmidt stepped inside.

"Close the door and have a seat."

Schmidt closed the door and sat down in the jump seat opposite Kessler, folding his arms on the tiny table. "Everything is ready for our departure. The first zug is ready. Chomping at the bit, as the Americans would say," Schmidt said.

"Very good. There are a couple of last minute changes, however."

Schmidt raised his eyebrows as Kessler handed him his precious G43 and ammo pouches.

"You are going to need this more than I. You will be leading the mission in the west. I will take the first zug to Georgia myself. Secondly, congratulations. You just became an American major," Kessler said, tossing a set of bronze oak leaves across the table, which Schmidt took with a small smile. "I will see to it you get the same promotion in the SS when…if we return to Germany."

"Danke. It has been a privilege to serve with you, Sir."

"Now listen. Both missions are difficult ones, Schmidt, and equally important in their way, but I feel that the operation in the west is the more complex of the two. I know, however, that you can handle it."

"Thank you. I appreciate the vote of confidence…but I was under the impression that I would be commanding the first zug."

"Does it matter?"

"Nein. I am here to serve in whatever capacity you deem best, Herr Sturbannführer."

"You owe the kitty ten bucks, Major," Kessler said, making Schmidt laugh.

"I did not tell you until now that you would be leading the second zug because of our friend from the Luftwaffe. The last thing I need right now is him second-guessing me. He's still making his reports?"

Schmidt smiled. "Yes. I've been getting every word of them from the ship's radio operator. I have to tell you, if that little prick is really Luftwaffe, I'll eat my hat."

This speculation had come up before, and it was not a big jump to assume that their Luftwaffe "liaison" was in fact fourth directorate Gestapo.

"Well, sadly I feel that Herr Gothe's usefulness to the Reich is at an end. A shame really, but a ship at sea is such a dangerous place. He never really did get his sea legs, did he?" Kessler said, looking at Schmidt meaningfully.

"He will be sorely missed," Schmidt said with a wry smile. "You know how well he's liked by all the men."

Kessler snorted, then wiped the smile from his face and looked at his second-in-command intently. "I just want to say good luck, Schmidt. This may be the last time we see each other before I leave the ship tomorrow. It has been an honor serving with you. I know you will make the Fatherland proud," he said, offering his hand.

Schmidt grasped it and looked at his old friend. "Thank you for this. I am looking forward to this mission. You can count on me to complete it."

"Destroying Hoover dam should cause quite a stir as well, Schmidt. Los Angeles without any power will not be a pleasant place. I just wish I could have seen the Hortens in the air. Perhaps after this the Americans will not be so smug."

"I was looking forward to killing Roosevelt myself. I envy you," Schmidt said.

"All we need is a few more months to finish the master weapon, Schmidt. This will buy us time. Now, all official business is concluded. Let's have a drink. I have some excellent American whiskey which I liberated personally from Reichsführer Göring's private stock."

Schmidt smiled. "Sounds good. I am looking forward to seeing this Arizona I've heard so much about."

"Maybe we can both retire there when the war is over, Schmidt." The two men looked at each other then laughed, both knowing the likelihood of either of them reaching old age slim to none.

43

A S IT turned out, Morrie was tired of studying and glad to see them, but she took one look at their beat-up appearance and immediately asked them what had happened. "You guys look like you've been blown up or something."

"Prospectin'," Dick said, earning a look from Jake.

"Let's go get some breakfast and talk about it," Jake suggested.

"Only if you both promise me to tell me just what in the hell you've been up to."

On the way to the restaurant they filled her in on everything that had happened so far; their meetings with Ed Shelton, going to see him and the explosion which had killed Gruber and nearly them...although Jake downplayed that part when he saw how much this appeared to disturb her.

"So, he said there was nothing in the letter he'd translated for her right?" Morrie said, reaching for another slice of toast.

"He said he translated a letter for her, but she seemed disappointed. Then she came back a few days later with another note in German, and it translated as the title of a book, and an address. She was happy this time."

"So, she decoded the letter somehow," Morrie said, eyeing the leftover sausages on Jake's plate.

"Apparently, but wouldn't it be even harder to decode in English than the original German? It doesn't make sense. Where'd she get the second note? We needed that information from Gruber, but unfortunately..."

"You're both lucky to be here. I have an idea. Do you have the letter with you?"

"As a matter of fact I do...but we've both been through that thing a million times. There's nothing there we can see."

"Exactly," Morrie said smugly, stuffing the last of Jake's breakfast in her mouth.

"Huh?"

"Haven't you guys ever heard of microdots?"

Jake looked at Dick and smiled. "Did I tell you she was brilliant or what?"

"We can use a microscope in one of the labs over at the college. Let's go," she said. "You're paying for breakfast right?"

44

A BOARD THE U-1238 Kessler faced his men over a map stretched across the table in the mess.

"The sub will approach the coast line here," he said, pointing at the nautical chart he'd been working on for weeks with the captain.

"I know these boat handling drills have been difficult in the cold, but it's important that we work smoothly and quickly, that's why I've been driving you so hard. As you know, our mission is critical to the survival of the Reich. Der Führer has tasked us with this mission. *We cannot fail.* Verstehen?"

The entire zug of twelve men, dressed in dark wool pants and black sweaters, nodded their agreement.

"Now, let's get to the details of the mission. Our target is a place called Warm Springs, Georgia. It is the vacation residence of Franklin Delano Roosevelt."

At the mention of the name of the U.S. president, Kessler felt the men all stiffen around him. Their attention was absolute.

"At 0300 hours tomorrow the U-boat will rise to periscope depth here, he said, pointing at the map again. "When we reach our debarkation point, the captain will fully surface and we will deploy the boats with the help of his men, just as we have practiced. The water will be rough and cold, and we cannot have any mistakes. Mistakes at this point could kill the mission. Verstehen?"

The men spoke as one this time. "YES, HERR STURBANNFÜHRER."

Kessler ran his finger along the line he'd scribed on the map, leading inland.

"From the time we hit the beach we have just three hours of darkness. We must bury the boats, change clothes, and get inland as quickly as possible. We may be driven off course by the current and come ashore further south. That is to be expected. We will simply take a compass bearing and adjust our course.

"The other difficulty is, we have very little intel about the terrain, other than knowing it is a salt marsh - swampy and overgrown. Such terrain can be very difficult to move through, and few of you have had much training in an environment like that…but I'm sure we will do fine," he finished, looking up at the men under his command with a confident, winning smile. The smile was contagious, and the men grinned back at him, knowing they could handle it. They were the crème de la crème - the finest soldiers Germany had to offer. Of course they would succeed. A mere swamp would not stop them from their task.

"Our agent will meet us at the rendezvous point. Remember those mock-ups of the Warm Springs compound we practiced storming outside Berchtesgaden? These are the real thing. The mock-ups were built using information from our agents, so the layout and your movements should seem familiar.

"This is a health spa, not a top secret facility, but do not underestimate the Americans. There may or may not be Secret Service agents or Marines where we were told…as you remember, most of them are roaming, so it will be a fluid situation. It is critical that we take as many of the guards out as silently as we can. Once gunfire is heard, they will rally around their president and rush him out of there. We cannot allow that. As we trained, we will use suppressed pistols for the initial phase, to get inside the compound itself.

"First squad, you will be with me, just as in training. Roosevelt will be in this structure here, usually in his bedroom or the sitting room. We will enter the structure here, here and here," he said, stabbing a finger at the hand-drawn layout in front of them.

"We will shoot the President, and I will take pictures and recover his glasses and cigarette holder as proof of our success, to be returned to Germany directly to the Führer, by his order. If I go down, they will be in the top left pocket of my blouse, the camera in the other. The next man will take them and if he goes down, the next, and so on. Don't worry, I'm not planning on getting shot," he finished, showing them another dazzling smile, which provoked another round of laughter.

"Damn, And here I was looking forward to finally getting that promotion," Meier, now a corporal, joked, provoking another round of laughter.

Kessler smiled. He was glad to see them in such good spirits, especially at this stage in the war. Things had not been going well for the Reich since December and frankly, it looked grimmer every day. He credited their good spirits to having a chance to strike back at the Allies finally, to make a difference. No doubt, the killing of their beloved president would be a great blow to the Amis indeed, as would destroying the Americans largest hydroelectric dam, also named after a president, despite the Americans calling it Boulder Dam at present. He never had understood politics, even in his own country. Regardless, the loss of electricity to critical war production facilities in Los Angeles would be a huge blow to the American war machine, as would the loss of their biggest armament depot. Could they do it? Kessler shook off his doubts, dismissed them and went back to his maps.

45

MORRIE RUBBED her eyes with her fists. "Great. Well, I've been over this stupid letter a dozen times and I don't see a thing.

"Did you check all the punctuation? They may have hidden it in a period or a comma."

Morrie gave Jake a look that would curdle milk.

"Sorry. Can I give it a whirl?"

"Knock yourself out, but I'm telling you there's nothing there."

"We need to make sure though, right?"

Morrie had to smile. Jake had just blunted her anger without apologizing. Unlike so many men she'd met, he was honest and real to a fault, and as she watched him hunch over the microscope she realized that she was falling for him.

"So, I hate to bring you two back to earth, but are we going to eat again today? I could eat the other half of that cow now," Dick said.

"How could you, Dick? Here we're trying to solve a girl's murder and all you can think of is your stomach?" Morrie said, regretting it immediately when she saw the effect it had on Dick, who had learned from the war that there were things bigger than him that he was unable to control. The horror of where he'd been, of the terrible things he'd seen and done was etched on his face, the pain in his eyes plain to see. It made her heart go out to him. To come back from such horror and find the only good thing in your life dead…

"Dick, look at me. I was just kidding, I'm really sorry. Actually, I totally agree with you, I'm starving."

"I have to finish this first," Jake said from the microscope.

"No, you don't. I *told* you, there's nothing there," Morrie said, an edge of steel in her voice. She looked at Jake, his eyes glued to the microscope, ignoring her.

"Fine. Let's take a vote. Who's hungry and wants to find a restaurant right now?" she said, raising her hand. Dick raised his too and grinned at her.

"That's that. Two to one. Jake, you can either come with us or we're leaving without you."

Jake sighed, raising his head to look at Morrie. "Know what I like about you Morrie? You're the shy, retiring type."

"What's the matter, Jake? Didn't anyone ever warn you about redheads?"

As they walked to the car the three of them went over what they knew, which was very little. If Gruber had just been able to give them that information maybe they'd know something, Dick said. Frustrated, they turned the corner of the building and a bumblebee flew straight between Jake and Morrie, startling them, the sound of the shot coming a split second later. Before she knew it Jake and Dick had each grabbed an arm and thrown her to the ground.

"WHAT THE HELL?"

"Somebody's shooting at us, Morrie," Dick said a little too calmly.

"Why would someone..." she began.

"Who cares? All I know is, we don't want to be here right now," Jake said.

"The car's right there, Dick said. "We need to go now, before they flank us."

The next thing Morrie knew, the two of them had each grabbed her by an arm, jerked her to her feet, and were hustling her to the car. Another bumblebee buzzed past their heads and whined off into the distance, a hollow boom following it.

"Sounds like a .45," Dick said. "That means he should have five, possibly six shots left. I'll drive, Morrie can shift for me."

Jake tossed him the keys as they hustled down the short slope to the car and Dick sprinted around to the driver's side as Jake yanked the front door open and pushed Morrie in unceremoniously, then jumped in after her.

Dick was already cranking the engine as Jake slammed the door and the rear window exploded from another bullet, showering them with glass.

"Time to go," Dick said, the tires squealing as he dumped the clutch and sped away.

Morrie looked back but didn't see anything. "Bad enough being shot at by someone you can see, let alone someone you can't," she said.

"Sorry if we were rough, Morrie. No offense, but you learn to just react to incoming fire. If you're slow, you're dead," Dick said.

"Unless you have two big, strong war heroes to save you," she said.

Dick and Jake looked at each other, then back at the road.

"The only heroes are the ones who didn't come home, Morrie," Jake said.

"Where to?" Dick said, changing the topic.

"I've kind of lost my appetite, but we need to talk. Let's find that restaurant, Dick. Any preferences, Morrie?"

"Just somewhere no one's shooting at me," she replied.

46

IT WAS cold and dark, worse than it had ever been during their brief training, and the sea was rough, the submarine rolling and pitching with each swell. Waves rolled over the low transom, giving even the submariners trouble. The folded rubber boats were dragged up through the narrow hatch from the belly of the ship, inflated and tied off with great difficulty to the ribbed deck, which became wet and slippery within seconds.

Kessler's men struggled alongside their U-boat comrades on this task, while Kessler and the captain hunched in the conning tower with another crewman, watching for patrol boats. The training they had done alongside the submariners made the task possible, but this weather was worse than anything they'd trained for.

"This is madness, Kessler. You'll swamp the boats getting to shore." Captain Hauer yelled against the rising wind.

"We have no choice, Kapitan – the operation is scheduled to dovetail with another operation. They must be carried out simultaneously."

The captain nodded, turning back to his field glasses. As excellent as they were he could see nothing through them. It was as dark as he'd ever seen it. The weather wasn't the worst he'd seen, but if he hadn't been under orders he'd never send his men out on the deck to launch rubber rafts. This was madness.

As if answering his thoughts, a shout came from the deck as another crewman was washed overboard. Two men dropped what they were doing and grabbed the safety line of the man swept overboard, pulling him back through the freezing water to the boat, where he was pulled aboard - a limp, shivering rag doll.

Hauer reached down to grab the injured man as he was handed up the conning tower ladder, the submarine rolling between the swells violently as he gripped the sailor's arms, pulling the soaked man up to him as his fellow submariners and one of Kessler's men pushed from below. It was Denzel, from engineering, and he didn't look good, his face pale, his eyes rolled up in his head, which lolled from side to side as they hoisted him, just pure dead weight made even heavier by his sodden clothing.

Kessler grabbed him on one side and they hoisted him into the tower as Hauer yelled to the ensign who was still trying to keep a watch while at the same time keeping an eye on them to see if they needed help. He yelled down the hatch and men ran up the ladder to take the injured man, who chose that moment to puke up the last meal he'd eaten as well as what seemed like several gallons of saltwater onto Hauer's oilskin. Hauer didn't flag. It wasn't the first time he'd dealt with such inconveniences, but he could see Kessler holding his breath and grinned.

Once Denzel had safely been lowered into the ship, Hauer straightened and looked at Kessler with a big smile. "Anytime you want to join the U-boat corps, you let me know, Kessler," he said, Denzel's dinner still dripping from his slicker.

"No thanks, Herr Kapitan. No offense, but after this operation I hope to never see the inside of a U-boat again."

Hauer was about to reply when the ensign yelled "CONTACT, ENEMY SHIP, BEARING ONE ONE ZERO DEGREES."

Both Hauer and Kessler struggled to the rail and raised their field glasses in the direction the ensign was pointing as a sailor popped his head out of the hatch to report that sonar had picked up engine noise, bearing 112 degrees.

'Lot of good it does us now,' he thought grimly, as he watched an American destroyer escort emerge from a curtain of rain.

"KESSLER, WE HAVE TO DIVE."

Kessler looked at the deck where his men were struggling to get into the boats. Without another word Kessler grabbed the waterproof bag with his civilian clothes and gear, handed the field glasses to the ensign, and swung onto the ladder. He was halfway to the deck when the submarine hunter began shelling the ship. Huge geysers of water erupted on each side of the submarine, and he could hear the captain screaming orders to his men, preparing to dive.

Kessler had just placed one foot on the deck when the world exploded. He felt himself being lifted up, as if by a huge, unseen hand, the air pressed out of his chest making it impossible to breathe. Then he hit the water, and it was like falling onto concrete. He fell into a dark, silent void, trying to remember what he was doing there and trying to understand what had happened, then he realized a shell from the American warship must have hit the sub directly. He suddenly felt the pressure in his lungs. He needed air, and weakly he began clawing his way to the surface, which was lit like a window from a fire within, dotted with the black forms of human and mechanical wreckage above him.

47

JAKE WAS tired. Driving so much the last few days was taking the starch out of him. Just pushing the pedals was making his legs ache, and he wondered about the wisdom of driving back to Sedona by himself.

It had been a rough couple days, nearly getting blown up, then shot at, but after dropping Dick off at the bus stop he and Morrie had spent the rest of it together, wandering downtown Flagstaff, window shopping and holding hands. It'd been a brief but nice break from worrying about Lily's murder, although he'd kept an eye out nonetheless.

Finally he said he had to go, despite not wanting to, and the goodbye kiss she'd given him had Jake flying pretty high. It was getting dark now, however, and he wanted to get down through the switchbacks before it got any darker. The canyon was dangerous at the best of times, let alone at night.

As he started down the slope into the first curve, Jake noticed some headlights pull out behind him from a Forest Service road. Probably kids necking he thought, but suddenly the lights were right behind him, and he turned the mirror down to avoid the glare. The maniac was driving way too fast, and as Jake started into the next turn he felt a bump as the car hit him from behind, making the his car slide towards the outside edge.

"WHAT THE HELL?" He yelled angrily, hitting his horn to show that he wasn't pleased. The car stayed right behind him, though. It was like one of those gangster movies with Jimmy Cagney, he thought, where the car comes up behind you in the dark and…BAM, another hit, this time jerking Jake around in his seat. Who was this crazy bastard trying to kill him? Jake decided to speed up, but when he accelerated around the next tight bend, the car sped up to stay right with him.

The wheels skidded on the loose gravel as he took the next hairpin, just trying to get away from the guy, but the car stayed right with him, moving to the outside and hitting him yet again. "Okay bud, this isn't funny anymore. We get off this mountain I'm going to clean your clock," Jake said to the mirror, his teeth gritted in concentration as he downshifted for the next curve, his feet jabbing at the clutch and brake, the ache in his legs forgotten for the moment.

The Buick slid on the loose surface as Jake tried to stay ahead of the crazy fool behind him, but he heard the car accelerate again, its headlights looming in the rearview. He felt a sickening lurch as the car hit him yet again, the bumpers screeching loudly as they scraped together. The next hairpin was coming up fast...too fast. There was a good 75 to 100 foot drop straight off the outside – it was one of the hairiest turns in the switchbacks leading up out of the canyon. Jake stood on the brake, his legs aching with the effort as the car behind him slammed into him a final time, pushing him towards the edge.

48

KESSLER WOKE up and vomited up half of the Atlantic, or so it seemed. He was soaked to the skin, and cold...so cold. Springtime was coming to Georgia, but the wind chilled him nonetheless. He knew he had to move or die. He raised his head with great difficulty to find that he was lying at the high tide debris line of the beach, tangled in driftwood and huge strands of seaweed with monstrous, bulbous roots like something from another planet; long strands of them, some hundreds of feet long, cast up on the beach with the other detritus the sea coughed up on its shores daily: an old shoe missing its mate, laces unbelievably still intact, a small white bottle that had once held cologne on someone's dresser, dimensioned lumber broken scarred and worn from the sea's caresses, stones so smooth and round they looked as if they'd come from a factory.

Normally Kessler loved the beach, having spent many happy summers as a boy in Odessa, on the Black Sea, building castles and combing the beach for treasures...but at the moment he hated the beach - this damn American beach.

As he pushed himself to his knees he wondered about his men. He cast his eyes up and down the sand, the sky growing gray above him. He saw no one, no bodies, no rafts, no nothing. The sea had swallowed them whole, choosing to save only him. For what reason? Why had his men died as a result of a vagary of fate; a warship out of position for some reason, crossing their path at the worst juncture possible? He shivered, the wind a sharp knife through his sodden uniform.

Still on his knees he automatically checked his equipment. He had still been wearing a belt and Y-harness, and the first thing he checked was his pistol. He was surprised to find it still there, as was the ammo pouch for his MP40, and the small assault pack he'd attached to his Y-harness.

He felt quickly for his gravity knife, relieved when he found the familiar shape. He had lost his watch cap, his slicker, his weapon and pack. His breadbag had been torn from his belt, but he found a sealed tin of Scho-ka-kola; a caffeinated chocolate made for the Luftwaffe which he was partial to, in one breast pocket, under his wet sweater.

He knew he would need to clean the pistol, suppressor and ammunition of the salt water residue immediately, hoping that the ammo had not been spoiled by its brief dunking in the ocean. He suspected some of it would be all right, but how to tell whether a cartridge would ignite or not just by looking at it? He had no choice. He could not test fire a round for fear of bringing the shore patrol. He had to assume they were all good and just clean them as best he could.

The thought of the shore patrol sent him back onto his belly, this time with his pistol in hand. He checked it quickly, shaking as much water as possible out of it and the magazine, then rechambered a round, looking around him quickly, realizing that now he was a hunted animal. Knowing they had fired on a submarine and probably hit it, the American ship would undoubtedly report to its base, who would send out men to comb the beach as soon as it got light, which was now. He didn't have much time before he'd be discovered. He needed to get off the beach immediately.

He was about 75 yards from the tree line, which was made up of huge pines and scrub willows, thin at the shoreline, then growing thicker and closer together as he made his way inland. Several of them lay on their side at the sands edge, giants that had crashed to earth with the help of some long-forgotten gale off the Atlantic. He struggled over one, gasping with the effort, then had walked the long way around the others, struggling through the sand dunes covered with elephant grass and morning glory.

Finally he made it to the cover of the forest, his relief at being off the open beach ameliorated immediately by the swarms of insects that found him as soon as he was out of the wind. He pulled off the sweater, tying it around his waist, hoping that it would dry quicker that way, rolled down his sleeves, and plunged into the underbrush.

49

JAKE WAS hanging on a branch in Jordan's cherry orchard, trying to reach a juicy bunch of black cherries hanging tantalizingly just out of reach. Rosa was standing beneath the tree, shading her eyes with one hand, stamping her foot on the ground and telling him to get his tiny butt out of that tree right now or he was going to get the switch. Didn't he know that cherry trees were prone to breaking branches? There was a loud crack as the branch he was on...

But he wasn't on a branch. He was in the Buick, not in the orchard, and he was twenty-six years old, not five. His head hurt where he'd smacked it on the doorjamb, and he had blood in one eye from a cut on his scalp, making it hard to see. He realized that he was jammed up against the door, but it took him a moment to realize that the car was tipped crazily, and gravity was what he was fighting.

The headlights shone straight out into blackness, broken only by an occasional wisp of fog. He could hear the light patter of freezing rain on the roof. The wipers had stopped when the engine stalled because they ran off vacuum from the running motor, and he realized he was hanging off the edge of the third turn - the bad one - just as there was another groan from beneath him.

He could hear a slow waterfall of dirt clods rolling down the cliff, and realized the heavy wood and cable guardrail had caught him, but by the sound of it, wasn't going to hold the car much longer. He had to get out, and the quicker, the better.

The problem was, the car was tilted at nearly a 60 degree angle with the cable running across the driver's side door - the only thing keeping the car from a 150 - foot drop. He would have to climb up and out the passenger side. He managed to pull his legs up and get them under him, although the recently healed muscles screamed with disapproval.

He pushed up against the door, stretching up and over to the other side, pulling the door handle down and pushing the passenger side door open by straightening his legs. The car shifted suddenly again, and he heard more dirt falling. He knew suddenly he didn't have much time. He pushed himself up and out, squeezing through the tight triangle of open door, trying to ignore the groans and creaks coming from the guardrail...or what was left of it.

He got a third of his body out of the car, but suddenly had nothing to push against, bottomed out as he was across the seat with his feet against the driver's door. Not only that, but he was having trouble holding the heavy door open – the weight was pinning him to the doorframe. All he could think about was Cates slamming the door when they'd first gotten the car, commenting on how solidly it was built.

He made the mistake of putting his foot against the partially open driver's side window glass and it shattered, dropping him back down inside another foot, his leg plunging through the window, the passenger door scraping his torso, the broken glass tearing his leg. Jake hardly noticed. He felt the car lurch again and his stomach lurched with it. He had to get out, and right now.

With everything he had he pulled himself up and out over the open door frame, scrabbling frantically through the narrow opening, not caring how much he got scraped along his back as he pulled himself through. His searching fingers found a piece of steel cable, part of one of the hawsers that had once tied the wooden guard rail together. It had snapped, and he gouged his hand on the sharp needles of the torn end as he grasped it frantically, not caring or noticing the pain.

There had been two of the cables running through the posts, but one had clearly broken, the other - still holding his car - was about to. He pulled himself hand over hand up the cable, dragging his body out of the car, until just his left foot was still inside, the heel of his shoe catching on the door.

He tried to reach the door to pull it open in order to free his foot, but he was too far above it – he couldn't reach. Worse, the cable was slick with rain and grease, and his hands were slipping on the cable as the car pulled him slowly but inexorably off the cliff. Metal slivers ran into his palms from the cable, but he didn't dare let go.

He fought with it, rolling on his back and trying to lever the door open with the toe of the other shoe when the second cable let go with a loud crack and the car dropped, tearing the shoe - and some skin - from his foot. The cable whipped overhead and Jake instinctively ducked as the cable ends missed him by inches, the whizzing sound reminding him of being shot at. There were a couple seconds of silence, then a gigantic crash like a train wreck as the car hit the first of the rocks and continued rolling to the bottom.

Shaky with adrenaline, Jake managed to pull himself up the cable, up and over the steep slope over broken glass and cactus, to finally collapse on his back in the road. When he'd caught his breath he raised up on one elbow and peered down to the road below where the Buick lay on its roof like a crushed beetle, one headlight miraculously still working, illuminating the trees at the edge of the road, its wheels still spinning in futile mimicry. Then he saw the other car, the one that had been behind him - a beige Ford coupe with one hubcap missing.

It was just uphill from where his car had come to rest, just sitting there with its engine idling, its headlights illuminating the scene. Jake felt anger course through him. They wanted to make sure he'd been killed.

He tried to get a better look at who was driving it, then there was a low "crumph" as the Buick's gas tank ignited and it began burning merrily. He watched as the other car rolled forward, slowly picking its way around the burning wreckage, then calmly, almost sedately drive away towards Sedona. It was dark, and their windows were up. He couldn't see a face or even the license plate.

Jake lay back on the road, his fury at nearly being killed quickly replaced with shock. He was in one piece but sore all over, scraped, cut and beaten by the impact...and missing one shoe. His foot ached where the door had nearly torn it off, and his head felt like someone had used it as a football and was still bleeding from hitting the doorjamb. He felt dizzy. Probably a concussion, he thought. Coming so soon after the explosion at Gruber's he felt as though he'd just crawled out of a plane crash, which was a feeling he was well familiar with.

On top of that, it was beginning to rain in earnest. He pulled his suit jacket around him tighter, having lost his hat in the crash as well. Then it hit him how close he'd come and he really began shaking. He couldn't help it. If the Buick had hit the guardrail head on instead of skidding and hitting it sideways he probably would have gone straight through, arcing out into space like a comet.

He was pretty sure it must be the same person or persons who had shot at them, and who had likely set the bomb at Gruber's. They had waited for him on that forest road, up near the first turn with their headlights off, waiting for him to come by. It also meant they knew somehow that he would be passing by around a certain time, and what his car looked like. He shivered as the cold rain soaked his suit coat. He needed to find shelter, and soon.

Almost in answer to his prayers he heard the low growl of a truck engine being downshifted, and moments later he was bathed in the warm but dim glow of big six-volt headlights. He raised his arm instinctively against the light, unable to move, hoping they would see him and not run him over. Wouldn't that be ironic?

Fortunately the big truck had been going slow, and stopped just shy of him. He heard the driver pull the emergency brake on and shut the engine off, and he tried to stand, but his ankle gave out and he went down on one knee again. He heard two doors slam, then there were strong hands helping him into the warmth of the cab, which smelled strongly of horses and tobacco, but their voices seemed far away, as if through a haze...then he was gone.

50

KESSLER CONSULTED the waterproof map in the fading light, ignoring the mosquitoes and black flies which swarmed around him. The flies were the worst, raising huge welts from their painful bites. He thanked the stars again that he hadn't lost his compass.

He quickly lined up the azimuth on the map and did a quick time and distance calculation in his head. With any luck he would reach the rendezvous site by midday tomorrow if all went well, but that would still put him quite a way from Warm Springs. He would need a car to make it the rest of the way. The contact would wait in the same spot for fifteen minutes every morning at 7:00. If he could make it there by tomorrow there was still a chance he could regain his timetable.

He wondered for the hundredth time where Canaris had gotten such a detailed floor plan of the objective, but frankly he didn't care. He found himself picturing the layout of the house in his mind, over and over, looking now for the perfect one-man assault plan, wondering where the Americans would place their security.

He had only one chance at this, and the sentries had to be taken out quietly to avoid spooking the principal target. Kessler knew there would be surprises. There always were. The terrain surrounding the facility was clearly fairly rugged, and the obvious approaches were sure to be heavily guarded.

Some chance, he thought, refolding the map and returning it to his breast pocket. What could one German commando do against all the Secret Service men undoubtedly guarding the president – each of them sworn to protect him with their lives? Kessler wasn't sure what he would do if he made it that far, but he had to try. It was his duty. He would either kill Roosevelt or die trying. He took a deep breath and stepped back into the trees dripping with Spanish moss and kudzu, the heavy mud sucking at his boots.

The rest of that night Kessler struggled through dense underbrush, fighting the invisible lianas that grabbed at him, the sharp branches that poked at his eyes, and worst, the thirst. He found some low, clear trails through the dense forest, made by wild boar most likely, and tried using them for a while but soon grew tired of walking hunched over or crawling on his knees.

Near dawn he finally found some water, dark and stagnant, but he drank it anyway, lying on his belly to slurp at it, wishing he had a canteen. It left a taste like algae in his mouth, and he was afraid it would make him sick but he had no choice. Another few hours in the heat without water and he would've collapsed.

The humidity was like someone sitting on his shoulders, heavy, grim and unrelenting even at night. He slumped against a tree near the water he'd found, planning to drink more after he rested briefly then be on his way. He closed his eyes and was suddenly asleep.

51

THE ARADO AR196 seaplane skimmed through the moonlight, barely off the water, carrying Schmidt towards Mexico. The pilot didn't seem perturbed at their low altitude. Moreover, whenever he turned back to look at Schmidt his lips were spread in the permanent rictus of the perennially cheerful. He looked as though he were having fun. He said he was flying low to escape radar, but Schmidt had a feeling he didn't have to be quite this low.

"Having a good flight?" the pilot's voice came to him through the earphones, his voice ghostly from the throat mike.

"Oh yes. Can't we get any lower? Perhaps we should just land. I mean, we're skimming the waves now," Schmidt responded.

The pilot laughed. "Herr Sturmfürher, you *do* have a sense of humor, Das iss gut. You may call me Rudy. You needn't worry, but let's go upstairs for now."

The seaplane rose in a surprisingly gradual, restrained manner, as if floating up on a cloud, and Schmidt knew once again he was in the hands of an expert. Once they had reached a higher cruising altitude Rudy came back on.

"Better?"

"Ja. Danke."

"This plane reminds me of when I learned to fly. Do you like flying, Rheinholdt?"

"Not particularly, and you may call me Herr Sturmführer."

The pilot laughed again. "Bravo, boss. Now, let's see if we can find the coastline. We don't have much fuel left...ought to be around here somewhere." The link went dead as Rudy applied himself to his charts and flying the plane. Schmidt knew he was baiting him, one officer to another, but what Rudy didn't know was that Schmidt always got even. An officer brought up through the ranks had certain advantages over university-taught flyboys…

It was much warmer here than in Europe, but March had turned out to be a troublesome month weather - wise. The Hilfskruezer *Orion* (Now the "*Tropic Sea*") had a rough time of it, and his men had suffered, to the amusement of the Kriegsmarine sailors who now hated them. The animosity was palpable below decks, and Schmidt couldn't wait to get his men off the ship.

In some ways he supposed the bad weather was a blessing - they hadn't been discovered by either British or American patrols, and had managed to evade all radar contacts. With the lone exception of one tense moment when one of their own U-boats had nearly fired on them because the damn radio operator had typed one too many strokes, changing what came out of the Sonderschussel code machine they had done well.

Only twice had they been challenged, and "Danny Boy" Stein had been able to fake them with his impeccable cockney accent. Their only problem was trying to keep from laughing. He'd done such a good job that the radioman on the frigate *HMS Halcyon* told him they should get together for a pint at a pub in Chelsea he knew "…once this bloody war is over."

They were close now, close to Mexico. It had been a long voyage from Germany, to Brazil, then up through the Caribbean. He could smell the equatorial rot from the jungle and see birds silhouetted in the nighttime sky, frozen for a moment as if on a string as they passed beneath the plane, the powdery clouds backlit by the moon, the smell of salt water an ever present scent, the roar of the big rotary engine in his ears.

"There it is." The pilot pointed at the horizon, but Schmidt couldn't see anything. He strained his eyes looking and, sure enough, gradually a black line appeared on the sea, then got thicker, and thicker again. Then he got tired of looking at it and stared up through the canopy at the moon playing hide and seek in the clouds.

Schmidt closed his eyes for a moment, fell asleep briefly, and when he awoke the sea was brightening; becoming silver with the morning light, the sun not yet over the horizon, but as Schmidt looked behind them he could

would be mere minutes. Ahead he could see not only land, but trees.
It went on in each direction seemingly forever. Mexico. At last.

It took another 45 minutes for them to reach the bay where the pilot
landed the Arado with a calm aplomb that Schmidt did not share. He
closed his eyes as they came closer and closer to the water. As a paratrooper,
heights did not bother him, but he had crashed in several planes, and he
hated landings, especially glider landings. Something about landing on
water just didn't seem right to him.

They motored over to the tiny backwater dock where a man in a white
linen suit and Panama hat stood waiting for them with some workers, who
promptly took the seaplane's lines and pulled it in while others ran to refuel
the plane. The man in white yelled at them in Spanish to hurry, while
Schmidt and the pilot got out to stretch their legs.

Schmidt's gear was handed over and taken up the dock to a small house
with a large, wrap-around screened porch. The pilot would return to the
ship after doing another radio check with the compact radio set Schmidt
had brought with him. This would be his only lifeline to the ship, so it was
critical that it work. It had a smaller version of the Enigma machine in a
separate case, which created a code that Schmidt had been assured was
unbreakable. He had trained on the machine while in Berlin, but was a
little nervous that he would not get it right.

"Herr Schmidt? I am Kurt Jahnke. Welcome to Mexico," the dapper
man in white with piercing grey eyes said as he stepped forward to take
Schmidt's hand. He was older, in his sixties, and although Schmidt had
been briefed about this legendary spy who had served Germany in the First
World War, in a way he found it hard to believe that this dapper old
gentleman was a legendary intelligence agent.

"Thank you. I am looking forward to my vacation here," Schmidt
responded in English, making Jahnke smile. The Arado had been repainted
to resemble a civilian transport, and Schmidt felt suddenly uncomfortable
in the civilian clothes he wore, perhaps simply because it was so damn hot
or perhaps because he was out of uniform, and eligible to be shot as a spy.
Shot as a spy or not, he would have to lose a layer or die from heat

exhaustion. He had served in Afrika and Italy, and thought himself used to heat, but this was a damp, wet, humid heat which had him sweating bullets now that there was no longer a breeze from flying.

"Let me show you to your room and then we'll get a drink."

"Fine, thank you."

Schmidt followed Jahnke up a narrow, much-used path to the bungalow, which was larger than he had at first thought. The thatched roof and primitive exterior belied its comfortable interior. The wooden floors were covered with colorful rugs of every description, and the chairs were leather, overstuffed and softer than they looked.

The windows were shuttered to keep the interior cool, and two large ceiling fans turned lazily in the humid air, running off a long leather belt connected to a motor mounted in the corner. Schmidt was surprised to find they had electricity out here, but he didn't complain about the ice Jahnke put in his drink.

"May I propose a toast?" Jahnke said, holding up his glass.

"Certainly, Herr Jahnke," Schmidt said, standing with relief after sitting in that infernal airplane for so long...

"To the Reich, to Adolf Hitler, and to being in the company of another white man."

They clinked glasses and drank. It was some more of that wonderful American whiskey called bourbon which Schmidt had first tasted on board ship. It slid warmly down his throat, the slight breeze from the large ceiling fans cooling the sweat that had collected on his brow, probably during landing.

"Ahh. That is really excellent, Herr Jahnke. I thank you."

"Nein, Herr Schmidt. It is I who should thank you. I thought we might share one toast as countrymen before sliding into our respective roles as it were. After tomorrow, however, remember that you will be Major Peterson from the American Army Air Forces."

Schmidt told him about their efforts on board to create the illusion of being Americans, of the money they each threw into the pot each time one of them slipped, and how well his men had adapted. They had found to their surprise that they liked the Americans, and their gear was all top shelf material. Then Schmidt and Jahnke discussed logistical details for a bit, before being called to dinner by a servant. Schmidt was famished, and the food, while exotic, was very welcome. He particularly was fond of an odd, green condiment called guacamole.

The sun was fading through the windows as they ate, and it occurred to Schmidt that their window to find the correct landing spot had been very small. If the pilot had made the slightest navigation error they might be still flying over the ocean, or worse yet, the jungle. He shivered thinking about the consequences. Schmidt didn't mind heights, didn't mind jumping out of an airplane, or standing on a cliff looking down, but airplanes for some reason gave him a slightly queasy feeling. He just didn't trust them. How ironic that his mission was entirely about and dependent on airplanes, he thought.

Cigars on the wide, covered porch followed dinner, the citronella candles perched on the rail guttering in the gentle, welcome breeze as the overhead fans turned lazily. Casual conversation in English was the rule here, and Schmidt realized in a way that this was a test, that Jahnke had been sizing him up, trying to decide for himself if Schmidt was up to the job. He hadn't become the premier German spy in the western hemisphere by not being a good judge of character.

Schmidt was exhausted by the heat, the flight, and the large meal, and could not help yawning repeatedly. Finally his host made note of it, and despite Schmidt's apologies, suggested that there was nothing wrong that a good night's sleep wouldn't cure, professed exhaustion himself, and suggested they retire early and discuss business over a good breakfast. Schmidt agreed wholeheartedly, and that night he dreamed he was flying over an endless sea by moonlight, flying the path cast by the moon as if it were a wide, white, shimmering road.

52

FRANKLIN DELANO Roosevelt slumped on the pile of pillows propping him up on his bed, a cigarette burning in the ashtray next to him, the bedside table nearly covered with glass bottles of pills and reports from the War Department. He was exhausted, and it seemed to him lately that there had never been a time when he was not exhausted. The memories of his youth, of running, sailing, rowing…all seemed like a dream, like something that had happened to someone else. Now there was only the exhaustion, the pain, and the constant stream of assistants, nurses and hangers on.

He had come to Warm Springs for rest, but he wasn't sure whether he was getting any or not. The stress of the past ten years hung over his shoulders like the weight of a chain mail cloak he couldn't take off. He shook off the depression and feelings of malaise every morning and greeted his staff with a smile, but there was nothing behind it, and he was sure at times that they must see through him, see what a fraud he really was.

He was encouraged by the reports from the ETO until he remembered all those brave souls who had already made the ultimate sacrifice. He wondered how much more tragedy he would see in his lifetime. First the Depression, then the war…his generals said Hitler couldn't hold out much longer, but then they hadn't foreseen the breakout in the Ardennes either.

The worse news had come just yesterday. Germany had apparently succeeded where they had not, and had detonated a small atomic device as early as October according to a witness, a captured German pilot who had been interrogated by the Army Air Forces. If the report was true, and if they were given the time to develop it further, London and even possibly New York and Washington were at risk.

They had known for a year that the Germans had heavy-lift aerial capabilities, and were capable of hitting New York with long range bombers, but until now they had thought the only reason Germany hadn't attacked was that their bombers didn't carry enough fuel for a two-way journey. Now they knew better. A one-way mission with an atomic weapon against New York or Washington would still be a success. The Japanese weren't the only ones who had experience with kamikaze pilots.

The weapon had been tested in the four corners area, near Silesia, not far from Prague. Eisenhower had sent Patton south, and his fears seemed justified; huge columns and trains of men and materials were reported heading in that direction. The Russians had met fierce, almost fanatical resistance in the Balkans as well, which held several passes which were, according to the analysts, being held open for the retreating troops heading for the Alpenfestung, or "Alpine Fortress" as the Germans called it.

Reports of huge, underground factories churning out munitions and even underground airbases had been verified as much as could be expected, but information was sketchy. One witness had seen a Messerschmitt 262, one of their new jets, literally fly off the side of a mountain. Trains loaded with supplies were also headed in that direction, and Berlin was being emptied of both critical personnel and records, all headed in the same direction - south.

The analysts had all come to the same conclusion: If the German army succeeded in retreating into the Berchtesgaden area, or even the mountainous area around Munich, the Allies would play hell getting them out. An offensive undertaken there would make the Normandy landings look like a kid's playground. This spring and summer would be critical; if they didn't stop the Germans from reforming in the Alps before the next winter…well, the analysts estimated the war might go on another two years, possibly longer. "The Bulge times ten" Eisenhower had called it.

Roosevelt wasn't sure he could take another two years. He needed the men and resources to throw at Japan, who although defeated at Midway, Iwo Jima and in the Philippines was still very much a threat. They had begun kamikaze attacks against U.S. ships and convoys, and it made him wonder just when this madness would end.

Berlin was surrounded, but it didn't matter. It was no longer the most critical objective, which is why he and Churchill had decided to let the Russians "liberate" it. What was more important now was Czechoslovakia.

The Skoda works in Prague were said to be at the center of the German nuclear program. If they developed a fielded weapon before the Manhattan Project, well…all bets were off.

As a result of this news, FDR wasn't getting much sleep. He couldn't seem to rest his mind, even for a minute. His chest had been paining him lately, and when alone he had private conferences with his broken body, telling it not to fail him now, that he was the only one who could handle this burden, at the same time secretly wishing someone else would shoulder it and leave him to simply enjoy the warm springs he had so come to love. The waters had not had their usual rejuvenating effect this time, however. He just couldn't seem to shake the feeling that something was about to happen…and not something good.

53

"MY GOD Jake, what on earth happened?"

Jake awoke with a start to find Morrie grasping his hand. He was still sleepy from the sedative Doc had given him, and still so sore he wasn't sure how he had slept, even with the drugs, but after his rescuers brought him home from the car wreck, he'd passed out on the couch in the library – hadn't even made it to his room.

"Hey, gorgeous. What are you doing here?"

"I came to see you, dummy. Aren't you glad to see me?" She was wearing a yellow sweater over a white blouse, and it was like someone had suddenly opened the curtains to the room and let the sun in. She was radiant, even with the worried look on her face. The phrase "light of my life" popped into Jake's head.

"I sure am, buttercup. Be happier if you gave me a kiss."

Morrie smiled, bent over him and filled the request.

"I feel much better all of a sudden," he said. "How'd you find out about the accident?"

"Cates called me. I drove straight here. They were winching your car, or what's left of it, onto a truck when I came by. It's so horrible, Jake. You could have been killed."

Jake reached up for her cheek to wipe a tear away, but she got there first, smearing it away with the heel of one hand.

"I'm sorry, Jake. I'm just so tired of all the death and destruction. I've lost so many people I love to this damn war…now this. I just don't know what I'd ever do if I lost you too."

"Shhh. Everything's fine. *I'm* fine," he said.

"Jake, Cates told me what happened. You've got to go to the police. Give them the letter, tell them what you know, then drop this damn thing."

"I don't know anything, that's the trouble."

Morrie looked at him, a troubled look on her face.

"What?"

"Uh. Well, I think I figured it out."

"Figured out the letter?"

"I found the microdot and I know where to look. I just don't know what we're looking for."

"You're kidding."

"No, Jake, I mean it. I just think we should give this to the authorities and let *them* handle it."

"They couldn't find their ass in the dark with both hands."

"JAKE."

"Sorry. Anyway, tell me what the message said."

"Well, I took a little German in school, and found my old textbook. What I think it says is to look for a specific book in the library of Mars."

"Oh. Yeah, I can see how *that's* helpful."

"I have the name of the book too, you idiot."

"Now if we just knew where the library of Mars was," he said.

Morrie couldn't hide a self-satisfied smirk.

"You know where to look, don't you?" Jake said.

"Well, I have a pretty good idea."

"So tell me."

"Not unless you promise me I can come with you."

Jake shook his head. "Honey, this could be dangerous."

"Less dangerous with two people looking."

Jake sighed. "Okay. Lemme get dressed. Can you drive?"

"After you drove off the side of the mountain? You bet I'm driving."

"Hey, that wasn't my fault."

"That's what they all say."

54

THE RENDEZVOUS point was a roadside stand that specialized in Georgia peaches. Closed this time of year, it was quiet and remote. Just beyond the stand was a turnoff which led to a small, little used parking area, nothing more than a circle of hard-packed dirt in the shade of a copse of magnolia trees lining the side of a slow-moving, muddy river. In summer, fisherman would fill the area with their trucks and jalopies, but this time of year it was used only by lovers looking for a quiet place for their tryst, and then only occasionally, and at night.

Kessler's contact would stop at the peach stand and check for three vertical hash marks; three tiny marks on the right hand lower corner of the stand, where they were not likely to be noticed. If the hash marks were there, he'd drive down to the parking area and open the hood of the car as if having cooling problems.

Kessler reached the stand two days late, in the early morning just as the sun was coming up. He'd lost the chalk along with the rest of his gear when the submarine had been destroyed, but had salvaged a piece of charcoal from an old campfire he'd run across.

He made the three hash marks in the agreed upon spot, then retreated to the river to wait, secreting himself in the dense undergrowth, exhausted from fighting the woods all night, and a damp uniform which had never completely dried. After drinking his fill from a small spring feeding the river he lay down in the shelter of a rhododendron bush and fell asleep.

The thunk of a car door awakened him, and his hand went immediately to his Walther. Peering out through the leaves, he saw a thin, tired-looking man with straw colored hair and round tortoise shell glasses looking around nervously. Then he looked at his watch, making Kessler check his own, a good Swiss watch that had miraculously survived the attack on the U-Boat and a good dunking in salt water. It was 7:15; the rendezvous was set for 7:30.

The man walked over to the produce stand, bent down straightened and looked around. Then he walked back to the car, around nervously as he unlatched the hood and raised it, the signal that everything was clear. Kessler knew he was an operative from the local German Bund, but nothing else about him. He clearly hadn't had much training in espionage, and Kessler was a little worried about his steadiness from what he'd already witnessed, but he had no choice. He took a deep breath and crawled from the undergrowth.

He was almost to the car before the man noticed him, which clearly startled him, reinforcing Kessler's already tepid opinion of the "agent".

"Good morning, friend," the man said.

"Now, you know I'm not your friend, I am your brother," Kessler replied, completing the identification. The man visibly relaxed as they shook hands.

"My name is Hesse. Freidrich Hesse."

"I'm Kessler."

"Where are the others?" Hesse asked, looking over Kessler's shoulder.

"There are no others."

This raised an eyebrow, then the bund member noticed where Kessler had torn the rank from his collar, and the placards from his shoulders, and he gave him the once over.

"Mein Gott, you are still in uniform. Are you mad?" he whispered urgently.

"There was an accident coming ashore. I lost my men and our gear. I will require clothes and papers."

"Schiess," Hesse exclaimed. Opening the rear door of the sedan, he reached in and pulled out a long raincoat and handed it to Kessler.

"Bitte – put this on and turn the collar up. No one must see that uniform."

Kessler did as he was bidden, a bit amused at the man's nervousness, but he understood it. If caught they would be shot or electrocuted like the last group of German spies to come to America. Still, Hesse would soon learn who was in charge here.

"We'd better go," Hesse said, looking around nervously. Kessler decided right there that Hesse was going to be a problem. Nervous looking men with German accents tended to get questioned. Once he got Kessler what he needed, Hesse would have to be taken care of. The mission must not be compromised.

55

SCHMIDT WAS rubbing his tired eyes when Giesler burst in the door.

"Major, I just got word there's a plane requesting landing instructions. It's Mexican military."

Scheisse, Schmidt thought, here we go.

The technicians were nearly done. They had told him they had one more day assembling the Horten Nurflugels despite working around the clock. They were ahead of schedule but Schmidt was still nervous. Mexico had come in on the side of the Allies, and every minute they had to hide here the more likely they were to be detected, and with detection came failure.

Galland had assured them that the Hortens could take off fine from a grass field, as opposed to the Me 262 jets, which required a much longer runway and a higher takeoff speed. He had gone into a long explanation about wing loading, at which point Schmidt's eyes had glazed over. He didn't care how the damn things worked, just that they did, although they looked nothing like any plane he'd ever seen.

The Hortens were small enough to fit into a three-car garage, so were happily hidden from view in the small outbuildings which had been hastily converted into workshops by the advance team, but the C-47 sat in full view on the runway, and Schmidt had nightmares about someone wondering what an American C-47 was doing way out here at the edge of the Mexican jungle, just miles from the coast. Now it seemed as though someone was.

Ostensibly they were a crack unit of U.S. Commandos getting jungle training in preparation for a mission in Burma, but Schmidt had no desire to put their cover story to the test. Now it looked as though they had no choice.

"Let the others know. Get a card game going if there isn't one going already. Remember, this is just like on the ship. We drilled for this. NO

GERMAN. Officially this is our day off from training. If there's a ranking officer on the plane, bring him to me. Remember, we're Americans. Keep Meier away from them, and tell him to keep his damn mouth shut."

Schmidt sat down at his desk and spread the fake intelligence reports on Burma around just enough to look real, his stack of fake personnel files for each of his men, carefully fabricated by the Abwher neatly stacked to one side. He was reading a personal letter from his "wife" in St. Louis when Danzig knocked on his door once again. Schmidt was vibrating inside the way he did just before battle.

"Major? There's a Captain Gutierrez from the Mexican Army here to see you, Sir."

"Show him in Sergeant," Schmidt calmly told Giesler - aka Sergeant Driscoll.

Gutierrez was a short, immaculately groomed officer with a slightly pompous air about him. Schmidt lowered the letter he was "reading" and stood, stepping around the desk to greet the captain with a warm smile.

"A letter from my wife, please excuse me. It's our day off," he said, wondering if he was already overdoing it.

"Major Peterson? I am Captain Ramon Gutierrez, of the Ejercito Mexicano," he said, coming to rigid attention and saluting. Schmidt saluted him back, then extended his hand.

"A pleasure, Captain, but allies should not stand on ceremony. What can I do for you?"

"Please, Major, excuse my intrusion," the Mexican Army officer said in his best ass-kissing voice, "We had reports of an American C-47 at this landing strip, and...well, no one seems to know why you are here in Mexico."

"Ahh. Well, that's because no one is *supposed* to know, Captain. This is a highly classified training operation. It's been cleared at the highest levels of your defense ministry."

"You do, of course, have documents to that effect?"

Schmidt smiled widely. "Of course. However Captain, they are classified themselves. I'm afraid I can't show you them without authorization."

Gutierrez frowned. "This is highly irregular," he said, his English nearly as good as Schmidt's, obviously a product of an exceptional education. He would be from a wealthy family, well-connected - perhaps having studied in America.

Schmidt winked at him. "Yes, yes it is, but you see, we needed the highest operational security for our mission, even during the jungle training phase...which is why, in fact, we are operating out of a remote airstrip in your beautiful country."

Schmidt hated Mexico, hated the jungle, the heat, humidity and most of all the bugs, but he figured a compliment couldn't hurt. It certainly didn't in *his* army.

"I will have to check with my superiors to see how I should proceed..." the young, chubby captain began. Schmidt held up a hand.

"Tell you what, Captain. Let me contact my people first and ask them how much I can tell you. Perhaps then I can show you my orders and the letter from your ministry authorizing this operation, and we can clear this right up."

The captain smiled uncertainly.

"Of course, you must stay for dinner and leave in the morning. It's getting late. Not a good time to be flying over the jungle eh? Now, would you care for a small drink? It's a bit early, but it's five-o'clock somewhere I believe."

The young captain smiled this time. "A drink would be quite acceptable major, thank you. You see, I do not like flying."

"Then perhaps we should make it two drinks – I don't like flying either," Schmidt replied, slapping the captain on the back. "Now what did you say the rest of your name was?" he said as he moved to his desk where he kept a bottle, two glasses, and an American .45 automatic.

"My full name is Ramon Egberto de Calves de Santorio y Gutierrez."

"And what do your friends call you, Ramon? Bert?" Schmidt said, pulling the drawer open, contemplating the pistol momentarily, then pulling out the bottle and two tumblers instead.

"My American college pals used to call me Eggy," the captain replied, almost demurely.

"Eggy it is. Eggy, how do you feel about good Kentucky bourbon?"

56

O N THE way up the canyon Jake couldn't stop looking at Morrie. There was something about the fiery, trim little redhead that really made him feel alive. She looked at him and smiled, and he couldn't help but smile back.

"So, are you going to tell me how you found it?"

"I think we should get something to eat before we go up there. We have to wait until it gets dark."

"C'mon, don't leave me hanging. Spill."

She grinned at him. "Get this. It wasn't on the letter at all. It was in the inside of the *envelope*."

"Really?"

"Yup. You know how they print patterns on the inside of envelopes so people can't just hold them up to the light and look through them?"

"Yeah…"

"The microdot was hidden in one of the patterns," she said smugly.

"So, it had this Mars library and the name of a book and that's all?"

"That's all."

"So where's this 'Mars Library' it mentions?"

"Well, that got me for awhile, so I went to both libraries in town and asked if they'd ever been called the Mars Library. I mean, the one is pretty close to Mars Hill. They said no, but there is another library in town; the one in the rotunda at Lowell Observatory, *on top* of Mars Hill."

"So, how are we going to get permission to look through it? Isn't it private property?"

"Oh Jake, you're so naive sometimes. We're going to wait until dark, then we're going to sneak in. Which reminds me. After we eat we have to stop at my house and get a flashlight."

They ate at Gino's, one of their favorite restaurants, and Jake couldn't believe how Morrie packed away the antipasto and lasagna. He wasn't much hungry himself, he was just antsy and curious. Why a book? Could a book be a location of another clue? Why Lowell Observatory? The spy or spies had to have access, otherwise how would they get to it? He had more questions than answers at this point, and Morrie wasn't helping. They waited until it was well after dark, and Jake buttoned his coat as they walked out the door into the chill of a March night. The snow had hardened and crunched beneath their feet as they walked to the car.

They parked on North Thorpe Road in the same place they had the night they met. Mars Hill rose up in front of them, its flanks covered by towering pine trees. Morrie turned off the lights but left the Chevy running.

"Sure you want to do this? Jake said. "It's snowing to beat the band."

"Chicken."

"I'm just not sure it's a good idea."

"Why not?"

"Oh, let's see; trespassing on private property, breaking and entering…it's wartime. If there's security we could be shot."

"On a night like this any security guards will be huddled in their guard shack nursing an Irish coffee. This is *perfect*. Besides, it's not like it's some top-secret government installation or anything."

"How do you know? Maybe it is."

Morrie sighed. "Fine, whatever. This is your thing Jake. I thought you'd be excited."

Jake had to admit she was right, he was, He just didn't want to get her in trouble, or worse yet, get her hurt. The name of this book was the first decent clue they'd had, and clear proof that Lily had been involved in something. Could she really have been a German spy? Jake had a hard time believing that, despite the evidence stacking up. His gut told him that she'd stumbled onto something, something dangerous. One way or another though, he had to know the truth.

It was cold, but warmer in the trees, which broke the wind, and the snow was only deep in places. He was glad they hadn't waited a day later though, despite his reservations, because it was snowing like hell.

Flagstaff's combination of high altitude, clear air and lack of light pollution seemed the perfect place for an observatory when Percival Lowell built his first telescope in 1894. Lowell had that rare condition known as "astronomy" which presented itself as an overwhelming need to stare at the stars through a telescope for hours on end. He built a small one, then a bigger one. Astronomers from all over the world were drawn to it like moths to a flame, and after Lowell's death in 1916 the small seed he'd planted atop Mars Hill sprouted into full flower.

In 1896 a larger telescope was built next to and just uphill from the original site, with a dome which had been modernized and rebuilt in recent years, now rotating on Ford truck tires, with a complex but ingenious rope and pulley system to open the viewing doors. Percival Lowell was interred in a lovely dome shaped mausoleum built of Vermont marble and purple leaded glass on the original site of his first telescope. "Uncle Percy" was laid to rest in his own private observatory atop the hill he loved.

Over the years several houses were added to the site besides Lowell's original cabin. Eventually the rotunda was built to store reference material, and a few years later a more conventional, two - story rectangular structure with a matching stone face was added to the north side of the rotunda to serve as office space; a rectangle of stone embracing the original rotunda dome.

The rotunda building crouched in a shallow swale just to the west and below the main observatory, the walls built of volcanic rock; a building material of which there was no shortage in the area. The beams and roof were built of local fir, and the domed roof which gave the rotunda its name also gave it more than a passing resemblance to Monticello, or at least another observatory.

After trying several doors they found the door to the coal cellar was open and squeezed in. It was pitch black, so Jake turned on the flashlight briefly and saw a door in front of them. On the other side the furnace growled softly, making the steam pipes tick as they warmed. In front of them was a short staircase, and he shut off his flashlight as they went up them by feel, Morrie holding the hem of his coat so as not to lose him.

Dim light came through windows on the north side, just enough to see the small, angled stairway leading upstairs. Two huge, iron-strapped doors led into a great, 42 foot diameter room, furnished with an eclectic mix of sturdy, over-stuffed mission style furniture.

Long oak tables with converted Yale oil lamps stood against one wall, providing workspace for the scientists, and a narrow walkway ran in a semi-circle around the top of the room with two curved, ladder-like steps positioned at each end to provided access to the upper shelves. The natural light coming through the valances dimmed periodically as storm clouds filtered the moon. By library standards the place was small, but large enough to make Jake groan inwardly.

"This is going to take forever," he whispered.

"Oh, don't be a baby. They have to have some kind of system. C'mon, let's find this thing and get out of here before someone comes. I'll check up there first."

Since they only had one light, Jake held the flashlight on her while she scurried up the ladder, then handed it up to her while he stood guard. He stood in the dark, listening intently, but besides the occasional thump of snow falling off a tree onto the roof and the howl of the wind he heard nothing. What could be hidden in the book? Another message? Stolen blueprints for war material? He was curious as hell. What had Lily found? She'd obviously been killed for it, but why? What could be so important?

Morrie just fit on the narrow walkway, and worked her way along on her knees. She'd been right, the books were alphabetical, but also broken into sections by subject. Not being a scientist, she had to go through an entire section on radiotopography. Then telemetry, then finally astronomical physics. She missed it the first time, as it was hard as hell to read the spines sideways, especially in such cramped quarters, but as she moved the flashlight back she saw it: *Elementary Treatise on Elliptical Functions'* by Arthur Cayley, 1895.

"I found it."

"Shhh."

The book was tightly wedged between the other tomes. she wiggled it out and tried to open it but it wouldn't open. It was as if all the pages were glued together, making the book one solid piece. She peered intently at it with the flashlight but saw no reason it wouldn't open. Maybe it had gotten wet? A roof leak perhaps?

"Huh."

"What's the problem?" Jake hissed from the floor.

"Just a minute." She decided to just take the book with her – they'd figure it out in the car. She doubted it would be much of a loss to the library anyway. She crawled quickly to the other ladder, which was closer, and tucked the book under one arm. Jake met her at the bottom after bumping painfully into a heavy chair.

"Next time we break into a place let's bring two flashlights," he said, rubbing his shin, already sore from the long hike up the hill.

"Shhh. I think I heard something," Morrie said. They stood silently, and sure enough, it sounded like someone was moving along the lower hallway, then they heard the scuff of feet coming up the stairs and saw a light come on outside the doorway, shining up from below, the way they'd come in. Someone was coming.

57

KESSLER UNFOLDED the road map again and checked it, the eight year-old Ford idling roughly. He'd been a little concerned with the lumpy idle at first, as, with the window open he could hear a loose tappet clicking lightly, but all the car had to do was get him to Warm Springs. After that he didn't care.

Unlike the owner of the car, whom he had buried the night before in his own vegetable garden, Kessler had no illusions about surviving this mission. After killing Roosevelt his life wouldn't be worth a plug nickel, as the Americans liked to say. He wondered briefly what a plug nickel was, then his mind clicked into gear as he considered the problem ahead of him.

He dropped the map back onto the seat, put the old Ford in gear and pulled back out onto the road; a decent but rural terracotta red clay affair which wound lazily through a verdant, gorgeously green Georgia spring, the buzzing of locusts loud in his ears as he shifted gears, enjoying the drive, something he hadn't done in years.

When he arrived in Warm Springs he was immediately struck by how casual the atmosphere was. America might be at war and there were clearly shortages, but there was none of the tension he had felt in Berlin, none of the despair of people being bombed day and night, no rubble, no stink of dead bodies trapped in the wreckage, no starving children. He ate well, and because his English was so good and he had no discernible accent, people accepted him as one of them, or at least as a "damn Yankee".

A few discrete inquiries led him to the linen company that supplied the Warm Springs resort with clean towels, linens, and uniforms for the employees. Posing as a new hire, it was an easy matter to secure not just one, but three brand - new uniforms; white jackets almost military in cut with black linen pants, a black bow tie and cummerbund. They even offered to send two of them out to the resort with the next delivery, but Kessler politely declined, explaining that he wasn't due to start his new job on the wait staff until the following week and didn't want to appear too anxious.

After glancing at Kessler's shoes the clerk suggested a shoe store which could supply him with the proper black oxfords. Kessler had thanked him, left a small tip, and with a smile on his face, had gone to find the shoe store, his new disguise draped over his shoulder. So far it had been almost too easy.

The original plan of a direct frontal assault by a 12-man zug had been a tactic that he had felt was sure to succeed, even with Roosevelt surrounded by Secret Service and Marine guards. Kessler's men had trained tirelessly in an exact replica of the resort compound until they had it down to a six minute operation from the time they hit the front gate. Kessler had been confident in their ability to overwhelm the guards and kill the president, but now he was alone, with nothing but a Walther P-38, a suppressor and his wits to get the job done.

The clerk at the shoe Store had been more than happy to give Kessler directions to "The Little White House" as it was known, and even warned him about the Marine sentries at the gate, who had been added when FDR became president in 1933 and who'd been there ever since, telling him to allow time to clear the checkpoint so he wasn't late.

Kessler had decided that a closer look was necessary, and had bought a second pair of shoes from the salesman, a pair of dark, non-descript, ankle height walking shoes in supple, dark leather, suitable for a day in the woods. Thanking the clerk, he put his purchases in the car and went into the men's store next door which had a sign across the top spelling "LaRocca's" in big letters. He pawed through the suits for several minutes until he could sense the clerk salivating at the thought of a big sale.

"May Ah help you, sir?"

"Huh? Oh, just looking. You have some beautiful suits here. I really just came in to buy a sweater, maybe a hat. It's chillier at night than I'd expected."

"Still early in the year. Here on vacation?"

"Yes. The wife came down to visit the spa…she has trouble with her legs."

"The springs should help her."

"Yes, but in the meantime I'm bored silly. Any hunting this time of year?"

"Just rabbit…and of course squirrel. You should really have a dog for that though…at least that's the way Ah like to hunt."

"Mmm. I agree. Wish I'd brought my shotgun and old Barney now, but the missus would've used the gun on me if I'd tried to put him in the car."

"Barney your dog?"

"Uh-huh. He's old, but what a nose."

The salesman pursed his lips for a moment. "Say, Ah know a feller might rent you a hound cheap. Ah've got an old 16 gauge Ah could loan you if y'all don't mind a 16."

"Why I think I'll take you up on that…where'd you say I could find the fella with the dog?"

58

"QUICK, OUT the front," Jake whispered.

Morrie unlocked the door and they squeezed out into the snow just as the lights in the library came on. Jake eased the door shut and they ran uphill, back the way they'd come, expecting at any minute to hear a cry of alarm from behind them.

"Turn off the damn flashlight," he hissed. Morrie complied, and they stood behind a large tree for a minute, catching their breath, letting their eyes adjust to the gloom. The moon lent a feeble glow to the landscape, filtered by the snow which was coming down harder now. They made their way past the "Pluto Dome", where Clyde Tombaugh had discovered Pluto in 1930, and turned north, following their tracks coming in, turning on the flashlight periodically to get their bearings.

Finally the trees grew thicker, and the light grew dimmer. They'd walked into a herd of sheep about here on the way up, which without the flashlight on, had scared the hell out of them both until they realized what they were, so as they started down the hill Jake told Morrie to go ahead and turn on the flashlight. They were safe. Now if they could just get back down the hill to the car without breaking their necks, he thought.

Although his legs were stronger now, they still trembled from the effort, but he gritted his teeth and pushed on. The combination of snow on mud made things slippery, but somehow they made it back to the car without breaking anything, and they both breathed a sigh of relief when the car came into view, covered with almost four inches of fresh snow. The way it was looking, they'd have a foot by morning, and here it was the beginning of April.

Jake brushed the snow off the door for Morrie and she got in while he went around brushing off the windows. When he got in it felt colder inside the damn car than it had outside. He started the car, and the heater began blowing cold air, which wasn't helping any.

"Brrr, it's like a meat locker in here."

"At least we didn't fall on our keisters like we did going up," Morrie said.

"I nearly did." He rubbed his legs, which ached worse than they had in a month. "Now that we're thieves as well as trespassers, let me see that book."

"Don't feel too bad about it, Jake, it's not much of a book. See? It's all glued together."

She handed him the book and he turned it over in his hands. It looked completely real until you tried to open it, then you realized it was all one piece. Odd. He put more effort into it, and suddenly it gave, cracking open in the middle, with a hollow chamber in the middle, carved into the now solid pages.

"You got it!" Morrie said.

"Yeah, but it's empty. Look here, they used a little rubber cement to keep it shut."

"Why bother? Once you put it in the stack between the other books it'd stay shut."

"It must have been something valuable, something they didn't want falling out under any circumstances."

"You're sure it's empty? There's not a second compartment?"

"Here, look for yourself," he said, handing it back to her.

"Hmm. You're right. Pretty neat though."

"Well, it is confirmation that we're not totally crazy."

"No, just you are."

"What's *that* supposed to mean?"

"Jake, this is beginning to worry me. Your friend Lily was murdered, you and Dick were nearly blown sky-high, the three of us were shot at, then you were run off the road...all for a lousy glued-together book?"

"Well obviously there was *something* in there, something small...and valuable in some way. Look at the size of the compartment."

"Jake, you're missing the point. There are dangerous people out there who would do anything to get their hands on what was in this book. We don't even know who they are. We could literally walk right past them and not know…but they obviously know who *we* are. It's beginning to scare me, Jake."

"You're right. I never should have dragged you into this," he said, taking her hand.

"Jake, for a smart guy you can be pretty dense. I'm not worried about *me*, I'm worried about *you*. Why, if anything ever happened to you I'd…"

Morrie looked at him seriously, then without warning, kissed him, her lips warm and soft, then she threw her arms around him and buried her face in his neck. Jack put his arms around her and pulled her closer, the only sound the rush of air from the defroster and the soft tones of Artie Shaw's clarinet from the radio. He could taste the salt of her tears at the edges of her mouth.

"Morrie, I have to tell you something."

"Uh-oh. Here it comes," she said, pulling away a little.

"No, no. Look, you know I've been trying to get back in shape to fly again right?"

She nodded, looking past him

"Well, Elliot got me a job with Lockheed testing a new plane. It's the hottest thing they have. Unfortunately it means me going to California for awhile."

"So this *is* goodbye."

"Will you stop already? Spending time with you the last few months has been wonderful. If it wasn't for this thing with Lily I'd be the happiest guy in the world right now… Funny, but all I've been hoping for the last several months is to get back in a plane, and now that I have the chance I just want to stay here with you."

Morrie put her hand on his face again. "Stupid, stupid boy," she said, then she was kissing him again, and all Jake could think about was that if you could bottle this feeling a guy could get rich on it.

– Part Three –
April 11ᵗʰ, 1945

59

THE PLANE was fast...faster than any plane had a right to be. Jake estimated it was nearly 200 mph faster than the P-38s he'd flown. The Lockheed P-80 Shooting Star was definitely no slouch. At first he thought it was sluggish in responding to controls, then he realized that he was just going so fast that it just had a wider turning radius. He'd have to remember that in a dogfight, he thought, then he realized he would likely never have this plane in a real dogfight, which made him grin. There was no pressure here, he thought. Just fly the plane.

He pulled back on the stick and punched a pedal. The plane spun upwards through the atmosphere like nothing he'd ever experienced. His control on the ground was yelling something at him. Suddenly the stall warning horn blared, and he felt a lack of control...the plane was stalling. He leveled the aircraft's attitude and as it stalled, rolled it over onto its back. The P-80 began falling back to earth, the nose slowly swapping places with the tail as it fell through 180 degrees of arc, tipping over backward into a Split-S, a trick Jake had learned as a kid flying the Jenny.

The plane fell like a rock, there was no controlling it. Jake pulled back on the stick, but it took a superhuman effort. Jake hit the igniters with a prayer on his lips. There was a short pause, and he fought with the stick briefly, until the engine suddenly reached full operating thrust, blasting him straight at the ground at near Mach 1. He passed 20,000 feet with the stick braced, pulling for all he was worth.

He wasn't sure he could do it, but the plane finally leveled out at just 7,000 feet. He blinked at the airspeed indicator and G-meter and smiled. The radio was still spitting at him, and he finally responded.

"Eagle Two under control and returning to base," he said into his new oxygen mask with built-in mike.

"Roger, Two. We were a little worried."

"Sorry about that, grandfather. Had my hands busy for a few minutes."

"That's a hundred thousand dollar aircraft, Eagle Two. Try and land without crashing it will you?"

"Roger, Base. Just one thing…where's the landing gear switch again?"

Jake smiled into his mask as he said it, playing the game of control pilots have played since planes were first invented.

"Just bring it home, Two."

"Roger, base. Eagle Two out."

Jake pointed the jet back in the direction of Cottonwood and gave the engine full throttle making the jet take off like a scalded cat. For once Jake was happy. Moving the planes here to Clemencau Field from California had been his idea, but he was still surprised Elliot had gone along with it, and been able to swing it. It was a more remote, secure location for their testing, sure, but the main thing was that he was home, in love with Morrie and he was flying again. For the moment, life was good.

60

THE DOG Kessler rented was a young, friendly spaniel unimaginatively named Pepper, being mostly white with a black head and a coat that looked like someone had shaken out their paintbrush over him. He sat panting in the front seat of the car while Kessler drove around for an hour, familiarizing himself with the roads and the lay of the land. He passed the turnoff to the Springs, and could see a low, white fence with diagonal braces flanking two small sentry booths whose fresh paint sparkled in the morning sun.

The borrowed 16 gauge lay wrapped in a blanket in the trunk, wrapped in oilskin, and he'd gone to the trouble of buying a visitor's hunting license for small game with his false ID at a local gas station, along with a box of shells. The friendly clerk at the men's clothing store had thrown in a lightweight hunting vest with loops for shells, big pockets in front, and a huge game pocket in the small of the back. He'd purchased a pair of binoculars, the smallest he could find, and they just fit in one of the front pockets although he couldn't button the flap. They'd been expensive, but he didn't care.

Pepper's rental had cost him three dollars a day, an exorbitant sum he was sure, but Kessler didn't argue. He paid the owner in advance for three days, and gave him a ten, telling him to keep the change, thus cementing his cover as a visiting small business owner. It had been agreed that Kessler would return Pepper to his owner each evening to be kenneled and return for him after breakfast the next day.

Kessler drove back to the road he'd seen on his first time by, a dirt track which led off into the woods. It was on the same side of the road as the entrance to the resort, but about three miles further down. It looked as though it mainly saw use by woodcutters and hunters, perfect for his purposes. He turned down the muddy track, the red Georgia clay sticking tenaciously to the tires. He hoped he didn't get stuck.

Pepper whined anxiously as Kessler opened the trunk, donning his vest after loading the shotgun he had no intention of using - rabbit or no rabbit - although the thought of hasenpfeffer had him salivating. He closed the trunk and opened the door, and Pepper leapt out happily, dancing at his feet, ready to go. Kessler couldn't help but smile at the dog's youthful exuberance.

"Okay, boy, let's go," he said, catching himself as he nearly spoke to the dog in German. They struck out into the woods at a right angle from the direction of his objective so as not to make a beeline straight to the target. Kessler had an excellent sense of direction, and followed a rambling, seemingly random zigzag path through the forest, the dog bouncing through the underbrush ahead of him, nose to the ground, his exuberance contagious. Kessler kept his eyes open, but not for rabbits. There were Marine sentry posts out here – he was sure of that, but they wouldn't be painted white this time.

After an hour and a half, Kessler estimated he was getting close to the line where he'd find the Marine sentries and, sure enough, a few minutes later he found a sign which said "No Trespassing – No entrance this side, by order U.S. government." Pepper didn't read the sign, so he pretended he hadn't seen it either and kept going, the dog tearing through the underbrush, nose to the ground, everything around them fresh and bright green with the promise of spring, the smell of wet, fertile earth and new life everywhere.

Fifty yards or so later they came to a fence, this one simple barbed wire, not razor wire fortunately, with the same white signs with black lettering hung off the fence with wire every hundred feet or so. Kessler mentally added wire cutters to his list of equipment.

He stopped and stood absolutely still, watching for movement in the forest beyond the fence. He saw nothing for several minutes, the woods quiet except for the soft patter of Pepper's feet on old, wet leaves...then he saw it - a tiny wisp of smoke rising from where the ground dropped off ahead of him into a natural swale about fifty meters away. He turned to his right, moving quietly, following the fence up the hill until he reached the top of a small rise. He squatted down, took out the binoculars, and after pushing Pepper away aimed them back towards where he'd seen the telltale wisp of smoke from a cigarette.

He couldn't see much, but finally found a dark, hard edge nearly hidden by the contours of the land. Trees don't have angles like that, and finally the image resolved itself as the trailing edge of a shake roof, just large enough to be a sentry shack. He waited patiently, and soon saw another telltale wisp of smoke rising like steam through an errant beam of sunlight near the shack. He smiled.

There were likely two Marines in each shack, and from what he could tell they would be no closer than one hundred meters from each other, undoubtedly well-camouflaged by their position and the use of olive drab paint, but the Marines manning them would be bored and inattentive, and he doubted they patrolled much. It would be an easy matter to penetrate this first line of defense. Closer to the compound there would undoubtedly be roving patrols, but he guessed that they would be as regular as clockwork, and while he'd have to be careful not to run into one, he had no doubts as to his ability to avoid them.

After searching for and identifying two more guard shacks, Kessler returned Pepper to his owner, explaining that he and the missus were leaving early due to a family emergency, thanked him for the use of the dog, complimented Pepper, and told him to keep the deposit for the other two days. The dog owner shook his hand happily, having made ten dollars for renting his dog for one day.

He took the shotgun he'd needed only as a prop back to the store clerk who'd lent it to him, giving him the same story as well as another ten, which made the clerk as equally amenable to his return. Kessler was running low on money, but it didn't matter.

After treating himself to a big steak dinner accompanied by a mysterious substance called "grits," Kessler returned to his room and cleaned the pistol and silencer one last time even though it didn't need it, the familiar, cold steel of the Walther like an old friend, relaxing him as he field-stripped it, rubbed it down, oiled it and loaded the magazine with fresh rounds, knowing this would be the last time he'd ever go through this little ritual.

After reassembling the weapon, he checked that his new uniform was neatly folded in a linen bag, laid out the third pair of black pants, the dark blue shirt and sweater, then lay down on the bed after calling the desk for a 3:00 a.m. wakeup call. He couldn't sleep – he never could just before an action, so he lay there in the dark, the radio playing softly, the gleam of the pistol on the table a reminder that soon he would kill the president of the United States...or die trying.

61

JAKE AWOKE to a hammering in his head, and a soft weight on his left side, which turned out to be Morrie. She was snoring softly, her warm breath a soft breeze against his chest. She was wearing a silk slip, and his hand cupped her shoulder. He blew some of her hair out of his face, then stuck his nose in her hair and took a deep breath.

The pain behind his eyes was intense, and his leg was starting to ache where she'd thrown hers over his, but he didn't want to move, didn't want to wake her. He just wanted the moment to last, and so he closed his eyes and just breathed, comfortably uncomfortable, until he fell back asleep.

When he woke the second time she was gone, and the pounding in his head had reduced itself to a tolerable level. He stretched, and even the constant ache in his legs didn't feel so bad. Then he heard the shower running in the bathroom. He lay there a few more minutes listening, then pulled himself up so he was sitting against the headboard, wishing he had coffee. Then he remembered he was in a hotel, and picked up the phone to order a full carafe and two cups.

He had just lit a cigarette when he heard the water stop. Several more minutes went by, then the door opened, pouring steam into the room. Morrie came out rubbing her hair dry with a towel, wearing a bathrobe that looked as though it were two sizes too small. Jake found himself growing hard as he looked at her. She smiled at him from beneath the towel.

"Hey, sleepyhead. How you feel after all the beer you drank last night?"

"Not too bad considering. I've got coffee and aspirin coming from room service."

"Bless you. My thoughts exactly." She stopped toweling her hair and dropped the towel on a chair, then walked over to the end of the bed, looking at him with those bedroom eyes of hers. She reminded him of Bette Davis when she did that, and reminded him of something else when she crawled onto the end of the bed and made her way slowly towards him on all fours, her eyes never leaving him, the robe no longer concealing what was underneath, a female lioness on the hunt. He could see her cleavage clearly as she came towards him, straddling his damaged legs gently, her hands running under the sheets and up his torn thighs…

She stopped and looked at him, a look of ineffable sadness on her face, then pulled the sheet down to look at his injuries.

"Oh, Jake."

She caressed his wounds with the airbrush of her fingers, the light touch only a woman can provide, tears coming as she touched him.

"It's okay, Morrie. I'm getting better."

"But Jake, your legs…"

"It's okay."

She came to him then, gently straddling him, her tears wetting his cheeks as she kissed him, her hands cupping his head as she kissed his forehead, his eyes, his cheeks…then their lips met again. He kissed his way down her neck to her breasts, and someone knocked on the door.

"Dammit. YES? WHO IS IT?"

"Room service, Sir."

"LEAVE IT OUTSIDE THE…" he began, not caring for coffee now.

"NO, WAIT," Morrie yelled at the door. "I'll get it." She swung off him, belting her robe as she moved across the room, her lovely hips swinging. She found a couple of dollar bills on the dresser next to his wallet and went to the door. He heard a muffled conversation, then the door closed and she came back with the tray. The smell of coffee filled the room.

"They sent cinnamon rolls. Are you hungry?" she asked, stuffing one into her mouth as she came back to the bed, setting the tray on the bedside table, sitting beside him. He nuzzled into her back, ignoring the pain in his legs, nuzzling her neck.

"Yeah, I'm hungry," he replied. "Hungry for you."

"Mmmm" was her only response as she turned to kiss him, the sweet icing from the cinnamon roll on her lips passing to him, the warmth in her green eyes all the sustenance he needed.

62

"IT IS very kind of you to give me a ride on your plane back to my garrison, Major Peterson," Capitan Rafael Gutierrez said as the C-47 climbed into the humid morning air, the jungle gradually receding below. "I must return your generous hospitality somehow. Perhaps after the war you might come visit me at mi tio's hacienda. He has a cook with an amazing talent for enchiladas con pollo, and we can shoot some skeet, run some horses…perhaps I can even introduce you to some señoritas."

Schmidt looked at the plump Mexican captain with a disinterested smile. The cockpit door opened and the copilot stuck his head out.

"We're cruising at six thousand feet, Major," he said to Schmidt.

"Thank you, Otto, that'll do nicely," he said.

Unbuttoning the flap covering his .45, Schmidt pulled the big American automatic out and racked the slide, chambering a round, then he swung it to point at the Mexican officer's nose. Gutierrez couldn't help but notice – he was staring straight down the huge, open muzzle, just inches away.

"Your sidearm please, Captain."

"What…what are you doing?"

"Your sidearm. NOW."

The young officer slowly pulled his revolver from its holster and presented it butt first. Schmidt took it and nodded to one of his men. "Horstmann, open the door," Giesler and Horstmann, obviously working on previous orders, moved immediately to the jump door and unlatched it then pulled it back inside, and set it out of the way, the Mexican army officer's mouth nearly as wide open as the hole in the side of the aircraft as he tried to grasp what was happening.

"It's unfortunate that you had to stumble across our little operation Captain, but at least you had a good dinner and a fine cigar last night," Schmidt said loudly.

"I've known many a fine soldier who went to his death on an empty stomach, lying in a snow-filled trench, so cold they couldn't feel their toes. Death was a blessing to them."

Guiterrez' eyes were wide with alarm now. "But...but you *can't*. Don't you know who I am?" he said, yelling now to be heard above the wind howling through the open door.

Schmidt just looked at him calmly, as he'd looked at a hundred others.

"I'm sorry, Herr Kapitan. Giesler, Horstmann, throw him out."

He tried to fight, but the corpulent captain was no match for the two battle-hardened SS commandos who simply picked him up like a sack of potatoes and tossed him out of the plane. Once Giesler helped Horstmann replace and seal the door shut the wind noise dropped appreciably, although the inside of the C-47 was still far from quiet. At least there was no more screaming.

Schmidt stood up and grasped one of the safety rings hanging from the ceiling to steady himself . They were flying low to come in under the radar, and turbulence was worse here nearer the ground.

"All right, everyone. Let's go over it one last time," he said.

63

AVIATION MACHINIST Mate Dan Goodman looked blearily out the window of the airfield office, bored to tears. His Garand leaned haphazardly against the desk, his .45 sitting next to it in its holster. He hated the weight of the damn thing and took it off whenever possible. It was against regulations of course, but who the hell cared? The war had passed Daniel Goodman by, and no one had showed up in weeks except for his relief. The early morning light cast a funereal pall over everything he looked at...or perhaps it was just his mood. Debbie had left him for "a real Navy flyer" as she had put it, and when they closed Naval Auxiliary Air Station Clemencau and the pilot was transferred to San Diego she went with him.

As he yawned, he heard a sound like a freight train passing overhead, then another. He tipped his chair forward, slamming the front legs back to earth, suddenly very awake. What in God's name was that?

He slung his belt and holster back on, grabbed his rifle and ran outside just as he heard a call come over the radio, and heard the tower respond. Jamie sounded excited, and with good reason. No one had landed a plane here in months, except for the old coot with the tired old biplane who seemed to think he owned the place, and of course the two Army Air Forces jets that had recently moved onto the base.

Goodwin looked up into the gradually lightening morning sky, saw two bat-like shapes sweeping around the end of the valley in the fastest turn he'd ever seen, just as the phone rang. He ran to the wall and literally snatched it from its hanger.

"Ground Control."

It was Jamie in the tower. "DAN, GET THOSE RUNWAY LIGHTS ON – WE'VE GOT TWO OF THEM COMING IN FAST,"

"ROGER THAT," Dan yelled back. He slammed the phone down and hurled himself at the knife switch near the door and watched the lights on

Runway one four flicker once, then begin burning ever more brightly until they were fully lit. He saw that a couple were burnt out and cursed, hoping he wasn't reported. Goodman was responsible for replacing the bulbs, and he'd been slacking a little, not having checked them in weeks, although he'd checked them off on his nightly list. He vowed to replace them first thing tomorrow.

The first plane landed so fast he couldn't believe it. Sleek, black…and had no tail. He guessed it was one of the new jets, like the other two in the hangar at the end of the runway…the two he had the misfortune to miss when they came in, but had heard all about. It seemed like he was always off duty when they took them out to test them and the rest of the time they were locked in the hangar. He still hadn't seen them fly and they'd been there for two weeks.

Goodman watched the jet taxi noisily towards him as the second one touched down. The jet engines were shut down, and the second plane rolled up beside the first, nose pointed towards the runway. The pilots were already clambering out as Goodwin ran towards them. The closer he got, the more amazed he was. They looked like something out of Buck Rogers. The first pilot was dropping to the ground just as he ran up, his wingman in the other plane just climbing out of the cockpit.

"Sir. Petty officer Daniel Goodman at your service, Sir." The salute was the crispest, cleanest one Goodman had given since boot camp, his chest stuck out, at attention as if the flyer were a visiting admiral or general.

The pilot looked at him and smiled. "I need fuel," he said. Goodman noticed a slight accent but didn't think twice about it.

"I'll get the fuel truck, Sir," he replied, snapping another salute as the aviator saluted back, trying to cover his amusement as Goodman ran off to get the truck.

"Does he suspect anything?" Mink asked Fullgrabe as he walked over from his plane.

"Are you kidding? He couldn't keep his eyes off the planes. I'll keep him busy here, why don't you go visit our friends in the tower?"

Wilhem Mink nodded his acquiescence and strode off towards the portable air control center, chambering a round in his silenced pistol and tucking it into his belt behind his back. Fullgräbe wasn't used to killing up front and personal, but he would do what needed to be done, and knew Mink would also. He looked at his watch. The commandos would be landing in Williams about now, he thought.

Once they refueled here, they'd kill the remaining personnel with the MP40s stashed in the cockpits, quickly stencil the German cross on the wings with the paint and stencils they had brought, and be in the air 20 minutes later. He took a deep breath as the fuel truck drove towards him, the red light above the cab flashing. He just hoped the bombs fit the American style brackets they had modified the Hortens to accept. They had good intel, but you never knew. Fullgräbe was just waiting for something to go wrong…something always did. He waved at the approaching truck, the sailor driving it unaware that this was his last hour on earth.

64

"WAIT UNTIL you see this thing, Dick. It's the future of manned flight."

"Can't imagine how you conned Elliot into letting you fly it."

"Hell, Dick, they need test pilots right now. With the war nearly over, Elliot says the next race will be to space."

"Who are we racing?"

"The Russians. That's not official of course…they're still our allies."

"For now. I don't trust them."

"Me neither. Personally I hope when this is over we never have another war. You know, at first I wanted to go back…do my part…but I don't know if I'd survive another dogfight or not, Dick…the legs have healed, but they aren't what they used to be. I'm just glad to be back in the cockpit."

"You'd better do something nice for Colonel Roosevelt. He's been mighty good to you."

"I know. I've been trying to think of something he'd like, but he's the son of the president, and rich besides. What do you get a guy like that? You know he invited me to the White House?"

"Now that's a place I'd like to see. Be interesting to meet FDR just once. I don't agree with everything he does, but he sure pulled us out of the Depression."

"I remember. I'm still not too fond of jackrabbit stew," Jake replied.

Dick laughed. "Jes' be glad you had that. Lots of folks went hungry them years."

"Yeah, I remember."

When they pulled up to the gate at Clemencau Field there was no one in the guardhouse. Jake honked the horn but no one came out to open up.

"That's odd."

"Navy boys. Probably in the bathroom," Dick said contemptuously.

Jake got out of the car and walked slowly to the gate. He could see something going on at the other end of the field…it looked as though they were fueling two planes, but he couldn't tell, the fueling truck was blocking his view. Then he realized Elliot had probably gotten the guards to help him fuel up and load ammo for the strafing runs, and they hadn't opened the gate.

Jake reached through and found the latch then slid the gate aside, the chain link singing as he slid it open. Then he got back in the car and they drove inside, this time Dick jumping out to slide the gate shut.

As they drew closer, Jake realized that the two planes sitting there in the dawning light weren't P-80s…but they were something special. He wasn't even sure they were planes. They looked more like spacecraft.

"Jesus, Dick. What the hell are those things?"

"Whattya' mean. Those aren't *your* planes?"

Dick had seen something else though in the dim light, the unmistakable outline of a machine pistol in the hands of one of the two men who turned towards them as they drove up.

"DUCK," he yelled, as he grabbed the wheel and spun it to the right, jabbing his foot over Jake's on the gas. The Ford lunged to the right, accelerating towards the gap between the hangars as bullets began stitching through the windows, glass shattering everywhere, the sound of bullets hitting sheet metal all too familiar to Jake. Then they saw the bodies on the tarmac.

"What the hell?"

"We're under attack. I don't know by who, but they ain't friendly."

Jake was too busy driving to wonder. He punched it, swerving to miss the bodies of the dead Navy men, but still hit one, feeling the sickening thump and bounce as he drove over him. "Sorry, buddy," he mumbled to himself. He reached the end of the hangar and shut off the car lights just as more bullets began hitting the rear of the car. He pulled left and stopped the car, but left it in gear.

"OUT."

Dick didn't have to be told twice. They both bailed out, the twinges in Jakes legs forgotten as they rolled away from the car, scrabbling towards the weeds. The car started forward again under its own power, moving drunkenly as if the driver had been shot, which was just what Jake was hoping for. They heard running footsteps and saw the killers sprinting down the side of the hangar, following the car. The sun was beginning to come up, and they got a better look at them, peeking through the brush.

"Those are Schmeisser machine pistols," Dick whispered as they watched them approach the car, which had finally come to rest against a corner of one of the hangars.

"What the hell would Germans be doing in these parts?"

"I don't know, but if we don't find some cover, we're dead as soon as they figure out we're not in that car."

Dick looked around at the surrounding vegetation, or rather the lack of it.

"Don't look good, hoss."

65

SCHMIDT FELT his body tense up automatically as the C-47 touched down at the airport at Bellemont, the chirp of the tires on the pavement telling him that things were now beyond his control. They had come a long way to strike at the heart of America, and it was now up to him and his men, disguised as American MPs, to take the mission into the next phase. He looked at his men for the last time before they disembarked. He paid special attention to the faux prisoners.

"Don't forget your roles. You are American military police escorting a group of German POWs. You POWs, don't forget, you are not proud soldiers of the SS, you are tired, beaten German scum."

Some of the men smiled at this, but Schmidt did not.

"What happens in the next 90 minutes is critical to the success of our mission. When we move, it must be quickly, but not so as to raise suspicion. We want them to be unaware until the last possible moment. There is no second chance. The fate of Germany lies in our hands, and only ours. We must succeed."

The men all nodded seriously as the plane taxied towards the hangar where a truck waited. The driver was American, and had no idea he was about to meet a group of German commandos. The truck had been arranged by their contact; to make it look like a real prisoner transfer, it had to be done through official channels. There had been some worry that the Americans would double-check their paperwork, but no one had even raised an eyebrow. They were about to drive straight into the most secure weapons depot in America, no questions asked.

The men were well prepared from the extensive briefings on board the *Orion*. They had watched films of American soldiers to see how they acted, and all the men, including Schmidt, had been amazed at the casual attitude and nonchalance of the American soldiers, sometimes even in the company of their officers. There was no such lack of discipline in the German Army, and the hardest thing for the men was to "unlearn" the desire to snap to attention in the presence of an officer. Schmidt cultivated the slouching, blasé look of the Americans in his men…not too much, because even the Americans had their limits.

In the guise of an American officer Schmidt hoped to control any situations that might arise. His stomach was doing flip-flops despite his outwardly cool appearance. Any man who claimed to have no fear before battle was, in his opinion, either an idiot or a liar. Schmidt was neither. How you controlled your fear was the important thing.

The plane came to a stop as the engines slowly died. Schmidt stuck his head into the cockpit to talk with the crew. "Stay with the plane. Refuel it as if everything were normal. Be friendly, but minimize your contact with the Americans."

"Yes, Major, of course," the pilot answered.

Schmidt turned to his men and smiled grimly. "Show time, gentlemen."

66

FOR SOME reason the two Germans hadn't spent very long searching for them. Instead they headed back in towards the hangars and disappeared. A few minutes later Jake and Dick heard the planes fire up, and watched them through the brush as they taxied around to take off. Neither of them had ever seen anything like the strange-looking jets, but from their vantage point they could see the recently painted German crosses on the wings.

"The hell kind of plane is that?" Dick wondered aloud. "Doesn't even have a tail. How does it fly?"

"I don't know, Dick, but they damn sure do fly, and they aren't here for an air show. C'mon, let's go."

They scrambled back down the rocky slope, reaching the tarmac just as the first jet took off and banked away. It looked like a huge, jet-powered bat, and it gave Jake chills. If the Nazis had planes like this, what else did they have? Why now? The war was over for all intents and purposes…wasn't it? What could they possibly be doing here?

They ran towards the hangar where the P-80s were kept as the second plane took off, its landing gear folding silently up into its sleek belly, the matte brown and black camouflage paint ominous in the morning sun…then it was gone. They heard the rumble of a hangar door, and saw Elliot Roosevelt, who looked at them with surprise.

"Jake, thank God. I heard the shots – I thought you were done for. I had no way to warn you without giving my position away. Who's this with you?"

"Colonel, this is my friend Dick Lawson. Dick, this is Colonel Elliot Roosevelt, my commanding officer. So, what the hell were those things, Elliot?"

"Those gentlemen, are Horten jets. They aren't supposed to exist. Jack Northrop's been working on something similar, based on the same work

271

the Horten brothers have been doing. It's highly classified stuff. Higher even than the P-80s we're flying. I shouldn't be telling you this, but I figure you're both in it now."

"Where do you think they're going? How the hell did they get here?" Dick asked.

"I don't know, but if we don't get these planes in the air we'll read about it tomorrow in the papers," he said as he ran for the towmotor to pull the planes out of the hangar. "Dick, Can you help load that ammo? Jake, help me get these planes outside."

Minutes went by like hours as they struggled to get the first P-80 ready. Elliot shrugged on his oxygen mask and leather flying helmet as Jake did a quick preflight.

"No time, Jake, I have to go."

"Soon as we can, I'm right behind you, Sir."

Elliot nodded, flipping switches.

"CLEAR."

Jake ran clear as the jet turbine began spooling up with a whine. He watched the engine fire up, then settling down to a ragged growl. Elliot slid the canopy shut and gave him a thumbs up. Jake returned it, then ran to help Dick, who was still struggling to get the last of the ammo into the second aircraft one-handed.

"Dick, can you stay and see if anyone here is left alive? Call the authorities and secure the base until they get here?"

"Will do. Now get your gear on and get going. Elliot's going to need you up there."

Less than two minutes later Jake sat on the runway checking gauges, watching the turbojet engine's rpm spool up as he fastened his oxygen mask. Dick gave him the thumbs up and then he was rolling, trundling slowly towards takeoff position, every fiber of his being vibrating with the huge engine, hoping he wasn't too late, wondering how he'd ever catch them. They must be miles away by now. He tuned his radio to the air-to-air frequency they'd agreed upon, and pressed the mike switch on the control stick.

"Eagle One, this is Eagle Two, come in."

Nothing.

"Eagle One, this is Eagle Two. Please respond." They'd had some trouble with the radios last time out, and he hoped Elliot was just out of range. This was not the time for a malfunction.

He reached the runway and lined the plane up with the centerline. He stood on the brakes, letting the engine spool up until it was like the roar of God directly behind him, then he let off the brakes and the plane started moving, faster and faster. He pulled back on the stick and he was in the air, going like a bat out of hell, flashing out over the Tuzigoot Indian ruins, headed towards Sedona, following his gut instinct as he tried the radio again, but again with no result. Come on Elliot, Where the hell are you?

67

SCHMIDT TRIED to be nonchalant as he stepped from the plane. The "POWs" were handcuffed, and of all the little details, finding six sets of American handcuffs had been one of the most difficult. They had rehearsed this over and over, but still he wondered privately if they could pull it off.

Heinz went first, "covering" the prisoners with his Tommy gun, looking every bit the American G.I. As Ganz and Meier, two of the "POWs" stepped from the plane, Ganz turned to Meier and said "How about these Americans, eh?" in German. Horstmann stepped forward and grabbed him by the collar, shoving him forward.

"Shut up, Kraut. No talking. No sproechen, eh?" he yelled at him, playing his part to the hilt. Schmidt was amazed – he even mispronounced sproechen enough that it sounded foreign even to him. Horstmann had spent 12 years in America, and had been chosen as the "point man." He would field any questions that came up.

Schmidt just stood by, smoking a cigarette, trying to look bored as the rest of the "prisoners" were hustled roughly from the plane. They were pushed a few times, and gave their oppressors dirty looks. Schmidt saw one man beginning to smile a bit and cleared his throat. The soldier glanced at him and scowled. It was everything Schmidt could do not to smile himself.

Horstmann was already talking with the American corporal who had brought the truck to the airfield. They were having a laugh by the look of it, and Horstmann was giving the man one of his Lucky Strikes.

"Major Peterson is it?" he heard from behind him. Uh-oh, here we go, Schmidt thought. He turned to see an American colonel striding towards him. He came to attention, a few droplets of unbidden sweat beginning to run down inside his collar.

"Yes, Colonel," he said, as the man returned his salute.

"At ease, Major. I'm Colonel Randolph. You bringing these prisoners into the camp?"

"Yes sir. Would you like to see the paperwork?" Schmidt asked as he began digging in his bag.

The colonel waved his hand. "That won't be necessary. I'm sure everything's in order. They'll check you in at the main gate as usual. Usually you come in by train. A bit unusual to see prisoners come in on a plane."

"We got lucky I guess – the plane was being ferried up here anyway to pick up a load of ordnance. Guess they figured they might as well fill it up both ways."

"Haven't seen you here before."

"No sir, this is my first time here."

"Normally they send Scapinsky. Everything okay with him?"

"I'm sorry sir, I'm not sure I've met Scapinsky."

"Really? Oh well, it's a big army now isn't it?" the colonel said with a wink.

"It certainly is, Sir."

"I'm just asking because normally Scapinsky brings me a little something from the boys at the other end. They have a great PX there."

"Oh. I nearly forgot sir," Schmidt said, as he dug into his bag again, this time bringing out a bottle of Kentucky bourbon wrapped in a paper sack, making the colonel's eyes light up.

"Ahhh. Now that's what I'm talking about," the colonel said, peering into the bag. "It's even my brand."

"I can't take credit for that, sir. I'm just relaying it."

"I understand. Appreciated though. Damn boring duty here. Nothing but planes and trains, planes and trains. Care for a quick drink in my office?"

"Thank you sir, but I don't drink." The last thing Schmidt needed was alcohol. He was having enough trouble as it was. He couldn't afford any slipups.

"Mormon?" the officer asked.

"No sir, Dutch Reformed Church."

"Well, I understand. Too bad – Scapinsky and I usually share a quick glass and shoot the shit a little."

"I really have to deliver these prisoners, Sir…"

"Fine, fine. Listen, you'll be staying overnight I assume, they always do. Flagstaff isn't Chicago or anything, but it's a sweet little town. You need anything, you be sure to let me know. Just ring the base."

"Thank you sir, I will."

They shook hands and they saluted each other again, this time more casually. Schmidt couldn't believe the Americans were winning the war…they seemed so blasé about things sometimes. The colonel turned to leave, then turned back.

"Oh, Major? One thing."

"Yes sir?"

"Better tell your men no more abusing the prisoners. No pushing them around unless they misbehave. We aren't Germans after all now, are we?"

"No sir. I'll tell the men."

"Very good. Carry on, Major."

"Yes sir," Schmidt saluted once again as the Colonel left. He strode to the truck and got in on the passenger side, nodding to Horstmann, who said something to the driver and climbed over the rear tailgate of the six-by, sitting next to his comrades and pretending to keep them covered with his weapon.

Schmidt remembered the first time they had practiced this in Mexico, and one of the "prisoners" had reached down to take the Tommy gun from a guard, who had calmly handed it up to him. Schmidt had stopped the rehearsal at that point, pointing out the mistake. It was a small mistake, but one that would get them all hung. He just hoped everyone was as aware as he was, now that they had passed the first test. He opened the door and climbed into the cab, slamming it shut.

"Ready, Major?" the driver asked, totally unaware that he was about to drive an entire platoon of German commandos straight onto the biggest ordnance depot in the country.

"Yes, Corporal. Let's go."

The driver put the truck into gear with a curse, grinding the gears a little. He grinned at the Major and winked. "They give us the old crappy trucks back here, Major. This one needs a new clutch."

Schmidt nodded, not knowing how else to respond, as the truck growled out of first gear and into second, heading away from the airfield. He looked in the rearview mirror and saw Otto Wessling, the copilot, standing there watching them as the fuel truck drove up. Then he turned to wave at the truck with a smile, and Schmidt consulted his watch.

They had less than 90 minutes before the Hortens landed and all hell broke loose. He knew his men were mentally counting personnel, checking machine gun emplacements and any other hard points they could see as they drove out of the airfield, which seemed lightly guarded to him. And why not? he thought. There was no danger here from either German or Japanese attack. The very thought of that made him grin.

"Something funny, Major?"

"No Corporal. Just good to be back home."

"Know what you mean, Sir. I spent three years in the Pacific before I got this leg wound. Just about healed, but I don't reckon they'll be sending me back. This is the sweetest, easiest duty I've ever pulled. Figure we got those damn Jerries licked don't you?"

"You never know, Corporal. Those Germans are tricky bastards."

"That they are, Sir. That they are."

If you only knew, Schmidt thought as they pulled up to the gates. Suddenly he felt very good about this mission. The Americans had no idea what was about to happen. Schmidt stared out the window at the mountains rising in the near distance above Flagstaff and thought of home, and the German Alps. Then he pushed it from his mind and brought his thoughts back to the task at hand...the bombs for the Hortens.

68

ELLIOT ROOSEVELT was busy. He'd gone with his gut and figured they'd head for Navajo Depot, since it was the only target he could think of. He hadn't seen any bombs on the Hortens, but if they strafed the supply trains backed up on the tracks outside Flagstaff all hell was going to break loose.

He was lucky. The Hortens had vectored north only after flying to Sedona. They didn't know the area obviously, and were taking the safe route, whereas he cut them off by heading directly towards Williams. They had appeared on his radar just as he flashed over Sycamore Canyon. He caught them over the Secret Mountain Wilderness, coming in on their left flank, the sun behind them, outlining them clearly.

If his guns had been calibrated properly he would have taken at least one of them, but he missed. They didn't give him a second chance and peeled off in two different directions, heading back towards Sedona. Elliot added power and rolled back elevator, going for altitude, not wanting them above him. By the time he rolled over they were gone, heading back to the red rocks. He knew he was being suckered, but he had no choice but to follow.

"EAGLE ONE, EAGLE ONE, COME IN, DAMMIT," he heard in his headphones, realizing the radio had been squawking at him for some time.

"Eagle One here. Eagle Two come in."

"Where are you, One?"

"Secret Mountain, headed for Sedona. Fired on two bogies, no effect. Now heading zero niner zero."

"Roger. I'm coming in on your right, heading three four zero, altitude 8850."

"We're at 9320 Two. You'll want to get above them."

"Roger that One. Going up."

Jake sent the P-80 hurtling upward, trying to get altitude on the two Germans. They hadn't counted on any opposition, that was for sure. Jake wondered what they were thinking. Why were they headed for Sedona? He and Elliot had talked about it, and the only possible target they could think of was Navajo Depot, in Bellemont. Regardless, he had to catch them. He throttled up a little more, mentally urging the plane forward.

* * * * *

Fullgräbe was wondering where the jet had come from. He thought it was just a regular fighter until they had turned to run. He planned on just leaving it in the dust, but the plane had turned and come after them far too quickly.

"I didn't know the Americans had jets," Mink's voice came over the radio.

"It doesn't matter. We'll take him into the rocks and bury him. I'll go left, you go right."

"Roger that, boss. Can I take him?"

Fullgräbe smiled. Pilots, All of them the same. "Yes, you may have the kill. Head for that rock formation over there; we'll take him through it then split on the far side."

69

J AKE WAS sweating. He and Elliot had practiced some high speed maneuvers in the P-80s, but hadn't done much dogfighting with them. He had no doubt that the Germans had far more jet experience, perhaps flying 262s in actual combat. He'd heard a few of the German aces had 200 or even 300 kills to their credit, far more than the two of them together. They were in over their heads and both of them knew it. He searched below the plane on both sides and finally saw them. They looked even more like bats at this angle, and they were going like the proverbial bats out of hell, heading straight for Cathedral Rock.

"Eagle One, Eagle Two. I have bogies in sight, heading zero niner five. Looks like they're going to try and lose us in the rocks. I'm attacking. Need you to head zero eight five for intercept. Expecting them to split up other side of Cathedral Rock."

"Roger, Two, I'm coming up at your 7 o'clock now. I'll take the one that breaks left."

"Roger, One. I'm right behind you." With that, Elliot rolled over and dove, Jake following him, going inverted into a split-S maneuver to enter a high-speed dive, looking up through his canopy to find the strange German fighters, even as black spots began swimming in his vision as he followed Elliot through the high-G maneuver.

The anti-G suits they'd been testing helped, but Jake still had to fight the dizziness as they pulled out of the high speed dive. Now right side up and going like a bat out of hell, Jake could see the Hortens as two fast-moving black specks against the white band of basalt running through Munds Mountain to the north. They were turning south, and Elliot was following them, pulling up into a high yo-yo maneuver in order to scrub off speed and stay behind them.

Dogfighting is the exact opposite of racing. Instead of trying to pass on the inside of a turn and get ahead of the other plane, the danger comes from not turning tight enough and overshooting the turn, allowing the enemy plane to get behind you. Elliot was going high to scrub off speed in order to stay behind the tighter-turning Hortens, arcing up in a parabola, standing the jet on its left wing, riding the limits of the plane until the stall warning screamed at him, then punching full left rudder to drop the nose, diving back behind the Germans again, Jake following his every move, mere seconds behind him, just as they'd practiced for the last several weeks, pushing the planes to their limits.

Suddenly the Germans broke formation, one going left, one right.

"Go right, Two, I'm going left," came Elliot's command.

"Roger," Jake yelled back even as he rolled the P-80 into a high speed turn, extending his speed brakes this time to stay behind the bat-like plane, which could turn like nothing he'd ever seen...and where was the tail section? The damn thing was all wing.

"Watch you don't get caught in their scissors, Two. I've got your six covered, but he's taking you right into the other guy's guns...DIVE, GET OUT OF THERE," Elliot shouted.

Jake didn't think, he just snapped the plane over and dove for the deck as tracers from the other German's 30mm cannon blew past his canopy in a deadly arc.

"He's past you now, Jake. I'm still on his six, but his wingman is turning back in on me."

"Roger, Eagle One, I'm pulling up to take him head on. I'll be right there," Jake yelled as he pulled the screaming jet back up out of the dive, climbing now with his back to the fight, watching his altimeter roll upward as he executed a fast snap roll into an Immelman turn to come level again, attacking the German head on, the two planes closing at over 900 mph.

Then tracers were blowing past his wings again, this time from the front, and Jake was firing his own guns as the black wing came straight at him, it's tiny frontal area presenting a meager target.

"I'm still behind the first one, Jake, but I can't get a shot – he's a slippery bastard...he's heading south now, towards Cathedral Rock."

Jake heard Elliot, but he was busy. Suddenly the two planes were head to head and Jake snap-rolled again, going inverted, rolling the plane just as the German jet flashed beneath him. He got a good look up through the canopy this time and verified that the plane had no tail section, just a point where the trailing edge of each wing met in a graceful curve. It reminded Jake of a picture he'd once seen in National Geographic of a stingray from the South Pacific. How it stayed in the air he didn't know, but it could turn amazingly fast, even faster than the P-80.

Jake rolled upright and climbed to scrub off speed, then stood the jet again on its left wing, looking below him to find that his adversary had broken right as soon as they had passed, just as he had thought he would, and was now speeding away, going after Elliot. He cursed silently.

"Eagle One, second bogey coming up on your six. Break right when I tell you and I'll light him up."

"Roger, Two. Keep your eye on the first one - I think he's going to try something."

Jake rolled over and dove, the three planes ahead of him arcing left towards Cathedral Rock, the wind screaming past his canopy as his airspeed rose above 500 mph. What were the Germans up to? He estimated them to be at about 4800 feet, not nearly high enough to clear the huge rock formation.

The lead plane was jinking back and forth, trying desperately to shake Elliot, but Elliot was staying with him, despite the second German coming up on his tail, trusting his wingman to cover him as he tried in vain to get a shot on the German in front of him.

Suddenly Jake saw tracers. "BREAK RIGHT, BREAK RIGHT – HE'S FIRING," he yelled as Elliot stood the P-80 up on its right wing in a high speed, back-breaking turn. Jake was finally coming into range now and was counting on the second German to follow Elliot right, bringing him into his sights. He flipped up the safety again and prepared to fire as the silver skin of Elliot's jet flashed across his vision…then he realized the German wasn't falling for it, and was instead following the first Horten left, straight at Cathedral Rock.

"He's not going for it. I'm following them down. I'm guessing they'll go around Bell Rock and Courthouse, then swing back north."

"Roger, Eagle Two. I'm come around back east to meet them head-on. Change your partner, dosey – do."

Always the comedian, Jake thought as he leveled out behind the second Horten just in time to see the first German roll 90 degrees, so his wings were vertical, and Jake suddenly understood – the crazy bastard was going through the notch at the top of Cathedral Rock...a notch like a gunsight only about 50 feet wide between the huge, heavy spires that formed a natural amphitheater reaching just over 4,900 above sea level. Jake had never seen Stonehenge except in pictures, but he was sure it paled in comparison to the majesty of Cathedral Rock. The single finger of rock stood in the middle of the formation, the forked rocks like a gunsight, and he watched in amazement as the German jet flew straight through the slot, tipped on edge at over 400 mph.

The second Horten was sideslipping and jinking back and forth, trying to lose Jake, and for a minute he thought the German was going to pull up, but at the last second he too stood the plane on the left wing and slid smoothly through the narrow notch.

"Jake, Pull up. Don't follow those crazy..." Elliot yelled over the radio.

"Too late," Jake mumbled into his oxygen mask as he rolled the plane up into position, canopy towards the spire. He wanted to close his eyes as the huge red rocks sped towards him, but he couldn't. One tiny miscalculation and he was dogmeat.

At 450 mph you don't have time to think, just react, and as he passed through the narrow notch it was everything Jake could do not to flinch as the canopy clipped off a piece of rock the size of his fist...then he was through the other side, pulling back on the stick to break left, following the Germans through a high speed turn towards Bell Rock, a formation that had drawn its name from its obvious resemblance to a giant dinner bell.

"Of all the stupid, crazy shit I've seen you do, that takes the cake, Eagle Two."

"The day is young. I couldn't let them get away now could I? Looks as though I was right – they're going to either bank around Bell and Courthouse or head up Jack's Canyon. They're headed right at you. Let's squeeze 'em."

"Roger, Two. Meet you on the other side," Elliot said.

70

SCHMIDT COULDN'T believe the line of vehicles waiting at the gate to Camp Navajo. The line moved, but slowly. Most seemed to be civilian workers on their way to work, but there were some large transport trucks moving in and out of the gates, presumably carrying ordnance.

He knew from intelligence that some workers lived on base, but many lived in Flagstaff or came in from the Navajo reservation for the week. His driver got out to talk to one of the MPs at the gate, explaining that they had prisoners, and they were waved to a second gate he hadn't noticed, off to the side, obviously just for vehicles not involved with carrying ordnance.

They showed their papers at the gate, and while Schmidt pretended nonchalance, he felt anything but. He hoped they didn't see the sweat on his brow, and apparently they didn't because they were soon waved through the gate and shuttled off to the left, following a neat white sign reading B-4a, and "PW camp" with arrows pointing opposite directions.

As they drove along the access road he could see long lines of bunkers off to his right. To their left was the railroad, crowded with cars waiting to unload. He would have never imagined such a large depot. It was larger even than the one in Frankfurt, which he had thought huge. The Americans did everything big. It was amazing, really.

It was just a mile to the prisoner of war camp, but there was a turn-off to section B-4a coming up soon. Schmidt put his hand on his pistol.

"Nervous, Major?" The driver asked.

"No, I'm fine," Schmidt responded as the sign for the turn came into view. He pulled his .45 out and pointed it at the driver's head. "Turn right here."

The driver looked at the gun, then at Schmidt. "You got to be kidding me. What is this? The prisoner of war camp is the other direction. What's with the gun?"

"I am not kidding. Turn right here or I will blow your brains out."

The driver made the turn, driving slowly down through the bunkers, row after row of them, until they came to a long wooden building with small windows. Two Navajos were strapping crates to a pallet as they drove up. Schmidt knew that in the back of the truck the "guards" were handing their sidearms to the "prisoners". They didn't have much time. He hoped everything else was in place. He double-checked the number on the building.

"This is it. Turn in here."

"Listen pal, I don't know who you are, but…"

Schmidt hit the driver in the mouth with his pistol and turned the wheel himself, pulling the truck into the packed dirt yard next to the warehouse.

"Stop here. Don't make me tell you again."

The driver stopped the truck, and Schmidt heard Giesler and Horstmann climb out of the back. They walked towards the workers.

"Prisoner work detail. Who's in charge here?"

"Major Ramsey. He's inside," one of the Indians said with a toss of his head.

"Take us to him will you?" Giesler said with a smile.

"ALL RIGHT. EVERYONE OUT," Horstmann yelled into the truck, still playing the game.

Schmidt hit the driver behind the ear with the pistol and felt him slump onto the seat. He quickly handcuffed him and stuffed a handkerchief in his mouth, then got out of the truck just as the door to the warehouse opened. A spit - and - polish officer stood there, hands on hips.

"Major Ramsey?"

"Yes?"

"I'm Major Peterson. I was ordered to bring these men over to clean up the grounds."

"This is a restricted area, Major, you should know that," Major Ramsey said, as Schmidt closed the distance between them. Giesler walked up on Ramsey's left, his Thompson slung casually under his arm.

"You know how it is, Major. Idle hands and all that."

"You're new here, aren't you? I haven't seen you around. Listen, I mean it. No POWs allowed in this area. You understand? I'm going to call HQ and have your crew sent somewhere else."

Giesler pulled the machinegun up and pointed it at the Major, as the rest of Schmidt's men did the same, several covering the Navajo workers, motioning with their weapons for them to go inside. The men needed no urging. Ramsey looked around at the POWs, who were all pointing their pistols at him, at the MPs who were supposed to be guarding them, and got a very, very bad taste in his mouth.

"Inside. NOW," Schmidt said.

Suddenly a jeep with two MPs in it came tearing past the corner of the building, then stopped. Schmidt motioned to his men to lower their weapons. The POWs hid their pistols. He looked at the American major intently.

"I don't have to tell you to stay quiet do I?" Major Ramsey shook his head in response, his eyes as big as dinner plates.

Schmidt turned to find the jeep backing up. The driver put it in gear, pulled in behind the truck and shut it off, letting it coast the last few paces. The sergeant in the passenger seat swung himself out and approached warily.

"Major Ramsey? Everything okay here?" he said, fingering his M1 carbine nervously.

"Hello, son. Forgotten how to salute a superior officer?" Schmidt said with authority, hands on hips. The sergeant came to immediate attention, as Schmidt knew he would. These Americans might be a bit slack compared to the German army, but they weren't that slack. Schmidt returned his salute desultorily, then took a couple steps closer.

"At ease, Sergeant. We're just cleaning a few things up for Major Ramsey. I'm Major Peterson. I'm new here. So, what's the problem?"

The GI relaxed noticeably. "Sorry, sir. It's just that POWs are not allowed in this part of the camp. It's off limits." He looked both ways, then at the "POWs" who had hidden their weapons and were again playing the part. "Live ordnance sir, if you know what I mean."

"Ahhh. Well, sergeant. We'll get them right out of here then," he said with a smile. "Since you know so much about the area, and I'm new here, let me ask you another question." Schmidt had moved closer and put his arm around the shorter man's shoulder conspiratorially, leading him between the jeep and the truck, using the man's body to block the movement of his right hand. "I was just wondering where a guy could get a bottle of…"

In one swift motion Schmidt drew the silenced 9mm pistol from beneath his tunic, pressed it against the sergeant's body, and shot him through the heart, close enough to feel his body jerk in response, then took a quick step to his right and brought the pistol to bear on the driver of the jeep, who had frozen, a cigarette dangling from his lip.

He made a half-hearted effort to get the jeep started and in reverse before Schmidt shot him, right through the windshield, in the middle of the forehead. He stared at Schmidt for another second as if he couldn't believe it, then collapsed over the wheel. Schmidt let go of the sergeant and he fell to the ground. He looked down at his tunic. There was blood on it.

"You bastard." Major Ramsey said hoarsely.

"Klein, Hess. Get the bodies inside and the jeep around back. Clean this mess up. Major, you look about my size," he finished, stripping off his tunic calmly.

71

J AKE FOLLOWED the Hortens into a high speed turn around Bell Rock
and Courthouse Butte, finally getting a good look at the things for the
first time as they banked left in front of him. They looked like one giant
wing, swept back to form a rounded triangle, with the wingtips dipping
back into the body at the trailing edge in a graceful arc, then meeting at the
centerline in a sharp point where the tail assembly would be on most
planes. He didn't understand how it could even fly.

The jet engine nacelles flanked each side of the cockpit, and the mottled
brown and black paint scheme was some of the most effective camouflage
he'd seen, nearly impossible to see from above. The belly was sky blue, and
matched the azure Arizona sky almost perfectly. He tried turning inside the
German jet so he could get guns on it, but there was no way; the damn
things were too quick, and turned on a dime.

As they came around the butte Elliot came back on the radio, but there
was static. "Coming in on you at eight o'clock Eagle Two. Will be passing
you in a dive and engaging targets."

"Roger, Eagle One," Jake replied as Elliot passed him high on his left,
having gone for altitude in a tactical loop on the west side of the butte as
Jake followed the Hortens around to the east. Elliot timed it perfectly,
firing his guns at the rear plane, holding the trigger down as he passed him,
then coming off guns as he passed below their altitude.

When Elliot finally pulled up Jake estimated he was no more than 500
feet off the deck, then he passed under the rear plane and pulled up out of
the dive into a scissors, and Jake saw Elliot's guns flash again as the lead
Horten passed through his gunsights again, but no joy.

The lead Horten immediately rolled twice, fast, then broke right as
Elliot followed, heading straight for the gap between Munds Mountain and
Twin Buttes, in the direction of Marg's Draw. They passed each side of
Submarine Rock as the second Horten followed, with Jake right behind

him. The second Horten suddenly pulled up into a steep climb, and Jake went after him but the German pilot rolled over, going inverted, and dove, reversing direction in a reverse half-Cuban eight. Jake cursed as he pushed the stick over and dove after him, thinking he should have seen that coming.

The maneuver bought the Horten a little room, and he used it to bank around right near the east side of Mitten Ridge, heading into Bear Wallow Canyon, and Jake saw that his plan was to get behind Elliot, who'd followed the first Horten in from the east, heading northwest towards Schnebly Hill.

Jake rolled right, then snapped left, going up and over the ridge to meet him on the other side. Having grown up flying in the area gave him an advantage, but he still hadn't picked up enough on the German to go to guns.

The Mogollon Rim loomed closer and closer and at 500 mph it was coming up mighty fast, but Jake broke left before the Horten did, cutting the arc and closing the gap further.

"Eagle Two, Eagle Two, this guy is *good*. Do you have eyes on the other Horten?"

"Affirmative, Eagle One. He's at your seven but not close enough to fire yet."

"Roger. I'd appreciate it if you'd keep him off my ass, Two; I'm a little busy up here."

"Doing my best, One."

"Eagle Two, he just rolled into Oak Creek Canyon, low as hell. I'm following him in," Elliot's voice came over the radio, beginning to break up a bit, reminding Jake they'd had some radio issues last couple of times up.

"Negative, One, it's too tight to turn in there. Pull up and take him from above."

"Too late, I'm passing Grasshopper Point now."

There was heavy static on the radio again, something they'd intended to look at before taking the planes up again.

Dammit, Jake thought, why is he being so dense? He needs to go high and pin him down coming up out of the canyon. This was too hairy a game at 500 mph.

"Negative Eagle One. Too dangerous." There was no response, and Jake cursed silently. Now was not the time to lose comms.

He let the Horten go left in pursuit, and he went high and right, knowing he'd pick him up on the other side, rolling inverted as he passed the Cow Pies on his right, keeping it tight as he passed over Mitten Ridge, and picking up a little more on the Horten who had gone around the north end, but as he rolled the P-80 back upright on the other side of the ridge he saw he was a little closer, but still not yet in gun range. The German had picked up too much time on him with the Cuban Eight move. Jake saw the Horten turn on its side and disappear into Oak Creek Canyon and cursed. I guess we're all nuts, he thought as he followed him into the narrow gap above the creek.

72

WHEN SCHMIDT and his men entered the building, everyone working at the benches looked up curiously at them, their eyes widening when they saw their guns and that some of them were POWs. Schmidt jabbed the now tunic-less Major Ramsey in the ribs with his pistol.

"EVERYONE LISTEN UP, Ramsey said loudly. "You are to do exactly as these men tell you. Their...officer has given me his word that you will not be harmed as long as you don't scream or panic. Just do what they say and everything will be all right."

"Who are these men? They think they can just barge in here..."

"Laurel, for God's sake be quiet!" Ramsey said.

"You would do well to listen to the Major, fraulein," Schmidt said.

Laurel's mouth dropped open and her eyes grew wide. "GERMANS. You're just a bunch of dirty, stinking Germans."

Schmidt slapped her hard enough to turn her head. She raised a trembling hand to her mouth. Her lip was bleeding.

"Is that how you got to be the master race? Beating your women?"

Schmidt slapped her again, backhanding her this time, spinning her head back in the other direction.

"Only women who do not keep their mouths shut," he said calmly.

"MAJOR. Is this necessary?" Ramsey asked, putting himself between Schmidt and the young woman, who was looking at him with a mix of amazement and hatred.

"It will be my pleasure to teach this hündin some manners. She comes with us."

Laurel turned to a man standing behind her, fists clenched. "Harry, Do something."

"And take him as well; the sullen one. According to his uniform he's a pilot and should be able to help us identify what we need. Tie up the rest and gag them. Lock the doors behind you. We don't have much time,"

Schmidt said. One of the 'POW's smiled at Harry just before he jammed the M1 carbine he'd taken off the dead sergeant in the jeep into his stomach.

"SCHNELL. LET'S GO PEOPLE. WE ARE ON A SCHEDULE," Schmidt yelled, looking at his watch briefly just before grabbing Laurel roughly by the arm and pushing her towards the door.

The commandos had practiced this also, sneaking into the SS barracks in Berchtesgaden and overpowering, then tying up their own comrades. They weren't very well liked for it, but they had become very adept. It wasn't long before they had everyone in the building restrained and gagged and were piling back into the truck and the jeep. Schmidt considered taking the second jeep, but felt the bullet hole in the windshield would give it away.

"Get in," he said, climbing in and starting the engine. He saw his other "guest" struggling with his captors. "Put him in back." The commandos dumped Harry unceremoniously into the back of the jeep, then ran for the truck, which was already running. Schmidt backed the jeep out into the road.

"Which way?"

"You bastard, did you have to hit me so hard?"

"They had to be convinced it was real, but I'll hit you again if you don't tell me."

"Then why didn't you hit Harry? That way," Laurel responded, gesturing with her chin while digging in the pocket of her denim work apron and coming out with a pack of Pall Malls, lighting one with difficulty as they bumped and jounced down the gravel path.

"What the hell you talkin' about? His guy hit me in the stomach with his carbine!" Harry whined.

"Turn here. Cigarette?"

"Think you could take these cuffs off?" Harry said.

"Bad idea. Wait until we get there. Then my excuse will be that you need your hands to help load the bombs...you did get them didn't you?"

"Yes, four," Laurel said.

"Excellent…and they have been repaired?"

"Re-arsenaled? Yes. Do you think this is my first rodeo?"

"What?"

"Never mind," Laurel said, blowing smoke out the side of her mouth as they turned in towards another building, this one with a loading dock. "Here. I was told to give you this. It's urgent. You are to read it immediately."

Schmidt took the narrow, dark brown envelope whose color reminded him of the brown uniforms the SA wore, and tore it open as he drove, reading the single sheet it held as the envelope fluttered away.

"Mein Gott, new orders. Foolishness. Our secondary target has changed. They have information that the vice-president of the United States is visiting Sedona, just a few air miles from here. They want us to capture him."

"The vice-president is next in line to the presidency. Kidnapping or killing him will be an incredible psychological victory," Laurel said.

Schmidt shook his head. "No. We are here, now. We could burn Navajo Depot and Flagstaff to the ground with the second pair of bombs we have and the trains holding that ordnance. There'd be a chain reaction – it'd take out the tracks halfway to Flagstaff. As a military target it doesn't get much better. The Werewolf training we had in Berchtesgaden was in preparation for just this sort of infiltration and sabotage. We have a chance to do something great here, but they want me to go chasing a ghost," Schmidt said, obviously unhappy.

"Besides, the odds that he is actually where they say he is are astronomical," he continued as they pulled up in front of another building nearly identical to the first, and the truck with the men in it pulled up beside them and stopped. The commandos piled out of the truck, surrounding the building, while Navajo workmen watched in amazement.

"From what they told me of you, Herr Schmidt, I did not realize you were one to disobey orders so easily," Laurel said.

Schmidt gave her a dirty look. "What assurance can you give me that he's actually there?"

"I verified the information personally. I assure you, at this very moment the vice-president is in Sedona, at Smoke Trail Ranch, more specifically at Jack and Helen Frye's new house. I grew up in the area. I will guide you."

"No. Our orders are to jump into the area."

"I will jump with you."

"Nein. You will not."

"That is where you are wrong, Herr Schmidt. I *will* be jumping with you," Laurel replied. "I was trained for this, and my orders demand it. I live in Sedona, so I can be of use to you. I can guide you to your objective."

"You are not qualified. Not for a low-level jump such as this."

"I *am* qualified, and I *am* jumping with you. I have my orders, same as you."

Schmidt shrugged. "Fine, but you break your pretty little legs, we're leaving you." He shut off the jeep, uncuffed Harry, and strode up the concrete steps to the dock. Laurel and Harry followed, Harry rubbing his wrists where the cuffs had been.

The large sliding doors of the loading dock were built like barn doors, and slid back and forth on rails. Harry grasped the handle of one and pulled it open, and there, gleaming blackly in the lights of the warehouse were four 1,000 lb. bombs. Schmidt inspected them quickly, checking the mounts, then running his hands over the sleek length of them. He couldn't help but smile. What a surprise the Americans had coming, and with their own bombs...

"HE, penetrator type, just as you asked. These babies'll cut fifteen feet of concrete like butter," Harry said, a used car salesman working a customer.

"How did you keep them on the dock so long?"

"Easy, when you have the right paperwork," Harry grinned. "They were scheduled for hot deployment, but someone asked for a re-inspect. Seems the girls in Building 17 have been turning out some shoddy work lately." He winked at Laurel as Schmidt looked at his watch and turned to his men.

"Let's get these on that truck and get out of here. We have to be back at the airport in 20 minutes."

73

A S HE rolled the P-80 up onto its left wing, Jake caught a glimpse of Elliot's plane a little further up the canyon, going like a bat out of hell, then the second Horten swung through his sights and he squeezed off a quick burst but missed as the pilot zigged back right, following the canyon.

At 500 mph things happen quickly, and as Jake rolled the plane back to the right to follow he heard trees scraping the bottom of the fuselage. This close to the ground everything happened faster, and it felt like he was doing Mach 2. He and Elliot had flown the canyon, but never *this* low. This was nuts. One little mistake and he'd end up a part of Wilson Mountain, which rose up on his left; a huge, unmovable massif.

He saw the Horten Elliot was following suddenly pull up to the right in a classic vector roll reversal, and Elliot went straight up, bending the plane over backwards to meet him at the top, but Jake saw tracers from the second Horten rising to meet him, and watched in horror as 30mm cannon rounds stitched through Elliot's left wing. There was a small explosion, then Elliot's P-80, still in a steep climb, began trailing inky black smoke from the wing. He saw Elliot invert the plane in order to bail out…

"ELLIOT – GET OUT, GET OUT!" he screamed into the mike, forgetting his radio wasn't working as he fought to get the second Horten in his sights.

The bat-like plane rolled right, then tried to follow the other Horten up, but Jake was faster. He rolled left and dove, then pulled out, using the extra speed to pull up and to the right seconds before hitting the trees lining Oak Creek. The plane came out of the dive screaming, and then the Horten was there, in his sights, right in front of him, passing left to right like the world's fastest kite, and he lined up the sights and pulled the trigger.

Tracers tore straight across the middle of the Horten, right through both engines, and the plane exploded in midair, pieces of the plane showering down into Oak Creek and the scree slope just below Wilson

Mountain. Jake pulled the plane up and climbed, going inverted as he rose above the lip of the canyon, searching feverishly for Elliot and the other Horten.

He saw a flash of sunlight momentarily, and Jake realized it was Elliot's plane, in free fall now, the left wing missing entirely, spinning too quickly now for him to bail out, trailing fire and smoke, until it hit the upper eastern slope above the rim and disappeared in a huge fireball.

Jake's eyes hurt from the strain of combat, so he pulled back again and shot upward, going for altitude to get a better perspective, hoping to find Elliot's parachute and with luck the other Horten as well, which even now could be lining him up in its sights.

He pulled out at 10,000 feet, rolled upright and pulled a large, relatively slow circle around the burning wreckage, hoping that Elliot had the presence of mind to bail...then he saw it, a white parachute with a man swinging slowly beneath it, just before it disappeared into the tree line on the eastern rim, on the Mund's Park side.

Jake breathed a sigh of relief as he saw the chute settle, hoping Elliot wasn't hurt too badly. Remembering the other Horten was now hunting him, he pulled back on the stick again and added power, going higher, pulling another circle, but he still didn't see it. He went around one more time, but the Horten was gone, and he had no idea where.

74

THE BOMBS were quickly loaded onto the truck and secured with cargo straps before the forklift was even clear. Schmidt's men had practiced this with dummy bombs and a captured American truck so many times that it was second nature to them. The men had grumbled about Schmidt's stopwatch during training, but it had paid off. Everyone knew just where they should be, and they loaded and secured the weapons in record time. Seconds after the forklift was parked and shut off, the truck was already rolling, the last man pulled into the back by the outstretched hands of his comrades. The jeep led the way, both vehicles tearing at a breakneck pace back towards the main gate.

He was afraid it would come to this. Given enough time they had planned to bluff their way through the gates, and he had no doubt that it would have worked...but there was no time now. The planes would be landing at Williams in a matter of minutes, and if Schmidt and his men weren't there to provide security and load the bombs the mission would be over.

They rushed headlong toward the gate, Schmidt honking his horn and waving at the MPs to get out of the way. Miraculously, they did, staring open mouthed at the jeep and truck which blew past two other trucks and a jeep stopped at the exit point, and through the gate, which had just been opened for another driver - a colonel by the looks of it - and who honked his horn angrily. Not a shot was fired, but through the guardhouse window Schmidt could see an MP on the phone, gesturing wildly.

They turned onto the frontage road leading to the airfield and picked up speed, honking their horns and waving to the oncoming vehicles to get out of the way. Schmidt was amazed that they moved, but they did. They still think we're Americans, he thought.

Halfway to Williams they entered the woods and Schmidt slowed, then stopped the jeep. He left it running and ran back to the truck which had stopped behind him. Jumping up on the running boards, he looked at Horstmann and Giesler.

"When we get to the gate at the airfield, no firing. I'll try and bluff us through. Get the "prisoners" down on the floor of the truck and point your weapons at their heads. I'll tell them we have an emergency delivery, planes are coming in, and they came to help with the weight."

"Will it work, sir?" Horstmann asked.

"I don't know, but it's better than being shot at, eh? That will come soon enough. I'll try and take out the guards with my pistol. Once I do I'll need two men to move the bodies and take their places."

"Yes, sir," Giesler said grimly.

"As soon as they hear firing, the two men placed there will fall back to the plane. Tell them not to miss it; we can't wait for them."

"Yes, Herr Sturmführer."

"Good luck."

"You too, sir. Heil Hitler."

"Heil Hitler. Let's go."

75

THE C-47 sat on the runway waiting for them. They wasted no time here; the men they had left at the gate couldn't hold off an attack forever. They could hear the sirens from Camp Navajo still winding up and down, and could imagine the chaos going on there.

Four of his men took the jeep and were on their way to the control center, run out of a tiny trailer, to silence the radio and the men manning it. Schmidt scanned the sky for the jets, but so far nothing. He cursed. If the planes were late they would all die here once the Americans figured what was going on. Schmidt had no doubt that they had just kicked over a hornet's nest, and they were running out of time.

Then he heard a roaring, which quickly grew louder, and looked south to find a black speck growing rapidly larger. It was a Horten…but just one. It overflew the field just as Schmidt heard the rattle of automatic weapons fire from the air control center where his men were machine-gunning the technicians.

The black jet banked, turning to come back to the field. This time it came in, landing gear down, screaming over the ground like some vicious phantom from a Wagner opera. As it touched down he yelled to his men, and they started driving out to where they thought the plane would stop. They had practiced this seemingly simple maneuver with Galland's aircrews many times, and it was deceptively difficult.

They had no problems this time, but as Schmidt's men jumped from the truck, some to secure the perimeter, others leaping to the back to cut the bombs free, Schmidt squinted at the sky again. There was no sign of the second jet. He ran to the plane with Meier and another man, and as it came to a halt on the warm pavement, they threw the simple wooden ladder they had brought with them on the C-47 against the side of the jet. The cockpit slid open, and he saw it was Fullgräbe.

"Where is the other jet?" Schmidt demanded.

Fullgräbe just looked at him and shook his head. "We had a problem. We ran into a couple of American planes... jets. I couldn't believe it. Wilhelm augered in."

"Which mission was yours?"

"Boulder Dam."

"Gut. That is the more critical of the two. We now have new orders but we will try and set some charges here nonetheless."

"Herr Major, we are almost finished loading the weapon," Giesler said from behind him.

"Gut. Prime the other three bombs with timers. We don't have time to set them on the tracks unfortunately. We will park the truck in the middle of the runway and time it to detonate once we are airborne. It won't stop some smaller planes from using the airfield, but it'll stop any jets from landing. SCHNELL." He turned to Fullgräbe and thrust his hand at him. "Good luck. You are a brave man to serve the Fatherland this way. Where will you land after dropping the bombs?"

"Why, I thought I might fly to Los Angeles. A low-level pass in this thing over the city might do much propaganda - wise don't you think?"

"But where will you land?"

"I'll figure that out when I run out of fuel," Fullgräbe said.

They exchanged a salute and a smile, then Schmidt helped close the canopy and climbed to the ground, pulling the ladder away and running for the C-47 with the others. He waved to the pilot of the transport to fire up the engines just as he heard the whine of the Horten's engines firing up behind him. He could see two of his men who had taken care of the control center running to the gate to support their friends, as the two men he'd left at the gate began firing at a convoy of jeeps coming down the access road from Camp Navajo as Horstmann and another commando ran to the plane.

The other six men were piling into the C-47, which was running up, the engines coughing and belching smoke as they caught, the props beginning to spin in earnest. His men at the gate were doomed, and they knew it. He knew they would not abandon their post until their comrades were in the air.

He said a quick prayer for them, hoping they made it away into the woods surrounding the airfield. Once into the woods they would be difficult for the Americans to find. Perhaps they would have the opportunity to blow a few rail cars carrying ordnance - the original plan. He thought about the damage a couple American 1,000 pounders would have done to the railway and once more he silently cursed his superiors for changing the plan as the American transport plane began bumping down the runway, gathering speed.

A couple of stray bullets hit the fuselage, but no one was hit. The feeling of the plane lifting off was the first time Schmidt had ever felt good about it. His men were already stripping off the POW and American army uniforms and donning their own. It was the one condition Kessler had made of Skorzeny; that they would fight, and perhaps die, as German soldiers of the Third Reich.

He watched as his men checked their weapons, and was not surprised that many kept the American .45 automatic pistols they had been "issued". They were excellent weapons, and he himself had decided to keep his as well, transferring the holster to his own belt, on the right hand side, American style. His smaller Hsc he kept in the regular clamshell holster at his left side, the four-cell magazine pouch attached to his Y-harness on the right, facing left, giving his left hand ready access to his MP40 magazines.

A double G43 pouch rode on his left hip behind his small holster, his breadbag in its usual place at the rear right-hand side. He tied the submachine gun off to his pack and slung the G43 which Kessler had relinquished to him with great regret. They would be forced to jump with their weapons American style because of the lack of drop containers, something they had never done before. He cursed General Lasch again under his breath.

For the hundredth time Schmidt and his men prepared to jump into enemy territory, but this time in the heart of America. It felt different somehow. He had given the pilot the coordinates from their new orders, and they were flying south, back towards Sedona, in the direction from which the Horten had come. Rocks and cactus, he thought. It would be a difficult landing.

He ducked into the cockpit. "How long?"

"About fifteen minutes," the pilot yelled back.

"Give me the light when you're ready."

"Of course, sir."

76

JAKE DIDN'T want to leave Elliot, but he knew he had to. He tried the radio again, to report the crash, but got nothing but static. He had no idea where the German jet had gone, so he gambled. The nearest military facilities he knew of other than their airfield in Cottonwood were Navajo Depot and the airfield in Williams. He could think of no other target. Why and how the Germans got two planes into the country and what they were doing here was beyond him, but he decided to fly to Williams, and at the very least he could report the incident since his radio didn't seem to be working. He could also direct search and rescue to Elliot. He just hoped he was all right. He rolled the P-80 over and headed north.

On the five-minute flight to Williams he had a terrible thought. What if this were part of a much larger attack? Could that be why his radio wasn't working? It seemed ridiculous on the face of it that the Germans could mount such an attack at this stage in the war, yet he'd just seen and fought two experimental German jet fighters that were like nothing he'd ever seen or even been briefed on. He decided to keep his eyes open, just in case.

Upon reaching Williams Jake tried the radio yet again, changing to the frequency the Williams air control used, but for whatever reason he couldn't raise the tower. He and Elliot had used the airfield quite often, sometimes loading dummy ordnance from Navajo Depot to test the different dynamics of the planes with a bomb load, and even practicing low-level bombing runs, which they found were more difficult in a plane with the speed of the jets.

As he flashed over the field, he saw a C-47 starting up its engines with a belch of black exhaust, then a 6x6 truck moving in the middle of the runway, which was odd. He came around and made the usual high-speed break into the landing pattern, pulling "G" to approach speed. Now lined up with the runway, he lowered his landing gear as he watched the C-47 taxiing into position for take-off. He saw men running from the truck to the plane and wondered what was going on, but lost sight as he waved off and went around to give the C-47 room to take off, unaware the enemy was aboard.

He tried the radio again, but again there was still no answer. The C-47 finally took off and headed south, but the damn truck was still sitting in the middle of the runway, blocking it. What the hell? He was on final approach again with reduced power and full flaps, determined to land and get Elliot help. If he came in and dropped it just the other side of the truck there was room to stop, but just barely. They'd have to move the damn thing before he took back...

The flash from the explosion nearly blinded him he was so close, and the shockwave buffeted the plane as he pulled up, slamming the throttle fully forward. The plane screamed as he passed through a column of flame and inky black smoke. 'What the hell is going on?' he asked himself as he fought for control of the jet as it wobbled in the turbulence.

77

THE PLANE seemed undamaged by the blast, but it'd been close. If Jake had been landing ten seconds earlier...he retracted the flaps and banked the P-80 around the airfield so he could look down at what resembled a huge fire pit in the middle of the runway where the truck had been. All that was left of the truck were a few pieces of torn metal a hundred yards away. He couldn't believe he was seeing this. Did that mean there were enemy soldiers on the ground? Did the Horten attack from above and he didn't see it?

He was glad now he hadn't landed because a takeoff was now impossible with the middle of the runway gone. He never would have gotten back in the air.

It looked like a couple of thousand-pounders had hit in the same spot, and he wondered what had been on that truck, and who had parked it there. Should he follow the C-47 heading south? It seemed suspicious, but his concern now was still the other Horten.

He saw American Army vehicles tearing across the airfield from the direction of Navajo Depot and tried the radio again, but knew they used a different range of frequencies, and he didn't even know if his radio still worked. Again, he got nothing but static. Raising his landing gear, he checked his fuel. Fortunately the wing tip tanks had been full when they'd taken off, and he'd been so busy he'd forgotten to drop them as he usually would in a dogfight. It looked as though he were down about a third. Not knowing what else to do, Jake went up, to get perspective.

Another key technique in dogfighting is to get above your enemy and attack from the rear. Jake had no idea where the Horten had gone, or if it were still in the vicinity, but if it had landed at Williams, perhaps to refuel, it couldn't be far. The possibilities hurt his head. Maybe he'd see it if he could get higher.

He leveled off at 15,000 feet, reduced his power to economy cruise and set the plane in a gentle bank to the left, circling the airfield. The P-80 was still faster than any prop plane, so he had to scribe a larger circle because of the airspeed.

On the third time around, just as Jake had given up any hope of spotting the Horten, he caught a glimpse of a flash of reflected sunlight several miles to the west, heading approximately 270. With no other options, Jake banked around and headed west, wondering for the hundredth time just what the hell was going on, and wishing his damn radio were working. Elliot would have to wait.

78

SCHMIDT WENT back and flashed both hands once to his men to let them know it would be ten minutes. They were as ready as they would ever be. They would be jumping at low level, something they'd all had experience with except for the two Americans. It was dangerous, but they had to jump low, around 500 feet, behind the bluff near the ranch so they'd be out of line-of-sight of the security men he was sure would be protecting the vice-president. They would make their way to the house on foot, following the blue line marked as Oak Creek on his crude map. Once on the ground they should be able to make it there in less than an hour, he figured. Still, he was glad he had the two Americans to guide him. The terrain they were flying over was some of the most rugged he'd seen.

The light by the door turned red and the fallschirmjäger stood as they had a hundred times before. Schmidt couldn't help but feel a little thrill go through him as his men tumbled from the open doorway just as they had over France, Crete, Greece, and half a dozen other places.

The landing was a little rough, with two men managing to land in some cactus, their comrades berating them with sly smiles as they helped them pull the spines from their buttocks and backs. The woman landed fine, but the American flyer managed to get off course in the wind, disappearing silently into the next draw.

Schmidt cursed as they buried their parachutes. He didn't have time to search for the man, but they had no choice - the Americans had been tasked with showing them a path to the ranch where they would find the vice-president, Harry S Truman. They shouldered their packs, slung their weapons at the ready, and moved off into the woods to search for him.

It took an hour, and they never would have found Harry had not Horstmann noticed the flapping white sheet above them on the canyon wall. They found him hanging from a tree on a ledge, with both arms, one leg and his neck broken. The wind must have swept him directly into the sheer rock face, and he had put out his hands and feet to stop himself, but was going too fast.

The impact was no less than that of a severe autobahn accident, and the results very similar. He expected the woman to cry a bit when they brought him down off the rocks. She didn't show any emotion, merely watching impassively as they buried him wrapped in his parachute while she stood by smoking a cigarette, and once more Schmidt saw the coldness within her. She was beautiful, but he had no doubt that she would slit his throat if she were ordered to. He recognized a little of himself in her; the part that would do anything required to accomplish the mission.

"It's up to you now. Can you guide us to the ranch?" he asked her.

She nodded. "We're just west of there. We just have to continue east until we reach Oak Creek, then follow it back upstream to the house."

"Let's go then, before the vice-president is warned and this entire mission is for nothing," Schmidt said, still wondering if he should have disobeyed orders and destroyed the rail cars full of ordnance as the original mission dictated. This thing with the vice-president was a fool's errand, but he had his orders.

"Horstmann, get the men in line. Let's go, single file."

79

CATES LED his mule slowly along the creek bed, his old Remington 14A pump in one hand just in case. After a mountain lion had killed several of their cattle a few years back, and attacked him, he didn't take any chances when in the backcountry. The mule had earned the unenviable but accurate name of "Cottonmouth" due to its penchant for biting, but Cates knew the ornery old cuss still was the most surefooted of his animals, and besides, the damn thing hadn't bitten him in awhile.

The last time it had happened Cates had promised Cottonmouth an early retirement via his .44-40 Colt, and that had seemed to do the trick...but he still kept an eye on him.

He was going to collect Harry Truman, Doc Edwards and Jack Frye, then take them hunting grouse near Sycamore Pass, the other side of the Cock's Comb, a rock formation named for an obvious similarity to a rooster's topknot. An Indian had told him there was an old trail from there all the way up to the Mogollon Rim, and that the deer got fat there. He believed him, as it was good country for rabbits and grouse as well.

The packsaddle creaked and moaned softly, the only other sounds the soft scuff of the horse's feet on the rock and the mule's breathing, which seemed to blend with the wind through the trees, punctuated by an occasional songbird or gecko skittering through the brush.

Supposedly someone had found a Spanish conquistador's helmet and dagger up in Sycamore Canyon somewhere, and Cates' imagination ran wild with thoughts of a chest full of doubloons hidden under an overhang somewhere. It was this fantasy that filled his attention, so he didn't hear the birds go quiet.

"Stop please. Drop the weapon and get off the horse."

Cates blinked the sweat out of his eyes as two German soldiers in tropical uniforms and strange camouflage smocks stood up from behind boulders on each side of the trail. He dropped the rifle on the ground, then dismounted slowly, while keeping his eyes on the two men. He recognized the look in their eyes which signaled their willingness to kill him. He had seen it before. What the hell were German soldiers doing *here* of all places? He just couldn't believe it.

Four more men appeared, two of them moving down the trail past him to take up security positions, a third coming forward to pick up the gun and search him carefully. His knife was taken along with his belt and tinder pouch. The man searching looked at him icily for a moment, then took the items back to the fourth man, who examined them carefully. He took the rifle with interest.

"Unusual weapon," he said in perfectly unaccented English.

"Where'd you learn to speak English, Jerry?" Cates said, as he dismounted.

The officer smiled at this, hugely amused. Then he became serious.

"Washington D.C. Who else is with you?"

"I'm an advance scout for the Seventh Cavalry, out on maneuvers. You'd better skedaddle, they'll be coming up behind me soon."

"Skeedaddle? I have not heard this term before," the officer said. "Hans, what does it mean?"

"It means run away with our tails between our legs," one of the first men who stopped him replied, also in flawless English. Cates noted that neither his eyes nor the muzzle of his weapon had wavered in the least. He had the distinct idea that this kid wanted to kill him. He just couldn't figure it. They all seemed to speak English extremely well. Germans who spoke English fluently, here in Arizona? Mysteries on mysteries. All in all, Cates was getting a very bad feeling about this.

"Your name?"

"Benjamin Franklin."

Cates could see the amusement bleed out of the officer's face. He nodded to the man who had taken his gear, and he stepped forward and struck Cates in the stomach with the stock of his submachine gun, doubling him over. He fell to his knees, gasping. The officer came over and knelt down before him, covered by his friend with the submachine gun who had just given him the good news.

"Enough joking. Custer is long dead and there is no one coming to help you. You are alone, and you have stepped into something you should not have. You will tell me whatever I ask you, or you will be no good to me and I will have you shot. Understand?"

Cates paused, then nodded. He had to live long enough to get word to someone about these Germans. He didn't know why they were here, but it wasn't to trade recipes for hasenpfeffer.

"Good. Now let's try again. What is your name?"

"Roman Cates...my friends call me Cates. You can call me *Mister* Cates." Once more the officer seemed amused, but Cates didn't kid himself this time. He knew he was in deep shit.

"Do you live near here?"

"Over those hills," Cates replied, indicating the wrong direction.

"No, I don't think so. I think you are lying. Sergeant, hit him."

This time the stock of the submachine gun loosened a couple of teeth. When Cates stopped counting stars he found himself lying on his side, head aching, blood running from his mouth. He spit blood on the ground. He was getting mad.

"Go to hell you German bastard. Go ahead, kill me...just get it over with."

There was a pause, and when Cates looked up he saw the officer standing there just looking at him, a scoped, automatic rifle Cates didn't recognize under his arm. The officer said a few quick words in German and Cates was pulled roughly to his feet. Then he saw Laurel Hausen standing there looking at him. She didn't seem distraught in any way, she just stood there. He could hear Old Cottonmouth raising hell behind him, and the soldier assigned to hold him cursing in German.

"What the hell is she doing here?"

"Never mind that. You will calm your animal and come with us. If you give us any trouble, I will have you shot. I have more questions for you when we reach our destination, and you may want to reconsider your willingness to answer. There are worse things than being shot. Have you ever heard of the 'Viking's Revenge,' Herr Cates?" Cates shook his head no.

"Disembowelment while alive. Russian partisans would do it to German soldiers who were caught behind their lines after dark. They would slit their bellies open and pull their entrails out while they were still alive. *Extremely painful*. Takes hours to die. Now get your mule. Friedrich, go with him."

As soon as he got to his feet Cates received a rough push from behind and started towards Ol' Cottonmouth, who had just demonstrated to a cursing German how it had gotten its name. His head was spinning. I've got to get out of here somehow. His mind raced ahead to the shotgun hidden in his bedroll on the mule. He had one chance, and it wasn't a good one.

"You want me to calm the mule, right?" he said. The German assigned to him nodded, and Cates moved to the other side slowly, running his hand over the animal's haunches. "Woah boy. Take 'er easy now," he said, trying to calm the animal. He looked back out of the corner of his eye and saw the officer going over a map with two of his men.

The soldier who had been holding the mule was standing on the other side, cursing softly and looking at his hand where Cottonmouth had bitten him. He held the reins loosely, his weapon slung over one shoulder. Another soldier, the one who had hit him, was watching him from the other side, his submachine gun at the ready.

He took a step closer to keep Cates in his sight and Cates knew it was now or never. He grabbed the shotgun out from under the bedroll, racking in a round as he turned and fired, the German soldier taking the blast in the middle of the chest, the submachine gun firing a burst into the ground at his feet as the German sat down hard, a look of shock on his face as his hand went to the hole in his stomach, but Cates didn't wait around to see, he just ran, using old Cottonmouth as cover as the other Germans began firing.

9mm bullets tore up the ground all around him, even at his feet, but somehow Cates made it to the brush and dove through, not feeling the thorns which tore the hat from his head and plucked at his clothes. He could hear the mule honking and kicking, and hoped they wouldn't hurt him. He heard the officer yell something in German as he ran up the hill away from the sure death behind him, his legs pumping, aching with the effort.

80

J AKE HAD never seen anything like these German fighters. Camouflaged, sleek and aerodynamic, with no tail section creating drag, he was having a hard time staying with it. It was headed west, towards Nevada...and California. He knew it must be carrying a bomb load now, that's what the business at Williams was all about. He thought of a bomb being dropped on Los Angeles and his heart jumped. What other target could there be? Then it came to him. The Hoover Dam! If that was the target then there was a chance, a slight chance that he could intercept him.

The German pilot, unfamiliar with the area, was following mapped landmarks, Route 66 in particular. Jake had flown this country dozens of times, and he knew a more direct route to the dam, basically cutting the corner on the German. If he was wrong however, and the dam wasn't the target, he would lose the Horten and the German would reach his target unhindered. That didn't make sense to Jake though - a couple bombs from one plane wouldn't affect Los Angeles much. Hoover Dam however, was a target of great strategic importance, and a couple thousand - pounders would crack it open like an egg. Once the water started through, well, it'd be all over, and a lot of defense industries in L.A. relied on the electricity generated by its turbines. It'd be a catastrophe.

He had to decide soon; the spot where he'd normally turn off was coming up quickly Then he checked his fuel gauge and wondered if he would have enough to catch the other plane. It would be a near thing. Grimly he fixed his eyes on the black speck ahead of him, mentally urging the P-80 faster as he swept it into a gentle turn to the northwest, hoping he could get ahead of him, hoping his fuel would hold out, hoping he could reacquire the Horten and shoot the damn bat-wing thing down before it got there.

* * * * *

In the Horten, Fullgräbe could feel the extra drag of the bomb hanging from the undercarriage. The slight oscillations caused by the strange aerodynamics of a wing with no tail were accented now by the extra weight, and he fought to keep the plane level. They had flown the Hortens with dummy German ordnance, but the American bombs were a different shape and caused more of a problem. Nothing he couldn't handle, but it was annoying.

He followed the compass heading provided by Intelligence, searching ahead and to the north for the chasm which would be the mighty Colorado, which would lead him to the hydroelectric dam. Boulder, or Hoover Dam as it was originally known, was the largest man-made dam in history, and he would be the one to blow it up...for the Reich. It would bring their war machinery in nearby Los Angeles to a screeching halt. Afterward he would fly to downtown L.A., strafe the streets, then fly the Horten into the largest building he could find.

81

CATES CROUCHED breathlessly in a dark overhang of rock, listening for footsteps. He had three shells left in the shotgun, and he knew the old Winchester Model 97 pump and three shells wouldn't be enough against a squad of German soldiers carrying automatic weapons. Nevertheless, he pulled himself into a squat and rested the shotgun on his knee, pointing it down the slope at the entrance to the narrow slot. Above him was a jumble of boulders leading to an overhang. A narrow slice of sky was visible far above him, but for all intents and purposes he was boxed in. If they found him here, Cates knew it was over.

His leg was cramping up in a charley horse but he didn't dare move, his breath loud in his own ears. A bullet had grazed his right bicep, miraculously his only wound, and although sore, it wasn't bleeding much. Sweat was cooling in the space between his shoulder blades, and he shivered involuntarily when the sun momentarily disappeared behind a cloud.

A twig broke nearby and his finger twitched. Cates gripped the shotgun grimly, peering down its short length at the bead sight atop the smooth, gray barrel. *I'll take a couple more of the bastards with me at least,* he thought. He could hear soft footsteps in the dry oak leaves now as the soldiers came closer. The footsteps came closer, and he could see the shadow on the ground from one of his pursuers below him, standing just out of sight around the corner of rock wall.

Any minute he would be facing a submachine gun. *Please God, just no grenades. I hate grenades,* he thought, looking up at the narrow slot of sky. His finger tightened again on the trigger as the shadow lengthened.

Then the shadow disappeared and he could hear them moving away, the crunching of last year's oak leaves fading as they moved slowly away. Cates drew a sigh of relief, letting it out slowly. He lowered the leg he'd propped the shotgun on and rubbed the charley horse out of it. It gave him a minute to think about what had happened. What the hell were German soldiers doing here in Arizona of all places? From their demeanor and their uniforms they were clearly some sort of special commando unit. What were they after, and why was Laurel with them?

Suddenly it hit him. It was the only explanation he could see. They were after the vice-president. All his curiosity as to how they had gotten here dissipated. He had to get to the ranch and warn them. He would give it a few more minutes, to make sure they were gone, then he'd head for Smoke Trail Ranch. He just hoped he could make it there before the Germans did.

82

AFTER TWENTY minutes of searching, Schmidt made a decision and called his men back to him.

"It will take him time to get out of here and raise an alarm. He has no water and he will be cautious, believing that we are still hunting him. Our objective is the same. We continue on. We are already behind schedule and do not have time to track him."

"And Erdhardt, Herr Major?"

"We leave him here. Take his water and ammunition. Lay him over there in the shade. We have no time to bury him."

The men did as they were told. Each of them had been in such a situation before, and knew what they were getting into when they'd volunteered. They were hardened veterans, yet they moved their companion's body gently, laying him in the shade of a cottonwood where they'd rested only moments before.

They took his canteens and his ammunition, and Schmidt unbuttoned the upper right hand pocket of his friend's tunic and removed the letter he knew he kept there.

"Follow the mule's tracks. He was headed somewhere, maybe the mule will lead us to water. Once we find this Oak Creek, we will be close to the objective," Schmidt told them. "Giesler, take point. Move out."

Once more the German commandos shouldered their packs and headed off, each of them looking at Erhardt's body as they passed it, each giving him a silent salute. They were angry now. They would make the Americans pay.

83

HARRY TRUMAN slumped into the soft leather-covered Mission-style recliner and sighed. Jack Frye and he had risen early to fish, Oak Creek a lovely painting in the early morning light, the soft burble of the water running gently through the pasture as ducks dove for minnows in the shallows and squawked softly like lovers in the high grass at the water's edge. The wildflowers this time of year put even his home state of Missouri to shame. Willow trees dipped to touch the water here and there, their frond-like tendrils trailing in the water, moving ever so slowly in the gentle breeze.

They'd caught several nice trout, including a fat 18 - inch rainbow which Harry was particularly proud of, then had retired back up the hill to the house for a delicious late breakfast of pan-fried trout, home fries and a frittata that he demanded the recipe for. Now full and happy, he felt like a nap, but Cates was due soon with a pack mule and was going to take them to Sycamore Canyon for a little rabbit and grouse hunting and an unlikely hunt for Spanish gold.

They planned to stay out in the field two or three nights, then ride back. Right now though, he'd be content to just sit here and sip coffee or maybe a little bourbon and look at the magnificent view. The house had been built on top of a tall hill overlooking Oak Creek and the ranch, and the view of the mountains and red rocks surrounding them was magnificent. He was at peace. Jack Frye came in from the kitchen with a pot of coffee.

"More coffee, Harry?"

"Why thank you, yes, I'll take a little warm-up."

The president of TWA leaned over to pour more coffee for his guest, then straightened as he heard the drone of an engine. "That's a plane," he said curiously, moving to the window to look out just in time to see what looked like a C-47 disappear behind a nearby butte. "My God he's low.

DC-3s can go low and slow, but he didn't have gear down. No place to land one around here anyway. I hope we don't hear a crash soon."

"What would he be doing around here?"

"Hell if I know, Harry. It looked like it was olive drab, so it's probably a military C-47. He might just be sight-seeing, but he was awfully low." The sound of the plane slowly diminished in the distance and Frye shrugged. "I guess he's all right. Helen and I spent a lot of time flying low around here ourselves when we were looking for a place to buy. It's how we found this ranch. You just have to watch yourself. Things happen quickly at that altitude, and with the big rock formations around here, well, you can imagine how it would ruin your day."

Truman laughed. "I'll bet. You know, I don't mind flying too much, but I don't think I'd make a good pilot; too chicken," he was interrupted by the doorbell.

"That's either Cates or the good doctor, I'll wager," Jack said.

"Damn, you know I'm half inclined to just sit around here all day, drink bourbon and swap lies. Twenty miles on the back of a horse just doesn't appeal right now."

"Sir, this is your vacation. As far as I'm concerned, we can do any damn thing you want. We can always go out there next time," Jack said over his shoulder as he went to the east entrance.

He was right, it was Doc Edwards, with saddlebags slung over one shoulder and a shotgun in a canvas and leather case in his right hand. Jack welcomed him and steered him through the kitchen and into the living room where the vice-president stood sipping his coffee.

"Mr. Vice-President, good to see you again," Doc said, leaning his gun case against the stone fireplace as Jack lifted the saddlebags from his shoulder.

Truman stepped forward to shake hands with his newfound friend. "Now I told you already Doc, two old artillery-men need not stand on formality. You don't start calling me Harry, we're going to have to arm-wrestle."

Doc grinned. "Okay, it's a deal," he said as he shook his hand.

"Harry was just saying he kind of likes the idea of staying around the ranch today instead of going for a long haul…how do you feel about that, Doc?" Frye said.

"Fine with me. We should at least walk around here a bit and see if we can scare up a few grouse for the cook pot though. I haven't had that shotgun out of its case in a coon's age."

"Why that sounds fine Doc. Think Cates'll go for it?" Truman asked.

"Oh, he might grumble a bit, but he won't care."

Helen Frye came into the room from the direction of the master bedroom, putting in an earring as Jack poured coffee for Doc.

"Why good morning, Doc. You missed breakfast. Harry and Jack caught some beautiful trout this morning," she said.

"Just my luck. I just had an old shoe for breakfast."

"Oh Doc, you did not," Helen said, slapping him on the arm as she passed him. "Jack, would you be a darling and pour me some coffee too?"

84

SCHMIDT AND his men moved along the creek like shadows, constantly on the watch for the Secret Service men he was sure would be there. He had led countless patrols in dangerous country, and was glad to see his men hadn't forgotten their movement skills or noise discipline. He wasn't surprised at their skill; they had brought the best of the best on this mission, but it was gratifying nonetheless. Suddenly Horstmann raised his fist in warning and they all faded down into the grass. He moved forward, staying low until he reached his point man, crouching beside him.

"Look." Horstmann said, pointing through the grass.

Schmidt didn't see it at first, then the outline of a house atop a high butte on the other side of the creek gradually appeared. It was built from native rock and perched right on the edge of a cliff which dropped right down to the water. No wonder he hadn't noticed it right away. He took out his binoculars and scanned the house. Nothing.

He waited, holding the binoculars to his eyes as minutes clicked by, then saw the first sentry. He was on the south corner, in the shadow of the house, the only giveaway a puff of smoke from a cigarette. The guard came briefly into view at the corner of the house, then disappeared again.

The part of the house facing them was two stories, but dropped off to a terrace on the other side. It would make a good observation platform facing east, but he had only seen evidence of one guard on the roof. How many men would they have guarding the vice-president?

"From here on out it will be slower going. We must not be detected until the last minute. We have one chance at this. Remember, we want the vice-president alive if at all possible."

He looked directly at Laurel. "You will do exactly as you are told. You will stay here with Horstmann and the others. Geisler, you come with me."

He took out his pistol and handed it to her. "I suggest that if for any reason it looks as if you might be captured, you do the honorable thing and shoot yourself."

She looked back at him coldly, replying in heavily accented German. "Have no fear, Herr Schmidt. I will do what is required of me."

Mein Gott, Schmidt thought as his men spread back out, the woman is an ice queen. He had no more doubts as to her ability to kill or be killed.

The commandos moved forward cautiously, their weapons ready, until they reached the bank of the creek. The Americans wouldn't be expecting anyone to attack up the cliff, but their gebirgsjäger training would enable them to climb it without difficulty. They would not be roped, which was dangerous, but it was only 75 feet high or so. They had free-climbed much worse in training.

He stashed the submachine gun and his pack in the weeds with the other packs his men had shed, and checked his G43 quickly. Then he slipped slowly into the cold water of Oak Creek, the current pushing insistently against him as he went in nearly to the waist, holding his weapon out of the water to keep it dry.

85

CATES HAD circled around the back of the house, staying up high where there was less brush, where he could make better time. His stomach was tied in knots and he was out of breath. He hadn't run so hard and so far in years. He was hot and tired, and thirstier than he had ever remembered being. The shotgun was heavy in his hands, and he could see that it looked like it was going to rain. The edge of the house came into view. He could see Duffy on the roof. He began running down the hill.

Inside the house, Jack, Doc and the vice-president were laughing at an old off-color Army joke. They were still drinking coffee, but Harry was getting a little antsy.

"Where the hell is Cates?" he asked, looking at his watch.

Doc looked at his. "I really don't know. To tell you the truth I'm a little worried. It's not like him. Cates says he'll be somewhere at a certain time, he's there. I hope he's okay…that mule of his can be downright ornery."

"You think he's laying out there somewhere hurt?" Frye asked.

"I certainly hope not," Truman said. "He seems like a nice fellow. Hate for someone to get hurt on my account."

Suddenly they heard gunfire from outside. A machinegun was firing and it was nearby. Then they heard yelling.

"What the hell?" Harry Truman said, putting into words what they had all been thinking.

Cates raised his hands wide. He hadn't even thought about being mistaken for a threat, and coming running down the hill with a gun towards the well-guarded house containing the vice-president of the United States had not been one of his better ideas in retrospect. Duffy had fired a burst right at his feet, and ordered him to stop, which he did.

"PUT THE GUN ON THE GROUND," Duffy yelled from the roof.

"DUFFY, IT'S CATES, LISTEN…"

"PUT THE GUN DOWN OR I WILL SHOOT YOU."

Cates gently set the gun down on the rocky soil, then stood back up, hands still raised.

"STEP FORWARD SLOWLY. RANDALL, GET THAT WEAPON," he yelled to another Secret Service agent who had come running up the hill from his post on the east side when he heard the shooting. He was red-faced and out of breath.

Jack Frye came out of the house. "The hell is going on?"

"Please go back in the house, sir," Duffy said.

"Jack, it's Cates. LISTEN TO ME…"

"Sir, go back in the house. We'll take care of this."

"Jack, listen to me. I was in the last war, and I might be a little crazy, but I know German soldiers when I see 'em, and there's a whole squad of them comin' this way *right now!*"

Duffy had come down from the roof and was holding the tommygun pointed at Cates' belly, which Cates didn't care for much. Randall had picked up the shotgun Cates had dropped and was pushing him down the hill towards the house, hands still raised high. Doc had come out of the house, after telling Harry in no uncertain terms that he should stay inside, an opinion the vice-president wasn't happy with but was willing to abide by. Doc could tell it chafed at him though.

"I'm telling you, there's at least a squad of Germans making their way along the creek, and they're headed here," Cates insisted. "They probably heard you fire that thing…which might be a good thing. They won't think we're pushovers that way."

"Mr. Frye, Doctor, would you *please* go back in the damn house now?"

"Duffy, listen. If Cates said he saw a German soldier, then I'm inclined to believe him," Doc said.

Randall laughed. "There's hardly any damn German soldiers left in France, and you think there's some here in Arizona? The sun's getting to the old coot, you ask me."

Cates turned to Randall. "Put down that weapon, I'll show you who's an old coot, you asshole," he said, giving the Secret Service man a dirty look. Randall just grinned back at him.

"I'm telling you, they jumped me coming down the creek trail. They're dressed in khaki tropical gear, they have packs, they have submachine guns and they have Laurel Hausen with them."

"What?" Doc asked, incredulous.

Cates nodded. "I know it sounds crazy, but I saw her plain as day. They must have captured her too."

"Germans? Here? Why would they be coming *here?*" Jack asked, and they all looked at him. He looked at the window, at Harry peering out.

"Of course. My God, we've got to get him out of here," he said.

"All right, everybody calm down, Duffy said. "Load every gun you have, Mr. Frye. We'll take the vice-president out the east entrance to the car. They'll have to come across the bridge at some point, and up the hill. The driveway is on that side, so it'll be risky, but we have to go and go right now. Randall, check the west side of the house."

"Duffy, you don't really believe this…"

"I do, and that's a direct order. I'm paid to be cautious. Check the west side of the house…NOW. See if you can spot them. Oh, and give Mister Cates his shotgun back. We're going to need all the guns we can get."

Cates gave Randall a dirty look as he took his shotgun back and went in the house with Doc and Jack Frye as Duffy began talking quietly to Murphy, another Secret Service man.

Helen burst out of the kitchen where she'd been making cinnamon rolls, looking at him in alarm. "What in Heaven's going on?" she asked, wiping her hands on her apron.

"Helen, get the car keys and find Harriet. We're leaving."

"What? I have rolls in the oven. What the…"

Frye crossed the room and grabbed his wife by the arms. "Listen to me. We don't have any time. We're all in danger. There are German soldiers on their way here to kill the vice-president," he told her as the big Secret Service agent they knew as Ron Murphy rushed past them on his way to the east entrance, his Thompson held vertical, at the ready.

"Time to go," Murphy said in an unusually calm voice.

In the living room, the vice-president of the United States was busy loading a shotgun, along with Doc and Cates who were loading rifles. Duffy came into the room to speak to Truman and nearly had a heart attack.

"Mr. Vice-President?"

"Yes, Duffy, I heard. We're under attack," Truman said calmly. Duffy almost smiled. He had always been a fan of Roosevelt's, but if someone had to replace the chief someday he hoped it was someone like Harry Truman. A commander-in-chief had to stay calm in unusual circumstances…and this was definitely unusual.

"We'll exit out the east side to the cars. Sir, I *do not* want you carrying a weapon. My job is to keep you safe, not put you in combat."

"Duffy, it looks as though we are already in combat, or will be soon. I have seen combat before and I would prefer to be *armed*, thank you."

"Sir, you may keep a pistol on you, but you have to follow my directions. You aren't just a citizen anymore, you're the vice-president of the United States, next in line for the presidency, and you are *my responsibility*."

Harry looked at him, a sour look on his face. "All right Duffy, you've made your point. I guess you know I'm under orders from the boss to listen to you."

"Yes, sir. Now, can we please go?"

86

RANDALL LOOKED up the hill and into the draw, scanning the slope opposite the house as he strode to the edge. It wasn't a true cliff here, just a steep slope. He stepped to the edge and looked down...straight into the eyes of a German soldier. Suddenly he was punched in the stomach, like being kicked by a mule, and he knew something was wrong because he couldn't get the Thompson up, couldn't use his hands at all, and then he was choking, and couldn't catch his breath.

He went to his knees, trying to just breathe and get the weapon up so he could shoot back, and then the German's shadow fell over him, and shot him again, and he knew it was over. The world spun crazily for a second, and he tried to take another breath but couldn't, then it all went dark.

When Duffy heard the firing he knew what it was right away. It was an MP40, and it was right outside. He pushed Truman down and the others hit the floor as well. "GET TO THE CARS. STAY LOW – MURPHY WILL TAKE YOU OUT OF HERE...NOW GO."

Doc, Harry and Cates didn't need any urging. As bullets began shattering the windows they duckwalked towards the kitchen, where they met Jack, Helen and Harriet Applewick, Jack's personal flight attendant, crouched in the kitchen near the door.

Jack was loading a rifle, Helen was fumbling in her purse for her keys, and Harriet was just sitting on the floor, eyes wide, in a state of shock. Suddenly they heard glass breaking, then the loud thump of the Thompson from the living room. Duffy was firing. Then all hell broke loose.

87

"GIVE ME COVERING FIRE, I'M GOING FOR THE CORNER OF THE HOUSE," Schmidt yelled in German. Giesler nodded. They would leapfrog towards the enemy as they had dozens of times. He reached for a grenade, but Schmidt shook his head no, and Giesler remembered they wanted to take the vice-president alive.

Personally he thought this was stupid.. It would be much easier to just throw a couple grenades in the windows, then finish off whoever was left with their submachine guns. It was the favorite tactic of the German armed forces, and it worked. It worked very well. Of course, if the other Zug completed their mission on the East Coast, then capturing the vice-president would really mean something. Schmidt rose to move and Giesler began firing, wondering how things were going in Georgia.

On the other side of the house Laurel watched as the four German soldiers began creeping up the hill, their submachine guns ready, their dotted camouflage tunics and khaki trousers making them nearly invisible. There was clearly shooting going on around the other side of the house. If she could get to one of the cars, she could get away from this madness. If nothing else, Laurel was a survivor.

She put the small pistol Schmidt had given her in her pocket, and began moving across the hill just as people began running out of the east entrance towards the cars and the shooting began in earnest.

88

MURPHY GRIPPED Jack's arm in the doorway leading from the drive to the kitchen.

"When I say 'go', I want you all to run as fast as you can to that big round raised flowerbed and drop to the ground. The rocks and dirt it's built from will give you good protection. I'll cover you. When we get there we'll do the same thing again, but this time, run for the cars. Don't wait for me. You get it running, you take off. I'll jump on the running boards. We have to get the vice-president away from here."

"I understand," Jack Frye said.

Murphy looked at the rest of them. They all nodded except Cates and Doc.

"Reckon you could use a couple extra guns," Cates said. "You go first and we'll cover you. Harry needs you more than us. We'll run last while you cover us from the planter," Cates said. Doc nodded in assent.

Murphy looked at the two grim older men and knew he was looking at veterans. What's more, they were right. His job was to get the vice-president out of there. Anything else was gravy. He nodded.

"All right. You run to us at the flowerbed when we cover the others going to the cars."

Cates and Doc nodded.

Murphy looked at Truman, who was watching the front. "Sir? Are you ready?"

"Damn straight," Harry said. "Not exactly how I'd envisioned spending the afternoon, shooting however." Cates and Doc couldn't help but grin.

"Then let's go. Things aren't getting any better out there."

89

DUFFY HAD been hit. It was just a crease in the arm, but it hurt like hell and was making it hard to hold up the Tommygun. It was a great weapon, his favorite, but it wasn't light, and with his injury he was just a fraction too slow when one of the Germans broke cover and ran for the corner of the house, just 35 yards away, the bullets from the Thompson kicking at his heels. He hoped Murphy had gotten everyone into the cars and out of there. He knew he was likely going to die, but he was Secret Service after all, and he'd always known it could come to this.

He pulled the empty magazine from the smoking weapon and threw it to the ground as a second German ran for the corner. Where the hell had these guys come from? How'd they get into the U.S.? He had one 30 round stick mag left for the Thompson, plus his .45 Colt and three magazines for it, one in the gun and two spares. He just had to slow them down, keep them away from the vice-president long enough for him to get away…then he heard shooting on the other side of the house and knew that the damn Germans had flanked them.

90

ELEN HAD never been as terrified as she was at that moment. They ran for the planter as Murphy opened up on the bushes below the house with his Thompson to keep the Germans' heads down. She couldn't see any Germans there, but she supposed it was a good place to imagine them. She knew she was right when the bushes fired back, the bullets whizzing overhead like angry bees. Then the fountain exploded, showering her with Mexican pottery and water. Harriet was right behind her, and she felt her grab her arm.

She uncovered her head and looked at her husband who was raising up to fire his rifle. Harry Truman was leaning over the fountain, firing a handgun despite Murphy's instructions. She saw the Secret Service man run from the door towards them, while Cates and Doc provided covering fire from the protection of the stone steps. Murphy and Truman made it to the flowerbed, crouching next to her and Harriet.

She put her hand over Harriet's and squeezed it. "You all right?" she asked, turning her head to look at her. It sounded as if she were whispering, and she realized the gunfire was making her deaf.

She repeated it more loudly, and Harriet nodded. She heard Murphy yell to Cates and begin firing again, then Jack was pulling her up by one arm and she ran for the cars with the others, wondering how well sheet metal stopped bullets.

91

SCHMIDT CURSED softly as he held his ear. A bullet had clipped it, and it was bleeding profusely. Whoever was using that Tommy gun was good with it. He dropped the hand back to his weapon. The G43 was hot, but it had a fresh 20 - round magazine in it. He turned the corner and fired six rounds into the window where he'd seen the muzzle flashes come from as Giesler got up and began his run to the far corner.

* * * * *

The living room was full of smoke and filled with the stench of cordite. Duffy had been hit twice, neither of them bad in themselves, but the pain from the wounds and the blood loss were taking their toll. What's more, the Thompson was finally empty. He dropped the gun on the floor and pulled out his 1911. He had three full magazines. He wondered how much ammo the Germans had left.

What he couldn't figure was why they hadn't thrown a grenade in. He'd fought the Germans through the vicious French hedgerows as a paratrooper and he knew their tactics. Out of the corner of his eye he saw one of the krauts sprinting for the opposite corner. He raised the .45 and fired one-handed. The German skipped, then seemed to stumble, and went down. The German rolled back to his knees and began to get up and Duffy shot him again. This time he went down for good, and Duffy smiled, just seconds before a high-velocity 8mm rifle round struck him in the forehead, freezing his smile on his face forever.

92

A S SOON as they saw Murphy and Jack Frye rise up from behind the planter and begin firing, Doc and Cates took off running. It was hard to go fast because they were running down shallow flagstone steps, not just dirt. Cates saw Doc trip and go down. Cates had his shotgun in one hand and a borrowed lever action .30-30 in the other. He had a bandolier of shells for the rifle slung over his shoulder. He fired the shotgun one-handed at a German running up the hill, who dropped to the ground. Cates couldn't tell if he had hit him or not.

"C'MON YOU BASTARDS, I'LL GIVE YOU A DAMN HAIRCUT," Cates yelled. He turned to see that Doc was lying on the ground and hadn't moved, and there was a red bloom on the front of his white shirt. "Dammit," he said under his breath as he ran back to his friend.

Cates didn't stop to check on him, he just dropped the shotgun and grabbed Doc by the back of his collar, dragging him towards the fountain as fast as he could. It didn't feel very fast. Bullets were whining and spitting all around him as they chewed up the earth. The women were already running for the cars.

Murphy turned to look, stopped for a minute as Jack and Harry stood and fired to cover them.

"He's hit bad," he said. "He's not going to make it."

"He'll make it," Cates said grimly. Then he felt Doc grip his arm. He looked at him. His eyes were glazed over and his breath was ragged. There was blood at the corner of his mouth, and when he opened his mouth to speak, Cates could see it was red with it.

"Go. I'm done," Doc said.

"No way, I'm not leaving you here."

"Good knowing y…" Doc spit out, then stopped, and was still.

"I am. I have to do my job. Sorry Cates. Good luck," Murphy said, and fired again, working backwards while firing his Thompson from a crouch, working his way to the cars.

Cates had seen enough dead men that he knew right away his best friend was gone. He laid his head back gently on the ground, picked up the .30-30 and Doc's favorite hat, and sprinted for the cars.

93

LAUREL HEARD the cars start up and come towards her. She crawled out of the brush and stood in the middle of the road, hoping the cars weren't going so fast they couldn't stop. It was her only chance. She heard the cars rev, then reverse, then the sounds of tires digging frantically at gravel, and then they were almost on top of her, flying around the curve, literally screaming down the driveway.

The first car was the Frye's custard-yellow Mercury convertible. Helen was at the wheel, with Harriet crouched down in the back and Cates hanging off the other side, one leg inside the car, one outside, riding the door like a horse, with a bandolier of rifle shells slung over his chest Pancho Villa style, wearing Doc's fedora on his head. He had a rifle and was jacking shells into it and firing as fast as he could back in the direction of the German troopers. The rear car was the black Lincoln the government had secured for Harry and which had been driven up from Phoenix.

Jack was driving the Lincoln, and Murphy was firing the Thompson to their rear while hanging off the running board like it was some gangster movie, and she assumed the vice-president was hunched down in the rear seat. Helen saw Laurel and stood on the brakes, and Jack did likewise trying to avoid hitting her, but they were traveling fast, downhill, on the rough, loose, red rock gravel that could be treacherous just to walk on. Both cars were sliding towards her without stopping, and Laurel could just see Helen's look of horror as she dove to the side, out from in front of the cars, just in time to keep from being run over.

Both cars slid to a halt, the front bumper of the Lincoln banging into the rear bumper of the Mercury, bending both of them.

Cates leapt from the side of the Merc and ran to her. "You okay?"

She nodded as he helped her up.

"Then come the hell on, it's time to go!" he said as he grabbed her by the arm, pulling her towards the two cars, which were now sitting targets.

Cates shoved her bodily over the edge of the open convertible, into the back, right on top of a very frightened Harriet and yelled "GO." Helen took off like a bat out of hell, driving that convertible like she was on a dirt track, the rear end sliding out on each tight turn, raising a hell of a cloud of dust,

Despite the dust she could see the Lincoln right behind them, Jack matching Helen's slides through the turns and coming on strong. She could see a couple German soldiers in the rearview run down the drive just in time to snap off another burst of automatic weapons fire, then they were gone as she swung around the next tight turn.

"HEAD FOR THE AIRSTRIP," Cates yelled. He was holding the rifle upright with one hand, while hanging on for dear life with the other.

"Well, I kinda figured," Helen said as she spun the wheel and the car skidded through the turnoff to Red Rock Crossing. They were taking Truman to Jack's plane. It was the fastest way to get the vice-president to safety.

Laurel knew the German commandos wouldn't be able to beat them there. There were only two roads out of Smoke Trail Ranch, one slow and circuitous, the other easier driving but nearly three times as long. Even if they could scare up a vehicle, they would never catch up. They were going to get away. How could she stop them by herself?

94

THEY MADE it to Red Rock Crossing and slowed down to ford the creek. It was shallow here, pretty easy but slow to cross. They were talking about building a bridge, but for now they'd just filled the big holes with concrete. You didn't want to get your sparkplugs or distributor wet. Helen knew that because she'd done it once, splashing through the creek in a hurry to get home one day. They'd ended up pulling her out with a team of horses, leaving her red-faced with embarrassment.

As they came to a stop at the water, Cates jumped off the running board.

"I'll get off here."

"Don't be crazy. Get in," Murphy said from the other car.

"No, listen. There's a phone in the Willow House, remember? I'm going to try and get through to someone who cares and tell them what's going on. Then, at the very least I'll try and slow those guys down a little."

"All right, I think you're crazy but I don't have time to argue. Good luck. Let's switch, Jack. I'll drive," Murphy said, ducking inside and slamming the door as Jack ran to the other car and jumped in front with his wife.

"Good luck to you too. Take it slow across here," Cates said. "Just follow her."

Helen was nearly halfway across, the car bumping its way across the rocky creek bed. Cates waved. Murphy nodded back, but then came a command from the back and the car stopped again. Harry Truman stuck his hand out the window. Cates stepped closer and took it. Truman's grip was cool but firm.

"You take care now, Cates. No sense getting yourself shot when the fight's over. We'll have those boys rounded up in no time."

"Sooner someone knows, sooner we can get them corralled. Who knows? There could be more around," Cates replied.

"That's right, so I want you to be careful hear me?"

"I will, sir."

"Here, call this number and give them the second number I wrote on the back for verification when they ask for it," he said, handing Cates a card. "Ask to speak to Admiral Ross Macintyre and tell him what's going on. Oh, and Cates?"

"Yes?"

"Keep your head down."

"Yessir."

Truman let go of Cates' hand and the Lincoln drove on. Cates watched them drive across the creek, then checked the lever-action to make sure there was a round chambered. There was. What he hadn't told the vice-president was that he was fairly sure there were only two or three of them left, and they had killed a good friend of his. He snicked the lever shut and moved into the woods, his face grim. He had every intention of going for the phone first, but after that, Cates was going hunting.

95

S CHMIDT BURST out through the kitchen door just in time to see the cars take off in a cloud of dust. He fired at them, and they returned fire, the bullets skipping all around him. He could see two of his men running through the brush at an angle, trying to cut off the vehicles. Why the vehicles were still operational, he didn't know. They should have been disabled.

He cursed quietly as the sound of the engines faded. He raised the rifle and rested it on his shoulder as he strode down the steps. The body of one of the Americans lay crumpled by a large, round raised flowerbed built out of rock. They had obviously used it as cover to escape. His men had not been in the right position yet. Furious, he cut quickly through the yard, finding the bodies of two of his men where they had fallen...where they had *failed*.

Schmidt cut over to the driveway and met his remaining two men coming back. They were winded and out of breath.

"They got away," Horstmann said. An excellent soldier, but with an occasional tendency for overstatement.

"I CAN SEE THAT. HOW COULD YOU FAIL TO STOP THEM? DUMMKÖPFES!"

"They were surprisingly well armed, Herr Sturbannführer."

"They were not."

"You said no grenades, sir."

"I said *under no circumstances* were you to let them escape. I'd rather have Truman dead than lose him entirely. You are idiots. There is no room for failure."

The two soldiers looked at the ground. He could see on their faces that he didn't have to lecture them. They knew that they had failed, and they felt it keenly. They were good men, and he felt momentarily bad for berating them.

Schmidt took a deep breath and let it out, turning to look down the hill at the wide creek flowing unhurriedly past, then at the willow trees and the pasture beyond. He pulled his cap from his head and wiped his forehead with the back of his forearm. He had failed. He was hot and sweaty, but practically shaking with adrenaline.

Then he heard it. Heard the sound again and smiled softly. He pulled the map from his pocket and spread it on the ground, the other two soldiers going to one knee on the other side of the map, awaiting orders. One looked at the other and they both shrugged as Schmidt stabbed at the map with his finger.

"Here is the road they took. *Here* is where they are going."

"How do you know that, Herr Sturbannführer?"

"Because this is where Herr Frye's plane is. Remember seeing it on the way in? the big silver one? I have no doubt that's how they're taking the vice-president out of here. That's what I would do."

"I see what you mean. If we could cut across this section here, we could beat them there…but it's miles away and we're on foot. As rough as the terrain was on the way here, we'll never make it in time," Horstmann said.

"You're correct. We'd never make it in time…*on foot*," he said, as the horses he had heard earlier whinnied again. "Follow me."

Schmidt ran across the swaying footbridge as fast as he could, his two men close on his heels. He ran straight for the barn, where he could see horses milling around the corral obviously disturbed by the gunfire. He swept up a couple of old wrinkled apples from an open bin next to the barn.

He used the wrinkled apples to make friends with the horses and calm them down, and he saw Horstmann doing the same thing. He'd obviously been around horses before. Schmidt held the grey that had come up to him first under his hairy chin and blew softly through his nose into the horse's nostrils so he could smell him. The grey jerked but didn't pull away. Meier just stood off to the side watching, and Schmidt saw some trepidation on his face.

"Never ridden before, Rudi?" he asked as he rubbed the grey under the jaw and offered him an apple perched on an opened palm.

"Not since I was ten, Sir. I never did like it much."

"But you *can* ride?"

"Yes, sir."

"Good, we won't have to shoot you," Schmidt said, only half joking.

"Now let's get these horses saddled. Meier, you take the bay mare."

"Yes sir." Fifteen minutes later they were headed west, to catch a plane.

96

HELEN COULDN'T remember ever driving so fast. They sped past the Loy ranch and up the hill through the tight switchbacks, the car jouncing and bumping on the rough road, raising a cloud of dust a mile high. When she looked behind her she felt bad for the two men in the car behind her – they must be choking - but she didn't slow down, nor did they. Jack had said something about finding Glen Knudsen, his copilot, but Helen doubted they had time. They had no time to lose. Once they were in the air, Truman would be safe. Then she had a terrible thought. She looked at Jack.

"Hon, what if they have German fighter planes here as well?"

Jack laughed. "That's the most ridiculous thing I've ever heard, sweetheart. There's no way they could get fighters into this country. Besides, once I get that Lodestar into the air, they'd need jets to catch me, and I *know* they don't have jets in this country."

Helen frowned. "So what are the odds that our house would be attacked by German paratroopers?" she asked him.

Finally they hit the main road, and Helen merely glanced each way before pulling out, blowing right through the hand-made stop sign at the top of the hill, swinging left towards Cottonwood onto 89A, the now dust-covered Lincoln right behind her. She downshifted and had her foot to the floorboards as she glanced over at her husband briefly after she made the turn, the car leaning way over, so far she was afraid it would roll, but it didn't. He was hanging on for dear life.

"Jesus, Helen."

"Now you know how I feel sometimes when you're flying."

"You *are* flying. I didn't know our car could go this fast."

Laurel gripped the armrest fiercely as the car swung through the turn, her other hand in the pocket of her dress, gripping the pistol. Harriet rolled away from her, then back, bumping against her.

"WATCH IT," she growled.

"So-rry," Harriet replied. She couldn't help it, with the damn car lurching back and forth the way it was.

Laurel looked behind them. The Lincoln was still there. She'd wait until they were at the plane to make her move. She had one chance, and she had to get it right. Harry Truman had to die.

97

CATES MOVED through the woods with a patience born of experience, the Winchester at the ready. Besides the dead body of a German he'd seen no one. The woods were silent, but he wasn't fooled. He knew more Germans were out there. They'd have sent their very best for this job, and as Truman had pointed out, if they had come after him, the president was likely in danger as well.

He followed the creek upstream, using the bank for cover to bring him closer to the Willow House. Unfortunately, it stood in a clearing and he'd have to risk it. Taking a deep breath, he broke from cover, sprinting across the open space, maybe 75 yards to the house, his legs pumping, rifle held up in front of him.

It was the second longest 75 yards in his life, the first being a similar sprint from his wrecked plane to the hedges surrounding the field where he'd crashed. That was in France in 1916, and he felt the same feeling now as he had then, the awful certainty that enemy soldiers were tracking him with rifles, and the shot would come any moment which would knock him off his feet and steal his life from him. It was not a good feeling.

The shot never came, however, and then he was in the lee of the house, back against the wall, shaded by the overhang, trying to get his breath back. He was in good shape for a man his age, but Cates had done more running in the last few hours than he had in the last 20 years. He was glad he had worn the knee-high Apache desert boots he preferred for hunting rather than the ropers he typically wore around the ranch. He peeked around the corner to the back door, but there was no one. He slipped through the cool shadow cast by the structure to the door and gently turned the knob, then threw himself inside, going in low, the Winchester in front, the door slamming open against the frame, but there was no one inside.

The house was small and neat as a pin, with a love seat, a rocking chair and two Queen Anne chairs turned together. He saw the phone on the wall, but checked the remaining rooms first, just in case. Then he returned to the phone, leaned the rifle against the wall and pulled the card the vice-president had given him from his pocket, but when he put the receiver to his ear, there was no dial tone. He tapped the lever a few times, but it was no use. The line had been cut.

"Well, it was worth a try." He hung the phone back up, picked up the rifle and went out the door, heading for the stables.

There was just one horse left in the corral, a mustang that Cates remembered from the first time he'd been there and Jack had asked him his opinion about his horses. The little paint came up to him and sniffed his hand. He set the rifle down and rubbed its nose briefly, looking around at the ground.

He quickly found the tracks of three men wearing identical hobnailed boots in different sizes. He could see where they'd saddled the horses and headed west. Were they trying to escape? Somehow Cates didn't think so. He had the funny feeling they had gone after the others, trying to cut them off on horseback. It's what he would have done, and these were trained killers. They didn't just give up.

He looked at the mustang again. Not much to look at, but half-wild and bred for this country, it was the best horse of the bunch, and he'd told Frye that. He wasn't surprised they'd taken the other horses, which were prettier, but he knew they couldn't match the stamina or guts of the horse they'd left him. He smiled as he slipped a halter over the ugly little mustang's nose.

"You an' me, we're gonna go kill us some Germans, boy," he said softly. The mustang shook its head and whinnied as if in agreement.

98

SCHMIDT AND his two men had followed a wide trail which seemed to go in the right direction. It had met another, wider, much-used trail, which looked as though it were on the verge of becoming a road, and there was a hand-painted sign which said "Elmerville", with an arrow pointing left. It led northwest, which was the general direction he wanted to go, so they took it.

"Keep your eyes out for civilians. We don't want to waste any more time or ammo. We'll avoid them if at all possible. Verstehen?" he told the two men. They both nodded in return and spurred their horses down the trail at a brisk canter.

The trail wound around the butte to their right, following the contours of the land. It was dryer here, more rugged, with the same stubby junipers and cactus they'd run into on their way in. Schmidt was amazed at how different it was from the lush area around the wide creek they'd crossed. He wondered where they'd find their next water. They'd filled canteens before the assault, but he wished they had taken the time now to fill the larger aluminum 5 - liter containers each man carried in his pack

They had only gone a couple of miles when they noticed a building off to the left. The trail they were on headed in that direction, but a smaller spur led off to the right, following the base of the butte. Schmidt guessed that the larger main trail led to Elmerville, whatever that was, so on a whim he followed the lesser trail, since it seemed more or less to lead in the direction he wanted to go. They came over a slight rise, the butte rising into red cliff outcroppings of rock on their right. Ahead of them in the distance were mountains such as he'd never imagined; sheer cliffs of vermilion, orange and purple, as rugged as anything he'd ever seen. It reminded him in a way of Gibraltar, but the color was strangely magnificent. Large red vertical pillars of sandstone and basalt stood in ragged pairs here and there like alien sculptures. He had seen some of it from the plane on the way in, but from ground level it was something entirely different.

As they drew closer to the large butte on the right he heard a car, and he stopped before they were seen. They watched an old farm truck pass directly in front of them, about a quarter of a kilometer away. Obviously there was a road there. They rode up to it cautiously, and saw that it went up the hill to their right and over a rise, down the hill to the left and around another butte. The trail they were on met the road and continued on the other side.

Schmidt consulted his map. He had to make a decision. Did they follow the packed gravel road, which would be easier riding, or did they try and parallel it? The map showed that this was the only road from Sedona to Cottonwood and would take them right to the plane. He decided to take the road as there was no cover beside it anyway. They would have to risk being seen.

They turned the horses onto the empty gravel road and kicked them to a gallop. Speed was essential. He didn't know where their targets were, but they would have to take this road as well. Were they ahead of them or behind them? Schmidt didn't know, but if they could make it to the plane before the cars did they had a chance of ambushing them. He thought about setting up an ambush here, but decided it was a risk he couldn't take. They had to set up at the plane. If the plane was not there when they got there, then they would know they had failed. If it was there, well then, Truman was as good as theirs.

99

THE SPECK was larger now. Jake could make out the plane's delta shape and the pregnancy of the bomb hanging from its belly. He was gaining, but slowly. He had the advantage of surprise - the German was not expecting him. He would be within range in two minutes, then he'd put some .50 caliber holes in the bastard and go home.

Finally Jake was in range. He armed the guns, lined up on the Horten, and fired a burst.

Fullgräbe saw the tracers slinging past his cockpit and heard the guns, and acted instinctively. He rolled the plane over and dove.

Jake followed the Horten over. He knew he had the advantage now, since he was not carrying ordnance, but he was amazed when the Horten pulled out of the dive sharply, the bat-like top profile of it suddenly directly ahead of him. He fired again, but it was too late. He swore. The plane was fast, and the pilot was no slouch. He'd heard that some of the German pilots had over 300 kills. He couldn't imagine that, but this guy was good, no doubt about it.

He cursed silently as he saw the Horten dropping towards the dam. He was nearly there. He followed it down, diving the P-80 faster than he ever had, hoping he could pull out in time. The angle Jake had dived at was intended to intercept the Horten, and it worked, but not well, he had only a split second on his guns before he had to pull out himself.

The tracers dropped from his plane like stones of fire onto the top of the speeding Horten, then he pulled up, saw the rocks coming too fast, too close, rolled the plane just in time for the wingtip to clear, then pulled up and out of the Colorado River canyon, just barely clearing the edge.

* * * * *

Fullgräbe knew he should dump the bomb, but he couldn't abandon his mission. If he could just get away long enough to drop it on the dam, then he'd again have an advantage over the other pilot in maneuverability and he'd get behind him and drop him. Inverted, he could see the U-shape of the dam and pulled back the stick to drop towards it, picking up speed. Then he rolled back over, coming in low towards the dam faster than he'd ever gone in the Horten.

The weight of the bomb had given him the extra airspeed he needed during the inverted dive, and once he rolled back over into an upright attitude, he was in his attack position perfectly lined up between the ragged edges of the river, coming straight in at the dam, faster than he'd ever gone before.

The tracers fell like rain around the Horten, and Fullgräbe couldn't help but look up. At 500 mph things happen quickly, and as he came around the last bend he saw the high tension power lines too late. Two of the rounds had blown through the wings, but that wasn't what concerned him. He pulled up to clear the power lines which ran across in front of the dam itself, and he would have made it if he hadn't had the bomb hanging beneath the plane.

He hooked the last cable with the tips of the bomb which flipped the plane end over end. It was a tribute to the German engineers that the bomb rack didn't break and the high voltage line did. The line snapped, but there was no transfer of electricity because he wasn't grounded, like a bird sitting on a powerline, but the plane was tumbling now, end over end towards the huge wall of the dam. With his last effort Fullgräbe armed the weapon and screamed "HEIL HITLER" at the cockpit hatch as he thumbed the bomb release.

The Horten was tumbling viciously end over end, but it was still traveling at nearly 500 mph. One wingtip clipped the stone railing of the walkway running across the dam, smashing a small section out of it, but the rest of the plane missed the dam miraculously, hitting the water in a huge gush of spray just 100 feet away. The bomb was still in the air, cartwheeling away, landing in the water several hundred feet from where the plane had augered in.

Hitting the water at that speed was like hitting concrete, and the plane and the bomb exploded, raising a huge geyser of water, so much water forced out away from the explosion that a wave of water five feet high washed over the dam.

Jake pulled a high G turn and came back for a closer look. Miraculously the dam was not damaged, other than the notch taken out of the railing. One broken power line flopped gently against its stanchion in the wind, arcing violently for a moment until the huge wind-up circuit breakers kicked and shut it down. He watched the Horten sink beneath the surface, then looked at his fuel gauge. He needed to find a place to set the plane down soon or he was going to have the same problem. He pulled back the stick and went up.

100

THE MUSTANG was running hard, the way its forebears had run, just for the sake of running. Cates didn't have to give it his heel, the horse just ran because it wanted to. It wanted to catch its friends and run with them. It was a horse bred in cactus and juniper, a horse that simply loved to run, and ran as its ancestors had, flat out, over the roughest country imaginable.

The Germans had headed west, towards Elmerville, then turned to take the smaller trail Cates knew led to the road. He figured they had at least twenty, maybe thirty minutes lead on him, and they'd be pushing hard as well, trying to catch the cars, or maybe even get ahead of them. His only advantage was that the mustang could run harder for longer than their mounts. Sooner or later their horses would flag and they'd have to rest them. That's when he'd catch up with them. He gripped the rifle in his right hand as he let the little paint have his head, the junipers whipping past in a blur.

101

THEY'D BEEN lucky; they hadn't seen a single car or truck the entire time they'd been on the road, but Schmidt felt they were pushing it. There was a knoll here each side of the road, and he swung his horse off the road and up the one on the right to see if he could see the plane. The horses were blowing hard by the time they got to the top, and he felt lather on his hand as he swung off, running up to a rock formation to look west through his field glasses, which were secured by a strap around his chest.

As he unclipped them and brought them to his eyes, the far hills came into sharp focus. He could not see a plane and his gut clenched. He swept the glasses left to right, then he saw the glint of sun on metal, like the shine off a highly polished fuselage, and smiled. They were still here. He remounted and kicked the horse forward yet again.

A few minutes later Schmidt could see the plane with his bare eyes. It stood at the far end of the runway, glinting in the sun like a huge diamond, hard to look at directly in the midday sun. There was a car parked near it, but it wasn't one of the cars they'd been chasing, he was sure of it. The horses were failing, and when he stopped to raise his field glasses one more time their heads drooped in exhaustion. There was someone working on the plane, a mechanic or something…which explained the car.

He saw a shallow draw just this side of the airfield where they could set up. They would leave the horses behind the last knoll, out of sight, and approach on foot. They would kill the guard or guards as they got out of the car, then take Truman and force the pilot to fly them to Mexico. Schmidt smiled. It wasn't over yet, he thought. We can still do this.

102

THE MUSTANG was beginning to flag a little. Cates had seen where they'd left the road but he hadn't followed. He knew where they were heading, and he stayed on the road, letting the mustang run. Just past the turnoff for Page Springs there was a dry creek bed with a rise on the other side. He topped the rise and dropped off of the heaving, lathered horse. He would leave the road here and come in on them from behind.

He walked northwest, leading the little paint away from the road, angling towards Sycamore Canyon, on a path he figured would intersect their trail. He knew he could be wrong, that they had just headed for the hills instead of angling west towards the plane, but he knew the kind of men they were, and he figured they wouldn't give up so easily. If he didn't cross their tracks soon he'd angle back north and find them.

Cates led the mustang through the scrub, an occasional buzz from a rattlesnake here and there like locusts in the brush the only sound other than the sound of the mustang's hooves on the rocky ground. His mouth was dry and he wished he had some water, but there had been no time, so he had broken his own rule of always taking plenty of water with him.

Ten minutes later he crossed the tracks of three horses heading west at a trot and he smiled grimly. "Got you now, you sons 'a bitches," he said to himself. The wind rattled through the sagebrush and a tiny ground sparrow darted out and away from his path as he turned to follow the tracks, the tired but game little mustang trudging after him.

103

HELEN COULD see the plane now, big and silver in the sun, and she smiled triumphantly at her husband, who was grinning himself, leaning forward as if to urge the car faster. If she went any faster, Helen thought, they'd lift off the ground. She checked the mirror again, and the Lincoln was still there. Then she caught Laurel's face in the mirror. She was frowning, as if she were deep in thought. It was a little strange, and made Helen wonder. How did she get kidnapped by the Germans? It seemed odd to her that Laurel would be there, just as they were attacked…and how did she get away from them?

Helen instinctively didn't like her; there was something strange and cold about the woman she couldn't quite identify. Just something wrong. She turned back to the road. The shoulders here were soft, and if she didn't pay attention she'd roll the car and kill them all. Laurel would wait, but she'd keep an eye on her.

104

SCHMIDT AND his men waited in the hot sun for the cars. They had left their packs with the horses on the other side of the knoll and had come in slowly, triangulating the plane between the three of them, low-crawling the last 100 yards to their positions. Schmidt wished he had more men, but it couldn't be helped. It would be enough. He lay in the dirt about 100 meters from the runway, hidden by some low brush and the color of his desert uniform. It was covered with dirt from the ride, and he knew that as long as he didn't move no one would be able to see him until he got really close.

Something to the left drew his eye and he realized it was the two cars, coming fast, speeding down the gravel road from Sedona, clouds of dust like twin dust devils whipping up behind them as they came closer. He checked the G43 to make sure there was a round chambered and flipped off the safety. They were ready. He would take out anyone holding a gun, then his men would run in and take Truman and the others hostage while he covered them with the scoped G43. It was a good plan. It would work. It *had* to work. He lowered his eye to the scope and waited.

105

"GOOD, GLEN'S here. He must be working on the plane," Jack Frye said as the car came to a stop nearby. He was out and running for the plane before Helen could shut it off. The Lincoln slid to a stop behind them and Murphy jumped out, tommygun at the ready. Murphy gave a quick look around, then waved Truman out of the car, hustling him towards the plane.

Helen sighed with relief as she saw Truman about to board the Lockheed Lodestar. One off the ground he should be safe. She heard the engines kick over, then fire, the propellers beginning to spin, then she heard gun fire and could see bullets kicking up the dirt near Truman and Murphy, keeping them from entering the plane. She dove to the ground, thinking that this was crazy. First her home had been turned into a war zone, now this?

Murphy had Truman on the ground and was covering him with his body, while Helen, Harriet and Laurel were lying on the ground, trying to make themselves small. Then two German soldiers were standing over Murphy and Truman, one stepping on Murphy's Thompson to keep it pinned, the other pulling him off Truman, and stripping his pistol from the hidden shoulder holster. The soldier looked at it briefly, then stuck it in his own belt.

The firing had stopped. The first soldier took the Thompson and threw it as far as he could, then grabbed Truman and pushed him towards the plane. The other soldier pointed his submachine gun at Murphy, then at the women.

"ALL OF YOU GET UP. Over there by the car. SCHNELL."

They did as they were told and the plane's engines were shut down. The soldier had them line up against the car and held the submachine gun on them. He was young, but looked tired and grim. Helen had no doubt he'd kill them all. In fact, she was pretty sure that's what was about to happen.

Then she saw the tall German she'd seen earlier at the house rise up out of the weeds, brush himself off and begin walking towards them, a grim smile on his face, a strange scoped rifle in his hands.

Then she heard someone yell and turned. Truman was at the door of the plane and had been about to climb in, the German's submachine gun jammed in his back, when her husband had appeared at the door, a bolt-action rifle in his hands.

"LEAVE THEM ALONE," he yelled. "THAT'S MY WIFE, YOU BASTARDS."

"NO, JACK, DON'T!" Helen screamed, sure that they would kill him.

The tall German raised the rifle. "Drop the gun now or we kill all of you. If you drop the weapon, you may live. I may even let the others live, but if you die I have no use for the plane or anyone in or around it. Everyone will die...do you understand me?"

Jack Frye looked around at the guns pointed at him and his friends.

"Do what they say, Jack. It's no good. They came here for me. No sense others getting hurt," Truman said softly.

Frye tossed the rifle and it clattered against the hardpan runway surface. The tall German smiled and raised his weapon, leaning it against his shoulder like a hunter taking a break. "That's better. Now just do as I say and no one will get..."

Suddenly there were three rapid gunshots. Murphy watched in amazement as the tall officer went down first, then the head of the soldier standing behind Truman exploded. He turned back to face the soldier holding the machinegun on them just in time to see him take two steps and fall to the ground, face down.

Murphy dove for the MP40, then grabbed for Truman who was still standing there stunned. "Are you all right sir?"

"Fine, fine. Getting a little deaf from all the damn shooting though," Truman responded. Murphy turned around to see Cates rise up from the brush about 60 yards away and walk towards them, a .30-30 Winchester resting on one shoulder. It was the same way the German had done it, and

Murphy nearly shot him, but Cates raised a hand and Murphy lowered the weapon.

"Cates! How the hell did you get here?"

"Same way these fellers did," Cates said as he came up to him. "Horseback. We came cross-country, whereas you had to follow the road. Cut quite a bit of time off that way."

"Where are the horses?"

"Behind that knoll there," Cates said as he turned to point. The blast caught him in the chest and he staggered back, looking down at the tiny red bloom on his chest strangely as the others looked on in horror, then he fell to his knees, then onto his face. On the other side of him stood Laurel Hausen, holding the little Mauser Hsc pistol Schmidt had given her. It was now pointed at Harry Truman. Murphy didn't hesitate. He pointed the MP40 at her and pulled the trigger.

106

JAKE TAPPED the P-80's fuel gauge and grimaced. He should have put the jet down in Nevada, but he was worried about Elliot, and wanted to warn Truman and the authorities that they were under attack. With the radio not working, he had no choice but to get back as quickly as possibly, and the P-80 had been the only real choice. He hit the radio again with the heel of his hand in frustration, glancing at the fluttering fuel gauge out of the corner of his eye. He had to get the plane on the ground before it just fell out of the sky. The P-80 was fast, but its glide ratio was for shit.

The raw slash of Sycamore Canyon appeared briefly on his left as he flashed by, the brown water of Sycamore Creek looking like a mere trickle at altitude, curving into the wide, muddy Verde River, swollen and brown with spring runoff, then a minute later he could see the tiny town of Cottonwood off to his right. He was following the Verde's east bank, planning on sweeping in from the north to land at the airport when suddenly the low fuel alarm began beeping loudly. He had 60 seconds to get on the ground before he flamed out and the jet took on all the aerodynamics of a rock. He'd never had to dead-stick a jet before, and with the small wing surfaces of the P-80 he wasn't looking forward to it.

He quickly ran through his options: he no longer had time for a normal approach to the airport, and there was no other smooth area on the west side of the river to put the jet down. He saw a bright flash to his left, about eleven o'clock, and Jake realized it was Jack Frye's bright silver Lockheed Electra shining in the sun. There wouldn't be room to land on the runway with the other plane on it, but it gave Jake an idea. In the blink of an eye he'd passed over Frye's private airstrip and banked hard left, pulling the P-80 into a tight turn, lining the plane up with 89A just beyond it.

Jake was lined up with the road now, the fuel alarm screaming at him, the true speed of the plane more evident this close to the ground. He knew it wasn't a good idea to land a jet on a gravel surface – one little rock into the turbine and the engine would self-destruct, but he was out of options.

He set the flaps at full, then reduced power and the stall indicator started shrieking at him as well, competing with the low fuel alarm, just as the engine which had been running on fumes, gave out, spooling down with the familiar whine he previously had only heard when on the ground as the airspeed dropped and the ground rushed up at him.

He shut off the fuel pump as the plane became a glider - a glider with all the flying properties of a concrete block. Flaps full, fuel off…what was he forgetting?

Landing gear! Jake slammed the landing gear handle down and watched the light on the panel begin blinking, showing that the gear was coming down. The low fuel alarm had shut itself off when he'd shut off the pump, but the stall warning was still screeching at him, and he fed in a little more stick despite all his instincts telling him to pull up, but if he stalled the plane this high he was dead. His only chance was to ride the bullet in and try and flare out just before he hit.

The ground was rushing up at him now, and it was everything he could do to keep it lined up on the road. With the engine finally spooled down, Jake had lost hydraulics and the gear wasn't entirely down and locked yet. He mouthed a silent prayer as the ground sped up at him, sure that he was about to die.

107

JAMES AND Marthenia Pickett were on their way back to Sedona from picking up feed in Cottonwood when the strange plane had flashed overhead in a roar. It was a beautiful spring day and James had his window halfway down. The sound of the jet engine had gotten both their attention.

"What on earth?" said Marthenia as they caught a glimpse of the black and silver streak as it crossed their path, then banked around to the east. James pushed in the clutch and stomped on the brake.

"Some sort of plane...but nothing like I've ever seen," James said.

"Isn't he flying just a bit low?" Marthenia asked,

"I'd say so. Look, here he comes again. Why, I think he's going to...OH SHIT," James yelled.

"James, There's no need for such language."

"HANG ON DAMMIT," James said, ignoring his wife as he jammed the truck into reverse and revved the engine, popping the clutch and throwing his wife against the dashboard as the pickup's tires dug in, spinning crazily, pushing the ancient truck backwards as fast or faster than he'd ever had it going forward.

"JAMES!"

"QUIET WOMAN, HE'S GONNA LAND ON THE DAMN ROAD!" James said, steering over his shoulder as he backed up as fast as he could, his wife's eyes growing wide as she looked out the windshield at the plane getting bigger and bigger, headed directly for them.

108

JAKE'S VIEW of the ground out of the cockpit wasn't great, so he had to go by feel. When he thought he was close enough to the ground he pulled back on the stick, flaring out, the nose of the jet coming up as he scrubbed off airspeed. Unfortunately he'd waited just a couple seconds too long and he was close enough to the ground that the tail hit first, nearly somersaulting the aircraft, a less than desired maneuver known to pilots as a "tailstrike." The last thing he wanted was a ground roll.

As the tail hit, it brought the nose of the plane down heavily, so heavily that the nose gear snapped and Jake found himself staring at gravel as the nose of the plane dug in at over 100 mph, plowing a narrow furrow in the road.

Jake closed his eyes and rode it out, and finally the plane shuddered to a halt, the nose just a few feet from an ancient Ford pickup whose occupants looked up at him with wide eyes, staring at Jake, who took a deep breath and pulled his clenched hands from the control stick. He was on the ground, and miraculously, in one piece. *Elliot is not going to be happy about this,* was all he could think, then he wondered for the hundredth time if Elliot was okay.

He shut down the electrical master switch, the raw smell of burnt wiring and overheated hydraulic fluid filling the cockpit. Last thing he needed now was a fire. He quickly unfastened his harness and unlatched the canopy lid, sliding it back with difficulty, gravity wanting to slide it back towards the crumpled nose of the plane. It reminded him strangely of trying to climb out of the Buick up on the switchbacks just a few months before.

Finally he got the canopy locked back and climbed out, slipping off the wing and falling ingloriously to the ground. He got up and was brushing himself off when he heard the truck door slam and saw the old man driving it shuffling up to him.

"Howdy."

"Howdy," Jake replied, not sure what else to say.

"You missed the runway by a bit, son," the old man opined.

"Don't I know it."

"Could'a been a lot worse I 'spose."

Jake nodded. "Well, I had an instructor once, said any landing you walk away from is a good landing," he said. The old man was eyeing the plane. Clearly he'd never seen anything like it. Jake doubted many had. In the truck his wife had her eyes shut and her hands clasped, lips moving, clearly thanking her God for watching over them.

"Mind if I ask you a question?" the old man said.

"Go right ahead."

"Your name wouldn't be Buck Rogers now would it?"

109

THE MP40 didn't fire. It was jammed, and Murphy could see where the .30-30 round had struck the receiver before angling up into its owners' neck. He cursed as he watched the tall German, the one with the scoped rifle, whom he was sure was the officer in charge, running through the sagebrush, away from the plane. He ran to the German who had taken his 1911, but by the time he found it the officer was gone over a small hill, and his duty was clear; he had to get the vice-president back to Washington and report.

Murphy was sure the German had been wounded – he had seen him go down. If the desert didn't kill him they'd hunt him down soon enough. Then he saw Laurel standing by Helen's convertible with the pistol in her hand and realized that *she* had been the one who shot Cates. He began running towards her, but she fired twice more and he ducked as she jumped into the car, raising a roostertail of dust as she pulled around and tore out of there. He fired a couple shots in her direction with his .45, but didn't hit her -she was gone. He cursed silently. He'd assumed she was the German's hostage, and all along she'd obviously been working with them.

He was recovering his Thompson from the sagebrush where the German had thrown it and was brushing it off when he heard a car and looked down the runway. "Someone's coming," he said.

Jack, Harry and Helen looked up, and as the old pickup came tearing up the airstrip, they could see someone standing in the back. "That's it, Boss, I'm taking him out," Murphy said, raising the Thompson to his shoulder.

"No, wait a minute," Truman said, putting a hand on the barrel of Murphy's Thompson.

"Boss, you need to get out of sight. Let me handle this," Murphy said angrily.

"Agent Murphy, there's been quite enough killing today. Now you stand down until I tell you otherwise. That's an order."

Murphy reluctantly lowered the Thompson, but kept his finger on the trigger as the truck sped up to them.

"Why, that's Jake Ellison in the back," Jack Frye said as the pickup slewed to a halt and Jake jumped out of the bed, then reached through the cab window and shook hands with the older couple driving, then walked towards them, a slight limp still visible. He was wearing a flight suit with an anti-G suit over it. He looked a little worse for wear and grinned painfully as he limped up to them.

"Hello Jake, couldn't find the runway?" Jack Frye said.

"Oh, I found it fine, but a bunch of civilians were standing in the middle of it next to a fancy silver plane, blocking the approach. Mr. Vice-President, you shouldn't be here Sir, we're under attack."

"Now there's a news flash," Murphy said wryly.

"Jake, we were attacked at the house by German commandos. What happened to you?" Jack Frye said.

Jake quickly covered the firefight at the airfield, the dogfight over Sedona with the two tailless German jets, and gave them the general location of where he'd seen Elliot bail out. Truman promised to send a rescue party out to look for him right away, and sent Murphy to the plane to try and radio Washington with the report. If they had come after him, then the president was clearly at risk as well.

"Jake, there's something else. Cates has been shot. We've got him lying down in the plane, and there's a doctor on the way, but it's not good," Jack Frye said.

"Cates? Oh no," Jake said, concern written on his face as he began limping towards the plane.

110

IT WAS dark inside the plane, but once his eyes adjusted to the light Jake saw Cates stretched out on a lounger, eyes shut, with a blanket over him. Helen Frye, who was holding a monogrammed towel on his wound, turned to look as he came in. The plane was set up more like a flying living room than any plane he'd ever seen, and he remembered that this was the Frye's personal airplane. Some people really know how to live, he thought briefly.

"Jake! How did you get here?" Helen asked.

"It's a long story, Helen. How's Cates?"

Cates opened his eyes partway and looked at Jake. "Ready to go dancin' soon as they let me up," he said.

"Now old man, what'd you want to go and get yourself shot for?"

"Hell, it's been awhile…I'd forgotten how much fun it is."

"Cates, stop talking and save your strength," Helen scolded him. "He saved us Jake. He got two of them."

"Hell, I shot all three, but one got away dammit. He waited until Laurel shot me."

"*Laurel* shot you? Laurel Hausen? What the hell does she have to do with this?"

"She's working with them, Jake," Helen said.

"The hell you say."

"The German is more of a danger," Cates said.

"Don't worry, Cates, I'll find him," Jake said grimly.

Cates gave Jake a hard look, one he remembered well from his childhood.

"Now son, you listen to me. That German's dangerous as a coral snake. I wounded him, knocked him right over, so you just let the desert take care of him."

"Cates, these bastards tried to kill you, me, Elliot, the vice-president…why, they nearly blew up Hoover Dam, can you believe it?"

Cates grabbed Jake's arm with surprising strength, giving him that hard look again. "Jake…they killed Doc Edwards."

Jake recoiled at the news. Doc? Dead? It seemed inconceivable. A black cloud of anger engulfed him.

"That sonuvabitch got away was the officer in charge," Cates said. "I know I winged him but good, so he won't get far. Let the authorities handle it, Jake."

Jake heard a car pull up outside and a door slam. "That's probably the doctor. I'm gonna go warn him that treating you is like trying to play baseball with a cactus."

"Jake, now you promise me. You leave that damn German alone."

"Now Cates, you and I both know I can't do that. I can't let him get away."

Cates sighed. "You got your stubbornness from your mother. I never knew a mule half as stubborn as that woman, bless her soul. Take the little paint – you'll find him just over the rise to the north. He's a tough little mustang and he'll do right by you."

The doctor rushed into the plane pushing Jake out of the way, and he recognized the Navy doctor who'd treated him a few times before Doc Edwards had taken over. He was glad. The Navy doc was a good man. "Take it easy, Cates, hang in there," Jake said, backing towards the door.

Cates waved weakly as the doctor bent over him. Jake turned to meet Harry Truman coming through the door with Jack Frye right behind him.

"Jake, don't you worry. We're going to fly him to Flagstaff, then an ambulance will take him to the hospital. We'll take good care of him," Truman said., but Jack Frye was already shaking his head.

They're repaving the strip at Pulliam *and* the one at Williams, or I'd say go there. How about Bellemont?" Frye said.

"You can't land at Bellemont. The Germans detonated a thousand-pounder on the runway to close it," Jake interjected.

"Dammit. Jack, what are our options?" Harry said.

"Well, there's Valle, but it's a bit far from Flagstaff…same with Winslow. I'd say we could land it just outside town on Route 66 and meet an ambulance, but there's bound to be traffic," Frye said.

Truman smiled. "Don't you worry about the traffic, you leave that to me…Jake, where are you going?" he asked as Jake climbed out the door.

"Sir, with all due respect, you have to do your job and I have to do mine. You see Cates to a hospital and find Elliot. I've got a German to track and kill." He saluted Truman smartly, who saluted back, suppressing a smile as Jake began a stumbling run off the runway and into the sagebrush to find a horse.

"God bless America," Harry said softly. "That boy has got some stones." Then he turned to yell into the cockpit. "MURPHY. Get me the Arizona Highway Patrol on the radio. I want Route 66 west of Flagstaff closed and an ambulance standing by. I might only be the vice-president, but by God, they will do it or feel my wrath. Jack, as soon as that doctor says it's okay, I want to be in the air."

"Yes, sir." Frye said with a wide grin. "TWA is happy to help any way we can."

111

J AKE FOUND the mustang grazing right where Cates said he would be, along with another horse he recognized as being from Smoke Trail Ranch. Out of breath from the run, he stopped for a minute, hands on his knees, leaning on the lever-action Winchester he'd found and picked up at the edge of the airfield. Realizing he was still wearing the anti-g suit, he quickly stripped it off and threw it aside.

He unzipped the flight suit to the waist and shrugged out of the sleeves, his T-shirt wet from exertion. He tied the arms around his waist like a belt, cooler already, then picked up the Winchester and checked it. Seeing it had three rounds left, he caught up the reins of the little mustang.

He swung into the saddle, pointed the mustang towards Sycamore Pass and gave him some heel. Soon the little horse was flying over the ground, and Jake soon realized just as Cates had that here was a horse that loved to run. He let him have his head for awhile, sweeping back and forth in large arcs until he ran across fresh tracks.

Pulling the mustang up hard, he quickly dismounted to check them, running his hands over them to find that the edges crumbled easily. They were recent. He measured the stride with an experienced eye and saw that the horse was running hard. Then he saw a small spot of darkness like a tiny moon crater in the dust and bent to look, touched it, and brought it to his nose. No doubt about it, it was blood. Cates was right – he'd hit the bastard. Well of course he was hit, he thought, Cates wasn't one to miss what he was shooting at.

Convinced now he was on the right track, Jake swung back onto the mustang and set off again, this time following the tracks at a fast trot, holding the horse back from the gallop he kept wanting to break into until he got the message. Cates and Tom Crow Flies had taught him all they knew about tracking - which was a lot - and Jake had grown pretty good at it himself. Several times he found dark splotches of blood cratering the dust beside the trail. The German was hit in the right side, from what he could tell, and bleeding freely. Jake fully intended to make him bleed even more freely once he caught up with him.

Cates had been right; the mustang had heart. Jake had run the horse longer than he normally would, and the little horse had taken it in stride. In fact, Jake got the feeling that it hadn't been getting enough exercise. He'd been forced to slow down several times when the trail had gone dim, places where there was more rock than sand, but a scuff on a rock from a hoof, a few drops of perspiration from a sweaty horse, or an overturned rock told the tale. Tom or Cates might have been a little faster, but they'd taught him well, and he was glad now that he'd suffered through those hard lessons. He shifted the carbine as he sat up, pulling up the mustang momentarily to listen.

One summer he and Cates had shot a mountain lion that had been killing heifers, and they tracked the wounded animal for three days into the Secret Mountain Wilderness, the same general area he was in now.

He remembered when Cates had told him casually not to look around, that the cat was above and behind them. The hunters had become the hunted. Cates had stopped his horse and had quietly snicked off the safety on the old Remington Model 8 he carried, presenting his back to the angry animal crouched on the ledge above him.

He had waited until the cougar was in the air, nearly on top of him, then spun his horse, bringing the Remington autoloader up and firing one handed, the big .35 caliber slug catching the lion in the spine, dropping it to the ground where it flopped and writhed, screaming angrily for long seconds until Cates could get his horse under control and put the big cat out of its misery with a second shot to the head.

Jake never understood how Cates had known that the cat was there, or even that it had begun hunting them, circling around to attack them from behind, but now he tried to reach out with his mind and get a sense of where the German was, as dangerous a prey as he'd ever tracked.

The German commando was holding a fairly steady course, due northwest, towards Sycamore Canyon; rough country in the best of weather, and Jake could see storm clouds gathering up on the rim towards Williams. Ironically, the trail he followed passed within just a couple miles of their ranch, and Jake made the decision to make a quick side trip home to change into more suitable clothes and grab some supplies. If nothing else he wanted more than three rounds if he ran into the German, plus if the weather came in on them, which it looked as though it was going to, a slicker, a hat and some food could make the difference between life and death. Even someone as experienced as Jake could die of exposure easily.

This was no time to get stupid. The German wasn't going anywhere - in fact, he was boxing himself in, hoping to lose himself in the wilderness, but he was in Jake's backyard now. Knowing he could easily pick the trail up again, Jake turned the mustang west and ran for the house.

112

SCHMIDT FOUGHT to stay awake. He had bound his wound as tightly as he could with strips torn from his tunic, but he was sure now that the bullet had broken at least one rib, and he'd lost quite a bit of blood. The horse was limping, head down, blowing frothy bubbles from its nostrils. He knew he should get off and walk, let the horse rest, but he was afraid that if he did he wouldn't have the strength to climb back on again.

Blood still trickled down his side despite the field bandage he'd tucked inside his shirt. His ribs on the right ached with every step. It had passed straight through, but he needed to stop and boil some water and clean the wound properly before it went septic. He'd seen enough men die from blood poisoning to know that wasn't the way he wanted to go.

He'd been surprised by the old man, who'd gotten three shots off quickly, yet had managed to hit all three of his targets, including Schmidt. If Schmidt hadn't been in motion at the time - and if the bullet hadn't lost energy when it ricocheted off a spare magazine - he would have likely been killed. He was surprised that a civilian could shoot that well, and even more, stand up in the face of danger the way the old man had. He didn't know what he'd shot him with, but whatever it was it had a punch to it.

The horse stumbled, badly this time, going down hard onto its fetlocks, folding forward and throwing him from the saddle. Schmidt hit the ground face first, the slung G43 smacking him in the back of the head, his broken ribs grinding together, but somehow he suppressed a scream. Groaning, he unslung the rifle and pulled himself up to sit, his back against a nearby rock, agony in every movement.

He looked at the horse, now lying on the ground, legs twitching, chest heaving. It was clearly dying. He took a deep breath and found that he was unable to, his battered ribs hitching in pain. He wiped his lips with the back of his hand and it came away bloody. A shard of rib must have punctured a lung or something when he was thrown.

The horse lay on its side, breathing hard, staring at him with dumb, unseeing eyes. "I am sorry for the trouble I've caused you, leibling," Schmidt said to the horse. "You and I have come to the end of our trail, but there is no need for you to suffer anymore."

Schmidt pulled the rifle towards him by its sling, bringing it to his shoulder and pointing it at the head of the dying animal. The sights swam in his vision and he couldn't seem to hold the barrel still. He took the safety off and pulled the trigger.

Schmidt was still gasping from the recoil of the G43 when he realized he needed to find cover; a spot where he could ambush his pursuers. He checked the magazine out of habit and found one round left. He checked the chamber and there was another round in it, but that was it, two rounds. Frantically he checked his magazine pouches only to find what he already knew: his last full magazine had been the one that had saved his life, deflecting the bullet which would have killed him, but it had bent the magazine and damaged the rounds beyond salvage, and he'd thrown it away, knowing he had more 8mm ammo and the submachine gun in his pack, which was now, of course, pinned under the weight of the dead horse.

He had all the ammo he needed, even another weapon - he just couldn't get to it. It might as well be in Germany for all the good it did him. Could he dig a hole under the horse and get to it? He dismissed the idea immediately; even if he were in better shape, the ground under the horse was nearly solid rock. It would be nearly impossible for a man in good shape with a shovel, let alone him, with his bare hands or maybe a stick.

He cursed his own stupidity. Why hadn't he refilled his magazines from his pack last night? He should know better – he was a better soldier than that. He closed his eyes for a moment, then coughed, wiping blood from his lips once more. He was so tired…

He opened his eyes again, then forced himself to his feet, knowing that if he closed his eyes he would never wake up again. He had two rounds left. He'd take two of them with him then.

Schmidt had always known this would be his fate, dying in battle far from home…it was a fate he'd accepted long ago, and now he embraced it, smiling grimly, coughing again, the blood running freely from his mouth now. I will show them how a German soldier dies, he thought, a grim smile spreading across his face.

113

JAKE CHANGED clothes while Rosa packed some food into the old homemade canvas saddlebags he'd had since he was a boy. By the time he went back outside Jose had already saddled the appaloosa they called Hank, after Hank Williams, a young country performer Cates had seen play locally, and had pulled the gear off the sturdy little mustang, who he'd let into a corral to cool off.

The mustang could smell water, and was letting Jose know in no uncertain terms that he wanted some, and right away. The horse kicked the fence for the third time as Jake crossed the yard, Cates' old Remington Model 8 in one hand, his bedroll in the other. The mustang stood by the fence, looking at him as if to say, *Just where do you think you're going without me?* He liked the tough little horse and wondered if Jack Frye knew what he had there, then wondered if he'd sell it to him.

He'd left the lever action in the gun case and loaded the semi-auto .35 caliber Remington and grabbed two more boxes of shells for it. He was wearing his new .45 Colt automatic Cates and Rosa had given him for Christmas on his right hip, with his stag-handled hunting bowie in a sheath on his left side, the curve of the stag-horn handle facing forward.

His favorite Filson tincloth hat was on his head, a hat he had bought in Alaska where'd he learned soon enough that Filson was simply the best outdoor gear there was. It wasn't a Stetson, but there was no better hat in a rainstorm, and his slicker was tucked in on top of his bedroll where he could get to it in a hurry. Cates would have said he was loaded for bear, and he would be right. Ramiro had just finished cinching the saddle up on Hank as Jake threw his bedroll up behind the saddle cantle and tied it off to the rear rigging.

"Once he's cooled down real good, and had a drink of water, give that mustang an apple for me will you, Jose? He's earned it and then some." Jose nodded in return, a man of few words.

Rosa came bustling out of the house with Jake's old saddlebags, two canteens, and a sandwich in wax paper. "Tomatillo, you eat this now. I pack some burritos, beans, y tortillas for jou later."

"Gracias, Mama," Jake said with a smile, taking the food from the woman who had raised him as one of her own. "Cates is all right?"

"Si. They called and are taking him to the hospital in Flagstaff. Jose will take me up to see him."

Jake could see tears glistening in her eyes. "He's tough – he'll be okay," he said.

She grabbed his hands in hers, holding them tightly so he'd look at her, her eyes black fire even in daylight. "Be careful, Mijo. That hombre es muy peligroso. Jou come back to your Rosa, jou hear me?"

Jake leaned over and kissed her forehead. "Si, Madre, Si. Don't worry," he said, then ignoring the moisture in her eyes, he slung the saddlebags across the horse's rump and tied them off, then mounted up. Ramiro handed the rifle and his sandwich back up to him, and with a final smile for Rosa and a nod to Jose and Ramiro, Jake turned the Appaloosa in the direction of the gate and gave him a firm kick in the withers, the big grey horse surging forward like the storm clouds now gathering and darkening over the Mogollon Rim.

114

MORRIE SAT at the kitchen table staring out the window, worried about Jake. She hadn't spoken with him since the previous day and they'd had a bit of a falling out over continuing to investigate Lily's murder. Truthfully, she was afraid for him. He had no business poking around a murder, even if that gal *had* been like a sister to him. He'd been shot at, blown up and run off the road, but he was still too stubborn to see that if he kept on the same path, he was going to end up dead, and that was something she just couldn't bear to watch.

Morrie knew that her knowledge of the world might be a bit naïve and innocent at times – her parents had taught her to trust people until they proved they couldn't be trusted - but she wasn't so naïve that she didn't know that the world could be a very bad place, that there was evil in the world, and she couldn't help but believe that Jake had been caught up in something very bad. Muy malo as the Mexicans would say.

A saucer rattled and she looked up to see her cross-eyed cat, Felix, on the counter again, picking his way through the breakfast dishes she was putting off doing. Morrie jumped to her feet, clapping her hands.

"SHOO. YOU GET OFF THAT COUNTER." Startled, the cat made a run to the end of the counter, knocking over a glass, and just before jumping off the counter managed to bump a half-full bottle of ammonia her mother had left there. Morrie managed to catch the glass before it rolled off onto the floor, but she didn't see the ammonia teetering on the edge until it was too late. She lunged for it, but didn't get there fast enough, and pulled back at the last minute, shielding her face as the glass bottle smashed on the floor and the acrid stench of ammonia filled the room.

"STUPID CAT," she yelled, choking on the fumes, but Felix had wisely made himself scarce, having exited the room at flank speed.

Morrie looked at the mess on the floor and sighed, then sneezed. Ammonia had always made her sneeze, which her mother had joked was her way of getting out of mopping the floors. She sneezed again as she moved to open the windows, then went to the mudroom to get a mop and bucket. Sneezing or no sneezing, she couldn't leave that broken glass on the floor.

By the time she'd swept up the glass, her eyes were watering and her nose was runny. She ran the string mop under some water to soften it, wrung it out, and plopped it down on the floor, producing another sneezing fit. Desperately she reached into her pocket and was surprised to find a handkerchief, then remembered Jake handing it to her when she was crying over her brother. Jake had been such a gentleman, she thought as she sneezed again, this time into the hanky, as she bent down to pick up an errant piece of glass that had escaped detection.

She sneezed yet again, silently cursing the inventor of ammonia, and leaned the mop against the counter to refold the handkerchief. It was then that she noticed the black stains on the cloth, and at first she thought a fountain pen had exploded in her pocket. She was going to have to buy Jake a new handkerchief…oh damn, I probably have ink on my face now, she thought, as she stifled another sneeze.

She went to the bathroom and looked in the mirror, breathing a sigh of relief as she saw she hadn't gotten any ink on her. She went to throw the ruined handkerchief away, then noticed an odd thing: the ink stains were fading! Quickly she flattened out the cloth on the sideboard, realizing with shock that the fading black marks weren't stains at all, but letters and numbers. Suddenly they were gone entirely, and she was looking at a plain white handkerchief again, with nothing but the initials LH embroidered in red in the corner.

She stood there for a minute, just staring with amazement at the handkerchief. Had she just imagined it? She decided almost immediately that she *wasn't* seeing things, that maybe it was invisible ink. She remembered writing secret messages in "invisible ink" made from baking soda and water as a child. To see the message, you needed grape juice as a reactive agent.

The only possible chemical she could think of that she'd been around was the ammonia. Morrie ran back to the kitchen and closed the windows. The smell of the ammonia was much weaker now, and she realized that it must have been the vapors that had reacted as a reagent with the "ink".

Holding her breath again and trying not to sneeze, Morrie knelt on the cold linoleum and held the handkerchief over the floor, just inches away from where the ammonia had spilled, so she could read it. For several seconds there was nothing, then a faint pattern began to appear. She could discern a few letters and numbers, but it was still unreadable. It just wouldn't resolve itself into the black, inky letters she remembered.

Her mind raced. The ammonia vapors must have to be more potent. She yanked open the cupboard under the sink and searched frantically for another bottle of ammonia, finally finding a new bottle way at the back. She pulled it out with trembling hands, took a deep breath, opened the bottle, and proceeded to pour a good portion out onto the floor.

Despite holding her breath, the fumes immediately tickled her nose and when she finally had to breath, made her head swim. She sneezed as she reached for the handkerchief and nearly dropped it in the ammonia, potentially erasing the message. She told herself to slow down, stood up and took another deep breath, then knelt again, holding the handkerchief just inches off the floor once more.

Several seconds ticked by as, heart in throat, she wondered if the ink somehow only worked once, then destroyed itself, but then suddenly letters and numbers appeared, coalescing miraculously on the white cloth as if by magic.

The words were in English, amazingly, and she realized that it was an address, one right in Flagstaff! Choking from the ammonia, she stood up and found the pen hanging on a string near the phone, but she needed paper. She yanked the pen loose and scratched the address down on a brown paper bag lying on the table before she forgot it. Her head was swimming now, and she realized as she sneezed once more that she needed more oxygen...the ammonia was displacing it.

She threw herself at the nearest window, black spots swimming before her eyes, and pushed it open, gasping as she hungrily sucked in the fresh air. When she'd recovered she opened the other windows again as well. The room still reeked of ammonia, but she could breathe.

Suddenly she heard the front door. She quickly put the ammonia back in the cupboard and stuffed the address into the pocket of her slacks. She was sneezing into the now white kerchief when her mother came into the kitchen with a bag of groceries in her arms. "My Lord, what on earth happened in here?" she exclaimed as Morrie sneezed again, trying this time not to use the handkerchief. It was evidence after all, though of what she had no idea.

"Felix knocked over a bottle of ammonia. I was trying to clean it up."

"Oh sugar. I must have left it on the counter again. You shouldn't have tried to clean it up, Morrison. You know how much ammonia bothers you. Now shoo, I'll take care of it," she said, setting the groceries on the table and pushing Morrie out of the room.

"Thanks, Mom. I just didn't want to leave it. I think I got most of the glass."

"That's fine. You go on now."

"Okay. Think I'll go for a walk and clear my head."

"Good idea. Dinner is at six."

"Oh, Ma."

115

JAKE HEARD the rifle shot clearly, but it was too far away to be directed at him. It might not be the German commando, but he was betting it was. The heavy roll of thunder made Jake look up from his tracking. He eyed the dark clouds to the north with trepidation. Where he was it was bright and sunny, with songbirds singing boisterously in the brush, but somewhere high above them on the Mogollon rim it was raining like hell.

The German had been following an old dry wash, the sides made narrow by juniper and wait-a-minute vine overhanging the sides, good for concealment. The floor of the wash was a rough, barren landscape of torn roots, boulders and sand, and you could hear a horse's hooves a half-mile away, but it was a bad place to be if the water came - as it always did eventually. Jake could tell from the fact there were no weeds growing in the bottom of the wash, and by the striations recently left in the sand by running water, that it had flooded there not very long ago, despite the way it looked now.

When it did flood, it would fill to the rim in seconds, and be 15 to 20 feet deep full of rushing, muddy water filled with boulders, trees and other debris, and from the way the sides had been cut so deeply, he'd play hell finding a way out.

Every nerve in his body told him to get out of that wash, that the German was up ahead, as bad as any wounded mountain lion, lying in wait, ready to spring, but Jake knew he couldn't let him get away, as he'd likely end up killing some innocent somewhere nearby for food and clothes. Jake concentrated on the ground and the tracks before him, while keeping his ears open for the sound of rushing water.

116

WHEN MORRIE had told her mother she was going for a walk, she'd meant it. She just didn't mention *where* she was going. The address on the handkerchief was downtown, across the tracks, just off Beaver Street. There was a late-night juke joint just down the street that she and Jake had gone to a few times, so the address had jumped out at her.

It was a beautiful, sunny spring day in Flagstaff, daffodils and tulips sprouting in yards and beside the churches. The sun burned its way down through a sky of pure cerulean blue, the San Francisco Peaks still tipped in snow; where Humphrey's and Agassiz rose above their green skirt of pine trees they were still brilliantly white - too bright to look at for long. It was picture perfect. It would make a great postcard, she thought as she strode down the uneven sidewalk on Cherry Hill as she headed downtown.

There was a slight chill in the air that bit through her sweater, but it was refreshing, and there was a smell everywhere of damp earth and new leaves, everything fresh and new. Morrie loved the spring. It always opened her heart and made her feel as if anything were possible.

Today, however, she felt a cloud over her heart. Jake had told her how he'd found the handkerchief in Lily's room, along with the book and the letter. What on earth had Lily gotten herself into?

117

SCHMIDT LAY in the brush, motionless, his G43 pointed up the wash. His only chance now was to let the cowboy find him, and then ambush him and take his horse. He had two rounds left, but Schmidt needed only one. His eyes burned with sweat, and he'd lost his cap in the fall from the horse. He missed it. It would shade his eyes and keep the sweat from pouring down his face as it did now. His scope had been broken in the fall and he'd removed it – now the iron sight image wavered in the heat, and he forced himself to concentrate.

Lying on his stomach like this was pooling the blood in his chest, and his breathing was unnaturally shallow and forced, with a faint, hoarse rattle beginning. He was beginning to wonder if he could hit anything with a rifle with his breathing this bad. Breath control was critical for a sniper, and he could hardly catch his breath let alone control it. Schmidt was pretty sure he was dying, but he would die as a soldier; as an SS man. He would go down fighting.

Suddenly the cowboy who'd been following him appeared in his sights, bent over the neck of his horse, staring at the ground, tracking him. Schmidt wondered why he hadn't heard the click of his horse's hooves against the rocks, then saw that the clever bastard had wrapped them with burlap to muffle them.

Schmidt centered the sights on the cowboy's chest, then raised it to his head, taking up the slack in the trigger, his breathing ragged, his eyes blurring from lack of oxygen. He shook it off and squinted at the sights, squeezing harder until the rifle recoiled against his shoulder.

118

JAKE FELT the air from the bullet as it scooped the hat off his head. If the horse hadn't stepped down off that rock into a hole at that very second his head would've exploded like a pumpkin. The report came a fraction of a second later, but Jake was already spurring the appaloosa forward. There was only one thing to do when you're ambushed, Tom Crow Flies and Cates had both advised him, and that was to attack, to drive straight into the center of it, so he drove the horse forward as he crouched over its neck.

He saw the German stand up about 50 yards farther down the wash and ran the horse straight at him. The German soldier seemed to be moving slowly, and there was blood on his chin and tunic. The horse leapt towards him, racing down the wash as he slowly got to his feet and raised his weapon; Jake pulled out his .45 and fired a couple rounds at him, but the German didn't move.

Then he was on him, the German swinging the rifle up to bear as Jake leapt, Apache style, from the running horse onto his enemy.

* * * * *

Schmidt couldn't believe it. He'd missed. The cowboy's horse had stepped down just as he fired, and was now bearing down on him. He forced himself up off the ground from where he lay beneath the cutbank, exposing himself, not caring. He had one more round and he had to make it count, but he couldn't keep the cowboy in his sights. The bottom of the creek bed was so rough and the horse moving so fast that he couldn't get a bead on him. Then the American pulled a pistol and started shooting at him. He heard a bullet hit a rock near his feet and go whining off, then a second one whir past his head, then before he could recover the enraged American was there, leaping from his horse like the Indians he'd seen in American westerns as Schmidt swung the rifle up to bear, too close to miss now, the sights centered on the leaping body, and he pulled the trigger.

* * * * *

Jake barely felt the second bullet tear through his shirt and slice through his side. He was too angry. The impact spun him a bit in the air, the horse running wildly down the wash, then he hit Schmidt hard, knocking him to the ground, and the rifle from his hands, but he hit his hand so hard on the stock of the German's gun that it knocked the pistol from his grip, and it went skittering across the rocks, his right hand numb from the impact - the German grabbing at him desperately with hands like talons. Jake hit him with a left, then another one, then again and again until he began to get the feeling back in his right hand and started giving him the news with his good hand as well. Finally he felt the German soldier's grip slacken, and he rolled away and dove for his gun.

* * * * *

Schmidt endured the beating with equanimity. The American had pinned him with his weight, but the punches he threw felt weak, until he got in a couple rights and Schmidt realized he was right handed. The second right cross made him see stars, then suddenly the weight was off him. The cowboy was scrambling for the gun he'd lost when he jumped, and Schmidt knew he had to stop him or it was over. He forced himself to his feet and leapt at the American, who had just picked up the pistol, and was turning around to shoot him. He grabbed the barrel of the gun and pushed it away just as it fired, then grabbed the American's other wrist, pushing his arms apart so he couldn't shoot.

* * * * *

Jake couldn't believe the German was so strong. For someone who'd obviously been shot, and had pink froth bubbling from his mouth, the man fought like a wildcat. He had Jake's left wrist in a death grip, the other hand clutching the barrel of the gun so Jake couldn't shoot him. It had surprised Jake enough that when the German hooked his leg behind Jake's he went down hard, the German falling on top of him, but as he fell Jake instinctively got his knees pulled up to his chin between the German and himself, and used the leverage as they went down to flip him over backward in a somersault move he'd learned from Tom Crow Flies.

It broke the grip the German had on his hands, and Jake rolled over quickly and came to his knees as the German did the same, preparing to lunge again, but as he raised the pistol to fire, Jake heard a terrible rushing sound, accompanied by a deeper, heavier rumble beneath it. He saw the German's eyes widen, and turned just in time to see a 25 foot wall of turgid, roiling brown water bearing down on them.

119

THE HOUSE was small and plain, with peeling yellow paint and leprous French vanilla trim. The small narrow lot which it sat on matched the house's general state of disrepair, with unruly weeds poking up here and there through the hardpan yard, giving it a worn-out, unkempt look. A small, scraggly patch of tired grass hung on at the back of the lot, protected by the shade of several large sycamores and a huge western oak which loomed over the corner of the yard, the feathery remnants of a rope swing on one huge limb twisting idly in the breeze.

Morrie approached the door apprehensively, unsure what she was going to say. What was she doing here? She caught a glimpse of bare wood floor behind a tattered lace curtain through the low window that looked out onto the porch. The place seemed deserted. She pulled the screen door open, raised her hand, paused, then knocked loudly, still unsure exactly what she'd say if someone answered, but there was no answer, nor even any sound from within. She knocked again, louder, waited for a minute, then let the screen door shut on its spring, which needed tightening and didn't pull the door completely shut.

She looked around her. The street was quiet, although she could hear the traffic across the tracks on Route 66 and the plaintive wail of a train horn in the distance. She turned back to the door and reached up, running her hands along the doorframe, checking for a key, but found nothing. There was no welcome mat to look under, so she stepped off the porch and circled the house, standing on tiptoe to peek in the side windows. The house was empty, no rugs, no pictures, just a couple of orphan chairs and a small, metal-legged kitchen table. Then she saw a glass on the sink sideboard. It still had water in it. Someone was clearly using the house, but was likely not there at the moment. She went to the back door, which had its own little miniature roof to keep the rain off your head while you were fishing for your keys.

Feeling like a criminal, she ran her hand above the door frame, but here too found nothing. Discouraged, she stepped off the tiny landing and stood there, looking around, hands on hips. Most people in Flagstaff didn't bother locking up unless they were going away for awhile, and an empty house, well, it made sense. Still, she knew most folks stashed a key somewhere.

She checked all the obvious places; under a clay pot, beneath every rock within ten feet of the door, on and around the window sill...then she noticed a broken slat on the sidewall of the steps. Pushing the slat aside, she reached up and groped around inside, and sure enough, found a finishing nail, and hanging on the nail, a key.

She brought it out into the sunlight triumphantly, then immediately looked around, remembering what she was doing was illegal. Why was she doing this anyway? She could be arrested for breaking and entering. The answer came to her immediately: she wanted to help Jake. After all the tears and pleading with him to please drop this thing with Lily and let the police handle it, here she was, about to break into a stranger's house, simply because she'd found a hidden message on a handkerchief.

She took a deep breath and climbed the stairs again to the back door and tried the key, half-hoping it was just an old one and the lock had been changed, but it fit perfectly, and turned smoothly, as if it'd been oiled. The door swung open silently, as if the hinges had been oiled as well. She let the screen door close quietly behind her and found she was in a mudroom, off the kitchen, and the house had that dry, slightly dusty smell that places get when they stand empty.

She stepped quietly forward into the kitchen, then into the front room, not even sure what she was looking for. A second doorway to the left turned into a hall, which led to two tiny bedrooms on the right and a bathroom on the left. There was toilet paper, a sliver of soap and a hand towel in the bathroom, and a man's safety razor sat on the sink. There was nothing else. Each bedroom had a small metal bed made up with a wool blanket military-style, so tight you could bounce a quarter off them.

The floor creaked slightly as she moved forward, and Morrie stopped, taking a deep breath, thinking she wasn't doing any good here, she was just scaring herself. She looked around each room, but saw nothing. At the end of the hall was a linen closet, its bi-fold doors wide open, its shelves empty. The whole place was odd. There were signs that it was being used, but no signs of clothes or personal items.

Morrie backed down the hall, trying to figure it. It just didn't make sense. As she went through the living room she turned and looked again. There was no furniture besides one very sorry excuse for a davenport - no chairs or side tables at all. Whoever was staying here clearly wasn't interested in creature comforts.

She went back into the kitchen, looking around. There were four water glasses, including the half-empty one on the sink sideboard, nothing in the sink. There were four plates and four bowls in the glass-fronted cabinets, so she could see everything inside without opening them. She pulled the drawers open one by one and found four forks, four knives, four spoons, a spatula, a ladle and a paring knife, nothing else. Everything was in one drawer, the way a bachelor would keep them – all the other drawers were empty. She found no napkins, but there were two dish towels and a small container of dish soap flakes under the sink. She closed the cabinet door softly, straightened up and turned around, to find Laurel Hausen standing there staring at her.

"What are you doing here?" she demanded, her face a thunderhead.

"Oh my God, you scared me!" Morrie said, taking a step back to lean against the counter as Laurel took a step closer.

"I asked you a question. What are you doing here?"

"This *your* place? It's *very* cute. Who's your decorator?" Morrie said, not sure what else to say, her mind racing for an answer. She instinctively didn't like Laurel, but she had to think quickly if she didn't want to get arrested.

"For the last time, what are you doing in here?"

"I'm looking for Jake. I got a message to meet him here."

Laurel shook her head, a look on her face like a disappointed schoolteacher.

"You're lying. Give me the key," she said, stretching out her hand, palm up. Morrie didn't know what else to do, so she put the key in her hand. Laurel's fingers snapped shut around it, and it went into the pocket of her slacks.

"Well, it's been nice visiting with you, but if Jake's not here, I guess I'll just be going…" Morrie began, as she pushed past Laurel, her panic so close to the surface she could taste it. She barely got to the doorway when a thin man in a badly fitting grey suit with no necktie and a face like a jackal stepped in front of her. He had a small, nasty looking gun in his hand, and the look on his face told her he wouldn't mind using it.

"You aren't going anywhere," Laurel said from behind her. "What do you say we wait here for Jake together?"

120

JAKE CAME to with the Appaloosa's warm, fetid breath in his face, and a sandpaper tongue licking him. He hurt everywhere, his entire body feeling like someone had gone after him with a baseball bat. He rolled over on his side as he felt his gorge rise, vomiting the putrid water he'd swallowed into the sand. His lungs hurt even more than the rest of him, and his side burned where the German had shot him. Finally purged of creek water, he looked up at the Appy who shook its head happily, then lowered its nose to nudge him again.

"Good horse," he said weakly, running one trembling hand over the Appaloosa's wide, hard nose. The appaloosa nickered in response as Jake took stock. His boots and one sock were missing, and his holster had been torn from the belt by the violence of the flood, but somehow he hadn't lost his knife, which made him glad. His head hurt like hell, which wasn't surprising, as he gently probed a gash at the top of his skull. In fact, now that he was more aware, his entire body ached worse than before…and he was *cold*. His new .45 was gone along with the holster. He didn't remember losing it, but it was not surprising really.

He wasn't sure what time it was, but the light was failing, so it was nearly dark. He realized his teeth were chattering, and that he was going hypothermic. The water had been mostly snowmelt and freezing rain from Flagstaff. He needed to make a fire, and do it now, before it got colder. He pulled the one wet sock he had left from his foot, then forced himself to his feet and staggered to his horse, who stood patiently waiting, nosing the ground for forage but not finding much. The ground felt dry beneath his bare feet as he untied the saddlebags and bedroll with trembling, bruised fingers that didn't want to work right. He had to put them in his mouth to warm them, the feeling coming back in tingles and sudden, painful heat. It hadn't done much more than sprinkle where he was now, which was good – it meant he ought to be able to find some dry wood.

He tried unbuttoning his wet shirt, but his shaking, still-numb fingers wouldn't work the buttons, so he simply tore it off, replacing it with the wool serape he kept in his bedroll. It made him feel immediately better, and suddenly all he could think of was a warm fire. He dropped the saddlebags on the ground and staggered around the perimeter gathering wood until he had a good armful, dumping it next to a good size boulder that would make a good heat reflector.

He had trouble getting the straps of his saddlebags open with his frozen fingers, but he persevered, and while he was still cold, his teeth had stopped chattering, and the serape was warm and dry. He pulled the fire sack in which he kept tinder, flint and steel from his saddlebags, found the waterproof matches he kept in a tin sealed with beeswax, and soon had a flickering infant of a fire going, which he bent over, blowing on the flames carefully, feeding it twigs and dry grass slowly so as to not choke it.

The wind had died down, and from the look of the stars beginning to emerge from the soft blue glow of the firmament he figured he should be safe from rain, at least for awhile. He had a small canvas tarp with him that he rolled his bedroll into, but he hadn't the gumption to set it up.

He probed the wound in his side gingerly, examining it in the flickering light as he fed the growing fire. He'd been lucky – it had gone straight through, hitting nothing but meat, but it still hurt like hell. The fire felt wonderful, and he wanted nothing more than to collapse, but he knew he needed more wood to get through the night, so he forced himself up onto his feet again.

When he was satisfied that he had enough wood he shucked off his soaked Levis, unrolled his bedroll, and climbed in naked, shivering, pulling the serape over him to serve as an extra blanket. Finally warm, he fed the fire with one hand, the Appaloosa standing nearby, content for the moment. Then he had a thought and forced himself from his warm cocoon again long enough to hobble the horse and give him a handful of oats he kept in his bags, then shivering, climbed back into his bedroll.

He had a bad moment when he imagined the German finding him asleep, drawn by the fire, but then that rational side of his brain told him there was no way the Nazi soldier could have survived in the condition he was in, with a gunshot wound and likely a punctured lung. Hell, that flash flood had nearly done for him, and he was in much better shape. If he hadn't had the strength to hold onto the tree roots he'd been washed into until the water went down, he'd likely have drowned, or been beaten to pieces against the rocky sides of the wash. As it was, he'd barely managed to pull himself up and over the edge before passing out. Besides, the German had no fire, no supplies, so if he did manage to survive the flood itself, hypothermia would do him in. He'd be dead by morning.

Jake looked at the Appy, wondering if he would've made it through the night if the horse hadn't found him. "You, my friend, are going to be apple-rich for the rest of your days. I owe you," he told the horse, who blew through its nose, shaking its head in response. It was the last thing Jake saw before falling asleep.

121

SCHMIDT'S EYES fluttered open, and he immediately rolled over and retched up water and blood. He lay there coughing and choking for interminable minutes despite the stabbing pain, hardly able to catch his breath, no matter what he did. He was lying on his back on the rocks of the now muddy creek bed, the high water that had swept them away gone now, the sun peeking out between clouds, low on the horizon.

It would be dark soon, and Schmidt understood it would likely be his last night on earth, and not a pleasant one. One lung was slowly filling with blood, and his chest felt as though it were filled with broken glass every time he wheezed out a shallow breath. Slowly he began dragging himself towards a low overhanging ledge, pain stabbing him in a different place with each movement, but he kept going; a wounded animal looking for a private place to die.

Finally he saw the low ledge above him, and grasping the dried grass clumps from the previous year's growth, pulled himself towards it, a dry buzzing filling his ears. He shook his head, unable to rid himself of the sound. One more huge effort and he was through the weeds, beneath the dark, rocky overhang. The buzzing in his head seemed louder now, and he stopped, looking up in confusion, finally seeing the big Mojave Green rattlesnake coiled in one corner, its tail shaking in fury, the head drawn back to strike. Schmidt tried to scream as the rattler struck him in the face, again and again, but he didn't have the lung capacity. Finally the snake pulled away and slithered off, leaving him alone to die as the sun dropped behind Mingus Mountain, the darkness slowly erasing his pain.

– Part Four –
April 12ᵗʰ, 1945

122

KESSLER PARKED the car by the small cairn of rocks he'd built to mark the spot where he'd come out of the woods. He was dressed in the second pair of black slacks he'd bought, leaving the remaining uniforms hanging unused and unneeded in the closet of the hotel. Over the T-shirt the clerk had suggested as an undergarment for the high neck jacket he wore the dark navy blue sweater, with the watch cap and thin, black gloves.

He had on the walking shoes, with the polished black brogues, a second pair of black pants and one of the Nehru jackets - the only one he would need - folded neatly in a brown burlap bag to which he'd sewn a simple strap to so he could sling it over his shoulder. It had rained the previous night, making the remaining leaves on the ground supple, soft and silent.

He had removed the lamp from the overhead light in the car in preparation, and now silently opened the door, slung the bag over his shoulder crossways so he wouldn't lose it, the sharp weight of the pistol tucked into his belt as he pushed the door shut silently, until it was closed, but hadn't latched. He left the keys in the ignition, hoping some troubled delinquent might find the car and steal it.

He'd have preferred to have his face blackened, but he couldn't risk it – he doubted he'd find anywhere to clean it off. There was nearly no moon so it was dark, and he barely had decent light to navigate by, but didn't dare use a flashlight. Kessler stood silently for several minutes next to the car, just listening, orienting himself, allowing his eyes to adjust fully to the darkness, then slowly, silently, he moved like a wraith into the forest.

After cutting the bottom strand of barbed wire and wriggling under the fence, Kessler slowed even further, moving almost imperceptibly, watching for the guard shacks which he found, amazingly, by the thin cracks of yellow light seeping past the blackout curtains. Murmurs and soft laughter could be heard when he strained his ears. No noise discipline. He shook his head in disbelief as he slid quietly past.

Abwher intelligence had reported a small ravine just to the north of the facility, and Kessler headed in that direction, steering through the darkness with only the dim light of the moon and his own unerring sense of direction to steer him. The ground was beginning to dip into a small swale populated by a prodigious colony of large rhododendron bushes, when suddenly a dog began barking nearby. Kessler immediately dropped to his stomach and crawled into the depths of the rhododendrons, curling into a ball to hide the white of his face.

As the patrol came closer, the dog began alternating between whining and barking, clearly excited, and Kessler cursed silently, seeing it in his mind straining against its leash as the Marine cursed. A flashlight played through the leaves as Kessler tried to make himself smaller, his head tucked under his arms. His back to the Marine, the dog's panting breath and sharp, urgent barks loud in his ears, just mere feet away.

"What do you think?" he heard one Marine ask another. They were closer now, maybe six feet from where he lay, and he forced himself to remain still as they stood at the edge of the bushes, the dog whining to be let loose.

"Just another goddamn rabbit I bet. We always see them down here. Probably a whole warren of them in them rhoadies. Rosy, stop it! HEEL!" the second Marine said sharply, and Schmidt could hear her yelp as he jerked on her lead.

"She's a good dog. Great nose, but she just can't resist rabbits. C'mon Rosy, let's go. I said let's go!" Another sharp yelp from another jerk on the leash and Rosy was dragged off in the direction of the other guard shack, still growling and whining.

Kessler waited until he could no longer hear their footsteps stirring the leaves, and uncoiled himself slowly from the tangle of branches, sliding deeper into the swale he was sure led to the ravine. He realized he had to urinate, but ignored it for now. He only had a couple of hours before daylight, and he would lose his moonlight as soon as it dipped below the horizon.

As it turned out it took him nearly four hours to move just a few hundred meters. He low-crawled the last 100 meters on his stomach, finally getting close enough to see the dim pathway lights of the facility, which they kept lit despite the blackout, apparently confident at this late stage in the war of the inability of their enemies to attack them at home. They were about to find out otherwise, Kessler thought smugly.

As he inched closer he was more aware than ever of the increase in security here, in the president's backyard. He lay on the ground in the shadows and timed the sentries. He saw no dogs here, and hoped that the pepper he'd sprinkled liberally on his back trail would prevent him being discovered by the one he'd encountered earlier. He thought of the young pup he'd rented for the day; Pepper, who'd been responsible for the idea, and smiled.

The Marine guards seemed lackadaisical, strolling by about every fifteen minutes in pairs, with Thompson or Reising submachine guns slung over their shoulders. As soon as the fourth pair of sentries passed, he pulled his dress jacket and cummerbund out of the bag, pulled off his shoes, then waited. Once the next pair of guards passed by, he rose up slowly from the ground, quickly pulled off the sweater and stuffed it into the bag with his hunting boots, exchanging them for the shiny, black oxfords and the clean pair of pants.

Quickly snapping the hooks of the cummerbund together in front, he turned it around so the hooks were now in the back and tucked the Walther into the small of his back. He then donned the white jacket, kicked some leaves over the burlap sack, and stepped out from behind the tree and onto the path, reaching for his cigarettes.

Kessler's heart was pounding out of his chest, his hands shaking from adrenaline, but he forced himself to act normally, and walked slowly as he lit a smoke, remembering to hold it American - style. The nicotine calmed him as he approached the main dining hall, and as he went up the steps he looked at the cheap American watch he'd bought to replace his much nicer Swiss one. He had two minutes.

He stopped in the alcove and leaned casually against a white, roman-style wooden column, his left hand in his pocket, facing the intersection of pathways while he smoked; just another employee taking a break. It was beginning to get light out; a dim glow in the eastern sky telling him he had maybe an hour before daylight. Out of the corner of his eye he saw the next pair of Marine guards approaching. Now in plain sight, he calmly crushed out the cigarette on the step and lit another as they approached.

123

JAKE WAS past exhaustion – he felt like he'd crashed yet another plane, then been kicked down the stairs by a mule. He'd heard stories his entire life about flash floods and had hoped to never run into one. He knew how lucky he'd been, and that he should be in bed right now, but he'd unfortunately found that rare place where you are simply too exhausted to sleep. Overtired, some called it, but he'd simply been through hell and was just glad to be breathing.

Everything in the kitchen seemed to jump out at him – the crockery pan Rosa had brought with her from Mexico and kept out of reach on the top shelf because it had been her grandmother's, taking it down only occasionally to make a special, traditional dish, the small crack in the corner of the window that Cates had been meaning to fix for 20 years now, the crude texture of the vigas running across the ceiling; the next best thing to having trees in the room with you, and of course the huge, black and chrome woodstove that Rosa wouldn't give up, despite the money that had been provided in his parent's will to do just that.

Jake had grown up in this kitchen, had eaten hundreds of meals here, and more than once had received a spanking here, or a sharp rap on the knuckles with a wooden spoon. He sighed, tired but content for the moment, and sipped coffee from his mug, the liquid growing tepid, more of a comfort than a desire.

He heard the dogs start barking and the horses in the exercise pen next to the house nicker and run around a bit, then the soft sound of tires on gravel, a car pulling in.

Normally he'd get up and go to the door to see who it was, but as sore and tired as he was he didn't feel much like getting up, figuring it was likely Rosa back from visiting Cates in the hospital, unless she had decided to stay there and send Jose home with the truck, or maybe a neighbor returning a casserole or something

A knock came on the door, the wooden screen door rapping against the frame, an old, familiar sound. He was too wiped out to get up, so he just yelled "COME ON IN," in the direction of the mudroom. He heard the squeal of hinges as the screen door was pulled open, then slapped shut by the spring. He looked up as a ghost walked into the room.

"Hello Jake."

Jake gaped at her, not really believing what he saw. Was he so exhausted he was hallucinating? He rubbed his eyes and blinked.

"Lily? But…it can't be."

She smiled at him sadly. "It's me Jake, really."

"But you're…you're…" he began, getting up from the bench.

"Dead?"

Jake swallowed. "Well, aren't you?"

Lily threw back her head and laughed, the sound of it so familiar and haunting Jake was sure now that he was dreaming.

"Do I *look* dead, Jake?" Suddenly her smile turned to tears, and she threw herself into his arms, hugging him tightly. Jake knew then it wasn't a hallucination, that she was alive - not just an apparition - and he squeezed her back intensely, still not believing that he had his "little sister" back.

"Jake?"

"Yeah?"

"You're squeezing me so tight I can't breath."

Jake drew back, suddenly angry. He still had her by the arms, and he looked her in the eye, his rage boiling over.

"You'd better have a damn good explanation for this, he said, "A lot of people have been torn up by your so-called 'death.' You've got a lot of explaining to do."

Lily sighed and pried his hands loose, then pulled out a chair, slumping into it and holding her head in her hands as Jake sat back down, pulling back his anger.

"Would you like some coffee?" he asked in a gentler voice.

"No…no thank you," she said, dropping her hands to the table in front of her.

"Just start at the beginning," Jake suggested.

She took another deep breath and looked at him. "Okay. Here's what I know for sure. Laurel is working for the Germans."

"I know. She shot Cates."

"Oh my God," Lily said, covering her mouth with her hand. "Is he all right?"

"I think so. It was a small caliber pistol. Rosa is with him at the hospital right now. I'll go up and see him tomorrow...I mean later today. I just have a hard time believing she's a German spy."

"Believe it. Remember when she went to Germany in '36?"

"For the Olympics, yes."

"And also to see our paternal great-grandmother. I would have gone with her, but I was down with pneumonia. Besides, I was still young, and Mama had to stay and run the orchard, so Laurel went alone."

"She was a senior in high school. I remember."

"Just graduated, yes. You had gone off to British Columbia, then to Alaska to work on a fishing boat. We called it your 'Jack London' trip."

Jake couldn't help but grin a little. He had indeed gone off to the Yukon in search of adventure, and the Jack London novels which had lured him there still lined the bookshelves in the library. He hadn't found much romance however, just backbreaking hard work. Still, he would always be glad he went.

"It began then, I think. She'd met a man, an officer in the Abwher I figure now, who wrote to her every month after she returned."

"You're kidding me. Every month?"

"Yes, but the letters were supposedly from our grandmother – they came from her address, but were in a different handwriting. If you were to read them aloud, they would sound like an innocuous letter from a grandmother to her granddaughter, but they were secretly encoded with a hidden message."

"A book code," Jake said.

"Yes. How did you..."

"Never mind. Go on."

"Well, I caught her decoding a letter in her room once, and made her tell me about it. I was a bit of a brat – told her I'd tell Mama – so she had no choice but to show me how it worked, even let me decode part of one.

"It seemed very harmless really, his protestations of undying love and affection and all that. Young girls find secrets incredibly exciting of course, and I agreed not to tell Mama anything as long as she 'shared' her secret letters with me. Of course, she didn't like it, but she didn't have much choice."

"So, they were just love letters?"

She nodded. "At first, yes, but I understand now that Heinrich…"

"Heinrich?"

"Yes, that was his name; Heinrich Schiller. Anyway, in 1936 it seemed so harmless, then mother died in '40 and everything changed. The Germans had taken over Czechoslovakia and Poland of course, and had just invaded France. I was in high school and was more interested in the boys there than any old boring letters from Laurel's secret beau - letters that had come fewer and farther apart in the past four years anyway.

"I'm really not sure when she stopped showing them to me, or if by that time she was just showing me the innocent ones…" She shrugged. "It really doesn't matter. I started dating Dick not long after that, and then there was the war. I was worried about him leaving to go into the Marines…" she looked down at her clenched hands unhappily.

"Lily, I meant to tell you, Dick is back."

"Dick? Here in the States? Oh, thank God!" she cried, grasping both his hands in hers. "Is he all right?"

"He's…fine," Jake said, not knowing how much to say.

"I want to see him."

"Just finish your story, then we'll go over there."

Something suddenly occurred to her and she looked at Jake. "My God, he thinks I'm dead, too doesn't he?"

Jake nodded.

"Oh Jake, I've made such a mess of this."

"It doesn't matter. He'll just be so glad to see you. He really loves you, Lily."

She swallowed, tears filling her eyes. "Thank you, Jake."

"Never mind that, just finish what you were saying."

Lily pulled her hands from his and wiped the moisture from her eyes with the heel of one hand.

"Well, after Mama died Laurel and I grew apart. She became distant – we hardly talked anymore, and when war broke out officially in '41 she got that job at Navajo Depot and I hardly ever saw her. She was the one who usually picked up the mail after Mama died, but I was waiting for an acceptance letter for college so one day I went to Sedona and got the mail. There was a ton of it, probably three weeks worth, and sure enough, my acceptance letter was there...and a letter from Grandma Hausen."

"Except it wasn't from her," Jake said.

Lily nodded. "I recognized Heinrich's handwriting on the envelope for one, but also, Grandma Hausen died in '40 just before Mama did, so I hid the letter."

"Didn't read it?"

"Not right then, no. Of course I didn't really think then that Laurel could possibly be spying for the Germans...I didn't know what to think, truthfully."

"Go on."

"Well, a few weeks went by, and Laurel was getting more and more agitated. When she had come home that weekend and found out that I'd picked up the mail, I thought she was going to have kittens. I played dumb of course, even waved the acceptance letter from Arizona State at her, saying how mad I was that it had come *days* earlier and was just sitting at the post office. Best defense is a good offense right? We had a *huge* fight over that, but there wasn't too much she could really say. It was my mail too right?

"Well after that she made sure she came home every day for awhile, to pick up the mail. Obviously she'd been waiting for that letter. Finally though, she told me she wouldn't be home that night and I decided to decode the letter. Well, I snuck into her room and looked for the key..."

"The book."

"Right, the book," she said, giving him a puzzled look.

"Never mind. I'll explain when you're done."

"Well, anyway, I'd found the book we'd used before, a copy of Don Quixote, but it didn't work anymore – it was just gobbledegook. So, I decided they must have changed the key - the book they were using - so I went back into her room and found what I was pretty sure was the new key." She looked at him directly, her eyes burning into his. "Then Laurel came home and caught me."

"She caught you decoding the letter?"

"No, not quite. I managed to hide the letter and my notes, and pretended I was just sitting there reading Jane Eyre. When she saw me holding that book she started yelling at me and snatched it away. I told her I had been looking for something to read and she didn't have to be such a bitch about it."

"And the letter?"

"I'm sure she knew then that I had it, but she couldn't very well bring it up now, could she?"

"So what happened?"

"I told her I was sick and tired of her and I was leaving. I got up to go and she grabbed my arm, hard...I won't go into details Jake, but a sister to sister fight is not a pretty thing." She took a deep breath. "Finally I got away from her and ran out. I stayed the night with my friend Marci."

"You still had the letter with you?"

She nodded. "I went looking the next day for a copy of Jane Eyre so I could finish decoding the letter, but I ran into another problem. It was gobbledegook again. It didn't even work in German. I just couldn't figure out what was wrong. I went back to the house, and Laurel had gone to work, thank God, but of course she'd taken the book, the key, with her. My room had been searched, but carefully, so as not to make a mess, you know?

"She'd left me a letter on the dining room table apologizing for going off the deep end, blah, blah. It was so sisterly sweet it made me ill. She claimed the book was a gift from a friend and meant a lot to her. Anyway, it was bullshit."

Even though she was sitting in front of him, Jake couldn't quite put together the image in his head of the little girl in pigtails who had brought him lemonade or ice tea on the porch with the young woman who sat before him now swearing like a paratrooper.

"See, I needed the same *edition* of the book, because different publishers format the pages differently, which changes the position of words on a given page, as would a change in font or page size, you see? So even though I was on page 114, when I began counting, I was on the wrong letter because of the different formatting. You see? I didn't remember where I had started before, or I could have figured it out."

Jake nodded, although he was so exhausted he was only getting part of it.

"So I racked my brain trying to remember the publisher's name and date. It had been opposite the stamp, on the title page, but it's not the kind of thing you remember you know? I was pretty sure it had been Simon & Schuster, a 1936 edition, but I wasn't positive, so I packed a bag of clothes and wrote Laurel an even *sweeter* note than the load of crap she'd given me, that I wasn't mad, that I still loved my big sister, but that I was going to stay with a friend for a few days."

"Marci?"

"Yes, but I didn't tell her that, which is where things got weird. The first couple of days everything was fine. I looked everywhere I could think of for a similar copy of Jane Eyre. I must have bought five or six copies trying to find one that worked, and finally found one in the Prescott Public Library that looked just like the one Laurel had...I had to steal it," she said guiltily.

"So then what?"

"Well, two things happened. I had noticed this car, a beige Ford coupe, near Marci's house the day we were leaving to go to Prescott. Later I was sure I saw the same car down the street from the café where we ate lunch, just before I went to the library. Both cars were missing their left rear hubcaps."

"You're a regular Nancy Drew," Jake said. She stuck her tongue out at him, and briefly he saw the young girl in pigtails he remembered so well.

"Anyway, by that time I'd collected several copies of Jane Eyre, which understandably Marci was curious about. Finally I decided I had to tell her enough so that if something were to happen to me, someone would know and could tell the authorities."

"No offense, but it sounds a little paranoid."

"Well Jake, that may be, but Marci's dead now because of me."

Jake stiffened. "That was *her* body they found, wasn't it?"

"Yes."

"She was wearing your earrings. I was sure it was you."

"You saw her body?"

Jake nodded. "The sheriff came to get me because he couldn't get hold of Laurel. I identified her as you."

"Oh Jake, I'm sorry. It was her idea... See, I don't think you ever met her, but she and I became friends because we looked so much alike. Much more than Laurel and I, in fact. Our friends sometimes confused the two of us. We have...had, about the same color hair, we're about the same size and weight. People thought we were sisters."

"So Laurel likely didn't have to look very hard to find you, then," Jake said.

A sad look came over Lily's face. "No, I suppose not. After decoding the letters I knew they'd be after me, but I never *dreamed* they would hurt Marci. I never would have told her anything if I had known... she paused to brush a tear away. "Just stupid I guess."

Jake took her free hand. "It's not your fault, Lily."

"Like hell it isn't!" she exclaimed, snatching her hand back. "She's dead because of *me*, Jake."

"Lily, calm down. You couldn't have known that they would kill her. Now tell me what was in the book that was so important."

"You found the book?"

"Yes, but it was empty. What's it all about Lily?"

"Diamonds, Jake. It's about lots and lots of diamonds."

124

A S THE two Marines passed by they looked over at Kessler, who had just lit another cigarette, from which he took a deep drag, then nodded at them, trying to be nonchalant; just another bored service worker waiting for his shift to begin.

The Marines nodded back, then went back to talking as they turned and continued up the path on their rounds, weapons slung, completely unaware that they'd just seen a German assassin.

"If you're here for morning shift you'd better get inside. Woolesly will have your ass if you're late."

Kessler turned to find a short, pixieish, pretty brunette with her hands on her hips, looking at him disapprovingly.

"Sorry, I'm new. First day. I'm Dave Johnson," Kessler said, sticking his hand out. She shook it and gave him a smile, showing him a row of small, even white teeth.

"Annie Sumpter, pleased to meetcha'. C'mon, I mean it, he'll pitch a fit."

Kessler followed her inside, doubting it was a good idea, but how could he get out of it?

She turned left and led him down a long hallway lined with shelves filled with trays, covered serving dishes, casseroles and other kitchen paraphernalia. They went right, pushing through swinging double doors, and Kessler found himself in a group of people, all dressed similarly, clearly all waiting for their shift to begin.

A short, florid man holding a clipboard pushed his way in, the group quickly parting to let him through.

"ALL RIGHT, ALL RIGHT, QUIET EVERYONE."

This must be Woolesly, Kessler thought, desperately trying to think of a way out. Woolesly was sure to know he was a fraud; he'd call the Marines, and that would be that.

"Same assignments as yesterday except for Sanford. Gaines, I need you to cover for Shorty. He won't be in today."

"Probably drunk again," a wit to his right commented *sotto voice*.

"Also, Maynard's are here…they came in last night. We need someone to…who are *you?*"

Kessler, who had been surreptitiously looking around the kitchen for another exit, realized that he was being addressed and turned to find his new little führer staring at him, and not kindly. "I'm Johnson, sir. Dave Johnson," he said.

"Johnson eh? Funny, the agency didn't call like they usually do to let me know."

Kessler tensed, ready to run. He'd go back the way he came, do his best to dodge the Marine patrols and find Roosevelt before he was taken down.

"Eh, never mind, we can use the help. Annie, would you please get Mister Johnson a time card and line him out on his duties please? Give him a map and a quick tour. *Quick tour.* We don't have time to dawdle today."

"Like we ever do?" the same wit behind him commented.

"Davis, you'll handle the little White House today. They like you over there for some reason. Johnson can help you if you need to move more than one cart, but under no circumstances is he to speak to, or even sneak a peek at the boss. Got that, Johnson?"

Kessler nodded, hardly able to believe his good luck.

125

"DIAMONDS?" JAKE asked, stunned.

Lily nodded. "Think about it Jake, it's the perfect way to carry a lot of money. They were to be split up into shares here and distributed among different agents around the western U.S."

"But how did they get here? Why not just have the courier deliver them?"

"Because that would compromise both the agent and the courier. This way, with a blind drop, it compartmentalizes things – neither can identify the other if one of them were ever caught. Gee, Jake, you'd make a lousy spy."

Jake grinned at her. "I guess so. I'm just a simple pilot. So, you have the diamonds?"

Lily nodded again. "All that was in the first letter I decoded was that the payment would be in the next envelope. The next letter had no book code. None...so I began looking closer at the envelope itself..."

"And found the microdot."

"Dammit Jake, you need to tell me how you..."

"Someone smarter than me figured it out. Go on."

"Anyway, like I told you, Marci pretended she was me, got in my car and drove away. I was wearing her glasses and we'd swapped clothes, even jewelry, in case they had binoculars. When I hugged her at the door I could see that damn beige Ford parked up the road with two men in it. I almost said 'Goodbye, Marci' and ruined the whole thing." She looked at her hands. "Now I wish I had."

"C'mon kiddo. That won't bring her back."

"Oh Jake, we just thought we were being so smart...she'd lure them away pretending to be me so they'd follow her, giving me time to leave the house and pick up the diamonds. Once I hid them in a safe place I went to stay with a girl we knew from school who lived in Camp Verde. Marci was supposed to call there when she got home…but she never did." Lily began crying in earnest then, her head on her arms, her sobs echoing in the empty kitchen.

Jake got up and went to his room, found a clean handkerchief and brought it back to her.

"Thanks," she sniffled, red-eyed, tears forming tracks on her cheeks.

"I have one of yours somewhere, but I can't find it," Jake said. "I think I had it in my pocket and gave it to Morrie by mistake." Lily looked up at him with a look of alarm.

"Wait. You have one of *my* handkerchiefs?" she said, her eyes suddenly sharp.

Jake nodded, feeling guilty. "I was poking around your room after you…well, when we thought you were dead. I found your hiding space by accident. The book was wrapped in it."

Her eyes widened. "*That's* where you got the handkerchief?"

"Yes. I'm sorry – I don't normally go poking around in other people's things…"

She held up a hand like a traffic cop. "So, that's how you knew so much about the letter and the book?"

Feeling guilty now, he took a deep breath and told her about the book wrapped in the handkerchief, with the letter tucked inside, how Morrie had found the microdot and the empty book stash at the observatory, the explosion at Gruber's and being run off the road. He had just begun telling her about Schmidt, the commandos and the German jets when the phone rang.

"That's probably Rosa. She went to visit Cates. Probably wants me to check the icebox for milk or something. Hold on just a minute," he said, rising wearily to pull the phone from its cradle on the wall.

"Hello?"

"Hello, Jake. It's Laurel."

He looked at Lily and held her eyes with his.

"It's not a good time right now, Laurel," he said, as Lily's eyes widened with shock. She shook her head violently as in 'Don't tell her I'm alive', which Jake had no intention of doing.

"I know that, Jake. I heard Cates was shot. There's a bit of important business I need to discuss with you, though."

"You *should* know he was shot, since you were the one who shot him."

"Well, he pissed me off. Hold on just a minute, sweetheart, there's someone here who'd like to say hello."

"Jake? Oh God, are you there?"

"MORRIE? For God's sake, get away from her. She's dangerous!"

Suddenly Laurel was back. "Dangerous? You know I should be insulted, Jake, but in this case you're absolutely right. I *am* dangerous. You know how I get when I don't get what I want. Now, you have something of mine and I want it back. I'll trade you straight up Jake, your little honeybunch here for the diamonds."

"I don't know what you're talking about."

"That's too bad, Jake, because I'm a little jealous. There's no telling what I might do. I mean, couldn't you have waited a decent interval?"

"You touch a hair on her head…"

"Cut the melodrama, Jake. It's simple. Bring the package to Gino's at midnight. Ask for the special."

"Laurel…"

"Jake, don't screw with me. Be here by 12:30 or you'll never see your pretty little redhead again."

Jake opened his mouth to respond, but she'd hung up. He hung up the phone and looked at his watch. It was 9:40 in the morning. They had fourteen hours to figure out what to do.

"Laurel's got Morrie. She wants to trade her for the diamonds."

"Morrie? Who's Morrie?"

"The woman I've been seeing. Where are the diamonds?"

"In a safe place."

"We need to go pick up Dick. We're going to need him."

"Oh God, Jake, what do I tell him?"

"You'll figure it out. C'mon, we gotta go."

126

KESSLER HAD developed a newfound respect for waiters and waitresses that morning. Except for one short break the frantic pace hadn't let up since 5 a.m. He hadn't realized that not only were he and Davis serving the president's cabin, but two other cabins as well. Davis had taken the breakfast cart by himself, sending Kessler to a different cabin, so he'd had no chance to recon the area and was just about to chance finding it himself when the lunch order for the Little White House came in. It was 12:30.

The main kitchen was a madhouse, but special china had been set aside with two spotless stainless steel carts that were only to be used for the presidential party, and bore the presidential seal. By ten minutes of they were pushing the carts out the service entrance when Woolesly's snide voice came from behind him.

"JOHNSON." Uh-oh, Kessler thought, here we go.

"Yessir?" Kessler said turning, wondering how fast he could get to the filet knife he had taped to his ankle in a primitive cardboard sheath, stab the little bastard in the heart and disappear into the woods.

Woolesly came closer, a displeased look on his face. "I called the agency, and they have no idea who you are."

"Well, I…"

"You know you aren't the only person who's tried to get a job here this way. Didn't they give you any paperwork?"

"No, sir. They just told me where to buy my uniforms and told me to report out here."

"Hmm. Well, report to my office after you deliver that and we'll get this straightened out."

"Yes, sir. Right after we deliver lunch."

"And don't think you can put one over on me, you hear?" Woolesly said, pointing his clipboard at Kessler.

"No sir," Kessler said as the little tyrant stalked away.

"Yankee asshole," Davis said under his breath, then cast a glance at Kessler, who smiled conspiratorially. "Let's get this done. The Boss hates it when lunch is late, and I don't mean Woolesly."

The cabin was further away than he thought, and by the time they got there Kessler could feel the tip of the filet knife poking through the cardboard and into his ankle bone. He could feel blood beginning to soak his sock, and hoped it wouldn't get worse and give him away.

As they approached the cabin he saw why it was called "The Little White House." Four 14 inch pillars supported a portico similar to that of the real White House, but in miniature. Compared to the Führer's Bergholtz it was positively plebian in appearance.

This was FDR's inner sanctum; the Marine guard apparently provided perimeter security, the Secret Service the actual bodyguard detail, but he hadn't seen any yet.

As they came up the walk to the house two gardeners straightened up from what they were working on next to the path. It wasn't until one of them held up his hand for Davis to stop that Kessler realized they weren't gardeners, but Secret Service agents.

"Hold it. Who's this with you, Davis?" the one who'd raised his hand said.

"This is Johnson. He's new. Why they always stick me with the FNGs I have no idea," Davis said.

The "gardener" smirked. "Life is like that. What about you, Johnson? Got a gun tucked away on that cart somewhere?"

Kessler tried to remain calm, remembering the American tendency to joke about anything and everything. He picked up the lid of the silver serving tray and made a show of looking under it. "Nope. I forgot the gun. Nothing but a Reuben sandwich, a pickle and some potato chips," he said, re-covering the food.

The agent laughed. "Another smart-ass I see. Fine, you'll fit right in. Go ahead guys, but Davis, do me a favor and bring us a couple of them Reubens will ya? We're starvin' out here."

"Turkey for me, Joe. White, not rye okay?" the other "gardener" said.

"Sure thing, guys," Davis said, and began pushing the cart past him as Kessler followed. He had a bad moment when one of the Secret Service agents grabbed his arm with one vise-like hand.

"Hey, Johnson?" This is it, Kessler thought.

"Yeah?"

"Don't forget the chips and some extra pickles, huh? Oh, and a coupla Cokes, eh?"

"Promise," Kessler said with a smile.

The agent let go of his arm and Kessler pushed the cart around the corner, past a large shrub and into the kitchen of the Little White House.

127

Jake had a strange sense of *déjà vu* as he pulled into the Lawson's driveway just as he had dozens of times during the last several months as he and Dick had searched in vain for the murderer of the young woman who now sat next to him, vibrant and alive, chewing her nails to the quick.

"You don't stop that, you're not going to have any fingers left," Jake said, shutting off the car.

"Can't help it. Oh God, Jake, you've got to go talk to him first."

"What do you want me to say?"

"I don't know…just…I don't know."

"Okay, don't worry, it'll be fine. I'll be right back."

Lily just nodded, as if afraid to speak.

Jake climbed out of the car, his legs giving him just the slightest of twinges now. He was still exhausted, and his head hurt. He made a mental note to ask Dick for some aspirin.

He went through the screen door into the porch and knocked on the kitchen door. The house had a front door of course, but it was rarely used. It was just like at their ranch – people who knew you came to the back; salesmen and drummers came to the front.

Mrs. Lawson opened the door, wiping her hands on her apron and giving him a smile. "Why hello, Jake, come right in," she said.

"Is Dick here?"

"Why sure. He's out in the barn. We're having flapjacks for breakfast, why don't you stay?"

"Thanks, Mrs. Lawson, but I'm afraid I can't. In fact, I need to steal Dick from you as well. I need him to go to Flagstaff with me."

"This time of the day? Why it's only seven a.m. You boys shouldn't be out catting around so much…" she said disapprovingly.

"I'm sorry, Ma'am, but it's important."

"Girls are always important at your age…you'll be missing a good breakfast."

"I'm sorry, Ma'am."

"Well, I am too, but get on with you. Go on, shoo," she said in mock anger, pushing him out the door. Jake couldn't help but grin as he walked back to the car.

Lily looked at him expectantly as he got in.

"Mrs. Lawson says he's in the barn."

"Oh God, I'll have to tell her, too."

"Let's tell Dick first, then you two can figure out how to break it to her that you're still alive."

Jake started the car and drove around back to the barn. The sliding door stood open, and as he got out he could hear a steady, repetitious thud, thud, thud from within.

Curious now, he walked to the barn, looking back over his shoulder once at Lily who sat in the passenger seat, chewing whatever was left of her nails.

Dick had his back to Jake, and was busy hammering a punching bag made from an old sea bag with his left hand, which he'd taped. He'd removed his shirt, and his muscles strained through his armless T-shirt as he jabbed at the bag, the sweat standing out on his neck and shoulders, his shirt dark with it.

Suddenly he spun on his right leg, bringing his left leg in a full circle to deliver a killer kick to the recalcitrant punching bag. He was so fast his leg was a blur, and Jake was still trying to convince himself of what he'd seen when Dick spotted him and came over to him grinning, wiping his sweaty face with a dark blue towel he'd snatched off the barn rail.

Some barbells and a bench were tucked off in one corner, covered in dust; a lone dumbbell in the middle of the floor all a one-armed man needed. This was a one-armed man Jake would never want to face in a fight though. He was glad Dick was on his side.

"Where'd you learn that fancy spinning kick?"

"Philippines. You wouldn't believe how quick those guys are. Got my clock cleaned in an exhibition bout by a little Filipino guy about five - four, maybe 125 pounds soaking wet. Looked like he hadn't eaten in a month. I decided right then I was going to learn a few a' them moves…so what brings you out here?" Dick said as he shrugged on a blue button-down shirt with the sleeves rolled up; a neat trick for a man with one hand, and Jake could see he was getting better dealing with his disability.

"Dick, maybe you'd better sit down."

"What is it? Somebody else die?" Dick asked as he buttoned the shirt one-handed.

"No…actually, just the opposite."

"Just spit it out, Jake. You know I don't like it when people beat around the bush."

Jake took a deep breath. "It's Lily. She's alive."

"*What?* The hell you say!"

"It's true, Dick. She's out in the car." Jake moved to the door where he could see Lily and waved at her to come in. He could see her take a deep breath, then open the door and get out, walking slowly towards the barn, uncertainty in every step. Then Dick was standing beside him, and when Jake looked up at him he was staring, open-mouthed at the woman he loved, whom he'd thought dead, now risen miraculously like Lazarus. Jake ignored the wetness he saw in his eyes as any good friend would.

"Oh my God," he said slowly. "Lily? Baby? Is it really you?"

Lily had stopped 15 feet away, a trembling hand over her mouth, tears welling in her eyes, then she was running forward, throwing herself at him as Dick pulled her into him fiercely.

"Oh Dick! I didn't know you were back. I missed you so, so much!" she said, looking up at him, their arms around each other, tears running freely now.

"But how? I don't understand…" he began.

"I'll explain it all later. Now kiss me, you big idiot."

Dick did just that, and Jake found himself smiling for the first time all week.

128

Once inside the kitchen, Kessler knew he had mere minutes, and that this would be the only chance he would get. There was one other person in the kitchen besides Davis and himself; a woman busy peeling potatoes for the evening meal stood at a dry sink, her back to them. She turned briefly and smiled. "Take the boss his lunch, will you? My hands are wet," she said, turning back to her work as Kessler quickly knelt to pull the boning knife from the ersatz sheath at his ankle.

Rising with it, he took a well-practiced step forward, clasping his other hand over Davis' mouth even as he jammed the long, narrow blade into the cavity at the base of his skull and up into his brain, dropping him as if he'd been turned off by a light switch.

Kessler threw the body aside just as the woman turned around, hearing the tray of food Davis had dropped clatter on the ground. She opened her mouth to scream, her eyes widening, just as Kessler reached her, flipping the knife around and striking her in the forehead with the handle - a wicked, brutal blow that rolled her eyes up in her head. He caught her as she slumped, lowering her unconscious body to the ground as the potato peeler she'd been holding skittered across the floor of the kitchen. It'd been noisier than he'd wanted, but nothing a servant dropping something in the kitchen wouldn't explain.

Moving quickly to the exterior door he closed and locked it. It wouldn't hold for long, but it would hopefully stop the Secret Service long enough to allow him time to finish the job. Pulling the Walther from where he'd hidden it under the cummerbund at the small of his back and screwing the suppressor onto it, he took a deep breath, pushing through the narrow, swinging door, and into the next room.

129

IT WAS everything Franklin Delano Roosevelt could do not to slump in his wheelchair out of sheer exhaustion, but his pride would not allow him to show weakness in front of Madame Shoumatoff — the artist his sweet Lucy had insisted paint his portrait. He hadn't wanted to do it, but when it came to Lucy, the love of his life, who asked so little of him he was simply unable to say no.

Trapped in a loveless marriage with Eleanor, FDR treasured these rare moments with Lucy, even if it meant sitting for a portrait as he signed a never-ending train of documents his secretary Grace Tully brought him from her desk in the second bedroom. He hardly read them anymore unless Grace told him it was important.

He trusted Grace totally, as he had Missy before her. It was a good thing he had her, he thought, because he knew he could no longer perform the duties that the presidency demanded by himself. He was dying, and he only hoped to live long enough to see the end of the war. Days like this, he had little faith that he actually would.

Still, the Germans had their backs to the wall, Berlin was about to fall, even the war in the Pacific was finally going in their favor. While horrified at the terrible expenditure in men and material, Roosevelt was satisfied that he'd done the right thing in prosecuting the war as he had, including the sacrifices at Pearl Harbor, a decision which still weighed heavily on him.

He reminded himself again that the United States would come out of the war stronger than ever, and was now truly the world's leader. It was Stalin and the Russians who scared him now, Stalin being every bit as bad as Hitler in his opinion. As far as he was concerned it was just a matter of time before the USSR and the U.S. faced off. The very idea of yet another war tired the already exhausted President. He put his unlit cigarette holder between his teeth and closed his eyes.

There was a loud clatter from the kitchen, as if a load of dishes had been dumped on the floor, followed by a loud thump.

"What in the world?" Elizabeth Shoumatoff said, turning from her place at the easel, brush in hand. Grace Tully, who had just come back into the living room with a fresh load of papers for him to sign, frowned.

"I'll see what's going on Boss," she said, turning to go out the door to the kitchen to see what the racket was about, but a man in a white and black waiter's service uniform stepped into the room first.

"What in God's name are you people doing out there in the kitchen?" Roosevelt demanded. Then he saw the pistol in the man's hand and his mouth dropped open, the unlit cigarette in its holder falling to the floor. Grace Tully screamed.

"President Roosevelt? I have a message for you from my Führer," Kessler said. FDR's shock didn't last long. He'd been living with the spectre of death for far too long not to welcome it. He just hoped that those who cleaned up the mess would have the forethought to cover up the fact that he'd been assassinated; the idea that a German assassin could penetrate their security at this level would be a devastating blow to the morale of the American people.

Roosevelt looked his killer in the eye. "Tell your Führer that I will see him in hell," he said, as the German pulled the trigger.

130

JAKE EASED the car into the Hausen's driveway, sunlight dappling the hood through shadows cast by the freshly minted cottonwood leaves, the leaves from the previous fall still on the grass, the grass uncut and stringy, sticking through the sodden brown mat of leaves here and there, several broken branches brought down by the wind lying randomly here and there, testimony to the lack of the owner's interest.

Laurel had never liked yard work, and it showed. It made Jake a little sad, remembering how it looked when Laurel and Lily's mother had been alive, neat as a pin, the sprinklers spoiling the grass into a lush carpet that begged you to take off your shoes and take a long nap in the shade, the huge cottonwoods and sycamores forming a leafy, verdant, green roof overhead. He'd spent many happy days here, playing Scrabble or Chinese checkers with Laurel, quite often with Lily as well.

Lily leaned over the front seat, arms crossed over the back, Dick in front riding shotgun. They'd put Lily in back just in case Laurel was home, so she could quickly duck down out of sight.

"Her car's not here," Lily said, voicing the obvious, tension filling her words.

"What's she driving now?" Jake asked.

"A yellow '39 Plymouth convertible. I have no idea how she can afford it - it's nearly new."

"Lily, I think we all know how she can afford it," Dick said gently, giving her a knowing look, but Lily was staring at the house. Jake stopped and shut off the car, the engine ticking as it cooled in the sudden quiet.

"Dick, you stay here and play lookout will you? If we hear you whistle, Lily can go out the back and meet us down the road, and I'll pretend I was leaving Laurel a note or something," Jake said. Dick could whistle through his teeth like a referee, a skill he'd tried to teach Jake once upon a time when they were younger, but that Jake had never been able to master.

"No problem," Dick said, then he turned to Lily. "Hon, while you're in there wouldja see if that evil sister of yours has anything to eat in the fridge? My stomach's beginnin' to think my throat's been slit."

"Since when are you *not* hungry?" Lily replied with a smile.

"Hey baby, you just give me an appetite, what can I say?" Lily slapped him on the arm, but Jake could see that she was pleased. It's good to see her happy, he thought, not to mention *alive*.

Jake went first and knocked on the door, just in case, then tried the knob. It was locked, which was unusual, the first time he'd ever known it to be. Folks in Sedona never locked their doors – there was no need. He couldn't recall Cates and Rosa ever locking the doors at the ranch, nor did anyone else he knew. He waved to Lily and she got out of the car, her shoes crunching on the gravel as she ran up to him.

"It's locked. Got a key?"

"Locked? Huh, that's strange. We never locked it before unless we went on a long trip. Mom used to leave a key for the neighbors…" she trailed off, looking around the flower bed flanking the door, hands on hips, brow furrowed, and in that moment Jake saw her mother in her. Laurel had never loved this place the way Lily and her mother had. When they were dating she'd talk non-stop about leaving and going somewhere exciting, like San Francisco or New York, maybe Chicago.

This wasn't Laurel's house at all, he found himself thinking; it was Lily's. Laurel had always been a big city kind of girl, and it had always been Lily who had helped her mother in the garden, and not because she had to. She was the sister with the green thumb, while Laurel had always said she could kill ivy.

"HA. There it is," she exclaimed triumphantly, stepping over the rock boundary into the weed-choked flower bed, then bending to pick up something from the ground. She held it up and grinned at Jake, who could now see that it was a large, white ceramic toadstool with a red top covered with white polka dots and a small, faded gnome sitting on top.

"I bought this for Mom one Christmas when I was young, not knowing at the time what a horrid thing it was, but she said she loved it and put it right out front anyway..." a tear escaped one eye as her voice broke, and she wiped it away with the heel of her free hand, then smiled self-consciously at Jake. "Sorry, I still miss her, you know?"

"It's okay. I do too Lily."

"She always liked you, Jake. She used to say you were better than Laurel deserved. I never really understood that until recently."

Jake gestured at the toadstool. "So, no offense Lily, but how's *that* help get us inside?"

She held it up and shook it and it rattled. She grinned at Jake, then held it upright and shook it again while holding her hand under it, until finally a key fell out into her hand.

"Mom started hiding a key in it when we went away so the neighbors could get in to feed the cats and water the plants."

"I don't think we even *have* keys to our place," Jake said.

Lily set the toadstool back down carefully and stepped out of the flowerbed. The key worked perfectly, and seconds later they were inside. The house had a stale, musty smell - the smell of old dust and stagnant air, and it was obvious Laurel didn't spend much time here. Lily shook her head and headed for the kitchen.

"Lily, I know Dick said he was hungry, but shouldn't we get the diamonds first?"

"Just shush," she said without turning around.

Jake had always liked the Hausen's kitchen because it was so different from the one he'd grown up with. Where the kitchen at the ranch had a low ceiling of rough vigas and alligator juniper cabinets, oiled but never painted, here the ceilings were higher, the walls painted a pale daffodil, the cabinets a glossy white. The appliances were a new, gleaming white that matched the cabinets, the countertop stylish, yellow ice cube Formica as opposed to the butcher block at home.

While the kitchen at the ranch made him feel safe and warm, comfortable with the color of old honey, this kitchen reflected Mrs. Hausen's sunny disposition, and he could almost smell the ginger snaps she was famous for lingering in the air. He remembered it sunny and bright, with fresh cut flowers on the table, a bowl of fruit on the counter, and usually something that smelled delicious in the oven. It was a woman's kitchen, but he'd always been made welcome there. It had been sort of a home away from home…now it just felt cold, sterile and silent.

Lily pulled a chair from the table and threw it in front of one of the cupboards with the easy familiarity of someone at home in her own house. Climbing up on it, she opened the cupboard, reached in and pulled out a cylinder of Quaker Oats. She got down from the chair, laughing when she saw the puzzled look on Jake's face. She pried the cardboard lid off the cylinder with her fingers, then poured the oatmeal out onto the counter.

A black lump fell out onto the pile of oatmeal with a small thump, and she snatched it up, setting the tube of oatmeal down and blowing the oatmeal off the object. She held it up in one palm after brushing it off so Jake could see it. It was a small, black velvet drawstring bag, still dusty with oatmeal residue. She untied and pulled open the drawstring and poured a small stream of diamonds out onto her palm. "Laurel always *hated* oatmeal," Lily said with a grin.

"What if she'd thrown it out?"

"Trust me, Jake, she's too lazy. Five gets you ten there's a bottle of spoiled milk in the fridge that she was too lazy to throw out," she said, returning the diamonds carefully to the tiny cloth bag.

"So what now? We've got to figure out a way to work it so she doesn't double-cross us. If I take the diamonds with me she could just take them and not let Morrie go."

"Or kill you both," Lily said.

"I don't think Laurel would kill me."

"No? What about Morrie? What about me? *Her own sister, Jake?* You really think she had nothing to do with Marci's death?"

Jake grimaced. "Point taken."

"Go get Dick. I don't think she's coming back anytime soon. We'll have something to eat and figure this out," Lily said, opening the fridge and looking in. She reached in and pulled out a bottle of milk.

"Sure it's a good idea?" Jake asked.

Lily popped the cardboard lid off the glass bottle and sniffed the milk, wrinkling her nose at the result. She looked at Jake. "Trust me, Jake, I know my sister. I've got an idea about the diamonds, but it'll take a little time. We might as well eat while I'm sewing."

"Sewing?"

"Just go get Dick will you? Hmmm, I wonder if these eggs are any good?"

131

KESSLER COULD not help but admire the American president's composure, despite his sickly appearance. FDR's last words rang in his head as he stepped forward to collect the president's glasses and cigarette holder as proof the mission had been accomplished, then turned to face the two women, one sitting at an easel, obviously painting FDR's portrait, her hand over her mouth, the other, likely a secretary, standing in the corner of the room holding papers, a shocked look on her face. Although there'd been little sound from the weapon, the smell of cordite filled the room. He had no rope to tie them.

"Tell your people the war is not yet over. The German people will never surrender. Heil Hitler," he said, raised his arm in salute, then ducked out the door on the opposite side of the room, the one leading to the porch, feeling strangely as if he'd lost something rather than gained it. There had been no fear in the American president's eyes, only contempt, and he knew then - despite his words to the contrary - that the war was over, and Germany had already lost.

The glass-paned door led to a wide, curved sundeck with a view into the woods. Kessler climbed over the rail then dropped the final 10 feet to the ground. If he'd been wearing the ankle - height hunting boots he'd bought he'd have been fine, but the low-cut, smooth - soled black brogues were not designed for such gymnastics, and as he landed one foot slipped on the damp leaves and when he took a step to recover he turned his other ankle, twisting it sharply. Pain shot up his leg as he fell, rolling down the slope in agony. He recognized the pain, having sprained his ankle badly once years before during airborne training, and cursed under his breath.

He came to a stop at the bottom of the lawn, and wanted to just lie there for a minute, but he could already hear the shouts of the Secret Service and the sound of men moving through the woods towards the house. He had no time for the pain. Gritting his teeth, he forced himself to his feet and limped away.

132

THREE TIMES Kessler had heard men running through the woods, and three times he dropped to the ground, lying as flat as possible, feeling conspicuous in his black and white uniform. They hadn't been close enough to see him though and passed him by, but each time he gripped the Walther grimly, raising his head tentatively just enough to look around.

About 200 meters to his left he saw a building and decided to try for it. They would get around to searching the buildings eventually, but for now he needed cover, a place to wrap his ankle, and hopefully find other clothes.

It seemed to take forever to limp the 200 meters, but in reality it took four minutes – four agonizing, painful minutes - to reach what turned out to be a garage, with another cottage just beyond. He tried the side door and to his surprise found it unlocked. He slipped inside and closed the door silently behind him.

The garage was dark, cool, and slightly damp in that way garages always seem to be, and after his eyes grew accustomed to the gloom he could see that it held not one, but two cars. The one furthest from him was covered with dust, but the maroon Ford near him looked as though it had been driven recently. He tried the driver's side door and again, found it unlocked. He found a set of mechanic's coveralls hanging on a hook and pulled them on over his clothes, tearing the bow tie from his neck.

Kessler slipped inside and slumped gratefully onto the overstuffed seat, totally exhausted. He didn't intend to fall asleep but made the mistake of closing his eyes just for a minute.

133

D ICK WAS finishing his second plate of eggs and bacon while Lily and Jake brainstormed. The radio in the kitchen was playing soft jazz when an ad came on for CBS's new show about Daniel Boone.

"We can't just give her the diamonds, Jake."

"I know, but how do we get Morrie back without them?"

"We interrupt this program to bring you a special news bulletin from CBS World News. A press association has just announced that President Roosevelt is dead."

Lily gasped and leapt to her feet to turn up the volume.

"The president died of a cerebral hemorrhage. All we know so far is that the president died at Warm Springs in Georgia. More to follow."

They all looked at one another as Lily sat back down heavily.

"I can't believe it," she said.

"Everyone knew he wasn't well, Lily," Dick said, putting his hand on hers and giving it a squeeze.

"This is horrible. Cates never liked him much, but I voted for him," Jake said.

They sat in silence for a few minutes, listening to the radio, which promised an update directly from Warm Springs.

"I just realized something," Jake said.

"What's that, Jake?"

"Harry Truman will be the next president. I hope he made it back okay."

134

"TWA 240, come in."

Jack Frye keyed the mike. "I read you five by five, Beacon Field."

"Turn to heading Two Eight Five and maintain at 5,000 feet. You are cleared to land, runway Three-Zero.

"Roger. Heading Two Eight Five for TWA 240… Is it true, Beacon Field? What we heard on the radio? Is Roosevelt really dead?" Jack asked.

"Sorry to confirm, but yes, TWA 240. The president is dead. Vice-President Truman is on his way right now from the Senate to take the oath."

Jack Frye looked back at Harry Truman, who was crouched in the jump seat behind the copilot. Harry raised his eyebrows and shrugged.

"Thanks for the info, Beacon Field. Turning left to Two Eight Five, maintain 5,000."

"TWA 240, begin descent at Cone intersection, report passing 2,000 and contact Beacon Tower on 119.2 - Please taxi to military gate Able Three upon landing to meet your party. See you on the ground, Two Forty."

"Contact Tower passing Two on 119.2, taxi to military gate Able Three. TWA 240 out."

Jack Frye turned to Harry as Glen Knudsen took the Electra into a wide left turn.

"What the hell is going on, Harry?"

The soon to be president of the United States took a deep breath. "Continuity of government, Jack. I don't know what happened in Warm Springs, but obviously someone smarter than us has come up with a cover story to make it look as though I were in Washington the entire time. They'll read you in on the ground and swear you all to secrecy."

"I guess it makes sense. Wouldn't do to have you vacationing in Arizona when the president died."

"Oh, it'll go further than that, Jack. They're very good at cleaning up messes."

"Including a German commando attack on Navajo Ordnance Depot, not to mention our house? A bomb dropped on Hoover Dam?"

"German commandos in this country? Ridiculous. Advanced German jet fighter bombers flying around? C'mon Jack, you *know* that could never happen, especially at this point in the war," Truman responded with a wink.

"I expect some help from the government repairing our house and the bullet holes in my convertible, Harry," Helen said from behind them.

"Why of course, Helen. I'll make sure of it. By the way, thank you for your hospitality and the interesting excursion. It was very…invigorating," Truman said.

"Harry, you've got just enough horseshit in you to make a wonderful president."

"Why thank you Helen, I'll take that as a compliment."

135

KESSLER AWOKE with a start to the sound of voices outside. He was trapped. Instinctively he slid over the seat into the back, lying on the floor, praying they wouldn't look in the car, but sure they would. The voices came closer, then the sliding door to the garage opened, and he realized it was two women talking. They were discussing their grocery list by the sound of it, with one of them being vociferous in her opinion about buying a pork roast if the butcher had one.

He had made himself as small as possible on the floor, and neither of them noticed him as they got it. He could hear the mellifluous lilt of Georgia in their voices, and the seat sagged against him slightly, but he had a bad moment when the driver dropped her purse onto the back seat.

He listened to the driver complain that the engine needed work as she tried to start the car, and he could hear her pumping the gas and fiddling with the choke, making him glad he hadn't tried to steal it. Finally she got it running, albeit a bit raggedly, then pulled it out of the garage to let it warm up a bit, the two of them continuing what seemed to Kessler an inane conversation about nothing in particular.

Finally the car's engine was smoothing out, and he could tell when she pushed the choke back in all the way because the engine's tone changed to a gentle burble which he could hear quite well with his head against the floor. She put it in gear and the car lurched forward, rolling down the gravel drive, then turning right. It was time.

Kessler raised his head slightly to try and peer over the seat, sneaking a peek at them. A tall, large-boned blonde woman in a mohair coat was driving, and there was a shorter brunette in a dark knit coat in the passenger seat. Kessler was about to sit up when he heard the topic change, and ducked back down.

"Hard to believe we'd have someone stealing valuables right here at the Springs," the passenger opined.

"They said on the phone he was dressed as wait staff...Ah suppose he thought he was being clever."

"But breaking into cottages during the day to steal jewelry? That's downright *bold*."

"Well, they're calling everybody with a place heah, so Ah'm *sure* they'll catch the degenerate. They said he's armed, probably dangerous."

"But he could be anywhere. Why, he could even be right in the back seat of the car with us right now, Norma Jean."

Kessler decided that was his cue, and pushed himself up with one arm and pointed the Walther at the driver's head as the brunette in the passenger seat let out a little shriek.

"Don't panic and I won't shoot you. Now pull over."

The driver did as she was told, her eyes in the rearview wide with fear. Kessler could feel her trembling as she sat absolutely still, holding the wheel with both hands. Just up the hill ahead of them the road tee'd.

"Which way to the main gate? Left or right?"

"Right," the brunette in the passenger seat said.

"Is there another way out of the compound?"

"Well...yes, there's a forest road, but it'll be muddy – probably impassable this time of year. We just got some rain the other night..." the driver said, obviously nervous.

"Draw me a map," Kessler said.

The brunette searched her purse, finally finding a pen and envelope, and dashed off a quick but accurate representation of the local roads. She handed it over the seat tentatively, as if Kessler were toxic, making him smile slightly.

"I marked both exits, but they'll have guards at both – they always do when FDR's here. Plus there are roving patrols...you should just give up."

"Quiet. If I want your opinion I'll ask for it. Now, set the emergency brake and leave the car running, then get out and put your hands on the hood."

The driver turned to look at him. "Both of us?" Her lip was trembling.

"You first, then I'll get out with your friend. Try anything and I'll shoot her."

The blonde did as she was told, setting the brake then getting out and going around to place her hands on the hood.

"Now you. Slowly."

The diminutive passenger opened the door, and as she stepped from the car Kessler slid out over the back seat and followed her out, but not without difficulty; he hit his injured foot on the steering wheel and it sent a pain spasm rocketing up his leg. He closed the passenger door and pushed the brunette towards the front of the car, limping as he followed her painfully.

"Put your hands on the…wait, stay quiet."

He could hear the whine of a vehicle coming closer, then saw the unmistakable outline of a military police jeep tear past the intersection ahead of them. Had they been seen?

He heard the jeep slow, then stop and begin to back up. He grabbed the blonde by the hair and pushed her towards her friend as she let out a small shriek.

He quickly raised the hood, setting the Walther on the running engine, but within reach, as the jeep reached the "T" and the driver turned and started down the hill toward them.

"Let me do the talking," he told them, looking them both in the eye. "Smile and act casual. One wrong word and I'll shoot you both, understand?"

Both women nodded, their eyes wide. Kessler pulled a rag from the pocket of the coveralls he'd found in the garage and reached in as if checking something on the engine, just as the jeep came roaring up with two serious looking marines in full combat gear, with Reising .45 submachine guns in the rack.

"Car trouble, folks?" The passenger asked. Kessler saw the insignia of a lieutenant on his collar, and gave him a wide smile.

"Transmission linkage. Won't go into second," he said.

"You folks shouldn't be out here right now, it's dangerous. Some madman killed two people we know of, one of them the president," the driver said. Kessler heard one of the women behind him gasp.

"My advice is to get this car off the road. Go home and lock your doors. Someone will call you when…"

"You BASTARD!" Kessler heard the brunette exclaim. He turned to find her giving him an evil glare. Grabbing the Walther off the intake manifold, he spun around and shot the driver, a sergeant, in the forehead. The officer was already bringing his submachine gun up to bear when Kessler put two bullets in his chest.

The jeep lurched forward and stalled as the driver's foot came off the clutch, then rolled a few yards down the hill and came to rest against a tree. Kessler turned to point the pistol at the women, who instinctively put their hands up as if they could ward off a bullet.

"They are dead because of *you*, Fräulein. If you had just stayed quiet, as I told you…"

"You killed the president?" the brunette said, the hate clear in her eyes.

"Yes, and the Reich will live because of it. I don't expect you to understand, but this is war and…"

Something hit him from behind, like being hit in the back with a sledgehammer, and an explosion of red painted the women's shoes as his ears registered the gunshot. One of them screamed as Kessler looked down at the bloom of red on his shirt. He turned slowly to look at the jeep - at the man who had killed him.

The young Marine lieutenant was leaning against the jeep, a smoking .45 automatic in one hand, the other clasped to his ribs, a grim look on his face.

The world spun and Kessler hit the ground hard, wheezing, his lungs filling with blood. He pulled the remains of FDR's glasses from his pocket; the trophy twisted and shattered by the slug exiting his body, and knew he had failed. He tried to take a breath but there was nothing but blood to breath.

136

GINO'S HAD become one of the more popular places in Flagstaff during the war, and as light fell through the plate glass windows onto pavement still wet from an evening thunderstorm. Jake took a deep breath of the cool spring air, the place bringing back memories of eating angel hair pasta and oysters there with Laurel when Gino had first opened up. Even now, at half past eleven, the place was doing a hell of a business.

He could hear the sound of a jazz orchestra coming from a jukebox inside, a little louder and clearer every time the door opened, and he could see a picture of FDR over the bar, wrapped in black bunting, and felt a twinge of empathy for Elliot, mentally reminding himself to call him. They hadn't spoken since Elliot was picked up by search and rescue.

As he pushed his way inside, the bouncer was giving the good news to a couple of sailors who'd been arguing over their 15th drink. One apparently hated FDR, and was "...glad that socialist SOB was dead." The other sailor - clearly an FDR supporter - had taken umbrage at the remark and decked his shipmate. What sailors were doing in Arizona Jake had no idea, but the bouncer, a gorilla the size of the Empire State building, wasn't having any of it. He had each of them by an ear, and Jake stepped aside to let him escort the two Navy pugilists outside.

The bar itself was an ancient oak edifice of unknown origin, although someone had once told Jake it had originally come from a closed bar in Jerome. It reached nearly to the ceiling, which was easily 12 feet high. A huge, rectangular mirror was set in the middle, with bottles of liquor staged cleverly in front, making it look as though they had twice as much booze as was really there.

Carvings of nymphs being chased by satyrs scampered between curling oak leaves so realistic you would have sworn they'd blown in off the street, sticking to the faux Corinthian columns set at each end, carved from the same straight-grained oak.

The top and face of the serving area of the bar itself was hammered, polished copper which gleamed in the warm, dim light cast by oil lamps which had been converted to electric; huge globes suspended in triplets from the high ceiling. A brass foot - rail ran in front of the bar.

Most of the seats at the bar were taken by women, many of them with men who stood sideways, foot on the brass rail, arm on the bar, leaning in to listen attentively to what she was saying, or placing a proprietary hand on her back to whisper something in her ear.

Some of the women looked attentive, flirting openly; others were clearly ignoring the men trying to make time with them, in the hopes they would go away. Some were alone - men being a rare commodity during wartime, and stirred their drinks languidly, chin on hand, sipping only occasionally to make it last. A few of them had checked Jake out when he'd come in, but he wasn't in the market. All he could think about was Morrie. Was she okay? Had they hurt her?

"What can I get you?" the bartender asked, drying a glass with a bar towel even as he spoke.

"I'd like the special," Jake said.

The bartender looked at him with a furrowed brow. "No special tonight, Pally. You missed Happy Hour by about eight hours."

"You the only one on?"

"Yeah, until midnight when Pete gets in, but I'm telling you, there's no special. You want a drink or not?"

"Just a beer," Jake said, feeling stupid. Laurel had told him midnight. He was early.

He pushed some money at the bartender in return for a beer, and looked around for a quiet place to sit until the other bartender came in, wondering if he was a Nazi too, or just a guy making a few extra bucks on the side from a little smuggling. Gino himself made no bones about his loyalties, cursing Mussolini for ruining his beautiful country, bemoaning the bad luck that kept him from strangling the bastard with his own hands, which definitely ingratiated him with his patrons, whether it was true or not.

He always wore an American flag pin on the lapel of his suit coat, which he tended to put on whenever he left the kitchen, often right over his apron, playing the obsequious clown with half a dozen good customers, fawning over the women, kissing their hands while clapping the men on the back like long - lost friends.

The act didn't fool Jake any, he knew Gino was a shrewd operator. Everyone said he had mob connections, which made it a good place to have dinner - despite rationing, Gino never seemed to run out of anything, especially booze.

Just before midnight Jake saw the relief bartender duck under the entrance flap to the bar, lifting it just enough to get underneath, rolling his apron expertly, passing the strings around the back and tying it in front, tucking the knot under the roll, his movements those of a professional who'd done the same thing many times.

Jake waited until he'd served a couple of drinks, then approached the bar. The new guy was arranging something back there to suit him while the guy Jake had spoken to earlier schmoozed with his customers at the other end. The new bartender looked up as Jake set his empty beer mug on the bar.

"Another one?" he asked, reaching for the glass.

"No, I'd like the special."

The bartender's hand froze for a second while he sized Jake up, darkening as he tried to decide if he were some sort of cop, then he turned his head towards the other bartender who was saying goodbye to a couple of regulars and beginning to untie his apron.

"Hey Sam. Give me another minute will ya? I gotta get more ice – you left me hangin' here."

"Bullshit. I filled it an hour ago."

"Yeah, well, I don't want to run out; it's melting fast."

"Well hurry up, willya?" Sam said, retying his apron and moving to take a customer, unhappiness written across his face.

"Putz," Jake's bartender said under his breath, raising the flap once more and motioned for Jake to follow him through the swinging doors to the kitchen.

The kitchen was bedlam. Gino's served supper until 11:30, but it looked as though the last orders were just now going out. Jake dodged a waitress holding a stack of plates full of steaming food, and she gave him a dirty look as she slid by.

"Tryin' to make a livin' here, pal," she said as she scurried past, turning expertly to butt the doors open, the five platefuls of food miraculously balanced in her arms like a circus performer.

Jake found a spot he hoped would be out of the way and waited. The bartender had slipped around the prep table to the grill, and Jake saw him talking to Gino. He pointed at Jake, saying something Jake couldn't hear, and Gino looked back over his shoulder at Jake, gave him the once over, then turned back to the grill. Jake saw him nod once as he turned something over and the bartender came back over.

"Wait here, Gino will cook you the special."

"But…"

"Wait here, and stay out of the way," he repeated, nodding at a worker pouring a huge pot of hot soup into a storage container for the night, his elbow inches from Jake's head. When he turned back, the bartender was gone.

137

LILY AND Dick sat in the darkness looking at the house. One light in the back showed dimly through the closed curtains. There was what looked like a dark blue or maroon Hudson and a beige Ford missing one hubcap in the drive. "You sure this is the place?" Dick asked.

"This is the address that was on Laurel's handkerchief. Marci and I drove by here once before she was killed, but we didn't have the nerve to go any further. It was just a game then..." she trailed off sadly, clearly thinking of her friend.

"Listen, I want you to stay here in the car," Dick began.

"Not a chance in hell. I got one sweet kid killed, I'm not going for another one," Lily said, and she was out of the car before Dick could even finish. He grabbed the .45 auto out of the glove box and chambered a round, which was a real bitch one-handed, but he was getting better at it. He was starting to wish he'd traded Jake for his revolver though.

He got out of the car, closed the door softly and tucked the automatic into his waistband in the small of his back, pulling his shirt out and over it so it didn't show. Lily was already halfway around back, and he cursed quietly. "Dammit, girl." He had to run to catch up with her.

They had nearly reached the back steps when the light came on and Lily froze like a deer in the headlights. Dick dove forward, grabbed her by the wrist with his good arm and yanked her over into the shadows at the edge of the yard, where they dropped to their stomachs just as the door opened.

"Keep your face down, white faces show up in the dark," he whispered fiercely in her ear. The screen door squeaked again and he heard someone inside say to the man at the door: "...and get extra garlic bread."

"Yeah, yeah," the guy at the door replied as he came out, closing the inside door, then the screen, then stopping to fumble in his shirt pockets for something. Dick watched him out of the corner of his eye, face to the ground as the stranger found what he was looking for - a pack of

Chesterfields and some matches. He stopped on the bottom step to shake one out, place it in his mouth and light it, inhaling with a sigh of clear pleasure.

He tucked the cigarettes back in his pocket as he walked towards the dark Hudson, which Dick could see was definitely maroon now in the light from the back porch, jingling out keys as he walked. Lilly was raising her head, trying to see.

"Keep your face *down*," Dick hissed as the car started up and its lights came on. The car backed out onto the street, and for a moment Dick was afraid they'd had it. If the driver turned their way and came in their direction they'd be caught directly in the headlights, but he backed towards them and went the other way, toward Beaver Street.

"We've got maybe twenty minutes before he comes back with dinner. Sure you want to do this?" Dick asked, looking at Lily. She nodded in reply, looking straight at him, and he could see no fear in her eyes.

"Okay. You open the door for me, I'll go in and get the drop on him. You hear shooting, you hit the floor and crawl for the door, got it?" Another nod. "Let's do it then," he said, as he pushed himself up one-handed off the ground and sprinted for the door.

138

GINO FINISHED serving up the entrees he'd been working on, wiped his hands on a bar towel and stabbed a big, half-chewed, stub of a cigar he recovered from a nearby ashtray into his mouth. He came around the prep table and walked up to Jake, who was a little surprised at how fast the big man could move.

"You here for the special, that right?"

Jake nodded.

"Let's go and talk in my office," Gino said, indicating a beat - up door with peeling paint marked "office." Jake followed him, and when Gino opened the door he could see it led down a steep flight of well-worn steps into the cellar, with a small, right -hand landing halfway down.

Gino went first, and Jake stepped down two steps, then turned to close the door, but there was a knife in his face, just inches from his nose, and it looked sharp. It was the prep cook, the one he'd seen putting away the soup for the night. He didn't look friendly, and the knife didn't waver.

He gestured for Jake to continue down, which he did, taking a few more steps backwards, the cook following him carefully, the knife at his throat. The door to the kitchen closed and Jake stood in the dim glow of a single bulb from a pull string lamp over the landing.

"Stop."

Jake stopped.

"Hands on head. Turn roun' slow."

The prep cook had a heavy Italian accent, and Jake wondered what else he did besides cook. He had a pretty good idea what, and it wasn't encouraging. He put his hands on his head and turned around.

The cook patted him down, finding the big hog - leg Colt and the box of shells in one jacket pocket, then his wallet and watch.

"Down."

Jake continued down the creaky wooden steps, wondering idly how they held Gino's girth, into a low-ceilinged room empty but for a scarred wooden desk, a few chairs which matched the desk and looked vaguely dangerous to sit in, and a black metal file cabinet older than both of them. A low haze of smoke was already creeping across the ceiling from Gino's cigar.

Gino sat behind the desk, leaning back in his chair, hands behind his head, contentedly puffing away. For a minute Jake wondered if the brown stains on his apron were tomato sauce or drops of blood, then decided he didn't want to know.

"Sit," the prep cook said from behind him, prodding him with the long, wicked blade. Jake sat.

The cook stepped forward and set the big Colt, the box of ammo, and Jake's watch, wallet and car keys on the desk in front of Gino, then stepped back again, behind the chair, where Jake couldn't see him. He didn't like the feeling.

Gino sat still for a minute, just puffing his cigar and appraising Jake, then leaned forward and picked up Jake's wallet. He opened it and took out the driver's license.

"Jake Ellison. That you?"

"It's what it says doesn't it?"

Gino looked at Jake like he was something he'd stepped in.

"Look Gino, I'm just trying to do some business...a girl's life is at stake."

"So you come into my restaurant, carrying a heater, asking nosy questions, then you disrespect me? Frank..."

Jake was suddenly pinned to his chair from behind, the prep cook's uncommonly strong arm across his chest, the filet knife at his throat.

"Look, I'm sorry, really. I was just following directions. I'm not being nosy, I just asked for the special."

Gino sighed. "And *that* my friend, is a very nosy question."

"I'm sorry. I didn't mean any disrespect, I just want my girl back."

Gino looked at him for another slow, lethal minute, as if deciding something, then his eyes went to the prep cook. He sighed dramatically.

"Let him go, Frank." Just as quickly as it had appeared, the arm that had been like a steel band across his chest was gone, and the knife with it. Jake took a deep breath. The prep cook was stronger than he looked.

The phone rang, then rang again. Gino looked at it as if it were an insect he'd like to crush. He let it ring a couple more times then finally snatched the receiver out of its cradle and held it to his ear with one meaty hand, pulling the ruined cigar from his face with the other.

"This had better be good, I'm in a meeting," he said, looking at Jake with flat, dead eyes. Then his eyes rolled to the ceiling.

"What? You should have called me first. Yeah, he's here now...well I don't normally answer the fuckin' phone when I'm cooking. It's Saturday night. I'm tryin' to run a restaurant here..." He looked at Jake, his eyes narrowing. "No, nothin' on him, we looked...unless you like old cowboy guns. All right, hold on, I'll let you talk to him, but I get twice my usual for this. Oh, and you need to pay your tab. Those two pals of yours are big eaters...hold on."

Gino took the phone from his ear and held it out to Jake, who took it gingerly, unsure what to expect.

"Hello?"

"Hello, my ass. Where are the diamonds?"

"Close by. I figured you'd try something like this."

"Gino will show you the way through the tunnels. You show up without the diamonds, you'll get to kiss your girl goodbye...*at the morgue.*"

"You've been watching too many movies. Who writes your dialogue?"

"You want her dead, Jake?"

"I guess not."

"Then shut up and get moving."

139

DICK PULLED the .45 from behind him and flipped off the safety, holding it low.

"Open the screen door very slowly so it doesn't squeak, then the inside door fast."

Lily did as she was told, and Dick brought the gun up in his left hand, following it into the room like a .45 caliber battering ram. He found himself in a mudroom that ran across the rear of the house. He could see into the kitchen through a doorway off to his right. There was a light on, and he moved towards it quickly, their only advantage surprise.

He stepped into the kitchen doorway just as Lily let the screen door shut a little too quickly, making it squeal slightly as it closed. There was a man in a chair at the kitchen table reading a newspaper. "You forget something?" he said as he looked up, then froze when he saw the one-armed blond giant with a gun standing in the doorway. His eyes widened, and he began to move, dropping his right hand behind the newspaper, and Dick knew he was going for a gun.

He didn't hesitate. In the Solomon Islands, hesitation got you killed. Dick simply took two steps forward and kicked out with his size thirteen shoe. The blow caught the German square in the forehead, and he tipped over backwards in the chair, hitting the floor hard, out cold, his pistol skittering across the floor.

"Pride of Germany, huh?" he said. "Get his gun and find something to tie him up with. I'll check the rest of the house."

Lily picked up the pistol. "Does this make me your gun moll?" she said, striking a Hollywood pose.

Dick grinned. "Sure does. You're in it for keeps now, doll. Now check those cupboards for some rope and get this guy tied. We've got maybe fifteen minutes before the other scumbag gets back."

"Okay, Capone."

"My people call me 'Pretty Boy'," Dick said in an Edward G. Robinson voice.

Lily shook her head. "Can't do it. If I called you that there'd be no living with you."

140

To Jake's surprise, Gino had given him back everything, even his hog leg and the box of cartridges. Then he told Frank the prep cook to get lost. One thing about Frank, he knew how to take orders.

As soon as the door to the cellar had closed, Gino got up and went over to the two file cabinets in the corner. "Gimme a hand here," he said.

The two men muscled the cabinets out of the way, revealing a small door with no handle or knob. It looked to be painted shut, but when Gino touched a certain place on the baseboard it popped open a few inches, swinging inward. Gino pulled it open, fumbled in the dark for a moment, then lights came on inside the hole.

A long, low, damp corridor of rock, concrete and brick stretched out before them. Steam pipes and conduits ran along the ceilings and walls, and a pair of single wires ran across the ceiling connecting a series of lights spaced every thirty feet or so, most of them working.

"How far does this go?" Jake couldn't help asking.

"Another nosy question. You never learn, do ya?"

"Sorry."

"For your information, these steam tunnels run all over Flagstaff under the streets. The steam generating station is over by the underpass on 66. From there it feeds both sides of the tracks. You can go all the way to the college, you know the way."

"As you do, obviously."

Gino laid one finger alongside his nose as he grinned back at him, then they began making their way through the narrow, rough tunnel. "Let's just say these tunnels came in real handy during Prohibition. Hell, they still come in handy at times…like now."

Jake followed him through the maze, amazed that anyone could remember all the twists and turns. Every now and then Jake could hear the rumble of traffic or people talking on the sidewalk above them when they passed grates open to the street above them, fed by the occasional access ladder. Every now and then there was an intersection where Gino would stop and fumble with the lights.

There was just enough room for Jake to see dark tunnels running off in other directions, and huge cast-iron handwheels to shut off valves on high pressure lines, which groaned and sang all around them as the steam passed through them, ticking in others like a room radiator as they cooled.

The lines were covered with asbestos batting, but still gave off a lot of heat. In some tunnels it was merely sweltering, despite the cool spring evening, in others it was an absolute sauna, making Jake sorry he'd worn a jacket.

Finally they turned right into a larger tunnel running east and west, or at least Jake thought it was east and west. After Gino turned on the lights ahead of them and turned off the lights behind them, Jake could see the steam lines here were much larger, and ran mostly overhead, strapped to concrete and steel with huge bands, the valves and handwheels gigantic. Jake figured they must be 12 inches in diameter. Other smaller pipes ran out of these lines in various directions, and Jake realized this was the main trunk line. He thought about what would happen to them if there was even a tiny rupture in one of these lines and shuddered. As if to feed his paranoia, suddenly Gino stopped.

"Uh-oh. A leak."

Jake looked ahead to where Gino pointed. A cloud of steam filled the tunnel, and Gino inched towards it, then came back to Jake, sweat running down his face.

"It's okay, I think. Just a pinhole, and it's pointed at the south wall. We'll stay on the north side, close to the wall where it's coolest. Do just what I do. Hold your breath and close your eyes so the steam doesn't scald them."

Jesus, Jake thought, he's done this before, the crazy bastard. He did as he was told, and as they inched closer and closer to the billowing steam Jake could hear a high-pitched whistle like a steam kettle, and could see a tiny jet of steam hitting the south wall of the tunnel. It looked as if it were cutting a groove into the stone wall, and Jake couldn't help but shudder thinking of what it would do to a human body. It was so hot here it made the rest of the tunnel seem cool by comparison.

"Okay, you ready? Hold your breath and follow me. One, two, THREE." The two men pulled their coats over their heads, closed their eyes, and plunged into the wall of steam.

141

ICK HADN'T found anyone in the rest of the tiny house, which made him really wonder. He'd fully expected to find Morrie bound and gagged in one of the bedrooms but there was nothing, not even a sign she'd been there. The clothing he'd found in both bedrooms was men's, undoubtedly belonging to the two guards. He went back to the kitchen, brow furrowed, gun lowered, ready to shoot someone.

Lily had found a spindle of clothesline under the sink, new from the look of it, and had tied their new friend to his chair, making a good job of it from what Dick could tell. The German appeared to be coming around, rolling his head and groaning. Dick set the .45 on the counter and found a water glass in the cupboard. He set it in the sink, filled it with cold water, turned off the tap and threw it directly in the face of the Nazi spy to bring him around.

The German gasped and choked, bringing his head up while trying to focus. Dick set the glass on the table and grabbed him by the hair...hard. He'd helped interrogate a couple of Japanese prisoners a couple times. It hadn't been pretty, but after finding two of his men who had disappeared skinned alive, hanging from a tree upside down, Dick's concept of mercy had changed. He didn't want Lily to see what he had in mind for the German, but they were running out of time.

"There's a cellar here isn't there? Is that where you're keeping the girl?"

The German just sneered at him, a look of disdain on his face.

"Okay, Fritz, have it your way. Lily, fill that tea kettle and put it on to boil."

The German's eyes widened a bit at this, but he stayed silent.

"Dick, no."

"Lily, if we don't find Morrie soon, they'll kill her. Put the damn kettle on."

Lily went to the stove and picked up the tea kettle. It was nearly full, so she shook a match out of the box on a shelf by the stove, struck the tip with one thumbnail and lit the flame. She turned it up all the way and set the kettle on it, then turned to Dick.

"I won't help you torture this man Dick, Nazi or not."

"Just think about what he and his buddy did to your friend, Lily."

"What separates us from people like these Nazi savages, Dick? Huh? I'll tell you what. There are some lines you just don't cross, no matter what. We cross them, we're as damned as they are."

"I pour that kettle over Fritz's head, I *guarantee* he'll tell us where Morrie is."

Lily went to Dick and took his remaining hand, still holding the gun, in both of hers, brought it to her lips and kissed it, then looked up at him.

"I don't know where you've been or what you saw that was so horrible that it changed you so, Dick, but I hate it. I hate the fact that you had to endure such horror, and I hate that it changed you so. Dick, I love you with all my heart, but if you do this, if you persist in hurting this man, no matter what he may be guilty of, then it's over between us."

Dick looked at her as if he'd been slapped in the face. He sighed and closed his eyes for a minute, then pulled Lily tightly against him, pressing her head against his chest. "Then I guess you'd better help me look for that cellar entrance before that other kraut gets back."

142

LAUREL LOOKED at her watch impatiently. "Dammit, where are they? Gino said he'd bring him right away."

Klaus just looked at her dispassionately. Of the three Germans, only Klaus gave her the creeps. The other two were stone killers, sure, but she got the feeling Klaus genuinely enjoyed it. He and Dieter had been the ones who had taken care of her sister Lily. The little bitch deserved to die, but Laurel had been a bit shocked at how violent Klaus had been. Dieter had told her about the cutting, the questioning, the stabbing, then the cold, hard excitement in Klaus's eyes when he'd finished, and how Dieter was afraid for a minute that Klaus was about to turn the knife on him just to continue his fun.

He had told her of how some of the blood had splattered on Klaus's face from the murder, and how he'd first licked his lips clean of blood before wiping his face with a towel, holding it to his nose when he'd finished, breathing in the coppery, metallic smell as if it'd been perfume, his eyes closed in ecstasy. It had scared Dieter a little and he was former Gestapo, and had seen and done some weird shit.

Yes, Klaus would bear watching, she thought. He would have to be the first one she killed once she had the diamonds and had disposed of Jake and her other little problem: his little tramp of a girlfriend. She looked over at where Klaus had hidden himself behind some stacked crates in the narrow tunnel, and he gave her a wide, feral grin, almost as if he knew exactly what she was thinking. It was everything she could do not to shudder.

143

JAKE GASPED in a lungful of air, pulling the coat back down. The back of his hands were red and sore from the momentary immersion in the steam cloud. It was if he'd stuck them in a pan of dishwater that was too hot to touch.

"Jesus. You do this often?"

"They'll find the leak tomorrow during their rounds and fix it, but I figured you couldn't wait," Gino said, bent over, his hands on his knees. "Come on, let's go, he said, straightening. "It's still a little ways."

"Right behind you."

The tunnel they moved down now was wide enough to hold some storage, and Jake began seeing stacks of iron pipe in various sizes, as well as wooden boxes and crates of various sizes. The power company undoubtedly stored their repair materials here, out of the way and close to where they'd need them, which made sense. Then he started seeing other boxes that didn't look so official, then a bicycle, even a couch. Jake couldn't help but wonder how the hell they'd gotten it down there, and why.

"Here we are. Let me find the damn lights," Gino said.

"Thank God, I feel like we've been down here in the pits of hell for a week."

Suddenly the dark side tunnel blazed with light, and Laurel stood there in front of a stack of crates holding a mean little pistol.

"Hello, Gino. Hello, Jake," she said.

"You crazy bitch, you nearly gave me a heart attack," Gino said, his hand in his jacket pocket where Jake had seen him stash a stubby little .38 before they'd left his office.

"Sorry, Gino. Thanks for the help."

"When are we gonna settle up?" he growled.

"Tomorrow at lunch. Soon as I conclude my business here with Jake I'll get you some cash."

"You say Tomorra' by noon, you better mean by noon, or you ain't gonna be so pretty no more."

"Gino, you always were such a sweet talker."

"Sweet as I get. By noon, you hear me?" he said, backing away into the tunnel. He gave Jake a look. "Good luck kid," he said, then he was gone.

"Okay Jake, first things first. You bring the stones?"

"They're nearby."

"They'd better be in your pocket or your little sweetie has eaten her last bon-bon."

"Last bon-bon? Where do you get this shit?"

Laurel's face darkened. "I'm the one holding the gun here, Jake, so just pull that big hog leg out and drop it on the ground."

"Why, so you can kill me like you killed your sister?" Jake, Lily and Dick had decided for now to keep Lily's "resurrection" a secret.

"I just gave the order, Jake, I didn't kill her."

"And the difference is…what?"

"You don't understand."

"You're right, I don't. How could you have your own sister killed? I thought I knew you."

"This is *war*, Jake. The Führer has said many times that one must make sacrifices in war."

"So you sacrificed *your sister*, Laurel? My God, when did you become so heartless?"

"Enough. Where are the diamonds? Tell me now or I give the signal and my associate cuts her throat."

"I meant what I said, Laurel. You hurt her and…"

Laurel laughed. "And what, Jake? You never did see things clearly. The big idealist, went off to the war, got shot up, and for what? You picked the wrong side, Jake."

"Then how come the Russians are marching through Berlin right now?"

"Propaganda."

"You don't like hearing about the failure of your precious Reich, do you sweetheart?"

"Drop the gun on the floor, Jake. Then you'd better have the stones or I swear, the both of you will die right in this tunnel. They won't find you for days…maybe weeks."

"I think I'll hold onto the gun…just in case."

"What's wrong Jake? Don't trust me?"

"Explain to me why I would."

"ENOUGH. Give me the damn diamonds or I'll shoot you and take them anyway."

Jake raised his hands in supplication, then knelt and reached down to his pants cuff. Sewing the diamonds into the cuffs had been Lily's idea. She'd divided the stones roughly in half, sewing them up into two smaller packages, then she'd sewn those into the outside cuffs of Jake's trouser legs, using just enough stitches to secure them, but not so many they weren't easily torn out.

He ripped the stitches easily with his fingers and fished out the two tiny, narrow bags, one from each leg. They had taken a wild guess at the value and figured there was at least $150,000 worth of stones in each bag, probably more. He stood up, a fortune in each hand.

Laurel gave him her sweetest smile. "You always were a clever boy, Jake. Now toss them here."

"Tell me where Morrie is first."

"Now Jake, don't screw this up. I really don't want to shoot you, but I will. I told you I'd take you to her. She's close by – just like your diamonds."

"Fine. Here's half," he said, tossing her one bag. "You get the balance when I get her back."

"You forget who's holding the gun here Jake."

"And you forget that I don't care if I live or die without her. You might get the first shot off from that little peashooter you're holding, but you know Cates taught me how to draw, and I'll kill you twice before you get a second shot off."

Laurel threw back her head and laughed, her peals of laughter echoing through the tunnels. "My God. Jake the gunslinger. You can't *live* without her? You were *never* that romantic with me. It's so sweet it's just positively...corny."

"Look, Laurel, be reasonable. You get the diamonds, I get Morrie back. That was the deal. After that I don't care where you go or what you do as long as you stay out of my life. I just want her back safe and sound."

The woman he had once wanted to marry stood before him, juggling the bag of diamonds he'd tossed her, eyeing the other bag in his hand greedily. Finally she smiled.

"All right Jake. No reason we can't be civilized about this. It's this way," she said, nodding toward the tunnel ahead of her.

"Fine, you first."

"Now Jake, you might shoot me in the back and take the diamonds for yourself."

"I think we both know it's more likely the other way around. No, Laurel, I'm not turning my back on you. No way."

She laughed again, and Jake felt a prick of warning as he realized she was enjoying herself, like a cat toying with a mouse, he thought. What's she up to?

"Fine, Jake. *I'll* go first, just to show you there's no hard feelings." With that, she lowered her gun, turned, and strode up the tunnel, Jake following warily.

144

"DICK, I FOUND IT! It was right here in the mudroom the whole time," Lily said excitedly, waving to him from the end of the hall. Dick had been checking the bedrooms for a trapdoor. He followed her back through the living room and kitchen, anxiously expecting the sound of a car in the driveway any moment, the signal that the second Nazi spy had returned.

The one they'd left tied to the chair in the kitchen had been struggling against his bonds, but stopped as they entered the room. Dick checked the ropes just to be sure, but Lily had grown up on a ranch, learning how to tie animals so they didn't get loose. He couldn't help but smile, despite the dire circumstances.

He followed Lily back to the mudroom, directly off the kitchen and the first room they'd entered. A washer with a built-in wringer stood in the corner next to an old hutch with chipped and faded cream - colored paint. She pulled back a threadbare Navajo rug to expose the floor. Even Dick didn't see the door right away, but she pointed to a small latch, and he handed her the gun, grasped the D-ring and with a grunt, pulled upward.

The door was heavy, but had some sort of counterweight system, so once he got it past a certain point, the lead counterweights took over and it swung up the rest of the way easily. Below them was a short, dark flight of concrete steps. There was a pull chain on the wall, and Dick turned the light on.

Most houses in the area just had shallow crawlspaces, but this one had clearly been built with a room beneath it – perhaps some sort of root cellar? Maybe it was even tied into the steam tunnels? Dick had heard plenty of stories about them, but had never been in the tunnels. He wasn't even sure they came this far south, but the house looked as though it had been built around the turn of the century and Dick wondered if it had been some sort of speakeasy or smuggling stop during Prohibition.

He locked the door in the upright position and motioned for Lily to give him his gun. "I think you should stay here," he said as she handed him back his automatic.

"Not a chance, handsome," she replied, brandishing the .38 she'd taken from the guard. "If Jake's girl is down there she's likely tied up. You're going to untie her one-handed?"

Dick looked down ruefully at where his right hand should be. She had a point. "I still think I should check it out first."

Lily shook her head. "No way, champ. We're in this together…up to our necks, I might add. Now let's go before our second pal comes back with din-din."

Dick sighed and started down the stairs. Why couldn't he have fallen for a gentler, more compliant woman?

145

J AKE FELT more than saw Klaus attack from his left, the Nazi reaching for
Jake's revolver while simultaneously slashing downwards with his knife,
narrowly missing as Jake pivoted into him, instinctively throwing his left
arm up to deflect the blow. The revolver was jerked from his waistband by
Klaus's other hand but fell to the floor as Jake spun and it was torn from
the German's grasp. Klaus swung back and their forearms connected, the
impact knocking the second bag of diamonds from Jake's hand as he
blocked the knife, the bag skittering across the floor.

Klaus reversed his grip on the knife, flipping it expertly to slash at Jake's
abdomen, barely missing him as Jake lurched backwards. His Colt had been
kicked away and was out of reach. He wondered briefly why the German
hadn't just shot him, then the Nazi gave him a wide, evil grin and Jake
realized he was facing one of those people who just really enjoyed inflicting
pain on others.

Klaus cast a greedy look at the tiny bag in the corner momentarily, then
lunged again, feinting left then slashing right, immediately reversing the
knife to swing left again, and blood welled suddenly through a cut on Jake's
arm. The German was good, but Jake had learned knife fighting from Tom
Crow Flies and his nephew, and the Apaches were the best knife fighters in
the world.

Klaus came at him again as they circled, coming in down low, slashing
for the tendons behind the knees, then stabbing overhead as Jake ducked to
protect his legs, flipping the knife over again to bring it down into Jake's
back. But the German was overconfident, and as he drove the knife down
towards his back, Jake knew this was the moment he'd been waiting for.
When the blade came in overhead, Jake spun on one heel, going
underneath and turning his back on his attacker as he reached up and
grabbed his knife arm, standing up straight to jerk Klaus's weight off his

feet and flipping him over, slamming him into the concrete wall upside down.

He heard a grunt from the surprised German as he hit the wall hard, then collapsed on the tunnel floor. Jake backed up as Klaus stood back up, still holding his knife. He wasn't smiling now. Now there was red murder in his eyes, but the reversal in position had put Jake where he'd wanted to be all along; closer to his revolver, and he dove for it as the German lunged.

Jake's shot went wide, as he had fired instinctively where the German had been, but the 250 grain slug tore through the asbestos covering of the four - inch steam pipe running along the ceiling and shattered the cast iron, punching a hole the size of a cigar in the heavy pipe before ricocheting away, as a jet of 358 - degree water at over 200 psi sprayed from the pipe directly at Klaus, nearly cutting him in half.

Klaus opened his mouth to scream, but the superheated air flashburned his lungs even as he took a breath, and the scream came out as a half-gurgle, blood running from his mouth as he fell to the ground, the shirt torn from his back by the pressure, the skin and muscles cut like butter by a surgeon's knife, his skin an instant mass of blisters where the steam had merely brushed him, the gash in his back flush with blood, the steam having cut deeper than any knife.

Jake lay on the floor of the tunnel, having rolled away from the blast of steam, the revolver in one hand. The temperature in the tunnel was already well over 100, driven up quickly by the escaping steam, and his shirt was already soaked with perspiration, the ceiling already dripping with condensate as he struggled to his feet. In the heat of the fight Jake hadn't noticed Laurel scurry back and pick up the second package of diamonds, then run back down the tunnel, but when he looked for them they were gone.

He glanced one last time at Klaus's scalded, twitching body before lurching away, down the tunnel in the direction Laurel had gone, knowing that if she had Klaus try to kill him, then Morrie had just become a liability - another loose end for Laurel to take care of before she left town. He didn't care about the diamonds, just Morrie. She was all he could think about. He just prayed he wouldn't get there too late as he began running down the tunnel in what he hoped was the right direction.

146

AT THE bottom of the steep stairs was a door to the right. There was a bare bulb in a socket on the ceiling, but Dick could find neither a pull string nor a switch. He stuck his gun back in his waistband and tried the door, but it was locked. He put his shoulder to it and it creaked. Not much of a door even when new, he decided. Now, flimsy with dry rot and age, it didn't seem like much of a barrier. Down the hallway lay darkness, but when Lily shone the flashlight she'd found in the kitchen in that direction they could see another door at the end of the short tunnel.

"Let's try this one first, it goes under the house. I'm guessing that one leads to the steam tunnels. This hallway is longer than the house is wide."

"It's locked. Maybe the guy upstairs has the key?" Lily said.

Dick just grinned at her. "Just stand back, hon, and I'll unlock it," he said as he backed up, then with one jackhammer kick, splintered the door at the knob. One more good kick and the knob flew off as the door flew inward, slamming against the wall to the left. Dick already had his .45 in his hand again, and immediately plunged into the darkness on the other side.

Once his eyes had adjusted to the gloom he found a pull chain and yanked it, and the room was lit with a garishly bright light, practically blinding them both, illuminating a small 10' x 10' concrete room ringed with tired shelves holding ancient, dust-covered jars of peaches, string beans and botulism, but what drew Dick's attention was the chair in the middle of the fruit cellar, and the young woman tied to it. She was gagged, her eyes wide with fear, her arms bloody from fighting against the wire which they had bound her with.

"My God, You poor thing," Lily breathed as she pushed past Dick to kneel next to her. "It's going to be all right now, Morrie. Jake sent us to find you. We're going to get you out of here."

Dick saw Morrie's eyes close briefly as she realized she was being rescued, and when they opened again they were moist with tears, the most beautiful green eyes Dick had ever seen, set against hair as red as fire, and he could see why Jake had fallen for her.

She mumbled something behind the gag.

"Hold on, sweetie. Let me finish with your hands first. Dick, those bastards *wired* her hands so tight it's cutting into her wrists. What, they couldn't use rope?"

Dick stuck his head back out into the hall and listened for a minute, but heard nothing.

"There we go. Now the gag," Lily said as she untied the filthy bandanna they'd gagged her with. Morrie took in a huge gulp of air and coughed, her eyes watering as she tried to rub her numb hands together, but they were like two dead branches. She'd been bound so long she'd lost all feeling in them.

"Hold on, hon, let me untie your legs, then I'll rub some feeling back into them."

"Lily, we have to hurry. The other guy will be coming back any minute," Dick said, sticking his head out into the hallway again.

"You want to carry her, Dick? She'll be fine, she just needs a few minutes. There, there's your ankles, now give me your left hand. Can you feel anything in it yet?" Lily patiently rubbed Morrie's hand until she began to grimace.

"Pins and needles?"

Morrie nodded, unable to speak, her throat raw from the gag.

"I know it hurts, but it's a good sign. Now I'm going to rub your ankles some more, then as soon as you feel ready to walk we'll get you out of here and find you a nice glass of water."

"Lily, honey, we need to *go*," Dick said again, earning that look that women are always giving men when they think they're being obtuse.

"Okay, Morrie. Try standing up, hon. It's okay, I've got you," Lily said, her arm around Morrie's waist as she rose clumsily to her feet.

* * * * *

Morrie's hands and feet still felt stiff and wooden, but feeling was beginning to flood back into them, making them tingle and ache right through to the bone. 'I will not scream,' she told herself as Lily took her weight on her shoulder, holding her arm gently above the wrist, which were both chafed raw from the wires.

Dick backed out of the room and pointed his .45 up the stairs as Lily and Morrie staggered out into the tiny hallway. "Thought I heard something," he said, then he heard it again. It was unmistakable - the sound of a car door being shut. The other German had returned. They were out of time.

147

FOR AWHILE Jake just followed the path of lights in the tunnels, turning left with the lights, then right into a tunnel which ran parallel to the one he'd been in previously. The turns seemed about a block apart, which made perfect sense, as they were aligned with the streets - running beneath the sidewalks, but finally he came to the end of the lights, thinking, 'What now'?

He had no flashlight, no torch to light his way, then he remembered his Zippo. He'd been cutting down on his smoking ever since Elliot had told him test pilots needed strong lungs, but he hadn't been able to give them up altogether, and he kept his lighter on him just in case.

He fished it out of his jacket pocket and flipped it open. It lit on the second try, and while the light it threw was feeble and flickering, it was all he had. He transferred it to his left hand, and with the Zippo in one hand and the big Colt in the other he plunged ahead into the darkness.

He moved through the dark tunnel as quickly as he could, still managing to bark his shin twice on wooden crates hidden in the shadows. He had no idea where he was going, and no idea where he was, other than underneath Flagstaff, and no real idea of where Morrie was, but he had to try and find her. He swore to himself that if Morrie was hurt he would hunt down whoever was responsible and kill them, even if it were Laurel. He'd never hurt a woman before, but at the moment he was ready to kill a certain peroxide blond without a second thought.

148

L AUREL CAME out of the dark corridor, turning left into another lighted tunnel, which ran east, taking her closer to the safe house. She was nearly home free. She just had a couple of loose ends to tie up – the girl and her two "brothers in arms", the idiots. She had it all planned out. She'd tell them she had the diamonds and they didn't need the girl anymore. She'd have the muscle dispose of the girl in the desert, where her bones would be scattered to the winds by coyotes and buzzards. Then when they got back she'd propose a celebratory drink with a bottle of 12-year old McClellan she'd doctored with some rat poison via syringe in preparation for the occasion. She'd gotten the idea from *Arsenic and Old Lace*, where the two old ladies put arsenic in the blackberry brandy to euthanize indigent hobos, then buried them in their basement.

Of course it'd be a chore getting the bodies to the trap door, but once there she'd simply tumble them into the hole, close the trapdoor, and set the place on fire. By the time they found the bodies she'd be long gone. Then she had a deliciously wicked thought. Why have them kill the girl at all? She couldn't possibly survive the house fire, and it would speed things up, getting her away from Flagstaff that much sooner, and with less exposure. That way the two nitwits wouldn't have any time to even consider double-crossing her…well at least no more than they had already.

She shivered at the pure wickedness of it. Violence had always excited her. She fondled the two tiny cloth bags filled with her future and smiled as she turned into the final tunnel leading to the safe house and came face to face with her dead sister.

149

IT HAD been slow going with Morrie, who was barefoot, exhausted, shocky and dehydrated, but she limped along gamely with Lily's help, with Dick bringing up the rear. Once through the door they'd found themselves in a narrow concrete and stone tunnel filled with steam pipes and electrical conduits, the ceiling so low that Dick had to duck in places to miss the piping.

They had turned right coming out the door, which Dick's unerring sense of direction told him was north, towards the center of town. What they needed were lots of people around them. Harder to kill someone and get away with it in a crowd.

The steam pipes hissed and moaned like something alive, and Dick kept checking behind them, knowing that at any minute Morrie's two guards, the one they'd tied up and the one who'd gone for dinner, would be after them. They had to find an access shaft, and preferably not one in the middle of Route 66.

They reached the crossing of tunnels, and Dick was thinking there should be an access riser soon, when suddenly Laurel Hausen came running out of the connecting side tunnel to their left, a gun in one hand.

There was a moment of shock as they all stared at her, Laurel gaping back at Lily as if she'd seen a ghost, then she pointed the pistol at Dick who had been covering their escape with his pistol pointed back down the tunnel behind them. He was so surprised by her appearance that he was caught with his guard down.

"DROP THE GUN. Now, Dick, or I swear I'll kill them both," Laurel screamed. Dick figured he could probably turn and get a shot off, but Lily turned to look at him and shook her head "no." Then she did something odd; she lowered her eyes as if looking at the floor behind her, then looked at him, then did it again. He followed the direction of her gaze and realized what she was trying to tell him with her eyes – that the .38 they'd taken from the guard was tucked in the waistband of her jeans at the small of her back, where Laurel couldn't see it.

"Last chance Dick, Drop the gun or I shoot them," Laurel said again loudly. Dick could see that she was shaking from adrenaline, and she had never been that stable to begin with, so he decided to do as he was told, placing his precious .45 on the floor of the tunnel.

"Now, kick it away, back up the tunnel."

Dick did as he was told, and the gun went skittering away on the concrete. Laurel turned her attention back to Lily.

"You're alive," she said flatly, clearly not happy to see her younger sister, all pretense gone.

"No thanks to you. I knew you were a selfish, self-serving bitch, Laurel, but this is low even for you. Murder? Kidnapping? My God."

"This is a war, you stupid cow. Sacrifices have to be made for the Reich."

"That's it isn't it? Your stupid Reich? They turned you in Berlin in '36, didn't they? Well haven't you heard, Laurel? The war is over. Our troops are at the outskirts of Berlin, and your precious Führer is hiding like a rat in a bunker somewhere."

"SHUT UP," Laurel said, her voice shaking with rage.

Don't piss her off too much, Lil, Dick prayed as he edged closer to her.

"You and your friends have no idea what it's like to be a part of something greater than yourself, Lily. Something great, built by great men. The Reich will return, mark my words, and the Jews and the other scum of the earth will be swept away like the plague they are, cleansing the world and making it safe for good Aryans everywhere."

Lily shook her head as she stared at her sister. "You really believe all that tripe, don't you? Haven't you done enough? Just take your precious diamonds and leave us in peace."

Laurel shook her head. "Sorry, dear sister, I can't do that. I know you .You'd have the cops after me before I could get out of town. Now turn around. We're going back to the house," she said, gesturing with her little pistol, thinking "There will just be a few more bodies found in the basement than I had planned."

"Oh, and Dick? You try for that gun and I'll shoot them both right here. I mean it."

Suddenly Morrie, who'd been quietly listening to the whole thing, jerked her arm from Lily's neck, leapt forward and punched Laurel square in the face. Surprised, Laurel took a step back, but Morrie was on her, punching and slapping her, not caring that Laurel had a gun. Suddenly there was a shot and Morrie doubled over and fell to the floor.

Dick was already in movement and pulling the .38 from Lily's waistband. They had nothing to lose now, and he just hoped the other guards from the house didn't come up behind him as he fired.

150

KARL PUSHED through the back door of the safe house with two box dinners in a paper sack, ravenous from the smell of lasagna coming from the bag. Italians sure knew how to cook, he thought, then he nearly dropped their dinner as he tripped over the rug in the dark mudroom. The corner must have been flipped back when Dieter had gone to the cellar to check on the girl, and had forgotten to flip it back.

"Gott in Himmel, Dieter, you asshole, I nearly dropped din...." He trailed off as he came into the kitchen to find Dieter tied to a chair, struggling against his bonds, his mouth stuffed with dirty socks, the kettle screaming on the stove. "SCHEISS," he yelled, forgetting the lasagna.

151

EVEN AS he fired, Dick yelled to Lily to get down, but the roar of the guns in the enclosed space was unbearable, making his ears ache. He saw Laurel stagger away, then disappear into a dark tunnel, but he was pretty sure he'd winged her. Lily was already crouched over Morrie, who was looking at her, pale - faced and open - mouthed, her hand on her side, which was seeping blood. Dick crouched over them and set the pistol on the floor so he could check her wound.

"Let me see, Morrie," he said, gently moving her hand away and tearing the hole in her shirt larger so he could see the wound. It was bleeding freely, but it was in a spot he was fairly sure hadn't hit anything vital. He was no doctor, but he'd seen a lot of men who'd been torn up by bullets, and he was fairly confident that the small caliber bullet in her side wasn't going to kill her…as long as she got immediate medical care.

She wasn't bleeding from the mouth anyway, which was a good sign. He checked her eyes and they were dilated. She was going into shock. After all she'd been through, he was hardly surprised.

"Aw hell, Morrie, it's hardly a scratch. Just a little mosquito bite. Now here, put your hand back over it, here's a handkerchief. It's folded, now just keep mild pressure on it and we'll get you to a doctor," he said, watching her eyes relax a little, Lily giving him a worried look over her head.

His hearing was coming back, and suddenly he heard the sound of running feet echoing through the tunnels. Handing the .38 to Lily, Dick ran back down the tunnel and retrieved his .45 just as a man burst out of the tunnel to his left. He had the trigger halfway in before he realized it was Jake. He breathed a sigh of relief, lowering the big automatic.

"Jeez, Jake, I almost perforated ya."

Jake grinned, then saw Lily holding Morrie up off the ground and he dropped to his knees. "I heard the shots up the tunnel. My God, Honey, are you all right?" he asked, squeezing her free hand.

"Sure. I'm fine. Dick says it's jes' a lil' skeeter bite, huh Dick?" Morrie mumbled. She sounded delirious and Jake and Lily shared a worried look.

"Morrie here punched Laurel right in the kisser, didn't you, Morrie?" Lily said.

"Nazi bitch shot me," Morrie slurred.

"It was like watching a guy run straight into machine gun fire, Jake. Your girl's got some guts," Dick said.

"I don't feel so good," Morrie said.

"Come on, let's get you out of here," said Jake, giving Lily another worried look.

152

DIETER WAS rubbing his wrists angrily while Heinrich pulled the clothesline from his ankles. "I am going to kill them all...slowly," he said in German.

"Where is the damn Valkyrie? She should have been here by now." Karl asked Dieter.

"How should I know? She hasn't even called. She took Klaus and went into the tunnels. She said they'd be back in an hour."

"Perhaps she plans on leaving town without us once she has the diamonds. Maybe she's already gone," Karl said, voicing a thought both of them had shared at least once. They'd talked it over, and neither of them trusted her, and had planned on doing away with her once she'd recovered the jewels.

"No, Klaus is with her, but she needs to have an accident. Maybe she falls off a tall building," Dieter said, trying to get the taste of his sock out of his mouth.

"Or some other accident," Karl agreed, placing his spare pistol, a small Walther, in front of Dieter. "Kommen zie. Let's go get them," he said.

Dieter shook his head. "I want a quick drink first to get this taste out of my mouth."

"A quick schnapps first, then we go," Karl agreed, rising from his chair and going to the cupboard, being always agreeable to a little schnapps, a little too agreeable if you asked Dieter.

"Nein. Better yet, I saw her hide a bottle of good whisky on the top shelf of the cupboard, up there in the corner," he said, pointing.

Karl went to the cupboard and opened it, peering in. "I don't see it."

"Get a chair, you idiot, It's in the far corner, top shelf," Dieter said impatiently.

Karl spun a chair around to stand on, got up on it and looked. Dieter saw him smile, then reach in and pull out a bottle.

"It's Macallan…12 year old scotch," he said approvingly.

"A quick bit of this then we'll go find them, and when we're done we'll go find that Valkrie and teach her a lesson about screwing with us. Then we'll come back here and split up the diamonds."

Karl handed Dieter a tumbler with a generous two fingers of the dark amber liquid and the two men clinked glasses.

"To the Reich," Karl toasted.

"To Brazilian dancers and retirement in the tropics," Dieter responded. They both smiled at this, then drank, throwing back the scotch as if it were schnapps.

153

JAKE AND Lily took Morrie between them and gently helped her to her feet, an arm over each of their shoulders. "Dick, watch our six will you?" Jake said.

"Got it covered, Captain."

"I saw an access ladder back this way. Let's get the hell out of here."

"Jake, hold up. We're going to have a hell of a time getting her up one of those ladders, the shape she's in," Dick said.

"You got a better idea?"

"Well, I don't know about better, but I still think it's the only way we're getting her out of here anytime soon."

"I'm all ears."

"We go back the way we came in. Good news is, there's stairs. Bad news is, there's two Germans back there, and they'll be pissed off…but there's a telephone there too."

"Just *two* Germans? Hell, you can handle them by yourself, can't you?" Jake said.

Dick grinned. "I'll take point then."

"Lead the way, Geronimo."

"Keep it up. I take any scalps, you might be first," Dick grumbled.

They turned back the way Dick, Morrie and Lily had come, Dick going first, crouching slightly, his .45 automatic out in front of him. Just for a minute Jake felt sorry for the Japanese soldiers who had run into Dick in the jungle, and for the German spies who were about to.

Morrie's head was lolling dangerously by the time they reached the blue door which led to the cellar, and Jake and Lily lowered her gently to the ground while Dick held his ear to the door. He looked at Jake and shook his head, shrugging. "On three," Jake told him in sign language, cocking the big Colt.

Jake threw open the door as Dick went through it, his 1911 leading the way again. They were in the short hallway outside the room where Morrie had been held, and Dick held up his hand, surprised at the silence. Quickly he checked the fruit cellar where she'd been tied, then Dick started up the steep, narrow concrete steps, placing his ear to the hatch door to listen. After a minute he looked back at Jake, clearly puzzled. Why hadn't the two German agents chased them into the tunnels? Had they simply fled the house? Something seemed odd about the whole thing.

Jake came up the stairs behind him to help lift the hatch, which raised up with a soft squeal that made them both wince, expecting a shot from above at any second, but then Dick sniffed the air and wrinkled his nose, the smell of death in the air. He was well familiar with it from his time in the jungle. The smell of involuntarily voided bowels fought with a light scent of alcohol.

They climbed out of the cellar and followed their noses to the kitchen, where they found the two German agents, one on the floor and one in a chair, the one on the floor frozen in a rictus of agony, face bright red, the one at the table face down with his hand lying in a puddle of spilled whiskey. Jake hadn't much doubt that the bottle of 12-year old Macallan on the table had been poisoned.

"Care for a drink, Jake?" Dick said wryly.

154

LAUREL STRUGGLED up the access ladder, her wounded shoulder screaming at her to stop. Rung by rung she hooked her left arm over a rung, raised herself up, then held herself against the ladder with the fingers of her right hand, her shoulder throbbing, just long enough to hook her left arm over the next rung, the diamonds clutched tightly in her left fist. She had gotten almost all the way to the top when she realized that there was no way she could push the grate open with her injured arm.

She wanted to scream with frustration, but instead lowered herself achingly back down the way she had come, staggering back and slumping against the wall the second she hit the floor, shaky with blood loss and adrenaline. She wanted to close her eyes and sleep, but didn't dare. She had to find a way out. "Think dammit," she told herself. Gino's place had stairs, and so had the safe house, so logically they weren't the only places with such access into the tunnels…right? She'd just have to start checking doors until she found some stairs.

She looked at her watch. It was nearly 2:00 a.m.; no wonder she was tired. She took a deep breath and pushed herself up the wall where she'd collapsed, a wave of nausea nearly making her pass out. Then she thought about Jake, and her damn interfering little sister, and the bitch who had hit her just before Dick had shot her, and she felt better, feeding herself the anger to fuel her flight.

She forced herself to her feet, vowing that before she set sail for Brazil to meet Schiller - after she found a doctor - she would make them pay…all of them.

155

LILY AND Jake had ensconced Morrie on the lumpy davenport in the living room, trying to make her as comfortable as possible. Lily was holding a folded dishtowel over her wound while Jake held her head in his lap and stroked her forehead. Morrie had long since passed out, but he spoke to her anyway, telling her not to give up, that he loved her, and that she was going to be fine.

Dick paced the room like a jungle cat, the .45 stuck in his waistband, every now and then casting a worried look in Morrie's direction. Standing around doing nothing had never been Dick's strong point.

Finally Jake heard sirens in the distance, and he slipped gently out from under her, placing her head on a pillow and kissing her forehead. Her breathing seemed shallow, her forehead feverish, her hands cold, and it worried him, but he had to finish this. The sirens grew closer as he stood and looked at Lily and Dick.

"I have to go."

"I'll go with you," Dick said.

"No, you stay here and explain things to the cops. I have to try and find Laurel before she hurts someone else. She's wounded, so she couldn't have gotten far."

"I still think I should go with you."

"I need you here. That's an *order*, Sergeant."

"Oh sure. Pull *that* card."

156

LAUREL HAD tried three doors, all of them locked. Tears of anger and frustration filled her eyes, her shoulder throbbing worse than ever. Out of frustration she kicked the doorknob of the last door she'd tried, and it popped open. She stared at it in disbelief, checking the knob. It was still locked, but the frame must have swelled over the years enough so that it was barely latched. She didn't really care as long as there were stairs behind it. There were.

At the top of the stairs was another door, this one not locked, and it led into a small storeroom, which from the dim light coming in a high window looked as if it belonged to a restaurant. Long, narrow shelves held a variety of foodstuffs – boxes marked semolina, large jars of pickles, mayonnaise and ketchup, #10 cans of diced tomatoes and corn, narrow cardboard boxes of straws and paper napkins. The door was locked from the other side, but it was designed to keep people out, not people in, so she simply flipped the latch and walked out.

The room was pitch black, but she could see her way by the moonlight shining in the front window, illuminating a small group of tables and chairs crouched in front of a long, gleaming, white deli case, and she suddenly knew where she was. It was a delicatessen that catered to the lunch crowd; she'd bought sandwiches here for the idiot brothers several times.

She turned and made her way down a dark hallway to the back door, which was just where she remembered it. A coat hung on a hook near the door, and she grabbed it, sliding her injured arm gingerly into the sleeve, trying not to cry out, but an involuntary gasp found its way past her lips. She shrugged the other sleeve on, collected herself, then flipped a deadbolt matching the one in the storeroom and pulled the door open, pushing the screen door quietly before her. Then she was outside, the cool night air making her shiver despite the coat. After the oppressive heat of the steam tunnels, the cold April night felt like walking into a freezer.

She stopped for a minute to gather herself, marshaling her strength, shifting the diamonds back into her left hand, feeling them crunch satisfyingly against each other beneath the smooth, soft fabric. She'd lost a lot of blood and felt dizzy, so she called upon her anger again to sustain her, feeling it once again bubble to the surface.

She didn't have any friends she could count on, just those two idiots Dieter and Karl, but she couldn't risk going back to the safe house. If Jake, her sister and the others had succeeded in getting out of the tunnels the house would be compromised. Dieter and Karl were on their own - screw them. There was only one move, and that was to get to Gino's. He could get her a doctor, clothes and a train ticket, his loyalty secured with a few choice diamonds.

She gently squeezed the bags again in her left hand, feeling the stones shifting against each other. She needed to find something else to put them in, the cut-down bags with their flimsy stitching would likely burst if she dropped them, and the way she was feeling - about to pass out - it was a real possibility. She also needed a safe place to stash them until she was ready to leave town. It wouldn't do to show up at Gino's with all of the diamonds; she'd get robbed, maybe killed. She'd have to take a few out and hide the rest.

Her slacks had no pockets she could put them in, so she simply clutched the bags of diamonds in her left hand, pulled the thin coat around her and moved off in the darkness towards downtown. Staggering through the shadows, weak from loss of blood, her shoulder throbbing, only her rage kept her from collapsing. As she walked she imagined the horrible fates she'd visit on Jake, Lily, Dick and Morrie. Imagining Jake's skin being flayed from his bones by a whip was admittedly a fantasy, but it kept her mind off her own pain.

She could see the tracks now, just another block away, and once over them it was only two more blocks to Gino's and she was home free...and rich, she reminded herself, a toothy smile coming unbidden to her bruised lips, making her wince. She'd make that bitch who punched her pay as well. She stumbled over a curb and realized she'd made it to Phoenix Avenue; the last street before the tracks.

157

JAKE KISSED Morrie's forehead one more time, then with a hug from Lily and a nod from Dick, slipped out the back just as an ambulance and two squad cars came screaming up to the front. He slid through the hedge and ran toward Beaver Street, every muscle in his body protesting.

It had been a long couple of days, first the dogfight with the Hortens and crashing the plane, then chasing the German through the mountains and getting caught in a flash flood, now this. He knew he didn't have a choice though – if he waited to talk with the police, Laurel would be long gone. He'd wracked his brain trying to think of where she'd go, and since she wasn't the kind of woman who encouraged friendships - he figured Gino's was his best bet.

If she'd managed to get out of the tunnels on this side, she'd be headed for downtown, probably crossing the tracks at either San Francisco or Beaver. As if hearing his thoughts, a freight blew its horn as it sped through, past the long rows of freight cars full of defective ordnance waiting on sidings to be flagged through to Navajo Depot.

He ran towards the tracks hoping to catch her there, but when he reached them Jake realized that he had little chance of finding her like this. She could have crossed anywhere by now. He was stressed and beyond exhaustion from running on pure adrenaline for the last two days, and every part of his body ached.

He stopped beside the tracks, hands on his knees, out of breath, totally wiped out. Then he remembered something Cates had taught him about hunting: sometimes you just had to clear the mind and go with what your gut told you. He stood back up and looked up at the heavens, his breath fogging in the cold air. The sharp light of the stars he'd grown up under were thrown across a sky made cobalt blue rather than black by the light of the moon.

He looked up at the San Francisco Peaks. Humphreys and Agassiz were still topped with snow, making them strangely luminous in the moonlight, standing there like guardians above Flagstaff. The Hopi believed the Kachinas, their guardian spirits, lived in these high, sharp edged peaks, and on a night such as this it was easy to believe.

Jake closed his eyes as Tom Crow Flies had when hunting, saying a silent prayer to the Great Spirit, turning in all four directions slowly, arms outstretched, asking for guidance, for a sign, humble in the face of God, murmuring the prayer of a hunter in Apache the way he'd been taught.

When he finished Jake felt better, calmer, knowing in his heart he had done everything possible, and what was to be would be. Perhaps the hunter would find his deer, perhaps not, but he had asked the spirits to help him and it was in their hands now.

He looked once more up and down the tracks and saw nothing but a couple of drunk collegians making their way back to campus, holding each other up. He took another deep breath of the cold air and turned east, walking along the tracks at the edge of the cinders in the direction his heart had told him to go, the moon at his back, hoping for the deer to run from the thicket.

158

JAKE WASN'T sure it was her at first. She was staggering like a drunk, and wearing some sort of blue shift or coat he didn't recognize... then he saw her hair and caught the familiar edge of her face in the light of a street lamp as she crossed Phoenix Avenue, and knew he'd found his deer. He began running despite his aching legs, his anger at what she'd done bubbling to the surface.

* * * * *

Laurel heard the footsteps in the cinders even through her veil of pain, and looked up the tracks in time to see Jake pass through a pool of light thrown by a streetlamp, his revolver clenched in one hand, a look of grim determination on his face. She began running, stumbling blindly towards the tracks, Jake angling towards her just seventy-five yards away, then fifty.

"LAUREL, STOP. I SWEAR I'LL SHOOT," he yelled, but she just looked at him and kept running.

He saw her dodge between two engines parked on the siding and ran that way. He could hear another train coming from the east, blowing its horn, and he knew he'd lose her if the train got between them, so he forced his exhausted, aching body faster, diving into the same gap as the train sped towards them.

Laurel turned and ran east down the tracks towards Agassiz. The street didn't go through the tracks now, though it may have at one time, but she would cross there anyway. She could hear Jake's feet on the cinders behind her, closing the gap, and she forced herself to run faster. Why hadn't the fool used his revolver? She angled up the rise to the tracks, out of breath, stumbling past a parked freight car, looking for a place to climb through, finally finding a caboose parked front to back with a silent engine hooked to another string of cars lined up on the siding, patiently waiting their turn to continue west.

She squeezed between them, nearly falling when she stumbled on the second rail, her hand on the cold metal of the engine, then she was through, with two more sets of tracks to cross. The next set of tracks were empty, but as she looked both ways she could see a freight approaching fast from the east on the last set. She still had time to cross in front of it though if she ran, then the train would block Jake, giving her time to get away. She leapt the first set of rails and ran for the next, the diamonds clenched in her left hand, nearly home free.

In the dark she had misjudged how close the train was. It was hard to see, with only the small, tiny, blinding moon of its headlight as reference, and as she turned to look up the track at the speeding freight, her toe caught the trembling rail and she went down hard on the tracks, dropping the diamonds, her hands and knees smashing into the cinders and creosoted timbers as she cried out.

The rails were vibrating wildly as she cursed, running her hands frantically over the dark ground between the rails, her wound forgotten. The diamonds! Where were the diamonds? The train was closer now, its light casting her shadow down the track as a giant, then she moved back and saw one of the tiny black velvet bags. She snatched it up, hearing the squeal of brakes locking up metal wheels grinding against rails, the screech of metal against metal as she saw the second bag in the bright light, grabbing it and standing up to leap off the tracks, turning to look at the oncoming train as the engineer laid on the air horn again, the sound loud in her ears.

The 580,000 pound Union Pacific Challenger Model 4-6-6-4 was still doing over 50 mph when it hit her, the impact instantly breaking every bone in her body as both bags of diamonds burst, the shower of tiny stones glittering in the train's headlight briefly like a fourth of July sparkler; a thousand tiny falling stars scattered over half a mile of volcanic cinders.

From where Jake stood it was as if she simply ceased to exist. One second she was there, the next she was gone, so quickly that if he hadn't heard the thump of her body hitting the engine he would have guessed she'd made it to the other side and the speeding train had simply shielded her from his view… but he knew she was gone.

He closed his eyes and bent over to catch his breath, at the very end of his endurance. Finally he stood, took one last look at the slowing train, at the last spot he'd seen the woman he was once sure he would marry, then turned and started walking back to the house where Morrie lay, the cold, thin moon lighting his way as he found himself running yet again.

EPILOGUE

EXHAUSTED FROM working on the frame of the new barn, Cates was asleep on the porch in his favorite chair when he was awakened by the rumble of a large flatbed truck coming up the drive. Jake came out of the kitchen eating something Rosa had made, and Cates was glad to see his limp was nearly gone.

"What is it, Cates? Lumber?" Jake asked as the truck came to a halt. Whatever was on the back had a wooden frame built around it and was draped in canvas. The truck was an extra-long one, with California plates. The man who climbed out of the cab didn't look as though he missed many meals, and seemed jovial enough.

"Is this the Diamond S ranch?" he asked, walking up to the porch as Jake and Cates walked down the steps to meet him.

"Sure is. What can we do for you? This can't be the lumber I ordered – just called it in yesterday," Cates said.

"I'm looking for…a Mr. Roman Cates and a Mr. Jake Ellison," the driver said, looking at his paperwork.

"That's us. What's this about?" Cates asked.

"I have a delivery for you. Can you sign here, please? Both of you?"

Cates and Jake looked at each other as Rosa and Morrie came out of the house, Morrie drying her hands on a small hand towel. She threw a kiss to Jake who smiled at his new wife. Cates took the pen the driver proffered and signed, then handed it to Jake who did the same.

"What's on the truck?" Jake asked.

"I was told not to tell you until you signed for it. Help me get the tarp off, will you?"

They helped him untie the canvas, then flipped it off, to reveal a Curtiss JN4 Jenny in near-new condition with its wings stacked neatly beside it. They stared at it open-mouthed as Rosa shook her head and went back inside, the screen door slamming behind her as if declaring her feelings.

"Here's the letter that goes with it," the truck driver said, handing them a manila envelope.

"You read it, Jake," Cates said.

Jake opened the envelope and smiled. "It says – *'Gentlemen. It has come to my attention that you are presently without an airplane. Considering your combined skills as aviators, this seems a travesty and one that I hope this humble present helps correct. I was going to send you a Spad, but felt that a Jenny to replace the one lost in the fire would be more suitable. I salute you both for your service, and hope you enjoy her.'* It's a gift from Howard Hughes, Cates!"

"Well don't that beat all. We should burn the barn down more often. Got a new barn *and* a new plane out of it…" Cates said.

"Once is enough, Cates. Let's count our blessings."

"Well, I'm glad you're tickled with it," the driver said, "but I need to get back on the road. Now where do you want this thing, and how are you planning to unload it?" the driver said.

Cates and Jake looked at each other, dumbfounded, then started laughing.

"Well, sir, I'm not rightly sure. Why'nt you come on inside while we figure somethin' out?" Cates said, leading the driver to the porch. "How do you feel about Tequila in your lemonade?"

Author's notes:

Although this is a work of fiction, it is woven from the fabric of truth. Jack and Helen Frye were the owners of Smoke Trail Ranch, although the House of Apache Fires was not built until 1947. I wanted the house (which still exists as part of Red Rock State Park in Sedona) in the book, so I 'built it' earlier. It is currently being restored.

Elliot Roosevelt, Howard Hughes, Marlene Dietrich and Harry Truman were all good friends of the Fryes', and all spent time there during the war. At the time of the book however, Marlene was overseas entertaining our troops, and was nearly trapped at Bastogne with the 101st so I could not include her in the book.

In Elliot's case, he and Faye Emerson were married at the Grand Canyon in early December 1944 and spent much of their honeymoon at the ranch, although they spent a night at Mayhew Lodge in Oak Creek Canyon first. Howard Hughes is rumored to have paid for the wedding, lending credence to my personal theory that when he disappeared midwinter when Congress badly wanted to question him about the 'Spruce Goose' he was hiding out at Smoke Trail Ranch. I have no real proof of this, but it fits. Jack Frye was the president of TWA and got Howard Hughes to buy the airline. The two were very good friends.

The character of Kessler is a fabrication, but Otto Skorzeny is not. He was involved in many secret operations such as the daring mountain-top rescue of Mussolini in 1943, as well as 'Operation Grief' during the Battle of the Bulge in which English-speaking German soldiers dressed in American uniforms to work behind our lines, removing or changing road signs, sabotaging fuel dumps, and generally causing pandemonium. The concept of such an operation taking place here on U.S. soil was just too tempting for me to resist.

The German technology such as the Hortens and Q-ship raiders really existed, although the Q-ships were pretty much out of the picture by the end of the war, and the Hortens were (reportedly) still in the testing stage. I have read enough conflicting information that I suspect there were more Hortens produced than the record shows, and the 'UFO's' first sighted over Mt. Rainier in 1947 had the same odd 'skipping' motion that flying wings do due to their unique aerodynamics. The picture drawn of the first UFO is almost a dead – ringer for a Horten. Is it so incredible to think that our government kept them a secret after confiscating remaining planes? Could the 'UFO' that crashed at Roswell have really been a Horten? Imagine the uproar if the public knew the government was testing advanced Nazi aircraft.

We'll never know, but consider this – Northrup Aerospace recently built a 1:1 model of a Horten and verified in testing that it was indeed the first stealth aircraft. These are the folks who built the B2 bomber...

The more research I did on WWII, the more I came to realize what a near thing it was – the war was nearly lost not just once, but several times. In the end however, German fanaticism and technology was no match for the massive weight of American war production coupled with the sheer tenacity of the Brits and our other allies, and of course the American fighting man.

It was a dogfight to the very end, a fight two of my great-uncles participated in. It was a fascinating, horrifying, edge-of-your-seat time, a war where the tide could have easily turned against us, and several times did. Thank you for reading. I hope you enjoyed it as much as I enjoyed writing it.

About the Author

Morgan Jameson lives and works in the high
mountain regions of the American West.

Made in the USA
Middletown, DE
10 May 2022

65598888R00300